THE
LEAP YEAR
GENE OF
KIT McKINLEY

ALSO BY SHELLEY WOOD

The Quintland Sisters

THE LEAP YEAR GENE OF KIT McKINLEY

SHELLEY WOOD

UNION
SQUARE
& CO.

NEW YORK

UNION
SQUARE
&CO.

NEW YORK

UNION SQUARE & CO. and the distinctive Union Square & Co. logo
are trademarks of Sterling Publishing Co., Inc.

Union Square & Co., LLC, is a subsidiary of Sterling Publishing Co., Inc.

© 2024 Shelley Wood

This is a work of fiction. Names, characters, business, events, and incidents
are the products of the author's imagination. Any resemblance to actual
persons, living or dead, or actual events is purely coincidental.

ISBN 978-1-4549-5629-7
ISBN 978-1-4549-5630-3 (e-book)

For information about custom editions, special sales, and premium purchases,
please contact specialsales@unionsquareandco.com.

Printed in Canada

2 4 6 8 10 9 7 5 3 1

unionsquareandco.com

To Dad

"We seek constancy in heredity—and find
its opposite: variation.
Mutants are necessary to maintain the essence of ourselves."
—Siddhartha Mukherjee,
The Gene: An Intimate History

"I suppose it's like the ticking crocodile, isn't it?
Time is chasing after all of us."
—J. M. Barrie, *Peter Pan*

PROLOGUE: FEBRUARY 29, 2016

She told him to get some sleep before Udita gets there, but he's refusing, pretending to pout. The corners of his lovely lips turn down and he crosses his arms over his chest so that his elbows jut under the quilt. Outside, the rain is furious, slapping against the ferns and huckleberries. The branches of the cedars shudder, as if they want to punch back.

She's already read him the news off her phone. *Leonardo DiCaprio Wins Oscar at Last. Clinton, Trump, Gear Up for Super Tuesday. Chinese Scientists Use CRISPR to Edit Genes of Human Embryos.* He waves a hand at her to stop, then says: "*Your* story. Even the boring bits."

She tenses. The doctor had warned her to be on the lookout for lapses. Quirks. Any signs of forgetfulness. "Babe, you know my story."

His eyes are closed but his lashes rustle as if he's laughing underneath. He's like a little boy—stubborn and petulant. He can't be budged from the window of the candy shop. He wriggles lower in the bed, tugging the quilt up to his chin. "Everything. From the beginning."

As if he has all the time in the world.

The wind gusts sideways, chucking the fat raindrops against the glass to get her attention. She glances up. In the fading light, the green is greener than green. "Well, in the beginning, it was other people's stories."

His face is all mischief now, smug. He opens his eyes, then winks.

PART I

Ernest

(NOT QUITE) 1916

i.

Ernest McKinley stepped into the welcome gloom of his foyer, dropping his briefcase and shutting the door against the sun. First things first: he peeled off his shoes and socks, then took off his hat, tossing it to its hook, where it spun once, twice, before settling down like a dog on a rug. He shrugged out of his jacket, then tugged at the knot of his necktie to loosen it around his throat, it being too damnably hot for ties. If he could have been certain Marie had left for the day, he'd have stripped down to his underclothes. But his housekeeper worried about him enough as it was—unmarried and nearing thirty, both parents passed, and Thomas, his only brother, seven months dead having found himself shot to ribbons his very first week in France. Ernest closed his eyes against the images trying to jostle their way to the front of his thoughts and settled for yanking his shirttails from his belt. He wasn't lonely or singular. He was merely a busy man, and a private one. A man whose skills, during wartime, were in high demand such that thoughts of a wife welcoming him home, smelling of biscuits, her soft hands hastening to take his jacket, or of a child rosy from her bath waddling to the door to meet him: these were the furthest things from his mind.

The knock at the door made him jump. He caught a glimpse of himself in the hall mirror as he reached for the doorknob, his red curls unsticking themselves from his damp temples, his untucked shirt draping from his broad chest like a nightshirt. He snatched his hat from the coat stand and tapped it back on his head. Then he drew himself up and opened the door.

On the steps stood a young woman in a brightly patterned dress, at least six feet tall but no more than seventeen or eighteen, thin as a reed and wavering from foot to foot as if stirred by the heat rising from the flagstones. She had a toothy smile and was clutching a large purse in one hand and in the other a hat, decadent but squashed. The woman and her smile were recognizable without quite being familiar, as if he'd seen her in a toothpaste advertisement in a magazine.

"Can I help you?"

She darted a look at his bare feet, then his hat, which he sensed was askew.

"I'm sorry to disturb you, Mr. McKinley. I'm Natalie Kenilworth, Lillian's sister. We met at the funeral and—"

Ernest squinted up at her, trying to lift any features from her girlish silhouette, backlit by the sun outside his door, and find a match in his overstuffed brain. That he couldn't instantly place her was unsettling. Her nose and chin, even her small ears, were pointy, almost elfin, everything pulled forward toward a center point on her face as if cinched. Her skin was fair and smooth and her lashes pale and short, so that they seemed insufficient for warding off any stern scrutiny of her wide, blue eyes, which, Ernest realized, was what he was doing that very minute.

"Natalie?" she repeated. "Lillian's sister. So, Tom's sister-in-law? We met very briefly at the service for Tom back in May."

Ernest's head jerked and his eyes smarted, fleetingly, as if someone nearby were peeling a lemon. Thomas's funeral. That would explain it. If ever there had been a time when his powers of observation had failed him—well. He blinked the sensation away.

"Lillian's sister? My goodness. Is everything all right? Please." He ushered Natalie inside and felt a sudden flush, although he couldn't be sure if it was the heat of the afternoon sun sidling into the foyer with Natalie or a flood of grief and guilt. Burying himself in his work to keep from dwelling on Thomas's death, Ernest had all but forgotten about Lillian, his brother's young widow. He'd written to her at least three times, four surely, after the funeral, but she'd never replied, then he'd been swamped with new duties, and—

"Is she—is Lillian—all right?" His voice came out strangled. "What's happened?" Natalie raised her hands, fingers spread. He felt his breath catch in his throat.

"No, please," Natalie said. "I don't mean to alarm you. Lillian is fine." She sucked a deep breath of air. "Well, no, not fine. I mean—she is . . ."

She stopped, pinched her lips, then shook her head as if to start fresh.

"Mr. McKinley—I'm not sure Lillian has even told you. In fact, I don't believe Tom knew of it either."

Ernest prided himself on—indeed, in his line of work, was famous for—his poker face. But hearing his brother's name spoken aloud so many times, after so many months, he could tell: it showed. He could feel sadness pulling at his eyes with tiny ropes and pulleys.

"Lillian is . . . going to have a child," she told the loose knot of his tie, then risked a look at his face.

The words sent zaps of feeling through him: surprise, then grief, then joy. Then confusion.

"Lillian is with child," he repeated. He couldn't help himself and counted the months back to the day Thomas died, and to the day, not so many weeks before, that Thomas had set sail for Europe in the first place.

"With Tom's child?" he asked finally, a whistle of doubt creeping in. Natalie held his eye. "*Thomas's* child?" he said again.

"Tom's child." Natalie repeated it back to him firmly. "But Lillian—something's not right. She refuses to leave the flat. She's not eating as she should. She needs . . ."

Ernest had already snatched his jacket and jammed his feet, sockless, back into his shoes. "A doctor! She needs a doctor. Of course. It's wonderful news, wonderful. But is the baby coming now? It's time?"

Natalie stepped past him, deeper into the dim foyer, and set her purse down, rooting through it. "Well, she has a doctor, or at least she used to have one."

He watched her reflection in the mirror, her sharp face furrowed, then saw himself bobbing to and fro behind her, his hat lopsided, his face scrambled. After more rummaging, she gave a low growl of irritation and started raking the contents of the bag onto the table—writing utensils, lipsticks, several small pots of what looked to be womanly unguents, two dime-store novels, a small mallet, a packet of pin nails, a sheaf of folded leaflets, and—at last—a small notebook. She snatched it up and the paper pamphlets fluttered to the floor. She ignored them. As she paged through the book, he stooped to retrieve them. "VOTES FOR WOMEN!" the front of the pamphlet proclaimed in large block letters over a blotchy photograph of a lady with a long, stern nose. Yes, this rang a bell—Thomas and his bride had both been passionate about a range of social-ist and feministic causes.

A Meeting of the Canadian Alliance for Women's Suffrage
Thursday, August 17, 1915
Address by Prof. Carrie Derick
"Women in Academe" with Musical Numbers
by Mrs. Wendy Nightcap and Mlle. Nadine Dupré

"Dr. Percival Lawrence." Natalie poked at a name in the notebook, meeting Ernest's eyes in the mirror as if she expected him to know it. "I got his name from an advertisement in the directory because he did house calls and she was feeling so poorly. It was Dr. Lawrence who told Lillian she was pregnant, diagnosed her right after she got the news about Thomas." Natalie bit her lip. "But he wasn't nice about it. Said she was too young and pretty to be widowed and she'd be better off giving up the baby and starting anew. Lillian tossed him out and said she never wanted to see him again."

Ernest bristled. The very idea of his brother's child being handed off to strangers. He scarcely knew Lillian—Ernest was ten years older than Thomas and had been abroad when his brother was at university, where he'd met his bride. She'd had a missionary upbringing, as he recalled, somewhere exotic, parents now deceased, sharp as a tack with a passion for the natural sciences. Ernest had not returned from his overseas post until after Thomas had shipped out: the first time he'd met Lillian had been at his brother's funeral. Ernest was renowned for his photo-graphic memory, but grief had surely meddled with the shutter speed, leaving several months blurred and smudged. He had the wedding photograph Thomas had sent him on his mantelpiece, yet Ernest might have passed Lillian on the Montreal streets without a second look. He felt sick at the idea of this young lady grieving his brother's death, confined to her bed, then getting such heartless advice from some quack of a doctor.

Then he remembered his mental arithmetic and gestured for the door. "But it's time, is it? The baby is coming? We should hurry. Please—we can take my car."

Natalie had crammed everything back in her handbag and was shaking her head. "No, that's just it, Mr. McKinley. That's what I came here to say. Lillian is fine and the baby—the baby is fine, we think. We can feel her kicking." She smiled. "Lillian insists she's a girl."

Ernest smiled, too, the fact of a baby taking hold, squeezing something in his chest.

"It's not urgent, is what I'm saying." Natalie took a step toward the door. "And Lillian doesn't know I've come here. But it is time for the baby—it must be. Past time."

She paused, dabbing the back of her glove against her brow, her blue eyes edging to meet Ernest's again. "The thing is, the baby isn't coming. She won't come, it seems. And she shows no sign of coming soon."

For the entire journey across town from Westmount to the French side of the city, Natalie prattled like an auctioneer—the humid weather, the terrible sinking of the *Lusitania* by the German U-boat, the perils of automobile driving in the city. She directed him to park by a faded dépanneur on La Main, and they hastened through the door and up the stairs to the apartments above, passing a young couple on the first floor with a brood of young children. At her own door, Natalie's hands were so nervous or eager that the key seemed to buck at the keyhole, unable to find its way in.

When the lock finally relented, he hesitated, his eyes roving over the gloom and clutter: a living room, dining room, and kitchen all in one, smelling of rose water, boiled eggs, and the peppery tang of a laundry pile. The flat was big enough, perhaps, for Thomas and his bride—young students and newlyweds sharing a bed—but Natalie had told him she'd been staying with her sister ever since they got the telegram announcing Tom's death.

Grouped around a small table in the center of the room were four spindly chairs, their wooden backs heaped with blouses, skirts, and undergarments, one so heavily weighed down it had slumped against a wall, its front legs pawing at the air. The little table itself was taken up with neat piles of what looked to be the same pamphlets in Natalie's purse. Drapes in a drab green print were drawn over the tall windows, giving the room an underwater feel. Lillian, propped among pillows on the settee, was in shadow.

"Lillian?" Natalie turned to the window, tugging the curtains aside so that the evening sun streamed into the room. "You have a visitor."

Ernest squared his shoulders. "It's me, Lillian. Ernest McKinley. Your sister told me your excellent news."

Lillian blinked in the light and pushed herself higher on the pillows. To Ernest she looked much the same as she had at the service for Thomas—her thick, brown hair heaped high on her head, a lovely flush to her smooth cheeks, eyes deep blue pools under dark, bushy brows. She and Thomas had married so young—children, really, both of them scarcely very far along in their studies. Now, less than a year later, she was far too young to be a widow. Ernest stole a look at her stomach. Lillian, he recalled, was tall like her sister but with a more generous figure. To Ernest's unpracticed eye, she didn't look much more sizable around the middle than she had at the funeral. But when he stepped tentatively toward the sofa, her hand snaked protectively over her waist.

Natalie, as if thinking they needed a moment of privacy, made to slip into the adjoining bedroom but knocked over a clay umbrella stand, which toppled thunderously. Ignoring the broken pieces, she clapped the door shut behind her.

Why hadn't he tried harder to stay in touch with this poor woman? Lillian was grieving Thomas every bit as much as he was; indeed, far more. He held out his hand, awkwardly, and she reached out and took it, which had the effect of making his eyes tickle. She was so pale, as if she'd kept herself fathoms deep in the folds of this room. He recalled Natalie's words: *She refuses to leave the flat.*

"Is the baby coming soon, Lillian?" It took fortitude to keep from glancing at her midriff.

Lillian shrugged, idly stroking her stomach. "Not yet, I don't think." She smiled wanly.

"Should we call the doctor then?"

Lillian jerked her head. "I won't have that man back here! And I don't need a doctor. Natalie is taking good care of me."

"I don't quite understand," Ernest said. He scraped at his mustache with his lower teeth, a nervous habit that made him look like a bulldog.

"If the baby is . . ." His question trailed away. He cupped his other hand over Lillian's and cleared his throat. "Lillian, the baby must be due very soon, or else"—his voice caught—"or something's not right."

Lillian snatched her hand from Ernest's, balled her fingers into fists to shift herself higher on the settee, then swung her legs around, plunking them heavily on the floor and pushing herself to standing. He risked a glance at her waist, enough to satisfy himself that it was indeed substantially thicker than it had been in her wedding photo and at the funeral, but not, it seemed, burdened with a full-term infant. Straightened to her full height, Lillian stood almost half a foot taller than Ernest. When she inclined her head to his, her eyes were flashing like knives.

"This baby is Tom's," she said, slow and firm, as if to a child. "There's been no one else and there never will be. She's smart enough to know this is no time to be born into a world gone crazy with war. You, Ernest, are going to be an uncle, and you— Natalie? Natalie! Get back in here."

Natalie emerged from the bedroom, nearly tripping a second time on the broken umbrella stand.

"You, Natalie, should have let me tell Ernest when I was good and ready."

Lillian turned back to him, a frown still crimped across her features. Then her face softened. She put one hand on her belly and tapped her blouse where he could see the fabric pulled taut—the swell of her stomach seeming larger and firmer than he'd first thought. "There she is," she said, gazing down at her tummy. "Poking a foot to say hello."

And yes, as if his own hand was resting beneath hers to feel a tiny kick, he felt wonder wash across his own face so that his ears twitched and his forehead smoothed. Lillian seemed to sense it and nodded. Her words came out with a catch. "That's your niece, Ernest. Tom's baby girl, saying how do you do. Nice of you to stop by."

ii.

Each time he visited, Ernest tried to bring a surprise: an electric table fan in August, a duck-down comforter when the weather turned cold, a roast ham with carrots and butter potatoes that Marie put together, jams and jellies, licorice allsorts, and, today, a Christmas pudding. Lillian, he'd learned, had a sweet tooth. Today's other surprise, he feared, would be less welcome.

Ernest hesitated on the threshold. For once Lillian was not stretched out on the settee but bent over a notebook at the table, consulting a book with her eyebrows knitted, two fingers splayed to keep the pages flat. She looked up but didn't set down her pen.

"Lillian!" Ernest's voice was louder, jollier, than he'd intended. "You're looking well," he said. This wasn't the case. Both his lie and the truth pained him. Lillian had dark circles under her eyes, and her skin was so pallid it was almost blue. Her morning sickness had long since cleared, but according to Natalie, Lillian still refused to venture outside. It was understandable. More than ten months since Tom's death and fourteen since his departure, Lillian at last looked pregnant, enough that it might set people talking. Lillian regarded him with a long, blank look that suggested her mind was elsewhere, then returned to her scribbling. He cleared his throat and beckoned for the woman waiting in the hall.

"Lillian, I've brought someone to see you. A lady physician."

Lillian looked up again, startled, her book fluttering closed. He watched her size up the visitor. The doctor was wearing spectacles and a faded but fussy dress surely dating from the last century and was stout with jet-black hair combed back in a tight bun that framed her round, serious face. Thirty-five? Forty? It was hard to say. She grasped a black leather bag with both hands.

"Lillian, I'd like you to meet Dr. Margaret Hampston, from Boston, where she did her medical training." Ernest found he was bobbling, one foot to the other, his nervous habit. He had spent some time relying on his network of sources to find a doctor who was not only a woman, but also had certain special interests. "Dr. Hampston has some experience with"—he groped about for the right word—"unusual pregnancies." He then played his trump card. "And like you, Dr. Hampston is a member of the National Council of Women and one of the leading voices pressuring McGill and Laval to open their medical schools to women."

Dr. Hampston was already inching into the room, removing her hat and puzzling at the overburdened coat stand. Natalie hurried forward to take her things.

"Ernest and I will step out for a bit, shall we?" Natalie was already hustling onto the landing, the doctor's coat still draped over her own arm as if she intended to wear it.

By the time Ernest and Natalie had returned, stomped the snow from their boots, and mounted the steps to the top-floor flat, both Dr. Hampston and Lillian were seated on the sofa, discussing not babies or birthing, but rather the book Lillian had been poring over when Ernest arrived. It was, he swiftly learned, a collection of blistering satirical essays arguing for women's suffrage recently published by Mrs. Nellie McClung. "Some of it is very funny, but some of it I quite disagree with," Lillian was saying. "I'm happy to lend you my copy when I'm finished."

Dr. Hampston gestured for Natalie and Ernest to sit, which they did.

"Everything is progressing," she said in a flat, confident tone. "By all accounts, things are delayed—much delayed—but the mother is healthy and the baby's heart is lusty. It is unusual, but not entirely undocumented."

"But—" Ernest couldn't help himself. "When will the baby come?" All eyes fell to Lillian's stomach, which she swiftly covered.

Dr. Hampston's features were smooth and unworried. "Certainly not before Christmas. Late January, possibly, but I'm putting my money on February or March." Ernest was aware of Natalie beside him, pink-nosed from the cold, her jaw falling open at the words. He must have looked similarly gobsmacked because Dr. Hampston regarded them sternly over her glasses. "While the timeline is exceptional, nothing appears particularly out of the ordinary, although given the length of the pregnancy, there is certainly the risk of malformations and specifically polymelia, as I've explained to Lillian."

Natalie was trying to repeat the term soundlessly, her mouth moving around its shape, likely committing it to memory so she could look it up later. Dr. Hampston saved her the trouble. "Additional limbs," she stated, matter-of-factly. "A rare congenital abnormality believed to be caused by protracted gestation. Surgical correction is an option and the mental faculties of the baby are usually unaffected." This news had apparently already been shared with Lillian, who was looking stoically at the doctor.

"None of this is preordained," Dr. Hampston said, her face relaxing into a smile. "Everything seems, to me, to be perfectly in order."

iii.

Ernest paced. What a cliché! He paced between the overstuffed bookshelves and the table in his socks, one of which was wet on account of a leaky boot. He left a loop of spongy, unmatched footprints in the worn carpet and tried not to grimace at the sounds emitting from Lillian in the bedroom. Natalie, dispatched by Dr. Hampston to fetch more water and towels, had burst out of the bedroom and lunged for the kettle, whisking it off the stove and into the sink so that the teapot sailed across the room like a football, landing mercifully in a pile of ironing. Before she could hustle back to the bedside, they heard the newborn's first spluttering cries.

Later, tucked to his chest, the baby felt like a pot roast wrapped in flannel, not long from the oven. Curly, coppery lashes nestled on rosy cheeks, and a fuzz of ginger hair peeped out from under her cap. The warm heft of her sent him tumbling back to Tom's birth, twenty years ago. Ernest had been ten years old and someone—Father? Nanny?—had asked if he wanted to hold his baby brother. Ernest had held out his arms, just so, and Thomas had been nestled against the thump of his heart. Looking down at the tiny, crumpled lips of this child sipping at life, Ernest realized that whatever lingering doubts he'd had about the baby's parentage in the months since Natalie had knocked at his door had evaporated.

"She's a McKinley, no doubt about it," he murmured, saluting the fact as it sank in. Dr. Hampston had been induced to stay for a dram of whisky, then another, to toast the baby's miraculous arrival, on the leap year, no less. February 29, 1916. No spare limbs or ears, big bright eyes, and a robust set of lungs. All her fingers and toes were accounted for, with none to spare.

Ernest, Natalie, and Dr. Hampston clinked their teacups together softly in the living room while Lillian slept, the door ajar. Dr. Hampston nodded sagely. "I've never delivered a normal baby after such a long gestation, but there have throughout history been reports of women who've experienced a physical or mental trauma that appeared to have altered what we generally consider to be the normal incubation period. Lillian, with her background in the phytological sciences, is well aware of the impact of external stressors on successive generations of plant species, so she has a number of theories as to what might have happened embryonically here. And there is much we don't know about the breadth of what I'd term 'normal variations within the human species.'"

Ernest lowered his nose toward the baby, feeling the puff of her teensy exhalations against his cheek.

Dr. Hampston nodded, agreeing with herself. "This baby had a slow start, but she shows every sign of being a healthy, happy little girl."

For a long moment, she peered glumly into the bottom of her empty teacup. "Can I ask you, Natalie? Who knew that Lillian was pregnant? Family, friends?"

"Our parents are gone," Natalie said. "They died when we were young. Yellow fever." She saw the expression on Dr.

Hampston's face. "They were missionaries in West Africa. Lillian and I lived there, too, when we were little, but we were sent back to Montreal, to boarding school."

She shifted a troubled look at Ernest, as if ashamed. "I don't remember them well at all. Our grandmother lived here, in Montreal, but she's gone now, too."

Ernest, watching her solemn face, felt a fresh pang for these two sisters. They'd been through so much and were so very alone.

"During her pregnancy, did you do any entertaining here or did Lillian go out much?" Dr. Hampston asked gently. "You said she dropped out of university after Thomas died, but did she keep in touch with her classmates or attend any meetings of the National Council of Women? The local suffrage society?" Dr. Hampston spiraled her cup thoughtfully in its saucer, then peered over her glasses at Natalie. "What I'm asking is, how many people were aware that Lillian was pregnant, and for how long?"

"No one," Natalie said slowly. "Well, Ernest, of course, but no one else. Lillian was so miserable. People came to the funeral, but after that, she shut everyone out."

Dr. Hampston looked relieved as she smoothed her skirt over her knees. But Ernest saw that Natalie was winding her ankles, one behind the other, and had started gnashing on her lower lip. Ernest raised an eyebrow.

"Actually, Dr. Hampston, I'm sorry, but there was once, not long after Tom died, such a difficult time—it seems so long ago now. I'd only just graduated and moved straight here from boarding school. There were two women who visited Lillian, acquaintances from before the war who are also very involved with the Council of Women, I gather. Upper crust, Anglophone, looking around the flat with their snouts in the air. One of them had married into that big newspaper family and just had a baby, a girl." She flickered a timid look at Ernest. "Do you know who I mean? She and her husband were at Tom's service—this woman was still with child then, and he was the stuffy, sour-looking man in a top hat."

Ernest startled. She was referring to Harold Southam. The damnable fog of that funeral! He'd all but forgotten he'd noticed Southam there and been furious. The man was the worst sort of scandalmonger, likely hoping to get fifteen inches of sensational tattle for his battlefield column. How on earth had Lillian come to be friends with the man's wife?

"It was this lady, and another, who came by unexpectedly several months later, after the snooty one had her baby." Natalie swallowed. "Things were still very bad with Lillian then. She was sleeping most of the day on the couch, very indisposed, very low. She talked about her sadness as if it was a physical weight, pinning her down. I figured it was better for Lillian to have some company while I ran my errands, so I don't know how long they stayed or what was said, but I know they upset Lillian somehow, bringing that baby by. They left some tracts devised at a recent Montreal Suffrage Association meeting. Nothing to do with the franchise bills before Parliament but all about 'guardian mothers' and why well-bred women need to reproduce and preserve lineage during times of war, that kind of thing. You've probably seen their newspaper advertisements. Nasty stuff. I burnt them in the fire."

Natalie shot a sheepish look at Dr. Hampston. "Lillian was in such a stew after they left, I can only assume that they preached about their cause during their visit. She certainly never invited them back. And"—Natalie hesitated—"Lillian was showing by then, her belly was about so." She hovered her hands over her stomach, then held them up, looking from one to the other and widening them as though alluding to a fish that got away. "I assumed they would have noticed."

The baby mewed in the silence that followed, everyone thinking, no doubt, just how stubbornly tardy the baby had been, refusing to be born. Ernest felt a rising anxiety pushing against the feeling of deep calm radiating into him from the warm little loaf, asleep in his arms.

"And you, Mr. McKinley?" Dr. Hampston's round glasses fixed themselves on him. "You're Thomas's older brother and you have some high-up position in government, I believe?"

Natalie, he noticed, was also looking at him expectantly. "Just so," he said. "Department of External Affairs. International affairs, the Commonwealth, strategic relationships, and the like."

The two women regarded him blankly. Even the baby opened one sleepy eye, but it quickly drooped closed. "Diplomatic intelligence-gathering, if you will." In fact, diplomacy had less and less to do with it. Natalie drew her eyebrows together. "No legwork on my end. I'm merely—" He swirled a hand. "An administrator. Writing reports. Attending meetings."

Dr. Hampston looked dissatisfied, but only said, "Family? Your parents."

He shook his head. "Scottish. They've both passed." He felt the baby's heat, snug and reassuring. "Thomas was my only sibling."

Dr. Hampston gave another authoritative snap of her head.

"I don't mean to make you anxious." She gave a rueful smile. "What I might advise, if I may, is that we keep the details of the baby's time *in utero* to ourselves? As Lillian herself will have gleaned from McClung's book of essays, which I'm returning by the way"—she took a book from her black bag, the same book Lillian had been poring over before Christmas—"there is a growing concern in certain circles, including some of the more vocal heroines of the women's movement, unfortunately, about children born with any kind of mental or physical deficits, really anything particularly outside the bounds of normal. While this baby shows every sign of being a perfectly normal child, we can all agree that her protracted incubation time may raise unwelcome scrutiny."

Dr. Hampston pushed up her wire spectacles, digging the heels of her hands into the dark hollows of her eyes, then let the glasses drop back into place. "I think we'll let time be the one to decide what traits fall within the bounds of normal for this little one, shall we?"

A shout from the adjoining room made them start, and Natalie leapt to her feet so that Ernest had to reach out and steady the whisky bottle.

It was Lillian, growling sleepily from her bed. "Katherine," she said a second time. "That's her name. Katherine Margaret McKinley."

iv.

Whatever Ernest had expected to feel about his brother's baby—the warm truth of her in his arms, the way she smiled up at him from her cot, kicking her chubby legs in greeting—it wasn't this: this soggy mush of love that seemed to swell inside his chest, utterly unknown to him in his life so far, his heart soaking her up like a sponge. Kit, he called her, because she was such a compact and perfect bundle, everything fitting together just so. Even though the war effort was now in full swing and his responsibilities were great, he found a way to duck out of the office on his lunch hour once or twice a week to pay her a fleeting visit.

Natalie was equally smitten. Even after being accepted into the teachers college at Sainte-Anne-de-Bellevue, she insisted she wanted to continue rooming with her sister, never mind the commute, so as to be able to help as much as possible with Kit.

Lillian, on the other hand, having carried the baby so long, must have felt a lightness after Kit's birth that seemed chiefly to drive her back to the other pursuits she'd let lapse after Tom's death. These were women's causes, most notably the suffrage fight, but also some of her earlier fascination with plants and lichens—the focus of her university studies. Even with the baby dozing in her arms, Lillian seemed more intrigued by an iridescent moss that had grown in the groove of the kitchen window during the long winter. She forbade Natalie from disturbing it, carefully monitoring its progression with a series of neatly dated pencil marks along the wooden ledge. Fortified by this new energy and purpose, Lillian seemed even taller and more striking, so that Ernest felt he was finally seeing the young woman that Thomas had fallen for, razor-sharp and constantly buzzing. She just wasn't buzzing over her child.

In October, Ernest brought the sisters pumpkin pie as well as a flannel blanket for Kit. For Christmas Eve, he brought beef tourtière and a miniature porcelain tub fitted to a wrought-iron stand, a fountain pen for Natalie, and, for Lillian, a cashmere scarf in indigo blue that set off her eyes. On the last day of

February 1917, not precisely the right date, but still, he brought a birthday cake, plus a silver rattle shaped like a tiger for Kit and a rare first edition of Charles Darwin's *The Descent of Man*, a book Lillian had mentioned in passing. She had accepted the gift in a voice croaking with gratitude and amazement, stroking the leather cover as if he'd managed to procure an original Bible signed by Jesus himself.

For Easter, he arrived at the dépanneur on La Main bearing a maple-glazed ham, scalloped potatoes, and a plush toy rabbit. Also, a lapis lazuli bangle that had caught his eye on Rue Saint-Denis, its hue reminding him of the scarf he'd given Lillian for Christmas. He'd been unable to help himself. Was it too much? Probably.

He brought his gifts up the stairs, humming to himself. He smiled and tipped his chin at harried Mrs. Russo, who peered around the door of the apartment below, returning his greeting with a brisk jerk of her head. Once at the top-floor flat, he was surprised to find Dr. Hampston, who'd been summoned— and this was even more startling—by Lillian. A beam scale and a set of bronze weights were laid out on the low table. Seated on the settee, the doctor had a stethoscope inserted in her ears and was moving the bell over Kit's bare chest, so that the baby blinked in surprise.

"What's happened?" he said, his voice coming out like a braking locomotive. He hurried to the couch. Kit, tilting her head toward him, gurgled a happy greeting.

Dr. Hampston, listening with concentration, scrunched her nose to inch her heavy glasses higher but said nothing. Natalie, who'd let him in, was wearing her best coat and had taken some time with her hair, meaning she was likely on her way out to meet one of her beaus. But she stood with her long arms wrapped around her, her face pinched.

Lillian's cheeks were flushed, a silky tendril of hair spiraling down the nape of her neck. She glanced up at Ernest, and her eyes pooled. "She's not growing, is she? Not the way she should. Thirteen months old and she's nursing constantly, but not teething, her hair won't grow in. She's got no strength in her neck to support her head." She gestured at the balance on the table, and her voice cracked. "We've just weighed her and she's only fifteen pounds."

It was all Ernest could do to stop himself from taking Lillian in his arms. Ernest, too, had found himself noticing other babies and wondering more and more about what pace of development was normal. He felt swamped with relief to know that Lillian, always so guarded with her emotions, had been thinking these thoughts as well.

Dr. Hampston was plucking the instrument from her ears. "You were quite right to call me," she said in her comforting monotone, patting at the slicked hair over her ears, her tight, black bun. "There's nothing wrong, per se. Katherine—Kit—is healthy and hearty, responsive to stimuli, and her lungs are strong." She nodded at Ernest, as if she'd only just noticed him. "But it's true—" Dr. Hampston paused, choosing her words. "She's taking her time, just as she did in the womb."

"Will she catch up, then? With time?" Natalie, on her skinny legs, hunched and pacing in her white coat, looked like an egret.

The doctor raised a bushy brow above the tops of her wire spectacles. "No reason to think she won't, eventually. Unless—" She looked from Natalie to Lillian. "Do you recall either one of your parents looking particularly old, or particularly young?"

"Our parents?" Lillian blinked at Natalie, who looked equally discombobulated. "They just looked . . . parental."

"Of course." Dr. Hampston waved a hand. "To a child, all adults seem ancient, don't they? Timeless. And then they died young, you said. I just wondered whether there was anything in their ancestry to explain little Kit." Her face clouded. "Lillian, no doubt you've come across Charles Davenport, the zoologist?" Then she turned to Ernest. "Davenport was at Harvard when I was in medical school at Boston University, and we had our share of quarrels over the value of biometrics in human heredity. He's published dozens of papers and books on the genetics of everything from alcoholism to intelligence to manic depression, and several years ago founded the Eugenics Record Office—always on the hunt for threats to the continuity of the germplasm."

The words hung for a moment, then the doctor vanquished them with a shake of her head. "She's certainly progressing." Dr. Hampston waggled her pinkie finger above the baby, who snatched at it, trying to curl her tiny fist around it. "You see," she said, smiling. All their eyes fell to the satisfied grunts and lip-smacking of the baby, and it was probably only Ernest who noticed, or imagined, the flicker of doubt in the doctor's eyes before she blinked it away.

V.

"Excuse me, excuse me." Lillian edged her way awkwardly through the women already seated, bumping past their knees to reach the empty seats mid-row, Ernest trailing behind her. One of only a dozen men in the otherwise packed auditorium, Ernest was acutely aware of the faint smiles of the women standing to let him pass, then bending their heads to whisper together. In the two years since Kit's birth, Lillian had mumbled regularly about joining Natalie at one of the evenings organized by the Montreal Suffrage Association, but this was the first time she'd actually done so.

Ernest watched her gaze roving over the crowd, the flicker when she recognized a face. She gestured at a woman in sturdy shoes at the edge of the stage. "That's Dr. Derick," she murmured. Ernest recognized her face from the brochures Natalie had spilled from her purse that summer day in his foyer, before Kit was born. Derick was founder and president of both the National Council of Women and the local suffrage association. He'd since seen this same gloomy gaze and prominent nose presiding over a number of other circulars that had made their way into the apartment.

Ernest did his own appraisal of the mostly older, well-to-do women in the crowd. Unless he was mistaken, that was Education Minister Philip Devereux's jittery wife seated in the fourth row, quaking like an aspen, and farther back, the second violinist from the Montreal Symphony, now nodding her head as if to a secret rhythm. And there was an undeniable drumbeat. Several of the provinces had recently granted votes for women: the push now was to convince the newly elected Borden government to follow suit federally before this blasted war was over.

Lillian herself was sitting up very straight, puffed up and proud, her eyes shining. "Natalie should really be here," she had muttered earlier, even though Natalie, with a knowing look, had been the one to insist that Ernest accompany Lillian to the lecture. He'd have been perfectly happy to stay home with Kit so that the sisters could have gone together. She was the sweetest, giggliest, gurgliest baby he'd ever known. Even now his hands twitched for the love of having her in his arms.

The house lights dimmed. Lillian leaned forward and, without even seeming to notice she'd done it, reached over abruptly and clenched Ernest's wrist, letting it go just as quickly so that a damp warmth lingered.

After a brief introduction, Dr. Derick swept from her chair and strode to center stage. A hush fell.

"What a pleasure it is to see so many eager faces committed to the cause of women's emancipation!" Derick's voice was deep and stentorian, and the first minute or two of her speech came out like a lion's roar. Then her voice dropped low and ominous so that the crowd, as one, leaned forward to catch her next words.

"My friends, we have won some battles, but we have not won the war. Thoughtful, educated, well-bred women have demonstrated their stalwart courage in the face of global calamity, upholding Canadian civility in a time of tumultuous change."

Ernest stole a peek at Lillian and was surprised to see she was watching him. Her eyes, usually so inscrutable, were ablaze, suffused with excitement and eager to find him at her side. Derick was stoking an ember in Lillian, and she now looked transformed, ferocious and beautiful, like a bonfire. He managed to blink, a gesture of assent, and for a split second, he thought she might snatch again at his hand and not let go.

Derick, meanwhile, was quivering like a tuning fork, her voice rising again as she invoked the pressing themes of womanly standards, democracy, social hygiene, the scourge of urban vice and depravity, the influx of migrants, orphanages groaning at the seams. "Never before have we faced a moral imperative to ensure that a just and strong society can thrive!" she boomed.

"Hear, hear!" called an elderly woman, producing a wave of giggles.

"Our very humanity depends on the entwined paths of heredity and environment. It is the biology we are endowed with at birth coupled with the environs in which we are born and raised that constitute eugenics. Make no mistake! It falls to women to ensure the best strains of humanity are preserved and enhanced through successive generations."

Derick's rumbling voice was like a torrent plunging over a falls. Lillian's smile, however, had also dropped.

"War, for all its horrors, has helped to raise the status of women in unexpected realms, and for this we must be rewarded with the franchise. But many of our brightest sons are returning from the war seeking all manner of vice to help soothe the terrors of battle: brothels, whisky, and illicit drugs to numb their pain. I've heard it said that the number of unwed women birthing their bastard sons and daughters in our great city will soon surpass that of married couples if something is not done."

The room was too warm. Lillian shifted in her seat, twitching at her skirt to circulate a current of air. She had stopped darting looks at Ernest.

"To be sure, Canada has its fair share of war widows—fine, upstanding women, their husbands lost in noble sacrifice. Their fatherless children deserve our charity and our protection. But do not be deceived." Here Derick paused, wagging a stern finger. "Today, in 1918, the child of the soldier who went to war with those first battalions only to be felled at Ypres, at Vimy Ridge, at Passchendaele, is the little boy standing so high." She held a splayed hand at her hip and tousled the hair of the imaginary child. "He can pump his stout legs on the swing set and count to ten with his fingers. Beware the babies born of sin being passed off as the progeny of fathers lost in the valor of war."

Ernest shunted a glance at Lillian, anger stirring in his breast. She hadn't buttoned herself into her best suit to be subjected to this kind of sanctimonious hokum. Thomas was dead, not lost. And Kit was a million times more marvelous than mere "progeny." Lillian's hands now lay limp in her lap, and it was he who wanted to lace his fingers through hers.

"It falls to right-minded women such as yourselves to produce the leaders of tomorrow in stable, hygienic homes while the degenerates, the mentally deficient, and the morally bereft are prevented from propagating their kind. As science now makes clear, these children will only spawn the next immoral generations, further threatening humanity's finer lineages with extinction. More than war, more than pestilence, more than famine: this, ladies, is the greatest, most pernicious threat to the future of civil society. And the solution is within our grasp."

The applause was deafening. Dr. Derick closed her eyes, not a lion but a house cat, basking in the approbation as if in a ray of winter sunshine. A buzz of voices rose with the lights. Lillian sat motionless in her seat.

"Were you wanting to stay for the reception?" Ernest asked, apprehension pocking his chin. Lillian turned toward him blankly, then shook her head, blinking as if waking from a dream. "I should get back to Kit. I suspect she refused to eat her mashed carrot." She got to her feet and he helped her into her coat, sending a stern reminder to his arms of their specific assignment—coat-holding, not embracing or consoling.

"Lillian Kenilworth?" A stout, handsome woman in a fur collar was blocking their way to the main doors. "Lillian *McKinley*, I should say. What a pleasure after all this time! I'd assumed you'd moved away."

"Marjorie." Lillian paused. She was flushed, he saw, wearing her heavy coat in the warm foyer.

"Wasn't Professor Derick *something*! My Harold couldn't be here tonight, always working late, but he's running an exclusive interview with her in tomorrow's paper."

So this was Southam's wife, the one who'd so upset Lillian when she'd visited with her baby in 1915. She looked to be trying to rearrange her nosy inquiries into some semblance of empathy. "I've thought of you so many times, poor lamb. You were in *such* a state at the service for poor Thomas, and still so poorly when Lucy Fitzgibbons and I stopped by after my Ella arrived." Her eyes, as she said this, were latching on to Ernest. "And all went well with the child that fall, I heard? A little boy, was it?"

Lillian was turning a mottled purple. "No. I mean, yes. But it was— Well, it was a girl, Kit. Katherine."

Marjorie cooed like a pigeon and laid her gloved claw on Lillian's sleeve. "Katherine, how lovely. Was that your mother's name? You poor dear, an orphan, then losing poor Thomas. And now a child without a father." Her gleaming eyes leapt once again in Ernest's direction. He set his jaw so tightly he heard a ringing in his ears. He was thinking about what he'd do if he heard the phrase "poor Thomas" one more time from this woman's galloping mouth.

"Oh, we didn't have the best visit that day, but then I hadn't known of your delicate condition—certainly no one had mentioned it at the funeral for poor Thomas. But my dear, you should have reached out sooner! We're all here for one another, you know. And my Ella must be almost the same age as your Katherine, just a few months older." Marjorie twirled, beaming, to include Ernest. "Born the very same day the *Lusitania* went down, if you can imagine."

Lillian flinched.

"Oh, duckie! I'm so very sorry." She took a card from her purse. "We must get together. Do you have a telephone? You simply must stop by or drop me a line, any time. We'll get the girls together, shall we, at my place? Or we'll go for tea? My Ella is scampering all over and talking up a storm. She'd love a little playmate, I'm sure of it. We must introduce them."

Marjorie put extra emphasis on the word *introduce*, flinging another pointed nod at Ernest, who ignored it and turned his hat in his hands. Lillian took the card hesitantly, as if dazed. Perhaps she, too, was thinking of Kit at home, having scarcely started babbling anything remotely intelligible, pinching her lips belligerently against spoon after spoon of pulped carrot. Scampering? Kit had yet to pull herself up on all fours.

"We must go," Lillian said at last. It wasn't clear whether she meant this for Marjorie and her offer of tea or for Ernest, but before Marjorie could blather another word, Lillian was heading for the double doors, then out into the blowing snow.

Ernest and Lillian drove the short and slippery distance from campus to La Main in silence, mounting the steps to the third-floor flat as quietly as their winter boots would allow. On their ascent, they could hear Kit's howls and, to their surprise, found the door to the flat ajar when they arrived, the lamps blazing.

Kit, bless her, was in Natalie's arms, doing her best to drown out whatever might have otherwise taken place by way of conversation because their downstairs neighbors, the dour Russos, were seated on the settee. Another man, whom Ernest recognized as the landlord, Monsieur Langois—seldom seen unless a pipe was frozen or a window cracked—was striding around the apartment tallying the chips in the plaster walls, the dents in the wainscoting. Mrs. Russo, heavily pregnant once again, pointed a trembling finger at Ernest.

"That's one of the men, Monsieur Langois. Coming and going at all hours of the day and night, laden with packages." Mrs. Russo's eyes were wide and her chin wobbled, accentuating her underbite. "The other is a younger man, not quite so sharply dressed, who tends to come"—she jabbed in Lillian's direction now—"when Mrs. McKinley has stepped out."

Lillian turned to Natalie, her eyebrows raised. Natalie responded by peeling the baby from her shoulder and thrusting her at Lillian.

Mr. Russo got to his feet. "Monsieur Langois, you can understand. We have several children already, with another on the way. This is a respectable establishment. Two young women with a string of gentlemen callers, a baby. . ." His voice trailed away.

"A younger man, not as sharply dressed?" Lillian was addressing Natalie, batting aside the little hand pawing greedily at her breast.

"Just the one time," Natalie mumbled. "Maybe twice. Marty Thurston, I told you about him. He's a classmate at teaching school. Nothing untoward." She sniffed. "Nothing along the lines of what's being insinuated here."

Mrs. Russo bristled, turning her bulging eyes at the baby. "Thomas McKinley, God rest his soul, is nearly three years gone." She made the sign of the cross over her ample breast. "Three years! I have four children already, Monsieur Langois. I know babies. That baby"—she again speared the air with her thick finger—"is eight months old if she's a day."

Lillian took a step toward Natalie, who was making a show of rattling the cupboards open and closed. Lillian furrowed her brow at her. "Have I even met a Marty Thurston? I'm sure I don't know that name."

Monsieur Langois had stopped his pacing and was staring sternly at the baby, as if trying to place it. Kit squirmed, the cold, wet wool of Lillian's coat scratchy against her face. She took a gulp of air, gearing up for her hungriest yowl.

Ernest coughed, planted his feet wide, then pointed to the open door with a flourish. "This visit is over," he said flatly. He reached into his breast pocket and handed the landlord a card stating his senior position within the foreign services branch of government, along with his office address on the prestigious Rue Saint-Jacques. "Monsieur Langois, please telephone or call in at your earliest convenience if you require more," he said in French. Then he turned to the Russos and switched to Italian, which prompted more bug-eyed blinking from Mrs. Russo. "As you can see, the baby is hungry, you are upsetting her, and there is a risk she will catch a chill." He nodded curtly. "Good night to you both."

The click of the door set Kit caterwauling with fresh determination. Natalie and Lillian both started talking at once, Lillian trying to wriggle out of her wet coat, juggling the baby from arm to arm and showering her sister with questions. Natalie's protests were directed partly at Lillian and partly at the retreating Russos, her eyes flashing.

"Lillian!" Ernest said, loud enough that Kit's cries seemed to lodge in her windpipe and the quarreling sisters both turned to Ernest mid-sentence. He took the baby from her mother and nestled her into the crook of his arm, using the other to help Lillian out of her coat, then spinning her gently to face him.

"Lillian," he repeated, more softly. "Enough of all this. There is a simple solution before us, and a happy one." He cleared his throat. "Will you marry me?"

vi.

Time went by and the baby stayed a baby. Pink-gummed and plump-cheeked, with long ropes of glistening drool connecting her rosy lips to whatever she clutched in her miniature hand, eternally wailing or winsome. Kit's glacial development would surely have raised more eyebrows if Ernest's work had not kept them constantly on the move.

Immediately after they were wed, the new Mr. and Mrs. McKinley headed to Boston for six months, then New York, then Washington, DC, where Ernest was the eyes and ears of Prime Minister Borden's government amid the international mix of power brokers, industrialists, and political elites reeling from the war and vying for its spoils.

By the time the McKinleys returned to Canada in 1919, managing to avoid the Spanish flu, no one questioned whether Kit, with her strawberry curls and sparkling green eyes, was Ernest's child. Ernest, now approaching his mid-thirties, felt almost frightened by his own happiness. *What dumb luck*, he mused, while he huffed and flexed his way through his morning calisthenics. *What a change in tide*, he thought as he peered into the baby's bassinet to watch her furrow her sweet brow as if, like her papa, she hoped to solve the world's problems while she slept. *What divine fortune*, he marveled, as Lillian in her white slip tilted her head and fiddled with an earring at the mirror, and his ribs felt too tight in his chest. Lillian's loose chignon threatened to tumble sideways over her shoulder and his hand twitched with the urge to help it topple.

If only he could be sure that Lillian felt the same way. Reading Lillian's emotions was like decoding an enemy cipher. He'd watched her holding Kit, purple-faced and apoplectic, with a wooden stoicism that was just as likely to be the cause of the baby's upset as it was any sort of solace.

"Of course I love her," Lillian would say, her face a mix of hurt and bafflement.

"But she needs to *feel* that you love her," Ernest said. "It might help her flourish."

Because little Kit was still far too small. Now past her third birthday, the child had only just figured out how to stagger to her feet with the help of whatever leg or furniture was at hand. She showed no sign of cutting her first tooth.

"It certainly defies explanation," said Dr. Hampston, who'd since moved to Toronto, where her practice was attracting more of the sorts of patients eschewed by other physicians. She paid a special visit to the McKinleys once they'd returned to Montreal.

She pushed her glasses atop her round head. "My private diagnosis," she continued, "would be that her body's rhythm, that is to say, her internal calendar, is merely set at a slower tempo." Kit, seated on the rug in the middle of the room, smacked a disembodied doll's arm against a wooden box, grunting contentedly at the sound. "Time, for her, is different. She *is* aging, she's older than she was eighteen months ago, she's just not eighteen months older. There's nothing to indicate that she won't catch up at some point."

Dr. Hampston tapped her spectacles back down on her nose and lifted her chin to inspect Lillian. "And you? What will you do?"

"Me?" Lillian's brows hopped at the question. Kit, likely sensing she was losing the attention of the adults, hurled the doll's arm across the carpet, then scrambled after it on all fours.

"Quite the throwing arm!" Dr. Hampston said. "Yes, you. I'm assuming you'll now go back to finish your undergraduate degree?"

"Oh," said Lillian, waving vaguely at the tall shelves lining the room. They were crowded with books, most of them Ernest's, although her collection of texts and journals was slowly growing. "I keep up."

Dr. Hampston sniffed. "Crumbs and morsels," she pronounced. "Your brain will starve at this rate. I'll speak to the dean of the department myself. I bet he'd be delighted to have you back. And Dr. Derick is still teaching in the botany department, of course—as you likely know, she's decided to step down as president of the Montreal Suffrage Association."

Ernest could see from Lillian's expression that she wasn't up on society news, but there was a gleam in her eye that hadn't been there a moment ago. Ernest had assumed she was lonely. Natalie, after finishing up her teaching degree, had since accepted a job in New Brunswick.

Kit chose that moment to haul herself up using the arm of Ernest's wingback chair. "Pa-pa!" she said, beaming with pride. He hoisted her onto his lap and she whooped. Lowering his nose to her downy head and breathing deeply, he thought, *Of course*. Of course Lillian needed to return to her studies. He should have thought of this himself. Lillian wasn't lonely; she was bored.

Dr. Hampston was choosing her words carefully. "Kit is delayed, certainly, but she lacks all telltale signs of feeble-mindedness or congenital retardation." She hesitated. These terms were gunpowder in the women's league these days, where the sisterhood was increasingly fixating on mental hygiene and eugenics. It was the chief reason Lillian had little interest in attending any of the Montreal meetings.

Ernest set Kit down on her feet again, holding her as she swayed. He let his hands slide over her narrow shoulders and down her arms so that she clutched at his fingers with a ferocity that surprised him. After teetering for a moment, she lifted a foot and took an unsteady step toward her mother, then another, pulling away from his grip and half lunging, half stumbling into her mother's knees. Lillian finally seemed to snap to attention, breaking into a soft smile.

"If I may." Dr. Hampston cleared her throat. "I'd suggest you don't go discussing the particulars of Kit's slow progress with the likes of Dr. Derick."

1920

D r. Hampston took it upon herself to inform the McKinleys about the increasingly shrill eugenics research, which concluded that "degenerates" should be placed in specialized facilities and parents publicly denounced, or worse. Enclosed in her letters were nasty cartoons and sensationalist drivel from the local tabloids warning about deviants and imbeciles sullying the human gene line. Dr. Hampston's unwavering advice: until Kit's biological clock caught up with her contemporaries, it was best to keep her away from prying eyes.

So partly because of Dr. Hampston's warnings and partly out of some instinct of his own, Ernest made sure that Kit's circle stayed small and that the truth of her sluggish development remained a secret. This was only temporary, he assured himself— already Kit was showing hints of a superb intellect and other signs that she might soon start progressing faster and faster. A few growth spurts and she'd catch up. But had they, out of an abundance of caution, normalized fleeting connections for Kit that would make her distrustful of friendship? Of forging lasting ties? This was exactly the kind of pulp psychoanalysis the gutter press pandered to, and Ernest took special exception to, and yet it found its way under his skin.

When they first returned to Montreal, they had hired a live-in nanny named Olga, recently emigrated from Kyiv. By February 1920, Kit's speech was still a babbling brook, studded with the

occasional word in English or Ukrainian. When Natalie arrived
to celebrate Kit's first, true, leap year birthday, she surprised
them with a cake bearing a single candle as a joke. But Olga,
seeing this, seemed frightened.

"Today birthday?" Olga was turning this over, glancing
at the smoke snaking from the candle after Lillian had blown
it out. Ernest could well imagine what Lillian had wished for.
"So Kateryna is leap year baby? This explain everything! My
baba used to tell me stories about the leap year children and
their special—how you say—clock?" She backed away from
Kit, her eyes wide. "This explain much, Kateryna. You are
four years on earth, but today you are one."

Ernest would have liked to have learned more about Olga's
baba's stories, but Lillian was adamant. Olga must go.

It wasn't a sustainable strategy, hiring nanny after nanny,
but they did it for a time. Annette from Chicoutimi, Hortense
from Guadeloupe, then Angeliki from Greece—all of them staying four or five months, no more. Morag lasted nearly a year,
joining the household just as Lillian was preparing to start the
final year of her botany degree. Lately of Inverness, with a ready
laugh and a singing voice that could carry a choir, Morag's ruddy
face, accent, and red-bronze hair reminded Ernest of his own
boyhood nanny. To Lillian's enormous relief, Kit had at last
stopped lurching like a drunkard from room to room, but now
moved with an unnerving speed, oblivious to obstacles. It fell to
young Morag to follow Kit around, her big hands lifting Kit by
the armpits if she fell, dusting her off, and setting her back on
her feet.

She'd been nearly ten months with the McKinleys when
Morag had the great misfortune of falling in love with David,

a cub reporter trying to make something of himself at the *Montreal Gazette*. Lovesick desperation, Ernest conjectured. That was the only possible pretext for Morag mentioning to David that the child in her care was facile in French and English, and had a smattering of Greek, but never seemed to physically age. A perpetual toddler, nearly toothless, clumsy as a pinball careering around her nursery. The young man started poking around, asking questions, even tracking down Marie, Ernest's old housekeeper, who'd retired to Drummondville when the McKinleys first left for Boston in 1918, as well as Monsieur Langois, the landlord on La Main, who wrote to Natalie to let her know.

It was a kindly neighbor looking out her back window on one of the first warm days of spring who called Ernest at the office to ask about the strange man setting up a bulky box camera and tripod on the McKinleys' back lawn, while the child played on a blanket, the daisies blooming as backdrop.

No more than fifteen minutes could have passed before Ernest roared up the street in his Buick, tore around the side of the house, swatted the reedy man aside, and, hinging the camera open, snatched the film from its chamber. Ernest had to call in no small number of favors to make sure the *Gazette* story got quashed. Morag was summarily dismissed, and whatever it was her man had hoped to print about a baby that stayed a baby, it never saw the light of day.

Lillian was deeply shaken, waking in the night to prowl the house. Kidnappers might at any minute jimmy a window and abscond with the child, who would be thrust in a cage, poked and prodded like a freak. If he weren't equally rattled, Ernest might admit to being comforted by this rare glimpse of maternal instinct in his preternaturally imperturbable wife.

But Ernest, who prided himself on his steely composure, felt as if the lining of his heart had been flayed, exposing a raw underlay that trembled and quaked.

Ernest requested and was granted a transfer to Ottawa. Lillian took her first exam for her McGill degree the same week the Westmount house was put on the market, and her last on the day it sold. His little family had packed up and moved upriver before the month was out.

1924

On February 29, 1924, Kit tore through the pretty wrappings on her small stack of presents with a zeal for the crunch and rip of the paper that she was slow to muster for the gifts themselves. A stack of children's books chosen by her mother, a pair of ice skates—far too large—sent from Natalie out East, and a Meccano set that Ernest himself had purchased from a toy shop in downtown Ottawa.

"Construction in miniature," Lillian said, reading the words on the box, sounding dubious. "Couldn't she choke on the pieces?"

"Technically, she's eight years old," Ernest said, aiming for levity.

Lillian sighed deeply. They'd stopped talking about a magical growth spurt. Kit was less than three feet tall. The first of her back molars was only now threatening to protrude through the gums, which had turned bluish and mounded, making her fuss. But despite her physical shortcomings, time was proving a patient teacher. Kit stopped crumpling the paper and studied the cardboard lid of the Meccano box, which featured a smug boy in a red sweater presiding over a miniature crane. After a moment, Kit slid from her chair and scuttled in the direction of the study, returning with Ernest's letter opener in her plump fist. Ernest sprang to his feet before she could trip and impale herself. Kit was too fast. Back at the table, she overturned the box, then used the sharp tip of the opener to unseal the edges. He raised an eyebrow at Lillian.

"I think we can agree she's neither eight nor two," he said quietly. "She's somewhere in between."

That night was the wrong night to propose the idea pressing on him like a hand on his shoulder. Kit was fast asleep in her own room and they were lying in bed, man and wife, under the milky gaze of the moon and the stars. Lillian, her cheek on the pillow and her eyes almost closed, was roving her fingers over the rise and fall of his muscled chest, exploring the meat of his shoulders, the taut belly of his biceps. This was more than just youthful urge or appreciation on her part, he told himself. It was in her rambling touch that he knew she loved him.

"How are you like this?" she murmured. "So broad and strong. Tom was all rib cage, narrow as a rake."

He stayed still, quieting his heart under her silky caress. He didn't want this perfect moment to turn maudlin, although her voice was more curious than melancholic.

"I was always short and stocky where Thomas was lean and tall. Our mother used to say we were built using the same ration of clay but apportioned differently. And it was true, by the time Thomas was fifteen, he weighed almost as much as I did at twenty-six."

She was prodding at his pectorals the way you might size a cut of beef at the butcher. "This is more than clay, Ernest."

He could hear a smile in her sleepy voice.

"Well, the groves of academe, in my case, included some sanctioned pugilism."

"Meaning . . . ?"

"I boxed at university."

"Hmm," she said, smiling, sounding both appreciative and vindicated. When she lifted her hand away, he felt the chill of its absence.

He seized his moment. "Do you think, maybe Kit needs a little brother or sister?"

Lillian said nothing. They were always so careful about this. Counting the days of the month or using prophylactics. He pulled her awkwardly toward him. "You've said yourself, based on everything you've read, that Kit is likely a one in a billion mutation, her biological makeup affected at some critical juncture by the trauma of Thomas's death." In the dim light, he could see the whites of her eyes growing wider. His heart banged. "Dr. Hampston says the same, that Kit's anomaly is so rare it can't possibly be something heritable."

Her body was rigid in his embrace and stayed that way for a long minute. When she finally softened, letting her forehead come to rest against him, the sensation he felt was not warmth, not Lillian melting into him, but a hot-air balloon, stone cold, slumping to earth.

"Kit should be in school," she mumbled into his collarbone. "But we can't risk that when she looks so young, even if we lie about her age. She'll only fall behind and people will notice. Dr. Hampston says teachers can recommend children be put in special schools, separated from their families. We can't do this again, or I can't. She's taking everything I have already."

ii.

By the mid-1920s, Ernest's work saw him focusing more closely on European diplomacy and the League of Nations, grateful that doddering Joe Pope—bless him—had passed the baton to Ernest's top pick, Oscar Skelton, as undersecretary of state for external affairs. Ernest and Skelton had been perfectly aligned on the Dominion's stance on the Chanak skirmish. Lillian, who'd set up her microscope in the sunroom, paged through her botany books and puttered with seeds ordered through a catalogue, their new Atwater Kent radio filling the silence. Kit, armed with her own trowel, spent hours liberating scoops of soil from a sack and crafting small mounds around the room, as if the tile floor belied an underground network of gophers. Within a year, the whole arrangement, to Ernest, started to look more like a meticulously organized garden shop than botanical science.

Sensing her restlessness, Ernest taught Lillian to drive and traded his Buick for a Nash Special Six four-door sedan, large enough that Kit's carriage could be wedged in the back. Lillian took to driving like a bird to flight, intuitive and alert. Whatever risks the country roads might hold for his wife and daughter, Ernest knew these faded before the hazards of having them cooped up at home and tuning in too closely to some of the sensationalist drivel on the Atwater Kent.

For over a year, a plummy-toned windbag by the name of Vincent Donaldson, host of *Times Like These*, had been breathlessly regurgitating the proceedings of the Virginia circuit court case of *Buck v. Bell*, now destined for the US Supreme Court. The Amherst County judge had ruled that the Virginia State Colony for Epileptics and Feebleminded could legally sterilize seventeen-year-old Carrie Buck who, like her mother before her, had been transferred to the colony for intractable feebleminded-ness and promiscuity. Ernest had caught the tail end of Donald-son's interview with the colony's medical superintendent, who'd declared that a dozen specialists would testify under oath that eugenic sterilization should be mandated not only for Miss Buck but for Carrie's infant baby as well, on the grounds of hereditary imbecility. "Scientifically speaking," Lillian had said through gritted teeth, "on what grounds can the classification of 'middle-grade moron' be determined as a hereditary trait?"

It was far, far better, thought Ernest, striding the halls of Par-liament or meeting with associates on Laurier Street, to think of Lillian and Kit on the open road, exploring the lanes and byways of Southern Ontario. Ernest, seated at his desk looking out over the canal—the gongoozlers ambling the banks, the stream of cars huffing impatiently over the bridge—was surprised to feel a vicarious freedom and relief. His wife was not penned up at home, bored and fretting.

Sundays he joined them, perfectly content to be Lillian's pas-senger. When Kit wasn't asleep in the back, he'd nestle her in his lap, encouraging her chirpy chatter as she named the world's rich details in the mix of languages she'd picked up from her nannies in Montreal—*étang, oiseau, λουλούδι*. Lillian often brought along clippers or a spade, and when they stopped for lunch, she'd set off to collect cuttings that would end up under a lamp in the sunroom or find their place in the backyard, neatly numbered and labeled. Kit trailed proudly behind her, tasked with carrying gloves or a magnifying glass, and in her curious mix of words and gestures, she peppered her mother with questions about the migrations of birds overhead, the twitching complacency of horses in a pasture, the particular swirl of a river. Ernest marveled at the wealth of knowledge his wife had filed away: every species of plant and flower, their telltale features, how they propagated, and their tricks for surviving the Ontario winters—all their Latin monikers unfurling from her tongue like incantations.

In the fall of 1926, their Sunday drive took them out to Renfrew County, where they came across a country fair. The grounds were packed with people queuing up for wagon rides, bobbing for apples, or leading their prize pig for judging. The air smelled of hay and manure mingled with sweeter fairground smells: candy floss, kettle corn, and apple pie. Kit insisted on stumbling along on her stubby legs. *Baaaah*, they said to the lambs. *Oink*, they honked at the pigs. When they passed a man selling a litter of puppies, Kit, who knew the word for *dog* in four different languages, could scarcely be coaxed away. Ernest settled her on his shoulders, and she clasped her slim arms around his neck.

They paused in front of a building more cottage than farm stall, freshly whitewashed, with a queue of young couples curling across its porch. A petite, rosy-cheeked woman in a starched nurse's uniform was calling out to passersby. "Step right up to register your pedigree and learn your family's score!"

It took a moment for Ernest to register the purpose of this building and he kicked himself for pausing. *Walk on, Lillian*, he thought. *Walk on.* Even here in this pastoral paradise, the long arms of Vincent Donaldson and his shrill guests could reach out of the Atwater Kent to clutch at his shoulder. And sure enough, a man in a newsboy cap was chatting up the couples, making the men guffaw and the ladies blush, scribbling their replies in his notebook.

FITTER FAMILIES blared the towering words painted three feet high on the building behind the little nurse, while a tall placard offered a list of "Unfit Human Traits."

FEEBLEMINDEDNESS
PROMISCUITY
EPILEPSY
PHYSICAL DEFORMATION
CRIMINALITY
INSANITY
ALCOHOLISM
PAUPERISM
LOVE OF THE SEA

Did You know? the sign read. *Unfit human traits like these and many others run in families like color in guinea pigs. If all marriages were eugenic, we could breed out most of this unfitness in three generations. SELECTED PARENTS will have BETTER CHILDREN. This is the great aim of eugenics!*

Lillian, her mouth pinching in distaste, had already turned on her heel, but Kit, on Ernest's shoulders, her red curls aflame in the golden light, had attracted the attention of the nurse.

She bustled over, elbows jutting, thrusting a clipboard toward Lillian. "The questionnaire takes just five minutes, then you can get in line now or return with your husband tomorrow for the examination and competition. The Fittest Family prize for best breeding stock will be awarded at the end of the week. If this lovely baby girl is any indication, you might be in the running for the grand prize!"

Kit drummed the heels of her shoes against Ernest's clavicle, urging him forward. The nurse beamed up at her.

"How old are you, sweet cheeks?" She had clamped her clipboard under her arm but made to pull it out again. A look from Ernest made her freeze.

"I think not," Lillian said, and they strode out through the gates to the Nash.

iii.

The worst blizzard of 1927 struck in early March. That night, as the windowpanes chattered like teeth, Ernest built a roaring fire and gathered his family close, the wet birch hissing like a serpent in the grate. Lillian sat on the living room floor with her books spread out on the coffee table while Kit leafed through her battered *Peter Pan* picture book. Ernest sat in his green armchair, smoking his pipe and frowning his way through the major Canadian and US dailies, as was his custom.

"I see your mother's old professor has an op-ed in today's *Gazette*," he told Kit, snapping the paper smooth and studying the stern face in the blotched photograph "Dr. Carrie Derick. Mummy and I saw her at a lecture on campus."

Kit maneuvered herself under the newspaper and onto his lap, cushioning her head in his armpit. He fell silent, reading, but he could feel Lillian watching him warily. The editorial took its cue from the Carrie Buck sterilization case, now winding its way through the US Supreme Court. Derick, Ernest saw with a sinking heart, was still fervently embracing eugenics.

"Read it to me," Lillian said softly.

"'Royal Commission Required to Investigate Mental Deficiency,'" he read. "'The wise and humane solution is to provide, with compassion, a compulsory education for all children, but one that allows for a strict separation of the children with intellect and potential from the feebleminded and defective.'" He continued reading, regretting he'd ever spoken. "'In the same way that certain breeds of dog lend themselves to particular uses, so too can children be identified during their earliest years as having the genes that earmark them for one type of future and not another.'" He pulled the newspaper closer to straighten a crease, and Kit lunged forward, swatting at the words and offering a garbled opinion. He could well imagine what the likes of Derick would make of Kit. For an eleven-year-old, her physical development was profoundly delayed, but then no one would presume she was eleven. She looked for all the world like a happy, curious toddler. Indeed, next year she'd be three in "leap year time," as they privately called it, but three was wildly off the mark, too. It didn't capture her expansive vocabulary, her strength and agility, her uncanny sensitivity and intuition. Even now, he could tell, Kit was darting an anxious look at her mother, who was setting down her pen with a sigh.

He laid the newspaper on his knee, and Derick's eyes, disapproving, seemed to follow him from the page. He tried to encircle Kit, planting a kiss on the crown of her head, but she wriggled to dislodge him, bending forward with that marvelous elasticity of youth and snatching up his abandoned paper. He watched, bemused, as she jabbed a stubby finger at the page.

"Gins," she declared, pinning a word with her finger, then twisting her head to beam at her mother. Ernest leaned forward again to follow her finger to the word she'd selected: *genes*. He raised an eyebrow at Lillian. She met his look, then pushed herself swiftly to her feet.

Kit leaned in again, studied the words, then stabbed at the paper a second time, then a third, then a fourth, her pink finger skipping across the page. "Childwin," she said. "Mento intewect." She seemed to scan the text, landing ultimately on a word she recognized with particular glee. "Dog!"

"Start from here," said Ernest, pointing. "Each word in turn."

Kit's chin puckered in concentration as she leaned forward, then said, "Da. Wise. And. Hoomane. Sowution. Is. To. Pwovide. Wif . . . Com. Pass. Eon."

"Compassion," Ernest repeated, a whisper. Kit inclined her head to smile again at her mother. Lillian had come to stand beside their chair, relief scrubbing the lines on her tall forehead, a tear rolling down her cheeks and colliding with the brim of her smile.

1928

i.

Kit named her beloved mutt Spargo after Tony Spargo, the colorful drummer who led the Original Dixieland Jazz Band, one of her favorites on the Atwater Kent. Spargo's tail never stopped its steady beat, sleeping or awake. Just six weeks old and fifteen pounds when Ernest brought him home on February 29, 1928, Spargo proceeded to gain another five pounds every two weeks.

Lillian was incredulous. "Ernest, we discussed a dog for Kit, not a bear! He's already bowling Kit over. By the time he gets to full size . . ."

Ernest craned his chin to straighten his tie. "Well, it's not clear what breed the sire was, but certainly the pups looked like the mother, a German shepherd. Or mostly German shepherd."

"The mystery suitor must have been a wolf," said Lillian. She was easing her hand into the gloves she used for handling her plant specimens but paused when the ungainly dog came to stand beside her as if she'd just paid him a compliment. "Or a mastodon," she murmured, letting her hand fall to the scruffy fur at his neck, trying not to smile as the big dog leaned into her caress.

Kit, oblivious to Spargo's shambling gait, his sloppy black lips and patchwork coat, insisted he was the most beautiful, most majestic, most resplendent beast she'd ever laid eyes on. The chirruping adjectives were still hampered by short vocal cords so that her vast, polyglot vocabulary was at odds with her oral musculature: she knew far more words than she could properly pronounce. Ernest was teaching her to read in French and German—he already spoke German with Kit, who loved its guttural buzz—as well as some preliminary Italian that, she informed him, felt ticklish against the roof of her mouth. Kit herself had badgered Lillian to help her decipher the sheet music moldering in the piano bench and now could spend a morning plucking happily through her Schirmer Library Classics—never mind that Kit's hands could scarcely span five keys and her legs were too short to reach the damper pedal. Most nights, Kit fell asleep with her books splayed open around her, one arm thrown over the steady heave of Spargo's chest.

ii.

Lillian, surprising everyone except Lillian, had published a monograph on length of day and color intensity in tetrasporic plants in the *Annals of Botany,* then a second was accepted by *Genetics*. She peddled these, alongside her undergraduate degree, to land a laboratory assistant position at the University of Ottawa. Serendipitously, Natalie, for reasons she wasn't particularly inclined to elaborate on in her letters—which may or may not have involved an overeager suitor—had been looking to leave her teaching post in Moncton. Kit's latest nanny had moved out the day before, and Natalie would be arriving on the noon train. A growth spurt might make it possible for Kit to start at a nursery school the following year, but in the meantime, Natalie could feed Kit's hungry mind with history and piano lessons and multiplication tables, along with French and English grammar and spelling.

Kit and Lillian's safety and happiness—fresh fuel for their sharp minds—would be one less thing for Ernest to worry about. He was sleeping poorly and had for weeks. The falling stock prices of September and October 1929 had culminated in a week of frenzied trading that had blown the bottom out of the New York Stock Exchange the week prior and would have long-reaching implications for Canada. Abroad, Prince Maximilian had died in Baden. Regrettably. It had been a long time since the man had held any real sway in the volatile politics of the Reich, but still. Maximilian had been a moderate and a conciliator—something of a dying breed in Germany. Darker days were ahead, he could feel it in his bones. But on this bright November day, fine but cold, with his wife and daughter eager to take a stroll in Major's Hill before Natalie's train was due, Ernest was determined to put his sense of foreboding aside.

Ernest had Kit's warm mitten in one hand and Spargo's leash in the other, the big dog plodding obediently at his side. Each time Kit pounced at the frozen puddles, making them crack like mirrors under her boots, Ernest tightened his grip so she couldn't slip and fall. He needn't have worried. Stairs, taken at pace, could still occasionally trip her up, but on these smooth paths, Kit was agile and swift, almost graceful. Tiny, to be sure, but able to pass for a five-year-old.

They waited with the dog on the frost-chopped grass outside the station. Ernest, stamping his feet, caught the wash of happiness on Lillian's eager face as she strained to catch a glimpse of her sister over the waiting throngs. She'd turned thirty-two that summer, but working in the university lab, putting her busy brain to use again, had stripped away the years.

Then, to his surprise, she stiffened abruptly, dipping her head.

"It's Marjorie Southam," she mumbled, giving the brim of her hat a sharp downward tug. "You remember Marjorie, from the Montreal Suffrage Association. A busybody. And very involved with those horrible tracts." Lillian was struggling for a look of bland impassivity. "She was so nosy about Kit. I never returned her letters and calls."

Ernest could well remember the flavor of these particular pamphlets. *Preserving the Pedigree* and *Mothers for the Protection of Canadian Purity*. And the Southam dynasty had been snapping up newspapers and now radio stations all across the country. He cast an eye one way and the next, expecting to see Harold Southam toadying from party to party, straining to hear some salacious titbit to feed to his rabid columnists. Lillian hunched, trying to shrink her tall frame to the average height of the crowd, but Marjorie had already spotted them, her face lighting up in a pantomime of recognition and delight.

"Why if it isn't the mysterious Lillian McKinley! And of course, it *is* McKinley, isn't it? For the second time?" She leaned in, her lips pleated into an exaggerated pucker, then wheeled on Ernest, snatching his hand. "Marjorie Southam. We were introduced just the once, more than a decade ago now, at McGill. And Lillian was so enigmatic that night. Do you remember, Lillian?"

She swirled a coy look at Ernest, noticing Kit for the first time. She crouched low, bracing a hand on each knee to help lever herself into position. Kit blinked, jerking her head back from the force of the woman's perfume.

"Why, hello there, little one!" Marjorie lifted her round tortoiseshell sunglasses to expose a pair of small, beetle-black eyes and a wide nose, dusty with powder. She surveyed Kit, a pale tongue darting out to moisten her lips. Spargo, who'd plunked dutifully to his haunches, emitted a low, warning growl.

Kit's own eyes had locked on the desiccated face of some small, furred creature entwined around Marjorie's neck—a mink or a fox, its body shrunken and flat, one glassy eye looking to the middle distance, ashamed to be haplessly biting its own tail.

"Oh, you're a shy one, are you?" Marjorie, wincing, pushed herself back to standing and, extending a gloved knuckle, tilted Kit's retreating chin toward the sun. "I'd no idea you'd had another child!" She waggled a plump finger at Lillian. "And you're living here now, in Ottawa, is that right? Someone told me that." The tongue emerged again as she took a sip of air.

"Is that a real dog?" Kit was still staring, stricken, at Marjorie's fur stole. Marjorie's gloved hand fingered the rust-red fur. "And what is your name, darling?"

"It is *real*?" Kit repeated, almost inaudibly.

"Lillian!"

Lillian jerked around to see Natalie, her hair drifting out from under her hat like a halo. Marjorie revolved in a haughty orbit toward the voice.

"Kit!"

Kit, at last, wrenched her eyes from the flaccid fox and threw herself at Natalie, who bent gracefully to scoop the child in her arms. Ernest, when he thought of Natalie, typically saw the scrawny elf that first appeared on his Westmount door in 1915. This was a poised young woman glowing golden in the winter sun, materializing on scene with the timing of an angel.

Marjorie's gaze journeyed up Natalie's figure like a freight elevator, lingering on Kit's scrawny limbs, now clamped around her aunt, and on her beaming grin, all her baby teeth so stubbornly intact. Then, Marjorie's mouth was moving again, even faster, reminding Natalie of the day they met at the flat on La Main.

"I wouldn't have recognized you! Such a trying time for us all, Lillian in such a sorry state over Thomas and I so exhausted—the baby, my duties in the women's league."

Her beady eyes scurried back to Ernest and Lillian. "How time flies. My Ella has been at Havergal College since she turned ten, and Anna joined her last year. A very fine school. My youngest, Richard, is about the same age as this little one now, I'd say."

Natalie had turned aside, Kit in her arms, a slow revolution that served to inch them away so that Marjorie's next question was directed at the back of Kit's woolen hat.

"This little one is your first child then, together, is that right, Ernest? Or are there others? Because your eldest, Lillian—Tom's girl—Kathleen was it? Katherine? I've got a good memory for names. Is she at day school now or . . . ?"

A train's whistle made them jump, and Marjorie's yammering mouth paused at last. "Oh! My Harold. That's his train. You'll wait just here, won't you? You must. I know my Harold would be simply thrilled to meet you." She backed away with a simpering smile, her hands raised and splayed as if trying to hold them in place with an invisible net. "I'll bring him straight over."

Lillian looked limp with relief at Marjorie's departure, and Natalie, who had wheeled back on Lillian, raised her eyes in alarm.

"Come," said Ernest. Spargo sprang back to standing. "You'll be tired, Natalie, after your long journey."

Back home, Kit was sent outside to play in the yard, still bundled in her winter clothes, Spargo trotting happily behind her. Ernest could hear the scrape and rustle of Kit with her leaf pile, trying to heap it as high as she could before flopping into it. Hopefully she wouldn't try to climb the tree unsupervised. At some point, she must have tramped a path through the dry shrubbery that formed the border around the side of the house and stood on her tiptoes to peer into the living room, because Ernest could see the red pom-pom from her woolen tuque bobbing at the bottom of the windowpane and the occasional glint of her blazing hair.

Could Kit hear their conversation through the glass? He doubted it. Briefly he could see her pale forehead, as if she were struggling to crane her chin to the window. Then she dropped out of view and disappeared.

Ernest rose to look out at the yard. Dusk was steeling over the dry grass, but Kit's new red wagon glowed in the falling light, creaking as she tugged it over the paving stones. She noticed his face looming behind the glass and offered a cheery wave.

The sisters were communicating in some wordless way, Natalie blinking, long and slow, Lillian's fingers writhing in her lap. Ernest reached for her, and she dropped her cold hand in his. In the silence, he could hear the creak of the wagon wheels outside and the crunch of branches and leaves, Kit coaxing Spargo in a voice high and wheedling.

Natalie spoke first. "Have you thought, Lillian, whether through your work at the university, there might be someone you could speak with, confidentially. An expert in developmental biology or genetics who might have some insights into why Kit is so profoundly delayed? Whether that might be expected to change as she grows older? Maybe some tests, a treatment . . ."

"Delayed" was a euphemism Ernest had heard too often before. "No experts. No tests. No treatments. She's a perfectly normal little girl," he said, his teeth gritted. "She's simply . . . on her own schedule. She will get to where she's going in her own good time."

Silence, broken finally by Natalie. "I fully understand the need to keep Kit's condition a secret. You only need to look to the sterilization legislation that's been passed in the western provinces. It makes sense to keep her at home. But in time, she'll need to meet other children, to make friends, even if they're much younger, in years, than she is. She needs more than a dog. Others, who will be with her for longer. There are certain"—she grasped for the right word—"accommodations you'll have to make along the way, depending on how long it takes for her to grow up." Natalie's voice was unnaturally thin and tinny. "You are not such a young man, Ernest. If, perhaps, Kit's physical body is aging one year for every four, neither of you can expect to see her through to adulthood. Not if she doesn't start to catch up."

Natalie's words landed like a sucker punch squarely in the middle of Ernest's deepest fears. This was precisely why he'd so hoped to be able to convince Lillian to try for another child. Not just a companion and playmate: an investment for a future that he wouldn't and couldn't be part of.

Outside in the yard, Spargo barked, which Ernest should have known was a warning. Ernest spoke again, his voice gravelly. "This isn't some known condition, its course set in stone. It's possible, I believe, that her maturity will continue to quicken as it has already been doing. Her mind is far ahead of what you might even expect from a child in her early teens. It's her body, her physical stature, that is struggling to keep up."

Out of the corner of his eye, he registered a blur of red pom-pom, a white face with rosy cheeks, a pair of green eyes, anxiously blinking much higher up the pane of glass than before. But this realization was followed by a loud creak of wagon wheels, a shriek, and then the thud of something heavy hitting a drainpipe, which thundered. Then an awful quiet, broken by barking that didn't stop until Ernest burst out the back door into the yard.

iii.

Two years later, in late summer 1931, Kit would break her arm for the second time. Plummeting out of a chestnut tree after climbing onto a rotten branch, she'd fractured both her left radius and ulna. This was just before starting at Guigues Elementary, which was her second round of kindergarten—this time in French—and the second time she'd ended up with a chalk-white cast on her arm, which set back her piano lessons once again. Ernest had hoped the cast would help with the procurement of new playmates. Children always had such a macabre fascination with casts and splints and crutches, a charming frankness. That hadn't seemed the case with Kit.

On the subsequent hospital trip to get her plaster cast cut away once again, Ernest had watched the houses flash past, the red and gold leaves shifting fretfully in the streets, the brassy slant of the autumn sun. He'd found himself thinking of the night, nearly two years ago, when Kit had broken her arm the first time, falling from the red wagon she'd wheeled underneath the window so as to eavesdrop on her parents discussing her leap year secret with Natalie. He'd remembered the adults arguing in the car on the way to the hospital over what to say to the doctor—what age they'd give, what birth date, Lillian's quiet resolve, and his own prickling fears—while Kit whimpered on Natalie's lap. What had Kit heard that day through the window? How much of it had she remembered?

They lived on a different street now, in a different part of the capital—their route to the hospital now wound past a tawny, patchwork quilt of farmland, then a row of shuttered warehouses along the riverbank, one low wall blackened by fire. But Kit must have been rummaging through some of the same memories as her father because she said, "What do I tell the doctors if they ask, Papa?"

He caught her eye in the rearview mirror.

"If they ask what?" he said, but he was pretending and she knew it.

This would mark the moment that Kit joined the family collusion that would last Ernest's whole lifetime and beyond, the moment they tacitly agreed that, at least as far as Kit was concerned, they could set aside days, months, and years as reasonable markers and yardsticks. From this point on, Kit's public age would be whatever she could pass herself off as being. She would be the age of her appearance and her abilities, not bound by chronological or biological time, but some hybrid of the two. The truth, whatever that was, would be their family secret.

Kit dropped her gaze and turned to look out over the swollen river.

"Four." She said it so softly he almost didn't catch it. Four was the same age they had settled on in the car on the way to the hospital back in 1929, after the incident with the wagon. "I'll tell them I'm four."

1932

i.

Kit trudged up the steep snowdrifts pulling the Flexible Flyer to the top of the slope, bent with the effort, while her little friend staggered behind. The sleek new sled was her leap year birthday gift of 1932, and Reiner was the closest thing to a friend Kit had made at her school. In a year, he'd be taller than her; in another, they'd have to switch her to a new school and—the thought of this made Ernest feel deeply tired—they'd have to urge Kit to let this friendship lapse. For now, Ernest watched her settle Reiner between her knees with a solicitude she might have used with her own little brother. She looped her arms around him to reach the steering handles, then scooted her feet to bring them to the lip of the slope. Ernest was chilled to the marrow of his bones, could feel ice clumping his mustache and eyelashes, but the sight of his daughter and her friend whooshing down the blinding white hills, their shrill shrieks, Spargo dashing behind them—it warmed him as deeply as a swallow of Scotch. *You see there? That's my girl. That's my perfectly normal little girl.*

"I know it must be hard," Ernest would say to Kit, years later. "It must feel like life is moving so slowly for you, and try as you might, you can never catch up with everyone else."

She would slip her small hand into his, a habit she'd never grow out of in all the years they'd have together. "No, Papa.

It's not like that. It's just that try as I might, I can't get anyone else to slow down."

Ernest heard a crunching in the snow beside him.

"Reiner tells me your daughter is learning German."

It was Jakob Staedler, Reiner's father. They had met the last time the children played at this park, before the first snowfall. The man worked for the Hydro-Electric Power Commission, having emigrated to Canada before Reiner was born. To Ernest's ear, his accent sounded Bavarian.

"Her aunt is a teacher," Ernest said blandly. He had urged Kit to keep her multilingualism to herself, but the temptation to impress Reiner must have been insuperable.

Staedler nodded approvingly. "The young pick up language so quickly, I envy them."

They chatted for a time. Canada's gold medal hockey win in Lake Placid, the Lindbergh kidnapping earlier that week, how quickly the children grew out of their winter boots. Staedler said, "I read today we will be getting an early spring."

Ernest, burrowing his chin deep in his scarf, harrumphed. "Don't believe everything you read in the paper."

The man gave a snort. "There we can agree. What daily do you take?"

Ernest was surprised by the question. He devoured more newspapers in a single week than anyone else he knew. "Oh, the *Journal* mostly, more than the *Citizen*."

"I find there's very little of substance in the Canadian papers." The German man sniffed. "Sensational drivel, most of it. Conjoined twins, bank heists, and extraterrestrials. Serving to divert the underclasses rather than informing those desiring genuine knowledge. I rely on an Austrian weekly, although it is of course out of date by the time I get it."

"Which of the Austrian weeklies?" Ernest asked mildly, then merely blinked at Staedler's response as if he'd never heard of it. "And what is its slant?"

Staedler shrugged. "At least it's a paper for the educated man, not the masses."

The children were trudging back up the slope toward them, pink-cheeked and disheveled.

"Never underestimate the power of the media," Ernest said, his tone placid. "And the government's control over the media. That goes for the European papers every bit as much as it does our provincial press."

Staedler, in a more stentorian tone, as if the kindergarteners might benefit, launched into a treatise on press centralization and Aryanization as a critical tool of social improvement and political instruction. Ernest waited until he'd run out of words.

"Just so," Ernest said, his tone neutral. The children had almost reached them. With a sinking heart, he realized Kit's friendship with this man's child would be even shorter than planned. Softly, for Staedler's ears only, he murmured, "Certainly, if my government hadn't been so effective in glorifying the Great War to encourage enlistment, your brothers may not have killed mine on the battlefields of France."

ii.

These days, when the train brought him back to Ottawa from Toronto, New York, or Washington, DC, or when the taxi wound home from his office across town, Ernest's work and worries wore heavy. Chief among his qualms in the fall of 1933 was Germany's rearmament agenda, but also Japan's withdrawal from the League of Nations, the Assyrian massacre in Iraq, and, here at home, the growing relief lines and increasingly shrill calls to limit immigration. A melee had broken out at Christie Pits in Toronto last month after a group of hoodlums hung a swastika flag at the baseball diamond. Now young men everywhere were spluttering and emboldened, spoiling for a fight.

Indeed, it was a wonder it hadn't caught up with him sooner, he thought, as he stepped through the door, bracing himself for his family's reaction. "Hello?" he called and touched his finger to the cut on his temple, catching his wincing reflection in the hall mirror. He'd cleaned up as best as he could in the taxi. He made his way through the still of the house, cool and dim after the bright heat of the city. "Hello?"

He found them in the backyard. Lillian, cross-legged at the edge of a flower bed, her notebook in her lap, was touching her plants with a tenderness that made the hairs stand up on his arm.

"Papa!" Kit, grass-stained and filthy-footed, sprinted over and was about to leap into his arms when she saw his face and stopped. "Papa!" And this, at last, made Lillian look up and spring to her feet to lead him indoors.

Eyes wide and wet, she leaned forward and gently dabbed at his brow where he sat on the edge of their bed. Even so, he flinched back from her hand. "What in God's name were you thinking!" she said. He mumbled an answer, but his teeth sawed jagged against the swollen mush of his cheek.

"Ernest, you're scaring me."

"I'm fine, Lillian. Absolutely fine. Nothing broken. All my teeth still tucked in their beds. Just a bit of a misunderstanding."

"A *misunderstanding*?" She yanked herself backward, a bloom of blood spreading on the handkerchief in her hand.

"A dustup. Nothing serious. I took the boys from the office for a round at the Red Lion to celebrate Munro's retirement. There were some rough chaps already well ensconced at the bar and we exchanged some words." He shrugged, shooting a bolt of pain through his shoulder.

That's enough, son.

That's all Ernest had said. Gruff and forceful, but not impolite, not incendiary. Yet the sluice of beer—a full pint, it seemed, thirty cents wasted, when none of these rough lads had thirty cents to spare—had hit the back of his bare head like a whip. The liquor-loud sounds of the tavern fell so sharply it was as if a plug had been yanked from its socket; he could almost hear the trickle of ale, foamy as spit, seeping underneath his collar and down the knobs of his spine. Then a rough bark of laughter from the ragged pack behind them— four men? five? In his mind's eye, they'd seemed more sinew than brawn.

Slowly, slowly, he turned from the bar to face them, his fingertips curling into his palm. The blow caught him on the chin. Colors. A spray of sparks, yellow, pink, and iridescent green, popped behind his eyes before his lids could flutter open again. His tongue, tasting of metal and salt, probed clumsily at his teeth. But his weight was shifting where he needed it, his chin tucking. Force, a storm, quickened in his very center, even as the barstools squeaked and stuttered.

Shouts rose guttural from his own loyal boys, not a fighter among them. Then: grunts and thudding. The crunch of fists and flesh.

"Words?" Lillian repeated. She was steadying his head with a hand at the base of his neck, his curls still damp from beer and sweat. "What were you thinking, Ernest? What were *they* thinking? Taking a swing at a man like you? At your age!"

She took his chin between her finger and thumb and tugged it none too gently toward the window. It was worth it, and as rare as a rainbow in winter, to know from her crimped forehead and her angry touch that she loved him.

"A man like me?" he repeated. Even the effort of lifting an eyebrow and curling his lip toward a smile sent fresh tendrils of pain zigzagging through his jaw. With his face tilted to the mirror, he could see the gash over his eye, the skin puckered and puffed, a purple half-moon staining his cheekbone. In the hallway, the telephone rang and, over the throb of blood yet to settle in his ears, he heard Kit scampering to answer it, followed by a steady click of heels. Natalie, no doubt, dressed for an evening out.

Ernest grunted. "This is Ottawa. Men only come to blows over two things. Hockey and politics." He caught Lillian's eye. "And it wasn't hockey."

Her gaze darted to the door, and he sensed, rather than saw, Kit peering around the corner. Lillian forced her tone back into its normal register. "Your father's fine, but I need to have a word with him privately, please. Maybe you could bring me a wet flannel and some ice."

Kit dashed off on her errand, and Lillian watched him, waiting. They could hear Natalie tutting into the phone.

Ernest cleared his throat. "As I think you know, my department is fairly international, compared to others on the Hill. Tony's people are Italian and Joe is Jewish. I didn't know the gang of young smatchets. Out of work, would be my guess, based on the state of their clothes. Looking for trouble. And you know how it is. They were carping about immigrants, too many kikes taking Canadian jobs and that sort of drivel."

He pawed at her hand, intending reassurance, hoping she wouldn't notice his thickened knuckles. "My fellows, well, you can imagine. I didn't mean to get pulled into it, but there was no harm done." An image flashed through Ernest's mind—the barkeep at the Red Lion bellowing in warning as he pulled the baseball bat out from under the counter, the ragged men, pulling their ringleader off the floor by his armpits from where he lay, head lolling to one side and eyelids flickering, at Ernest's feet.

"Tell me about your day. What did you want to say in private? How's the flower experiment coming along?" He waved in the direction of the backyard, where he'd found her earlier, intent on her notes by her flower bed. She'd already tried to explain the project to him with a long string of incomprehensible jargon: *Mirabilis jalapa*, hypoxia and reoxygenation, photosynthesis inhibition, blah-blah-blah. The aim was to understand how stimulation and nourishment, as opposed to deprivation, might interact with the plant's underlying genetic intention.

"It's a failure, that's what it is."

"Surely not. It looks exquisite."

Lillian spoke quietly, the soiled handkerchief crumpled in her hand. "We've done everything, Ernest. Given her the best of everything." She wasn't talking about her flowers. "She's had every chance to catch up, to make up for lost time. She hasn't wanted for a thing."

Kit stepped cautiously into the room, cradling some slivers of ice in a cloth as if she had a baby owl cupped in her palms. How much had she heard? Her eyes bulged again at the sight of her father's mottled face, but he forced himself to smile.

"Hello, Kitty-Kat. Who was it on the phone?"

"It was the doctor, Mummy." Kit's gaze was like a pendulum between her mother and father.

Ernest started at her words, which only served to quicken the hammer strike at the back of his head. "Lillian, I'm fine. I most certainly don't need a doctor."

Lillian sank down heavily beside him, her face blanched, the cloth and ice falling to the floor.

"Hey, hey," he said. "I'm fine, Lillian. I didn't mean to give you a scare." He tilted her chin toward him and laid the flat of his bashed hand against his wife's brow, which was warm, but not hot. "Did you get too much sun in the yard?"

Lillian shook her head, her eyes bright. "Dr. Hampston, Ernest. I'm not sick, I'm late." She watched him process her meaning, while Kit edged forward, incomprehension twisting her little face. "Two months late, and I'm never late."

iii.

Dr. Margaret Hampston—grayer and rounder but in every other way unchanged—visited several times during Lillian's second pregnancy, even after it became clear that this one was very different than the last. Different, which is to say, normal. On April 13, 1934, Dr. Hampston delivered baby Helen, who proceeded to grow and thrive utterly on schedule.

All of which, instinctively, seemed suspect to Kit.

"She doesn't even look like me," said Kit, who didn't ask to hold the baby until six months had passed, then was rigid with discomfort, flinching at the baby's feeble kicks.

It was true—the baby was darker, taking after Lillian, with a tuft of chestnut hair and long, black lashes. Helen responded to Kit's observation with a throaty scream so that Kit, her head craning back, couldn't hand her back to Ernest fast enough.

When the baby was sleeping, Kit couldn't thunder through the house with Spargo or prance to Cole Porter blaring on the Atwater Kent. If she so much as sat at the piano bench to practice her Bach inventions—the tinkling voice of her right hand calling out to her plucky left, so solid and true—Helen's face wrinkled as if smelling something foul. When Helen started crawling, just eight months old, she tended to crawl away from her sister.

"She hates me."

Kit trudged to Ernest, burying her face in her father's stomach. Ernest rubbed her back and chuckled. "No, no, Kit. She's still getting to know you, isn't she. And you're getting to know her, too. Trust me, brothers and sisters are like this. Even when they're driving you mad, you love them. It was like this for me and Thomas, too." Kit liked to hear about her birth father—they'd never kept this from her and always indulged her questions. "It will be the same for you and Helen, I promise. You will love her, no matter what."

Ernest watched Lillian lift Helen from her crib, rocking her until her sobs subsided. In moments like these, his whole family around him, it seemed like his happy heart might punch a hole straight through his breast. The prime minister was insisting he make plans to relocate to Europe sometime in the next year or so to help firm up their network of ears and eyes, the same way he'd done before the Great War. Lillian had written to a professor at the Sorbonne in Paris describing her *Mirabilis jalapa* experiment with stimulus and deprivation, with an eye to continuing her work if they made the move. But they were so happy here, at last, his little family. How could he move them now? Even Kit, at a new school once again—this one with a strong music program—seemed adjusted and content. Her only source of sadness was her sister.

He rubbed Kit's back. "Helen will stop crying when she gets bigger."

Kit looked sidelong at the mewling infant in her mother's arms. "Bigger?" she snuffled. "Or older?"

"Both," Ernest said, his voice light.

There would come a day, decades hence—a blacker one, to be sure—when this moment would come roaring back to him: the wet of Kit's tears, her snotty nose burrowing into his dress shirt, the slump of her quaking shoulders. He'd recall with a visceral gratitude the look of doubt and longing she had cast at her baby sister, the rhythmic sway of his wife's hips as she soothed the baby, and the heady euphoria that had swept over him, as if love had him in a chokehold. Nearly thirty years later, the embers of the late-day sun would be every bit as golden and the crush of pride and pain beneath his ribs just as sharp, even as he struggled to draw air from the ruined muck of his lungs. On that distant day, Kit would once again be sobbing inconsolably, having climbed onto the starched sheets of his hospital bed to curl against him and nestle her quivering chin gently against his breast. Despite serving as witness to so many decades, she would still look and behave like a gawky schoolgirl, whatever wisdom she'd acquired in her long years on earth awash now in the stew of preteen hormones and insecurities: still far too young, too naive, to make her own way in the world, and he taking leave of her far too soon.

"Promise me, Kit, that you'll be a good girl," he'd say. "That you'll behave and be a help with your mother. And that you'll listen to Helen. Can you do that for me? Because Helen will need to be in charge, at least until you're a little bit bigger. And then, when the time comes, you'll look after Helen, won't you. Can you promise me? That you'll love each other and look out for one another, no matter what."

In that instant, idly joggling baby Helen at the window, Lillian was no doubt thinking of cryosectioning or binary fission, but she caught his eye, read the emotion in his face, and smiled.

iv.

The Sunday before Christmas 1935, Lillian, uncharacteristically festive in a red apron festooned with reindeer and holly, was sawing viciously at a roast while Kit glowered over a notebook at the table. Spargo was underfoot and drooling, watching for a piece of dropped gristle or bloodstained twine with the fixation he typically reserved for squirrels in the yard. Ernest hovered in the doorway with Helen heavy on his hip, his toe tapping to the music coming from the radio, his ear cocked.

"You know this one, don't you, Kit?"

Kit, who was nearly fluent in four languages but still struggled with cursive writing, seemed in danger of etching her letters into the tabletop itself. "Tchaikovsky number 14, Pas de Deux, Dance of the Sugar Plum Fairy," she muttered. "Helen's favorite," she added, sounding sour.

The music faded and the jolly voice of the announcer returned. "Isn't that something! There you have it, ladies and gentlemen, the little Beethovens and Mozarts of the future recorded right here in Ottawa in the hallowed halls of our very own Princess Mary Elementary."

Lillian's head jerked.

"Kit? This is your school? They're quite good, aren't they?"

Kit didn't look up. "The boy who plays the French horn is horrible and smelly and mean."

Lillian looked bemused, but Ernest was crunching his lips from side to side, making his mustache move like a caterpillar for Helen, who reached toward it, giggling.

"And who, pray tell, is playing the celesta, Kit McKinley?" he asked. "Is she mean and smelly and horrible?"

Kit fell for it. "No, silly! She's not smelly or mean OR horrible. She's me!"

Lillian's smile faded. "Pardon?" She put a hand on Kit's shoulder to make her look up. "You can't play that piece, can you, Kit? That instrument?" Lillian swiveled a look at Ernest, then back to Kit. "And we've never heard you practice that one, have we?"

Kit shrugged. "It's supposed to be on a celesta, not a piano. So I mostly practice at school. And anyhow, Helen doesn't like it. She doesn't like anything I play."

Ernest saw a new emotion replace the confusion on Lillian's face, one known to busy mothers the world over: wonder mixed with guilt, her mind scrambling backward, pawing mentally through Kit's satchel and wondering how she'd missed this particular notice to parents. This, *this*, was proof of her love, wasn't it: this doubt, this fear.

Lillian, as usual, was managing her emotions as if they were part of a hypothesis in need of validation or refutation.

Lillian turned her next question to Ernest. "How did you know?"

He pointed his chin back toward the radio. "He said it, the host. That the youngest member of the orchestra, Katherine McKinley, just six years old, was playing the celesta."

"How did they know your name, Kit?" A note of weary tenderness had crept into her voice, too faint for Kit to catch. "Did you speak with them?"

Kit shook her head vehemently. "I didn't even know they were there until the teacher talked about it after. She said it might go on the radio, but I forgot."

Ernest, with Helen growing heavier in his arms, glided back to the radio and lowered the volume. He lingered for a moment looking over the backyard blanketed in snow, the trees stooped in their thick white robes. If they hadn't been putting plans in place to move to Paris in time for Lillian to start in the Sorbonne cryogenetics laboratory next fall, and he to start the work for the legation, he'd already be researching a new school for Kit, perhaps even a new part of town. These days, the press was positively rabid about any hint of specialness in children. Just look at the ludicrous spectacle being made over those poor identical quintuplets in North Bay, attracting thousands of tourists a day, and their parents having no say in the matter.

He would have to impress upon Kit the need to keep her head down, just for a little while longer. Paris would be a new start for them all.

1936

"A unt Natalie! Come quick!" Kit sounded shrill and desperate. Ernest had hoped for a quiet Sunday morning to catch up on correspondence, but her cry made him set down his pen. Outside, the March sun was polishing the snowbanks to a gleam. The day before had been Kit's leap year birthday, February 29, 1936, and they'd given her a bicycle, her very first. But Ottawa in winter was no place for bicycles. The gift was propped against the wall in Lillian's sunroom, shiny red, a dormant specimen dreaming of spring, along with all the seeds and cuttings. In all likelihood, the bike would be boxed up again to be shipped ahead of them, to France, before the child ever got a chance to try it. Lillian had swaddled Helen in her woollies and set out on her walk, but Kit had declined to accompany them.

A moment later, he heard Natalie's voice, relieved. "My goodness, Kitten, you scared me. What's wrong?"

"It's Spargo." The despair in Kit's voice was enough to make Ernest rise from his desk and peer around the door. Kit was seated cross-legged by the hearth with her dog, his big chest rising and falling. "He's *freezing.*"

"Freezing?" Natalie kneeled beside them. "Right in front of the fire?"

"Look," Kit said, and pointed carefully at the streaks of white on Spargo's muzzle. "And here." She stroked the white flecks now powdering his soft ears. And it was true, Spargo's ashy hairs seemed to have appeared out of nowhere, like ice stealing across a pond in winter. The ungainly mutt looked almost distinguished.

"Oh, Kit, he's not freezing, honey, he's just getting older."

Kit frowned at her aunt, disappointed. "He can't get *old*, Aunt Natalie. He's a *dog*. He's getting white!"

"Well, gray, maybe." Natalie started scratching Spargo on the tummy. His tail increased in tempo under her touch. "Even humans turn gray as they get older, look at your father."

Spargo lifted his hind leg to oblige Natalie's long fingernails. No one noticed Ernest, eavesdropping behind them.

"But Papa already *is* old. What do you mean, getting older?" Natalie pinched her mouth, suppressing a smile.

"Well, yes, your father is a little bit old, but he's not *that* old. Only he's older now than he was last year and the year before that. That's what happens, Kitten. It happens to people and it's happening to Spargo, too. That's why he's slowing down."

"But I'm getting older and faster. Papa timed my laps at the park with the chronometer from Mummy's laboratory."

"But you will slow down one day, Kit." Natalie's voice sounded a shade less certain. The big dog rolled fully onto his back with his paws in the air. "It's what happens, to doggies and to people. We get older and slower and grayer."

"And what happens after we've oldened?"

Ernest edged into the room and Natalie cast him a pleading look. He'd meant to broach this topic with Kit—dog years versus human years, longevity expectations for a hound as large as Spargo. It might be a window into a bigger conversation, Lillian had urged, without offering to be the one to crack this window open. Ernest hadn't quite been able to bring himself to do it.

Just then the doorbell chimed. "Let me get that," said Natalie, standing briskly, leaving Ernest to face Kit's puzzled face.

Her rapid departure prompted Spargo to spring to his feet like the young dog Kit still presumed him to be, although he staggered to find himself upright so swiftly. When the bell rang a second time, he didn't seem to hear it, but trotted gamely after Kit, who followed her aunt to the door. Ernest paused to watch them, dog and child, Spargo matching his step to hers, then sitting promptly at the motion of her hand, panting audibly at the effort invested in this abrupt change of scene. How could Ernest possibly bring himself to tell her that Spargo wouldn't be making the crossing to Europe with them? That he'd be staying here with John, Natalie's latest beau, who had a property outside of town. Kit burrowed her fingers into the thick folds at the scruff of Spargo's neck the way she always did, a comfort to them both. The tip of Spargo's tail kept up its lazy tapping.

Natalie had gaily thrown the door wide, so that the sound of cars swishing by on the slushy streets flooded into the quiet of the foyer. She'd clearly been expecting John with a bouquet of flowers quaking in the frosty air or pastries still warm from the bakery. Ernest craned his head to see past her.

Outside stood strangers. A man with a hat pulled low over bushy brows that crawled down to his temples to meet his beard so that he looked like one of the furred beasts in Helen's picture books. An unlit cigarette was affixed to the shadowy curl of his lips. Beside him was a woman with painted lips, her cheeks flushed with rouge, her eyes wide and batting. Late twenties, was Ernest's best guess, but no friend of Natalie's by the looks of things—Natalie was darting a warning glance back at her niece—because already the woman was bending low and side-ways to look past Natalie, raising two plump hands in the air.

"It IS you, Kit! Oh, you beautiful bairn, I knew it was you, the minute I heard them talking about you on the radio at Christmas."

The woman's voice set something chiming faintly for Ernest, even if her appearance did not. Spargo stiffened, his tail growing still, his exhalation a thready growl. The woman seemed to sense it, because she straightened up and gave a little curtsy—more for Spargo, it seemed, than for Kit—then extended a drooping handshake.

"What a pleasure to make your acquaintance again after all these years," the woman said, still ignoring Natalie. "You don't remember me?"

It was a Scottish brogue, warm without warmth. Her broad burr summoned for Ernest a memory of his childhood, but also, more recently, spring grass, a blue blanket in a backyard, daisies nodding against a fence, and a boxy, black-snouted camera knocked to the ground. Ernest started for-ward with a jerk and now saw a third man, short and skinny, loitering on a lower step, with a face Ernest had never forgot-ten. This man, once again, was lifting a camera to his face.

"It's Morag, wee one. Your old nanny from Montreal."

Natalie had taken it in, all of it, and tried to yank the door closed, but the big, bearded man stuck out his shoe to stop it, his cigarette bobbing as he spoke. "Say, kid, that's some big doggie you've got there." In a flash, he'd whisked a pencil out from behind his ear, a notebook flapping open like the flick of a lighter. "Are you Kit McKinley, then, as Morag here says?"

"Are you getting this?" Ernest heard the woman, Morag, mumble to the cameraman out of the side of her mouth, even as Ernest thrust himself in front of Natalie, who fell back, blocking Kit.

He felt the shift of air behind him and Kit's gasp of alarm. A squirrel with the timing of a gymnast had chosen this moment to leap from the trunk of the maple tree to the birdbath, then make a hasty bid for the laurel that hid the house from the road. Spargo lunged past Ernest and down the steps, and in an instant, was charging through the hedge.

So what happened next wasn't Natalie's fault, for having thrown open the door so wide, or Kit's, for lifting her hand tentatively from Spargo to take the limp fingers offered by Morag as the camera man wheeled and clicked, or Ernest's for storming toward the visitors, which is the only possible thing that could have convinced Spargo that he didn't need to stand guard at Kit's side, that he wasn't on duty.

The next long crumple of noise would haunt Ernest and Natalie, not to mention Kit, to the end of their days: a squeal of brakes, a shout, a horrible crunch of flesh against metal, a piercing howl, and Kit's jagged shriek. Whether it was these or Ernest's bellow of rage that sent the visitors running, he would never know. His only thought was to throw his arms around his little girl to keep her from dashing out to the carnage of the street and seeing Spargo breathe his last anguished breaths, to bundle her back inside the house and slam the door.

"MIRACLE MUSICIAN IS NO KID," the headline in the *Citizen* would blare the next day, prompting Ernest to hastily bump up their plans to sail for Europe: ten column inches of newsprint accompanied by an inky photo of a little girl, her hand resting on the head of a large dog. "FIRED FAMILY NANNY PUTS TYKE'S REAL AGE IN TEENS."

ii.

Lillian and Helen had scarcely left the double berth since the SS *Montcalm* had steamed out of harbor. Lillian, her face the color of Palmolive soap, had a wet cloth pressed to her temples while Helen whimpered beside her.

"Eight days of this!" Lillian moaned. "Sick as a dog." She caught Kit's look and grimaced. "Sorry."

Ernest, feeling green about the gills himself, mustered the stamina to take Kit to the promenade deck. On the wide loop with few other souls pacing the perimeter, she tried to outrun her grief.

"I'll wait here," Ernest said, clutching the railing at the top of the stairs. His stomach was churning every bit as much as the gray-green wake spewing from the stern. "You run your fastest lap and I'll count."

If the sea was calm, she could sprint her loop and be back at his deck chair before he'd counted to 320. And she could go faster in one direction than the other, she said, because her feet fell farther forward in space—she could see it happen, right before her very eyes.

Which is how she managed to ram straight into Dr. Ayaan Gupta.

The man must have had his head bowed against the wind, because he looked up just as her head barreled into his stomach. Kit reeled backward, but the man's left arm shot out and caught her before she landed on her backside, while his other hand snatched a silvery object pinwheeling in the air. In one smooth movement, he pocketed the item and used this hand to push his spectacles back up his nose.

"My goodness, what kind of squall is this? A cyclone? A hurricane? A tiny tot typhoon? Are you lost?" the man asked kindly, then, seeing Kit's face, turned serious. "Did you lose something?"

She nodded, solemnly. "My dog."

He was tall and lean but with a broad, big-featured face with prominent ears, an overbite, and round eyes magnified by thick glasses so that everything above his shoulders seemed one size too large. His mustache was trim, and his shiny, black hair was parted severely and smoothed across the crown of his head, occasionally flapping in the wind like the wing of a crow. Thick eyebrows hopped upward at Kit's answer, as if to peer at her over the tops of his square spectacles.

"You lost your dog! Here, on the ship?"

Kit shook her head. Ernest saw the man's twinkling eyes grow soft.

"Ah," he said. "I'm very sorry. And did you hurt your head?" The man noticed Ernest hovering and blinked at him in greeting, then tapped his own belly, apologetically. "Not enough padding, I know. My mother says the same thing."

Kit seemed entranced by his voice. She'd never met anyone from the subcontinent before. Ernest braced himself for what she might say.

"You smell Christmassy."

The man straightened his bow tie, looking pleased. "What a relief," he replied. "My name is Dr. Ayaan Gupta. Delighted to make your acquaintance, Tiny Typhoon."

Ernest stepped forward and introduced himself, but a fresh lurch of the deck turned his smile bilious. "And this is Katherine—Kit—McKinley. I'm afraid I've rather loosened the reins on her while trying to find my sea legs."

"You are quick as lightning," the man said to Kit in his singsong voice. "I didn't even see you coming."

"I'm trying to get under three hundred," she said proudly.

"Give or take," said Ernest. He tapped his wrist. "My watch has packed up, much to Kit's chagrin."

"Ah, the salt and humidity play the devil with delicate clockworks," Gupta said gloomily as if discussing Ernest's own health. "I'd be happy to take a look. A hobby of mine." He poked his long fingers through the buttons of his green tweed jacket to rummage through an inside pocket, which clinked softly. Finding nothing, he delved into his outer flap pockets, first one, then the other, extracting a pocket watch on a chain, and dropping it back inside, then repeating the process with a gold wristwatch. Finally, from the pocket of his trousers, he pulled out another timepiece on a black strip of ribbon, its silver case burnished to a high sheen. This, Ernest realized, was the item Dr. Gupta had plucked so deftly from the air when Kit had nearly bowled him over. "I've got these ticking again, but I've no need for all three. Would you like to borrow one?"

Kit started bobbing her head enthusiastically, but she caught her father's eye and stopped.

"Very generous of you, Dr. Gupta, but we've not much use for time on the ship. Unless, of course, you can work some magic with this." Ernest lifted his own wristwatch to his ear, frowning, then fiddled to unlatch the band.

"Are you a doctor of clocks?" Kit asked.

Gupta beamed. "Indeed," he said. "A doctor of watches and men. The latter being a rather recent achievement. I graduated from the University of Bombay this spring and am indulging in a bit of a round-the-world tour before continuing my advanced surgical training at Oxford."

Ernest was impressed. "Congratulations, young man. A horologist and a medical doctor. Your father and mother must be very proud."

A shadow fled across the doctor's face as if, high above, a gull was soaring by.

The ship shifted just then, and Ernest toppled backward into a recliner, his lips clamshell tight.

"Never mind the watch, doctor. Any antidotes for seasickness? Kit seems fit as a fiddle, but my wife and I, as well as Kit's baby sister, have been under the weather since we left Montreal."

Gupta repeated the protracted exercise of pawing at every pocket, eventually producing a small tin of Meggezones lozenges. A smell assailed Ernest in force, warm and peppery, and he thought of Kit's words earlier. Christmassy. The box was crammed, not with lozenges, but with small, rough cubes, yellowish and wizened.

"Dried gingerroot," the doctor pronounced. "Works like a charm." He proffered the tin.

Ernest hesitated, then detached a sticky clump and popped it into his mouth, making his eyes water.

"Take the tin, please. I have more."

Kit tugged his tweed sleeve. "Can you time me, Dr. Gupta? Properly?"

"Now, Kit, Dr. Gupta has better things to do, I'm sure," Ernest murmured, stretching his legs the length of the chaise. "Why don't we try a game of chess."

"Not at all." Dr. Gupta once again fished out the silver watch on the black silk necklace. He crouched down to Kit, opening the lid. "You see here?" He pointed with his pinkie. "This one has a sub-second dial, so we can count the seconds."

Peeking out from under an eyelid, Ernest could see Kit was enthralled.

"Runner, take her mark!" Gupta proclaimed. He raised his hand in the air like a starter pistol, and Kit toed her shoe to a seam in the wood. "Ready, set . . . go!"

After that, Ernest and Dr. Gupta spent several hours each day at the oversize chess sets on the upper deck.

"Gupta! You put me in the unenviable position of taking candy from a child," Ernest crowed, strolling the length of the board, his bicep hooked around the neck of the doctor's knight.

"Are you feeling the sun today, my friend?" Dr. Gupta asked, mock concern scrunching his broad brow. He nudged his bishop from D2 to F4 so that it was standing in the same square as Ernest's queen. "Why else would you leave Her Majesty so shamefully exposed?"

Dr. Gupta also invited Ernest and Kit to see the workbench he'd set up in his own cabin, where he'd clamped to his desk a watchmaker's lathe with a cunning little tool drawer that opened, he told Kit, with a special coin. He pointed at a slim slot, then winked as a coin appeared out of nowhere, snaking fluidly between his fingers before hopping to his other hand. Kit gasped in delight, and Ernest gave an appreciative laugh. "A doctor, a horologist, *and* a prestidigitator. A man of many talents."

Dr. Gupta passed it to Kit for inspection. One side, like the Canadian penny, featured the mustachioed King George, but instead of maple leaves, the flip side was an ornate jungle of flowers and vines wound around three words.

"One rupee coin," she read, and Dr. Gupta grinned.

"Just five years old, you said, Ernest? She's a wonder."

Kit stayed silent, saying nothing, but her eyes wandered to Ernest as if to say, *Five?* She'd been six at home.

They were somewhere in the middle of the Atlantic, Kit plying her loop around the promenade deck while Ernest surveyed the muscled ropes of the sea, when Dr. Gupta materialized, pulling Ernest's wristwatch from his pocket.

"I believe it is keeping perfect time now, McKinley."

Kit was eyeing Dr. Gupta's jacket. "Do you have the magic coin with you today?"

Gupta frowned, his mustache curving steeply around his chin as his long fingers began scrambling in and out of his pockets.

He sighed. "I daresay that coin has absconded again, Kit!"

"What about there?" she pointed to the slit on his left breast.

"This one?" He fished inside and retrieved a stubby pencil, three paper clips, a brass button, and a handkerchief, neatly folded and pressed. "I'm afraid this particular coin has a nose for adventure and I . . . Wait a bit!"

Dr. Gupta peered around the side of her head. "Well, I never!" He put his fingers gently on the cusp of her ear, then showed her his open hand, where the rupee coin seemed to hop for a moment before settling flat. He set the warm coin in her palm, curling her fingers around it tightly. "You better hang on to this, Kit. It clearly prefers your company to mine."

When, at last, the Irish coast, then England, loomed into view, Dr. Gupta joined them on the promenade deck, watching the splodge of land take shape. He would be disembarking at Southampton while the McKinleys continued on to Le Havre. As Ernest watched, Kit slipped her hand into Gupta's. Their new friend had spent most of the voyage regaling Kit with stories about growing up in Delhi, timing her endless laps around the ship, and teaching her some sleight of hand. It occurred to Ernest that Ayaan Gupta, despite the age difference, was the first real friend Kit had ever made. In the next moment, he realized, doing the math in his head, Gupta and Kit must have been almost the same age.

"I'm indebted to you, Ayaan Gupta. Without your ginger-root, my family and I may not have survived the high seas. And your company has been consistently splendid, if I can't say the same for your chess game."

Dr. Gupta wobbled his large head, his smile stretching the width of his face. "The pleasure has been mine. I'm sorry you won't be settling on this side of the Channel. If you ever find yourselves back in England, or have a wristwatch in need of a doctor, please look me up."

All too soon the SS *Montcalm* was nosing into harbor. Dr. Gupta turned to Kit. "I don't suppose you've managed to hold on to that coin, have you?" This question was a variation on a theme. As Ernest watched, Kit arranged her face in a thoughtful frown.

"Gee willikers, I can't imagine where it could have gone!" She shrugged, raising her hands, palms up.

"Pity," said Dr. Gupta, dropping into a recliner beside her, looking dejected.

"But what do we have here?" she said, sweeping her arm in a wide arc before plucking the rupee coin from behind his ear as Ernest applauded their routine.

A moment later, Dr. Gupta sprang to his feet and gave a swift glance at the docks. "What do you say, Kit? Last chance to beat your record."

As Kit streaked off, Ernest was aware of the engines slowing, the brawling sea dropping its fists, the crew bustling with the lines. Boats big and small darted in and out of the busy harbor like bats at dusk.

Dr. Gupta's face lit up as Kit roared back toward them, and stayed smiling as she barreled right into him, just as she had the day they'd met. This time, she held her arms wide so he could sweep her up in his own, the bright sun making him blink. He set her down again, then reached for the black ribbon that hung down his breast.

"I want you to have this," he said, dipping his round head to lift the necklace watch from his own neck and looping it around Kit's.

Ernest opened his mouth to protest, but Dr. Gupta cut him off.

"No, McKinley. Kit has earned it. What use have I for a lady's timepiece? Think of it as an early birthday present. Or perhaps a belated one."

Kit cradled the silver watch in her hand, squinting at the worn engraving on the lid, then eased open the delicate lid to watch the dials whir. Looking at her, Ernest felt a stab of regret: Why on earth had they never thought to give Kit a watch?

She looked up at Dr. Gupta, beaming as he crouched down. "But when is your birthday, Kit? You never said."

"February twenty-ninth," she said, holding his gaze. Out of habit or superstition, they almost never told people the real date. And Ernest had already mentioned that Kit was five, which would be hard to square with this answer.

Dr. Gupta's eyebrows twitched as he straightened up and his eyes wandered for a moment to Ernest.

"A leapling! How absolutely unfair. But you've had a birthday this very year! All the more reason to accept this gift from me today. It's an auspicious date to be born, to be sure. I know a man back in India born on February twenty-ninth, and he always insisted it made him special." Gupta rested his hand on her curly head. "And in your case, I'd say that's unequivocally true."

He turned to Ernest, a card materializing from thin air in his long fingers. "My address, McKinley. In Oxford, but also my family's address in Delhi, which is where I hope to return when my studies are done. I very much hope our paths will cross again."

PART II
Lillian

CH1: AUGUST 1937

On the overnight train journey to Berlin, Lillian plunged into sleep as if dropped. Like an anchor. A stone. The train's shrill whistle woke her not long after dawn. Outside, the landscape flickered past as if on film. A pale mist skulked over the tawny fields. Every now and then, a farmstead or barn showed itself, ghostlike, before dissolving back into white.

On the facing bunk, Ernest was still snoring softly, his curly hair more coppery-blond than ever, his beard woven with strands of white. Under so much pressure, long days and late nights. Delicate negotiations and meetings he didn't discuss with Lillian, and she didn't ask. Mackenzie King, the Canadian prime minister, had agreed it would be prudent for Ernest to be based in Berlin for the foreseeable future, all the better to keep an eye on Herr Hitler. But he'd need to make regular trips back to Paris until the new envoy was installed at the legation. They had shrouded the furniture in the flat on Rue Madame for the time being and, in Berlin, had rented a house on Tiergartenstrasse just three blocks from the expansive city gardens. It was a short walk for Ernest to the British embassy on Wilhelmstrasse and just twenty minutes by tram to Friedrich Wilhelm University. If Helen hadn't already been curled in the back corner of his berth, Lillian might have crept in with Ernest herself.

Kit, on the upper bunk, was still dozing, or pretending to. Last night she'd been scared by the clack and clank of the train, had climbed down the ladder into Lillian's berth and asked in a whisper if she could stay. Helen, after all, had stamped and sobbed and wailed, turning crimson with the effort, until Ernest had agreed to let her sleep in his bunk. But Lillian had said no to Kit. She—Lillian—was too big, she'd said. And the bed was too narrow. But she was sorry for that now. Too often she responded to Kit with reason and argument. What Kit needed was simpler, Ernest always said. He'd said something similar when Lillian had first received the letter from Maximilian Dörr, inviting her to do her doctoral degree at Friedrich Wilhelm University, in Berlin. She'd only been working in the botany laboratory at the Sorbonne for a month when the institute's latest Nobel laureate, Irène Joliot-Curie, had introduced Max to Lillian.

Lillian's formidable intelligence, she'd said, was wasted as a technician, and her theories on mutagenesis would be an asset to Max's fledgling cytogenetics program in Berlin. But a *doctoral* degree. Such a thing hadn't been offered in Paris and was expressly prohibited for women at the University of Ottawa, where Lillian could only work as a laboratory assistant. Imagine if she, Lillian, could have the time and space, the support, to explore the ideas pecking at the edges of her thoughts? It could make a difference, she was sure of it. It could help to explain rarities like Kit's, lurking within the realms of human possibility. Not solutions, perhaps, but understanding. Illumination. This was what she tried to explain to Ernest. But he'd only shaken his head.

"This work—this field—needs you, and not the other way around, I understand that. So long as you remember that the girls and I need you, too. You must set aside some space for us in your busy brain."

And her heart, he might have added. He was always worried about her heart. How she was feeling, *if* she was feeling. "Of course I love them," she always told him, exasperated. Couldn't he see that love and worry were her driving force? To learn. To comprehend. One day, she often thought, there would be a diagnosis for her, too. For her type of mind. One that demanded order and answers. One packed as tightly with love and longing as anyone else's, just inept, wrong-footed at showing it. Lillian loathed ineptitude. But she loved her girls more than all the world's molecules put together. It was maddening that her family could possibly doubt this.

Ernest was dressed and seated at the little table by the window when she returned from the lavatory. Kit was on his lap, still in her pajamas. The train must have reached the outskirts of Cologne. Tractors and horses gave way to cars, trams, and narrow streets. Schutzpolizei, black-belted, stood stiffly directing traffic or stamped stern-faced down the streets. The new German flag snapped on tall flagpoles or against the walls of buildings. On the cathedral, with its twin spires like ears, the red banner lolled like a tongue from the snout of the thick central nave. Ernest and Kit were watching quietly as the city inched by.

Helen's voice, croaky with sleep, broke the quiet. "Are we getting off here?"

Lillian brought her face close, breathing in Helen's drowsy-child smell. "Not yet. We're on this train for the rest of the day."

Gertrude, the nanny, tried to keep Helen entertained by walking her the length of the train while she charmed the other passengers with her wobbly gait and easy laugh. Gertrude herself was smiling her strained, closed-mouth smile over her untidy clutter of teeth. Natalie's man, John, had connected them with

Gertrude, a distant cousin from Austria, who was nineteen at the time she was hired by the McKinleys. The girls loved her, tugging at her arm whenever she floated a demure hand over her disorderly mouth and climbing her skinny limbs like a vine, something they never did with Lillian.

Kit and Ernest took their own table at the other end of the dining car from Lillian, leaving her to her scribbling, and busying themselves with a stack of newspapers in who knew how many languages. Kit, intent on a crossword puzzle, was keeping up a steady patter that Lillian couldn't hear, while Ernest frowned and harrumphed, scanning one page before snapping to the next. Something Kit said made him glance up sharply and lean forward, asking a question that made the child nestle her chin to one side, ducking her head.

Lillian turned back to her own notes, the details of the project she'd need to share with Max. Not that she could tell him her deepest, truest aims. Her theories. If genetical instructions could be jumbled, fragments of their structure shuffled, this would lead naturally to different strains of maize, even very rare ones, despite environmental conditions remaining constant. This surely could happen in humans as well. The instructions for natural aging, for example. The external environment could allow for mental growth, even as physical maturation was kept in check. It might be like words getting accidentally shifted in a sentence.

Like a sentence getting its words shifted, accidentally.

If the words, the fragments, could be swapped out of place, then couldn't they also be put back?

None of this was written in her notes. Her doctoral work at Friedrich Wilhelm would stay focused on *Zea mays*. Her corncobs, as Ernest called it. Corncobs and jumping genes. Cytogenetical crossing over. That's what she would be telling Maximilian Dörr.

She started at the sight of Ernest, who'd seated himself soundlessly across from her, chewing quietly at his mustache, amused, and waiting for her to notice. But his face turned quickly serious once he had her attention.

"Kit's been telling me about an older boy at Saint Marguerite's *école primaire*, bullying a friend in her class. A little girl." He sighed. "Jewish, maybe? She didn't know, or wouldn't say."

"A real friend, do you think? Or imaginary?"

He shrugged. "To her, they're the same thing. You know I have my misgivings about a move to Berlin, given everything." He flapped a hand, which Lillian took to encompass more than the sugar bowl and tongs. "But I have to think it's a good time to get Kit installed somewhere new."

Lillian closed her eyes, and for a brief moment could picture Kit, her skinny arm waving above her desk, unable to stop herself from providing the right answer to every question. So eager to please. So hopelessly incapable of fitting in with the other children who looked her age and had so many of the same urges and interests, but who had been alive for such a meager fraction of Kit's own years on earth. Seven. That was the age they'd tell her teachers at her new school in Berlin. But there had been a reason, she was sure, that Kit had wanted to tell Ernest this story.

Lillian followed Ernest's gaze. The train was whistling through a small town without stopping. A sooty wall encircled the streets and homes, tall enough that no human life could be glimpsed. Stones lining a pasture jutted like teeth, blackened and chipped, through a pale, pinkish clay. Behind the wall was what must have been a factory, a chimney hung with the long red flag, belching black smoke into ashen skies.

"Munitions, certainly," Ernest muttered, his lids low. "Everywhere you look, this country is girding itself for war, and France is squabbling over two-day weekends and living wages. Important things, to be sure, but they pale in comparison to this."

She looked down again at her notes. There was certainly nothing particularly lighthearted about mutagenesis in corn. But there was joy in science, surely. In discovery.

A happy shriek made her startle up again. Helen. Barreling through the dining car, as if finding her family here was her own miraculous eureka. Helen trundled toward her sister. Gertrude emerged through the doorway, nodding, her lips tightly pursed in a shy smile.

Not alone, Lillian realized.

The man beside her, tilting his head as he spoke, was tall and fair and wore a dark double-breasted jacket. Ernest, too, had noticed and was sizing him up.

They stood as Gertrude made the introductions. The blond man extended a hand so smooth and white, Lillian mistook it for a glove.

"Dr. Heinrik Strauss. Good day, Mr. and Mrs. McKinley. Such a pleasure. I've been hearing all about you and your family." Lillian stiffened at his words. Instinctively, she disliked Germans. A German had killed Thomas. But that was ridiculous. This man looked to be scarcely in his twenties, around the same age as Gertrude. Likely a baby when Thomas died. An innocent. And there was something newly hatched about him. Small, pale eyes under a dusting of downy hairs that passed for eyebrows, his coloring not so much faded as insufficiently vascularized. Even his lips looked blanched.

"A medical doctor?" Ernest asked.

Dr. Strauss gave a small, stiff bow. "Indeed, I've just finished my studies—I was doing a research year at the Necker Institute in Paris and now return to continue my postgraduate work in pediatrics."

"Indeed." Ernest was now giving this young man his full attention. "And what is your particular area of interest?"

His voice was light, but something prompted Lillian to glance toward her daughters. Helen had clambered into the seat Ernest had vacated at Kit's table.

"Heart defects," Dr. Strauss was saying. "I plan to specialize in pediatric cardiology. And you work in government relations, Gertrude tells me?"

Lillian was only half listening. The girls were quiet, performing a pantomime with their hands. Some game of Helen's, no doubt, that Kit had been cajoled into playing.

Strauss, too, had been watching the children. "One of your daughters is deaf?" He addressed the question to Ernest, who looked as flummoxed as Lillian. It was Gertrude who replied in a mild voice, choosing her English carefully. "You might think so if you were trying to get them to come downstairs for supper, but no. I mentioned to Katharina that I learned some sign language when I worked for a family back home. She insisted I teach her. Now I would say she is trying to teach Helen."

All of them turned to look at the girls, who were matched in stubbornness. Helen was no doubt making up her own gestures that she wanted Kit to emulate; Kit was increasingly exasperated. *Pediatrics*, Lillian was thinking to herself, the

word sinking in. Defects. Dr. Strauss seemed perfectly pleasant, but still.

Ernest, it seemed, had the same instincts. He shuffled to one
side as he spoke, which served to block the girls from view.
"You've done some work with the deaf, have you, Dr. Strauss?"

The man smiled. "Not really. It's always been large organ
malformations I've been interested in. Ventricular defects of the
heart and the great arteries, that kind of thing."

There was a pause. Lillian's eyes flitted back to Kit and Helen.

Strauss turned to Gertrude. "It was very nice to meet you,
fräulein. You have my card. I hope you will be in touch. And
please." He turned his pale eyes, a watery blue, to include
Ernest and Lillian. "Do not hesitate if there is any way I can be
of service to you, in Berlin."

CH2: SEPTEMBER 1937

*T*his is where the magic happens!"

Maximilian Dörr threw open the heavy door to the laboratory with a flourish, ushering Lillian and Kit over the threshold.

Max, who'd swiftly become Uncle Max to the children during the weeks he'd spent in Paris last year, was a bachelor nudging fifty. He was small and round, with dark, wavy hair that was part black, part gray. Clean-shaven except for a slim mustache like a line of eyebrow pencil above his ample lips, he was as able and eager to lament the weaknesses of the Maginot Line with Ernest as he was to crawl around on all fours with Kit and Helen, playing Doctor Dolittle's baby pig.

When he'd met Lillian at the grand doors of the hospital that morning, he was neatly encased in a dark suit and broad bow tie, with his white lab coat folded carefully across one arm, looking more like a hovering waiter than one of the foremost geneticists in Europe. Bowing, he all but clicked his heels together before leading them through the long corridors to the Dörr Laboratory.

They stopped first at a foyer where his secretary worked, a panel of high windows letting in shafts of secondhand light from the adjoining laboratory. Mia Zimmermann bobbed up from her desk to greet them in eager if hesitant English, fluttering her eyelashes in delight when Kit piped up in her chirping German.

Fräulein Zimmermann showed Lillian her mail slot, already labeled with her name, in the wall of pigeonholes by the door.

Now, as they stood blinking in the long, bright laboratory itself, Lillian could count six, seven, eight rows of benches in the sprawling room and hear the soft steps and echoing clinks of others quietly at work, clearly accustomed to and unbothered by Max's booming voice. A man stepped out of a tall copper dome that looked like a cross between a diving bell, an elevator, and a telephone booth and smiled at them wanly before ferrying his tray carefully across the room.

"Oh, Max, it's . . ." The right word was lost on her tongue. She tilted her head back to admire the rows of electric lights.

"Wondrous," Kit supplied, breathing the word.

"Please," said Max, and Lillian stepped up to examine the microscope, the gurgling pipes and funnels, the seedlings straining toward the ceilings of their sphagnum jars, and contraptions for which even Lillian couldn't imagine a purpose.

Half a dozen glass reagent bottles, brand new, stood toward the back of the bench. Unable to help herself, Lillian nudged them into exact alignment. Better. Kit pulled away, stepping toward an imposing steel-fronted gadget fitted with gauges: pressure and temperature, by the looks of things, although one of them was surely a timer. Kit and her endless fascination with minutes, seconds, and dials. Lillian grasped her daughter's bony shoulder as she pulled away. "You can look, Kit, but no touching."

Max waved an arm to hail the attention of a small, balding man with a broad back, stooped shoulders, and no neck to speak of, which made him look like a tortoise. "Helmut? Helmut! Come and meet our latest colleague, Mrs. Lillian McKinley. Lillian, you'll already know Helmut Fassbinder—other than the

Lindegrens, Helmut is the world's premier authority on crossing over and second division in *Neurospora crassa*."

Lillian lingered for several minutes with Professor Fassbinder, while Max strolled with Kit to keep an eye on her. Smart man. Not that Lillian was worried. Kit had understood from a young age that she needed to keep her fingers to herself and Lillian's experiments uncontaminated. Helen, on the other hand, was still far too young and too prone to drama and arm-flinging. And Helen had no interest in being indoors, much less in a laboratory, on a sunny day. Ernest had taken her to the children's playground in the Tiergarten, giving Gertrude a day to find her bearings in the city. Lillian and Kit would join them later at the famous Zoologischer Garten.

Max steered Kit back toward Lillian when she'd excused herself from Fassbinder. "It's unusual, I know, to have botanists and chemists, mycologists, and geneticists working in such close proximity, everyone arguing over the Coolidge tubes! The cytochemistry and pathology departments are still being refurbished in the North Annex, so a great number of research projects had to be housed in here temporarily. You can imagine the grousing I've had from the intractable macromoleculists suffering the company of the biocolloidists."

Just then, a second set of heavy oak doors at the far end of the laboratory swung open. A lean man in a white lab coat, with a chiseled chin and thick, tawny hair slicked back from his brow and shaved short on the sides, stepped inside. He was speaking loudly to three men who followed closely behind. One was wearing some kind of uniform, walking stick-straight behind the others. The Germans and their endless uniforms. Lillian reached for Kit, to pull her close, but Kit had already backed away.

Max gritted his jaw, the color fading from his lower lip, his smile gone. The man moved with a masculine ease through the laboratory, tall on his toes, gesturing to his guests as he spoke. Lillian cursed herself for not trying harder to learn German, understanding only the words that sounded similar in English. *Intrazellulär*, she caught the man saying. *Mikroskop*. Perhaps she understood more German than she realized.

Then the man said a word several times that she couldn't place. *Taut-lish?* She glanced at Kit. Kit had drifted back to the shy Professor Fassbinder and looked to be tormenting him with one of her coin tricks.

The man finally noticed Max, his gaze a dark cloud passing over Max with a lazy distaste before scudding over to Lillian. He gestured to his guests to continue toward the far end of the lab.

"Dr. Amsel." Max's voice had none of the enthusiasm he'd shown for Professor Fassbinder.

The man slowed, as if he'd stepped in something unpleasant.

"Lillian, this is Dr. Karl Herman Amsel. Amsel, this is Lillian McKinley, joining the Dörr Laboratory in the pursuance of her doctoral degree. Lillian, you may have encountered Dr. Amsel's treatises on Mendelian units associated with harelip in the mouse."

In fact, she had. In spite of herself. In Paris she'd spent many happy hours in the library at the Sorbonne acquainting herself with the scientific journals she hadn't had access to in Canada. She'd encountered Amsel's name in the *Annals of Eugenics*, in an editorial where he reasoned that even if environmental triggers could be modified to reduce the likelihood of a cleft palate, or if surgical correction were perfected, the scientific aim should be to eradicate harelip from the gene line. And not just in mice, he'd argued.

Historically, Amsel had written, *the Spartans and Romans believed that children born with harelip or split palate harbored evil spirits, and they were thus put to death.*

Lillian shivered. She'd done her homework on Friedrich Wilhelm University. Eugenics research was the purview of the Kaiser Wilhelm Institute across town. And she'd been assured by Max that the Dörr Laboratory was rigorously focused on cytogenetics in its purest form. Yet in the space of ten minutes, she'd met a myocologist and a eugenicist.

Max seemed to read her mind. His fingertips nipped nervously at each other over his stomach, and rosy splotches bloomed on his cheeks.

When Amsel had strutted away to join his guests, Max said, "I'm sorry about that," in a whisper that Lillian might earlier have assumed he was incapable of making. "You likely won't have encountered much of Amsel's cant in English." One sorrowful eye squeezed open and closed, like the aperture on a lens. "Mind you, it was many of those same eugenic theories that drove me back here from the United States in the first place—requests to serve as an expert witness in some of the sterilization cases. Only to see my darling homeland enact many of the same eugenics laws as the Americans and stick Charles Davenport on the editorial boards of two of our most prestigious scientific journals! But I don't have any say over who is and is not housed in the Dörr Lab. For now. When the North Annex renovations are done, I'll be able to fill the spaces with staff and students of my choosing."

A giggle. Kit was back at Lillian's side, one small hand worming under Lillian's elbow. The other was pointing at Max's breast. He tucked his chin to his chest, the ends of his mustache also straining downward as if to catch a glimpse.

"Ah yes," he said, the warmth back in his voice. "May I introduce you to King Louis VII. Or is it VIII? I keep losing count."

It took a moment for Lillian to notice the mouse. A pair of beady eyes and a twitching nose poked out of the breast pocket of Max's lab coat, inspecting them briefly, before dropping again from view.

Max patted gently at his pocket. "Thankfully, this King Louis has no such problems whatsoever with his little palate."

CH3: SEPTEMBER 1937

A t the zoo, Kit sprinted ahead to find the penguins. Helen stumbled after her sister. And Lillian, too, felt slow and clumsy as she made her way with Ernest over the rise, her lungs overfull, her chest pinching at the effort. She paused at the top to catch her breath, and Ernest nudged her playfully with his elbow.

"So? I thought you'd be brimming with excitement after seeing Max's lab."

The muddy path sloped down toward the Penguin House and Lillian could see both girls straining to peer over the cement railing. Two penguins wobbled toward the girls, their wing tips brushing, bellies bulging white from their crisp black jackets. Something about their prim and bustling welcome reminded Lillian of Max.

"It's exquisite. Everything new and fresh and purpose built. It must have cost an absolute fortune. It's a dream come true to work there . . ." Her voice trailed off.

"But?"

"I would like to see the enclosure with the aurochs, if we can," she said, turning her head as if one of them might be sneaking up on them. "*Bos primigenius*. They're an extinct species of German cattle, genetically speaking, but two brothers have been trying to breed them back into existence."

"Lillian." Ernest breathed her name.

How could she explain this properly to Ernest? That she'd finally, at age forty, been granted the opportunity to loose the formidable powers of her mind in a laboratory like Max's, to take a giant leap toward solving the mystery of what was keeping Kit from aging. Lillian folded her fingers around his clammy hand. "You're chilled. Let's convince the girls to go inside to see the monkeys, shall we?"

The Ape House was indeed warmer. But sealed away from the outdoors, the monkeys seemed listless and irritable, their smell overpowering.

Helen scrunched her nose when they entered but seemed to forget the odor after spotting two macaques swinging through the branches of an enormous *Ficus elastica*. A chimpanzee approached the glass and put its wrinkled gray palm up against it, right at the level of Helen's face, which made her screech with laughter. Lillian could tell from Ernest's expression that he had more questions to ask her, but Helen was yanking bossily at his coat. Lillian trailed after Kit, feeling the brown eyes of a bonobo on her. She shivered. She didn't like animals in cages, never had. Not even in the quest for some greater scientific ideal.

A few other children and adults were braving the funk of the monkey house to escape the breeze outside. An older boy was pointing and laughing at the raw and swollen perineum of the matriarch of the baboon troop on the other side of the glass. Distracted by the loud boy and the lewd encouragement of his family, Lillian failed to see what Kit must have noticed instantly, a cautious smile widening on her face. A little girl, roughly the same height as Kit, perhaps five or six years old, was making a flurry of hand motions with her mother.

"Hallo, little one," the woman greeted Kit in German, her hands suddenly still, fingers twined, face guarded. She was dressed in a wool cape trimmed with fur the same hue as her honey-colored hair, which fell in sculpted waves. As Lillian drew closer, she saw a glint of fear in the mother's eye. The girl burrowed her hands into the folds of her coat.

"Guten tag," Kit said politely. Turning toward the girl, Kit lifted both hands and moved them slowly but purposefully to her lips, together, apart, around, and down. The face of the other girl changed from confusion to delight, and she responded with a series of counter-movements, which Kit watched with an intensity Lillian knew well. After a pause, Kit's hands and fingers were moving again—tapping, pointing, a curled fist, a finger to the brow, a hand to the chin. Lillian couldn't keep up.

The woman stepped to one side, effectively blocking the girls from the other family, and spoke softly in German.

Lillian shook her head. "I'm sorry, I don't speak German," she said. "Or sign language," she added.

The woman switched seamlessly to English. "I knew you must be visiting—we know most of the other deaf children her age in Berlin. I let down my guard, but sometimes Frida has so many questions. But your accent is American. You live here in Berlin?"

"Canadian, actually. We've been living in Paris."

A look of surprise passed over the woman's face. "And yet, your daughter is signing in German?"

Lillian blinked. She didn't know that sign language, too, had borders. "Her governess is from Austria and she taught them some . . . signs. My eldest is very good with languages. I didn't realize she'd learned enough for a conversation."

"She's not at all bad," the woman said, a ghost of a smile on her lips. She extended a hand and Lillian took it. "Mathilde Hesse," the woman said. "And this is Frida."

"Lillian McKinley," said Lillian. "And my daughter. Katharina." She didn't know why she said that. Katharina was what Gertrude and Max called Kit.

A cautious smile was inching across Kit's face, wrestling with the look of guarded self-doubt Kit so often seemed to wear around other children. But the smile was winning.

Mathilde turned to Kit, speaking in a low voice. "You're doing very well, little one. But you should know, in Germany, we almost never use sign language in public."

She stood and laid a hand on Lillian's arm. "Be careful," she said quietly. She took Frida's hand in hers and ambled away.

Kit looked puzzled. "What did that lady mean, Mummy? Be careful?"

Lillian pursed her lips. "That's a question for your father."

Kit did a little hop, about to dart in the direction of Ernest, but Lillian put a hand on her sleeve to stop her, remembering Amsel earlier, his commanding voice, the words she hadn't understood. She couldn't tell Ernest about Amsel, not when she had the chance to work with Max. To find answers. The opportunity of a lifetime.

"Wait. *Taut-lish* or *taut-leesh*," Lillian said. "Do you know what that means? In German?"

"*Tödlich*?" Kit furrowed her brows.

Lillian nodded. "That's it. Tödlich. That man in Max's lab kept saying it earlier."

"Fatal," said Kit, wrinkling her nose. For a brief moment, she looked like Helen had earlier, cringing at the monkey-house stench. "It means lethal. Deadly or causing death."

Later that night, Lillian asked Ernest, "Did you know that sign language is different in German? Kit tried out her sign language with that little girl at the zoo today, who was deaf, and they were actually communicating." Lillian shook her head. "It was something to see. But her mother told us that they don't usually use sign language, not in public. She said to be careful."

Ernest gnawed thoughtfully on his pipe. His bushy eyebrows nudged closer together, conferring. "Laws have been passed here in recent years decreeing that the mother of a deaf child be sterilized to prevent the birth of another, and the child too, when she's old enough. Physicians and teachers, even neighbors, are being encouraged to report families who may be trying to keep a child hidden. We'll need to tell Kit she can't be practicing it here, not with Helen, not when there are other people around."

Lillian felt the squeezy feeling in her chest again, just as she had when climbing the knoll to the Penguin House.

"She'll want to know why."

Ernest was quiet, nodding. "She always does."

CH4: NOVEMBER 1937

Usually her mind was like a river in springtime, rushing and roaring past one theory in order to get to the next.

gametic ratio
maternal transmission
paternal segregation

Ideas churning to the top of her thoughts, one, then another. This was how she made progress, by never letting her subconscious rest with its claws too long in an answer before pouncing to the next question.

Right now her every intelligent thought was buried under the din of this ballroom.

The different languages, music from the quartet in the corner, guttural laughter: all of it settled into one dense opera cake of noise. Her ear was too tired to pry one tier from the next.

Do noises have colors? Kit had asked her this just the other day. She was like Lillian that way, one question scarcely taking root before scattering its seed for the next. Do animals get to be ghosts? Do animals fall in love? Do ghosts? Lillian smiled, recalling Kit's circular theorizing. Helen was the opposite, so self-assured and content that her rare tantrums, sparking to a blaze at the most unexpected moments, were the jolting reminder that Helen did, after all, have needs of her own.

Lillian plucked at her clinging gown, trying to get the ruched fabric to sit smoothly over her hips. A party at the home of the American ambassador to Berlin was an invitation that could not be turned down, not with Britain and Canada waiting with bated breath for any news or insight into what Germany would do next. The green sateen dress set off her chestnut hair but made her feel like a tube of toothpaste. No. A link of sausage. She groaned. Too much champagne, then wine, then sherry. Unwise. Too many rich, heavy courses. Also unwise. Lillian had eaten everything set before her until the dining room, with its walls draped in scarlet tapestries, made her feel as if she, too, was being devoured by a gaping mouth. After dinner, the guests had repaired to another room lined in green damask nearly the same shade as her dress. If only she could disappear into it. Water. She needed a glass of water.

"Mrs. McKinley?" The voice was German and not unfamiliar. "I thought that was you."

The man was Dr. Whatsit, the podiatrist. No. Pediatrician. The one Gertrude had met on their train to Berlin. Lillian rummaged through her parched head for a name. Something to do with waltzing. The man's pale head looked even smaller than before, perched on a set of broad shoulders, his hands hanging long at his sides. Up close, it was as if the almost-translucent skin was stretched too thinly across his face.

"Dr. Heinrik Strauss," he reminded her, his lips thin.

"Of course, Dr. Strauss."

His gaze traced the air around her face as if following a fruit fly. *Drosophila melanogaster.*

"And Mr. McKinley?"

Ah. She waved vaguely. "Talking to an American industrialist. I'm trying to find a glass of water."

"Come." He chose a weaving line to the bar, buffeted by the other guests. Lillian struggled to follow, rolling like a ship in a storm. After an overlong, incomprehensible conversation with the barman, Strauss passed her a glass, which she drained in two gulps. Deeply unladylike.

"Peppermint?" He rattled a small tin, before popping the hinged lid. She couldn't imagine eating anything more for days. Weeks. And she'd never drink sherry again. Ever. She took two candies, out of politeness, and kept them pinched in her hot fingers. Her eyes roved. Where was Ernest?

"And the girls are enjoying their new school?"

They were, Lillian agreed. Kit's was close enough that Ernest could walk her there himself after breakfast. Helen spent her mornings with Gertrude, learning her numbers and letters. In the afternoon, she attended the kindergarten at Kit's primary school, leaving Gertrude a few hours to herself.

"They must love living so close to the gardens."

Lillian felt the tickle of a burp in her mouth and fought to suppress it. How did Strauss know where they lived? He must have seen the question on her face because he seemed riveted by the limp crescent of lemon at the bottom of his glass "Yes, I heard from Gertrude that you are nicely settled."

So Gertrude had been in touch with Strauss. Lillian's stomach gave a groan of protest. She feared the wurst. Ha.

"Dr. Strauss!" Ernest materialized in his quiet way. "What a coincidence."

Lillian let them talk, noticing the spidery gray veins on Strauss's temples, the triangular mustache, styled in the German way. A furry chevron. The uneaten candies, clenched in her hand, had suctioned to her palm like leeches. Only when Ernest had politely bid farewell to Strauss and started to steer her toward the cloakroom did she open her fist to pry them loose.

"Ernest." She held out her hand to show him. In the brighter light of the foyer, she could see both candies were embossed with a tiny swastika.

He frowned, passing her his handkerchief. "Those weren't being handed out here, surely."

"No, Strauss. Does this mean Strauss is a Nazi? Apparently he and Gertrude have kept in touch."

Ernest was holding her coat for her to shrug into so she couldn't see his face. "One gets the feeling you see that symbol on everything from postage stamps to toilet tissue," he said. "Who knows. Maybe you can no longer find a peppermint that's not sanctioned by the National Socialist German Workers' Party."

He turned her gently to face him and must have caught her woozy step because he held her elbow to steady her.

"My Lil, I'm sorry. I know you'd rather spend the evening with Max and your corncobs."

She wove her arm over the comforting bulge of his biceps, then whispered in his ear. "You know you don't need to worry about Max."

Ernest chuckled softly before brushing a kiss on her flushed cheek. "Of all the Germans I might be worried about, Max is not one of them. And unless I'm mistaken, you and every other woman in his orbit are absolutely safe from his charms. I like him. He's a decent man. A decent German, in fact. If I learned anything here tonight, that's an increasingly rare find."

CH5: DECEMBER 1937

Their first winter in Berlin, they went as a family to the Tiergarten on Sundays, bundled against the chill. Helen always wanted to go to the slides and the swings at the Spielplatz but Kit preferred the less manicured paths, the Wilderwald, she called it, where there were fewer children and more thickets, brambles, and tall, tangled trees. Fairies and sprites had forged secret trails through the undergrowth, Kit told Helen, whose eyes grew wide and hopeful. This was where the lovers retreated to promenade privately, arm in arm. Here also were the dog walkers, striding briskly as their hounds raced ahead. This explained Kit's preference for this part of the park, her face lighting up at the chance to pat any dog pausing long enough to allow it.

"But you must always ask first, Kit!" Lillian called out in vain. She was rewarded with eye-rolling from her daughter.

"I know everyone already, Mummy. This is Bruno." Kit squatted beside a dachshund, one finger stroking the cleft on his brow so that the little dog closed his eyes in pleasure. She turned her attention to a black dog, smaller still. "And this is Kaiser."

Germans had well-trained dogs and seemed to love them—more than their people, Ernest once remarked. There were very few strays in the neat German streets, but Kit naturally had managed to find a few in the park and befriend them. She pestered her mother and father to let her bring them home. Lillian had heard Kit telling Ernest in a whisper that she missed Spargo. Having a new dog would help, she reasoned with him. They were always saying she needed a new friend, weren't they? A dog was a good friend, a *real* one, not imaginary. The best kind of friend.

Ernest and Lillian, even Gertrude, had to tell her over and over, "Not now, Kit." Maybe back in France. Maybe back in Canada. These dogs probably had homes and owners.

"Hodgepodge definitely does *not* have his own home," Kit said. The shaggy hound she'd named herself was nearly as tall as Kit was and lurked skittishly in a lane at the edge of the Wilderwald. His coat was a tattered patchwork quilt of colors, dolloped haphazardly along his drooping tail. Even his over-size paws, Lillian noticed, were different shades: one black, one gray, one brown, one white. He came to Kit when she called his name, pressing his hulking frame against her as she combed her fingers through his tangled fur and fed him crusts of bread.

"You can feel his ribs when you pat him," she said solemnly.

"Katharina!" Gertrude strode toward Kit with a rueful glance at Lillian. "I've told you again and again not to pat that dog. It is filthy and infested with fleas."

Kit and Lillian had also bumped into Frida, the deaf girl they'd met in the fall at the zoo with her elegant mother, Mathilde Hesse. Lillian remembered what Ernest had told her, that the little girl would be sterilized when she was older, just like Carrie Buck, lest she pass on her deafness to any progeny, that this awful procedure would in all likelihood have already been performed on her mother.

Mathilde was a fidgety woman, jumpy. Her eyes never left her daughter. She remembered Lillian from their meeting at the monkey house and seemed to relax when Lillian told her they had impressed upon Kit not to use sign language in public. Frida herself seemed a happy enough child, shy but with a ready smile that lit up when she spotted Kit.

"She's very bright," Mathilde boasted. "She does not go to school now, but we have a private tutor for her who says her understanding of mathematics far exceeds her age."

They were hoping, next year, to emigrate to America, Mathilde confessed, tucking a silky curl behind her ear. But her husband had a building company with big projects that needed to be finished and paid up before they could contemplate a move.

"It is not so very easy here now," Mathilde said in her careful English.

They sat together on a bench watching Kit and Frida weaving and doubling back through a stand of linden, oak, and maple. Hodgepodge, after running with them for a time, settled on his haunches to watch them with the look of a laissez-faire uncle, surprised to find himself in a child-minding role but poised to fight to the death if it came to it. Frida was taller than Kit now. Everyone got taller than Kit sooner or later. But Kit was faster, and Frida seemed happy to pelt along after her, in and out of the long shadows.

Kit had made no friends like this at her new school, it seemed. No little girls or boys who asked her to play after class, no stories of lunchtime games. At home, if Lillian asked, Kit would shrug and deflect. They were boring, they were dumb, they were big, they were mean.

Lillian stiffened. "Mean, how?"

"They don't let me play with them. They say I throw like a girl."

Lillian lowered herself to the couch beside Kit and pried one of Kit's hands from where she had them balled against her skinny ribs, her arms crossed. Lillian was thinking of Amsel, the way he swished past her in the lab, nodding at the men but ignoring her utterly. As if she were a lamppost.

"Sometimes, as a woman, you have to be exceptional."

Kit opened her mouth. Lillian knew what Kit was going to say. Kit was exceptional, and she knew it. Now she thought of Irène Joliot-Curie, the Nobel Prize–winning scientist at the Sorbonne who'd introduced her and Max before being appointed to Prime Minister Blum's government. But she'd only lasted three months in the role.

"And when exceptional isn't enough," said Lillian, "you must also be loud." Another shrug. Chances were, Kit had also tried being loud.

"There was one nice boy at school, but the other boys pushed him and kicked him, even after he'd fallen down. They said his father is a filthy Jew."

Kit's eyes flicked at Lillian as she said the words, reluctant to repeat them. Lillian pulled her daughter's head to her breast, felt the tremble running through her. She was reminded of the story Ernest had told her on the train to Berlin, about a boy at her old school bullying her friend. How she'd thought at first the friend had been imaginary, then later had worried that the friend was Kit.

Lillian glanced over at Helen. She was seated cross-legged on the living room rug, building a tall tower with her wooden blocks, oblivious. If Helen had encountered bullies, she'd never said so.

"But the girls?" Lillian said, stroking awkwardly at Kit's hair. Comforting and consoling came so much easier to Ernest.

Kit's red head rustled back and forth against her, no. Her voice came out muffled. "When those boys make snowballs, they put rocks inside."

Lillian felt cold. Maybe they needed to speak to the principal. But Ernest was away again. One night, he'd said. Maybe two. To the south, or the west. She didn't know.

Helen looked up from her tower, her brow furrowed. "Is a Jew a dog?" she asked. "Like Hodgepodge?"

Lillian could feel her mouth falling open. This godforsaken country. "Absolutely not! Why would you say such a thing?"

"It was Kit who said filthy," Helen growled, peevish. "And Hodgepodge *is* filthy."

After supper, Kit bustled about, brushing her teeth and getting into her nightclothes before scurrying off to fetch her plush toy mouse, a gift from Max. Helen was always docile at bedtime, lifting her arms without being asked so that Lillian could maneuver her into her nightdress.

"Why, Helen, this is too small for you now! Isn't it sore, here, in the arms?" Lillian tugged at the fabric, which bunched under the shoulders, the hem scarcely falling to the knee. How had she not noticed before now? "You've outgrown it." Even saying the words gave her a rush of warmth. Kit wore the same things, year after year.

"Outgwown?" Helen repeated, her sleepy eyes widening. "Is that special?"

"No, no. Outgrown is normal. You're growing up so fast!"

Helen looked disappointed. Kit, edging back into the bedroom with her toy, had registered the delight on Lillian's face.

"What is it?" Kit frowned. "What's wrong?"

Lillian gave a brisk shake of her head. "Absolutely nothing. Helen's going to borrow your other nightie tonight, and we'll go shopping tomorrow, won't we. New nightclothes for you both."

When she checked on them later, Kit had her toy mouse in a stranglehold against her chest. Her precious necklace watch was clutched in her palm. Ernest had persuaded Kit to leave the watch at home on school days, and Lillian wondered now. Had someone teased her? Tried to take her watch away? Lillian gently prized the watch, warm to the touch, from Kit's hand and set it on the bedside table. She stepped quietly to the doorway, but before she could ease the door closed, Kit murmured something in the darkness. Lillian paused.

"Frida," Kit mumbled again. "Frida is my friend."

CH6: JULY 1938

L illian knew from Ernest's hopeful face that morning, his cheery tone, that he expected her home in time to try out Natalie's gift at the park. To pull away from her microscope, drag herself to the tram in her leaden shoes, sweat seeping from every pore, and join her little family in the Tiergarten, where both girls darted at her like swallows, swerving away if she didn't raise her arms to greet them. She'd begged off too often, working late, leaving Ernest to hurry away from his own pressing duties to relieve Gertrude of her charges. She needed to push through. Smile. Ignore the weight that sat like a hippopotamus on her breast. Maybe she should find an English physician in Berlin. Heinrik Strauss might recommend someone. In Paris she'd seen a doctor who told her the quaking in her chest, the jabbing in her heart, was anxiety. Very common in women. She didn't feel anxious. She felt emptied out. Exhausted. A group of scientists in Freiburg were approaching many of Lillian's own most private suppositions through a radical set of in situ experiments using identical and fraternal twins. The good citizens of the Reich were falling all over themselves to volunteer blood samples from their own children. Anything to curry favor with the regime, Ernest always said.

The package from Natalie had arrived that morning: a softball and three catcher's mitts, two small, one large. Helen had frowned at them, bewildered. But Kit had known right away what the gloves were for, snatching one up and working her hand inside. *They say I throw like a girl.*

Ernest, Lillian realized from the happy rustle of his eyebrows, wasn't surprised. He must have suggested the idea to Natalie.

This was a consolation gift, then, since Natalie and John had canceled a planned trip to Europe, given the political tensions.

Don't forget, Natalie had written in a separate note for Lillian. *If things deteriorate, you must abandon your research, promise me. You must come home at once.*

Lillian found her family on the wide gravel path bordered by flowers inside the north gate, Ernest gently lobbing the ball toward each of his daughters in turn: Helen screwing her eyes shut, then chirruping with excitement to find she'd managed to entrap the ball in her leather mitt, Kit hopping up and down in celebration, both girls hooting with laughter when Kit's overhand hit her father square in the stomach. Not hard. But he reeled backward in slow motion, arms wheeling, before landing on his bottom with a grunt and a grin. Lillian, watching, was struck with a sudden image: Kit, years ago, before Helen was born, throwing a ball for Spargo. The big dog thundering into her *Mirabilis jalapa* experiments in stimulation and deprivation. Today Helen was probably the same size and ability as Kit was then, but she didn't have her sister's stoic focus.

Helen ran to greet her mother, begging to head to the swings, her ball forgotten in a tall stand of *Dahlia pinnata*. Lillian started to shake her head. She was too tired. She would sit on this bench and watch them practice their throws. But Ernest shot her a look. They'd discussed Helen's palpable disappointment with Natalie's gift this morning. Lillian didn't have the energy to cajole an aggrieved Helen out of one of her tempests. She held out her hand and let Helen drag her to the Spielplatz.

By the time Lillian and Helen returned, Ernest and Kit had abandoned their game and were placing a row of round stones on a low wall. A moment later, Kit sped off. Ernest joined Lillian on a bench. Helen reclaimed the ball and started bowling it through the iron loops bordering the flower bed.

"What's with the rocks?" Lillian asked.

Ernest reclined in the seat beside her, Kit's watch around his neck. "Laps," he said. "Watch."

A few minutes later Kit came zipping back into view. As she looped past the wall, she slowed just long enough to knock one of the rocks to the ground before continuing back out.

"One rock for each lap," Ernest said, sounding pleased with himself. "So she doesn't lose count."

They waited. The flesh of Lillian's legs felt gluey in the evening heat. She could smell the day's effort overwhelming the talc in her underarms. The anxiety in her chest had eased. Kit came back into view, swept another stone from the wall, then sprinted back into the green gloom of the chestnuts.

"Why does she do this, do you think?" Lillian murmured. "This boundless energy and pointless running. She doesn't get it from me."

She said the words aloud but was already sifting theories through the fingers of her mind. Did Kit's speed and vitality stem from her stunted senescence? Or did the two qualities share the same genetic molecule? Maybe having four days' worth of energy packed into one required her to move faster, think quicker. But surely it should have been the opposite. She should have had to conserve and ration.

"Thomas was the same," Ernest said, interrupting her thoughts. He glanced down at the watch, hoping she hadn't caught the hitch in his voice. "Always racing, always buzzing. He grew out of it eventually, or at least learned to control it. But when he was a boy, he couldn't sit still. Never walked if he could run. He wore our mother to shreds."

Thomas as a child. She struggled to picture it. With the same wild red curls as Kit, as Ernest. But leaner, longer, and louder. Impulsive and headstrong where Ernest was thoughtful and measured. And yet she'd fallen for them both. She felt, almost physically, a prickling memory of Thomas in the year before they married, peppering kiss after kiss along her jaw, then her neck, pecking and nuzzling until she'd laughed and pushed him away. Ernest was more deliberate and unhurried, brushing his lips against the tender skin behind her ear, breathing her in until she shivered. And it wasn't fair, all these years later, to wonder whose affection, whose pace, she'd liked better. Steady Ernest or speedy Thomas. The only reason Ernest was here with her now was because Thomas couldn't sit still, had thought he might outrun the German gunners, too fast to catch a bullet.

She watched Kit pelting down the steps from the upper lawns, her chest puffed, her chin tucked. Lillian felt the tightness in her breast again, so sharp and sudden her hand flew to her sternum, groping at the gallop of her heart. Ernest's brow furrowed.

"What is it?"

"Nothing." She patted her breastbone. "My heartburn. Acid reflux. Or possibly an air bubble in my esophagus."

Ernest's eyes crinkled at her, his lips twitching.

"A bubble. Just so. Everyone has that feeling, from time to time."

He reached over, taking her hand, his smile still plucking at the corner of his mouth. "We tend to think of it as love."

CH7: OCTOBER 1938

In private, Max spluttered angrily about the speechifying and rallies around the city, the constant marching and saluting, the long red flags hanging like strips of meat. But Lillian had never known a different Germany, a different Berlin. This kind of patriotism struck her as shrill and unsavory, but not particularly unsettling. And it wasn't her concern. What she had to do was validate her technique for visualizing chromosomes in maize, linking regions to traits, then use this to establish the basis for genetic conservation, suppression, expression, and correction. In her mind's eye, at all times, she could picture Kit practicing her laps, Helen clambering on the monkey bars. Ernest, with Kit's silver watch swinging from the ribbon around his neck, would have one eye on Helen, his strong arms outstretched to catch her if she fell, the other one watching for Kit to careen back into view. Ernest's job was to keep them safe. Lillian's job was to decrypt the fundamental secrets of heredity. Universally, yes. But also intimately. Her own genes. Her own genetic inheritance. Kit.

Besides, everyone in Max's lab seemed as disinterested as Lillian in the ambitions of Herr Hitler. The Dörr Laboratory hummed like an engine, scientists from half a dozen disciplines sparring or conferring in German. *Nukleinsäure, Molekül, löslich.* So clipped and assured. Unable to understand much of what was said, Lillian could easily seal her mind shut to their conversations. It was a surprise to realize, as the months went by, that some of these German words had taken hold without her noticing.

Professor Amsel had not, after all, moved back to his refurbished North Annex. Instead, the north end of the Dörr Laboratory had been sectioned off by thick velvet drapes that Amsel and his staff could yank closed, a wide, black void walling off the rest of the sunny Dörr Lab. When Lillian asked Max, point-blank, what it was Amsel was working on, Max shrugged his round shoulders, his face drooping like a bloodhound. "Would you believe, I don't know. In my own laboratory. I'm not told, and I'm told I won't be told. In fact, I'm told *that* end of the Dörr Lab is not, in fact, the Dörr Lab."

Amsel had installed his own secretary in the laboratory foyer, a towering and sinewy woman named Karol Münter. Fräulein Zimmermann's desk still faced the door so she could greet visitors with her shiny smile. She cooed with delight on the rare times Ernest stopped by with the children, bustling around her desk to practice her English, pat the rosy cheeks of the girls, and ply them with homemade cake. Frau Münter, by contrast, ignored all visitors to the office and was especially frosty with the children. Most of the time, all you could glimpse of Münter, half hidden by a partition of cabinets, was the jagged ridge of her spine and her bony elbows splayed above her spotless desk. A falcon mantling over its nest. Lillian's only interaction with Münter had been when she'd come across the woman glowering at the long row of pigeonholes, an envelope pinched like a soiled cloth in her hand. Lillian recognized the stationery at once as Natalie's.

"Is that for me?" she asked in halting German. Münter muttered a short, unintelligible sentence. Straightened to her full height, Amsel's beanpole secretary stood eye to eye with Lillian, her breath an acrid mix of applesauce and cigarette. She replied in English, waving the envelope in the direction of Zimmermann's empty desk before handing it to Lillian.

"This one has potatoes for brains," she said, in a sandpaper growl. "Your mail is always in my box."

Ernest was abruptly recalled to Paris. In political circles, Ernest knew everything about everyone, always. Even predicting, ahead of time, that Hitler would march into Czechoslovakia. But Ernest had been broadsided when Chamberlain, Daladier, and Mussolini had agreed to the German Sudetenland.

"I need to go at once, you understand? Just for a week, if that. I'll be back by the sixth at the latest."

Ernest was unflappable, always. She'd never seen him flapped.

"But this means peace, doesn't it? That's what Prime Minister Chamberlain said in his radio broadcast."

Ernest looked dark and brooding and didn't answer. Gray pillows now lived under his sunken eyes. Instead he handed her a card bearing a phone number, nothing else.

"I've made arrangements for you if you need to leave quickly, if it comes to that. You call this number and a car will come."

CH8: NOVEMBER 1938

Whatever peace they might have hoped would settle after the Munich talks, allowing Ernest to cease his travels, was shattered in November. Kristallnacht—the night itself—Lillian and her girls slept soundly through it all, hearing nothing. But the shrill peal of the telephone before dawn on November 10 made her bolt out of bed.

Ernest, calling from who knows where. The girls were not to go to school today, he said. Lillian should stay home, too. He was returning immediately, on the next train.

Lillian's brain was slow to rouse, her tongue too woolly for questions. She rubbed at her eyes and realized Gertrude, too, had been woken, had crept down the stairs and was standing in the doorway, clasping her robe tightly closed, her face a scribble of worry. Lillian pressed the telephone to her ear. "Say that again, Ernest."

"It's Jewish businesses, homes, and synagogues," he repeated. "Destroyed, smashed, burning. All over the Reich. I don't yet know the scale of it, and I don't know when it will be under control. Indeed, I'm not sure the aim is to control it."

She could hear the strain in his voice.

"People are dead, Lillian. We don't know how many. I'm calling Max now and asking him to come by, just for the day, okay? And I'll be there by tomorrow night. I need you to stay indoors."

Max arrived a little after eight o'clock, more rumpled than she'd ever seen him, carrying King Louis the umpteenth in a small wire cage. His face was ashen and his eyes dull, even as he fixed a smile on his face for the girls, crouching to gather them in his arms.

"It's not good," he murmured to Lillian while the girls were distracted by Louis, whose beady eyes were blinking suspiciously at his new surroundings. Kit heard Max's words and glanced anxiously at her mother.

By midmorning there were more trucks rumbling in the streets, faces peering out from under the canvas tops. More men in uniform and civilian clothes, roving in packs. On the horizon, smoke. She glanced at Max, who had settled himself back on the couch with his feet up, ankles crossed. He was running an elegant finger across his slim mustache, deep in thought. A bulge rumpling the fabric of his shirt told her King Louis was back in his breast pocket. He wasn't the most menacing of male defenders, it was true.

Lillian nearly fell off her chair when the telephone rang once again. But it wasn't Ernest; it was Dr. Strauss, inquiring politely after Lillian and her family in a mild tone, as if it were a day like any other.

Gertrude hovered again in the doorway. So did Dr. Strauss call most days, midday? Lillian wondered. In those brief hours when both girls were at school? Lillian handed the phone to Gertrude and retreated to the living room, eyebrow raised. In a moment, Gertrude followed.

"Will you be staying in, Mrs. McKinley?"

Gertrude's wide blue eyes traveled to Max and back to her employer.

"Heinrik—that is, Dr. Strauss—is asking to take me to lunch. He says it's perfectly fine. I'll only be gone a few hours."

Lillian paced. The girls squabbled. Max was cajoled by Helen into mounting a puppet show, which helped to keep the peace. An hour crawled by, then another. When Gertrude at last returned, Max pressed her for details. He kept his voice mild, but Lillian noted the quiver in the extra fold of flesh beneath his chin.

The girl said there was not much to tell. There was a fire on Fasanenstrasse. At a synagogue. But fire trucks were keeping it from spreading. She'd seen some windows smashed and words painted on walls and buildings.

"What words?" Kit wanted to know. Lillian ran a hand over her eyes.

Gertrude pinched her lips into a line. "Not the kind of words a young lady needs to know," she said.

Anxiety pricked at Lillian's heart with its tiny knives, just as the doctor had described. Thank goodness Gertrude was home— she should never have let her leave. Helen, who'd been down for a nap, trudged back into the living room, her sweet face flushed.

"But otherwise things seemed normal," Gertrude was saying. "Completely normal. We went for lunch at Café Kranzler, and it was very busy. Every table taken."

Lillian pulled Helen onto her lap, and she snuggled close. Gertrude straightened herself again and smiled. "But it is absolutely fine to go to the park. Heinrik agrees. Everyone is in the park today."

And it was true. Men and women were promenading in the Tiergarten as if it were a Sunday afternoon, children dashing and shouting in the Spielplatz. Pleased to be finally out in the open air, Kit didn't grouse about the crush of other children in the playground, where Helen insisted they head first. Helen, in turn, was persuaded in time to link her arm through her sister's and head to the quieter paths in Kit's Wilderwald, where Kit could greet her canine friends by name. Hodgepodge, to her disappointment, was not among them today. She shrugged it off.

"Hodgepodge has other friends," she told Max in a confidential tone. "I've seen other nice people in the garden giving him scraps."

As they rounded the bend, heading back toward the meadows, Lillian heard someone call her name and turned. It was Mathilde, seated on a bench in the pale sun, Frida beside her. The girl sprang to her feet at the sight of Kit. Without a word, the two quickly clasped hands and fell into step side by side, silent. Helen, pleased to have Max to herself, set about negotiating a piggyback. Lillian dropped onto the bench beside Mathilde, who was neatly coiffed as always. Lillian was glad she'd tied a silk scarf over her own unruly mane.

Mathilde was blinking rapidly, a quaver in her voice. "Have you heard?"

"Very little," Lillian said softly, glancing around. "Ernest called this morning and described some of the violence. Insisted we stay indoors. But Gertrude ended up going for lunch with her friend and came home to tell us that things were fine, with the exception of the fire at the Fasanenstrasse synagogue. But we saw nothing, heard nothing, when we walked to the park. And this—" Lillian gestured at the busy park. "You'd never know anything was amiss."

Mathilde was staring at her, uncomprehending. "What does it mean, 'amiss'?"

She didn't wait for Lillian's reply, already scrabbling in her purse. "I have to show you." Mathilde held up an envelope. Her timid face, for once, looked not anxious, but alight.

"You haven't heard? The arson? The attacks? Ernest said . . ." Lillian's voice trailed away as Mathilde waved the envelope, excited. Lillian scanned the other couples and families strolling the forested paths, children playing hide and seek. For a moment, she couldn't see her own girls and panic flopped like a fish in her breast. Then she spied Helen and Max, crouched at the edge of the path. Kit and Frida were behind them, cross-legged under the spreading arms of a tall oak, leafless under the November sky. Her pulse slowed.

Mathilde, she realized, had extracted a single sheet of paper and passed it to Lillian, her eyes wide and bright. "We got this letter in the mail this morning."

Lillian smoothed the paper open on her lap, noting the big, bolded word at the top: *VERTRAULICH.*

Lieber Herr Hesse, the letter began. Dear Mr. Hesse. This much Lillian could understand. The postmark was an address in Wilmersdorf, not so far from the park. She scanned the rest of the German words, irritably. She'd picked up quite a lot of spoken German, but it wasn't helping her with these long, consonant-addled words in print.

Frida's name appeared, and she recognized the words for child, daughter.

Lillian handed the letter back. "Tell me what it says."

There was a bloom in Mathilde's pale face, despite the cold, and she was biting her lip, which couldn't stop her smile. "It's from Frida's physician, and another doctor, a Kinderarzt, for children." Mathilde swished the envelope in the air again, trying to translate.

"A pediatrician," Lillian said, thinking of Heinrik Strauss. A man who recognized sign language when he saw it. She glanced at the signatures at the bottom of the page, but she knew neither name. "And?"

"It says they are opening a new program for deaf children. They are researching a cure for hereditary deafness and are inviting Frida to join. I know you, Lillian, also study genes—I thought maybe you would know something about this. Will it work, do you think?"

Lillian stared at Mathilde. "A cure?" She repeated the word dumbly. If someone had isolated a gene for deafness and had a workable theory for how to rectify it, or suppress it, or nullify it in human subjects . . . If such a thing were achievable for deafness, a genetic fix, then it might be possible, surely, for other traits, too.

She struggled to navigate the lump in her throat. "But is Frida's hearing loss even genetic? You and your husband . . . ?"

Mathilde shook her head. "No, and not our parents either." She laid a hand fleetingly on her stomach. "And you know we have no other children," she said, her eyes downcast.

Lillian took the letter again, scanning the words in vain. "I'm sorry," she said finally. "My own work—" She looked to Max, his arms heaped with chestnuts being gathered by Helen. Would Max know anything about this? "My own work is in maize. Chromosomal shapes in relation to aberrant mitotic behavior, how mutants can appear in a germ line." She stopped. The look of joy and hope shining on Mathilde's face sputtered for a moment, as if her filament were faulty.

Lillian hastened to put her at ease. "Plants and leaves. Kernels of corn. That's my area."

"But you could possibly find out more?" Now it was Mathilde's hand squeezing hers. "Klaus, Frida's father, and I, we're thrilled, of course. But the facility is not so close. In Brandenburg. We won't make a decision until we know more. And—"

"This word, here." Lillian pointed at *VERTRAULICH* at the top of the letter.

Mathilde nodded. "Confidential, private. Because it's medical correspondence, and of course deafness is rather . . ."

"Taboo," Lillian offered in a low voice.

Mathilde's smile looked more hesitant. "Indeed. Please be cautious, with your queries."

CH9: NOVEMBER 1938

Lillian considered asking Gertrude whether Heinrik Strauss might know about the facility in Brandenburg. She didn't need to mention the Hesses by name. Gertrude, it seemed, went for lunch with Strauss a few times a week, but never spoke of him at home. But Lillian didn't know Strauss well enough to know whether he'd have any insights. Whether he would be discreet. *Cautious.*

When Lillian asked Gertrude whether she'd like to invite Strauss for dinner, she blushed and said no. She preferred, she said, to keep her life and work separate. Besides, Ernest predicted, if Strauss was serious in his intentions with Gertrude, it would be her own family, not the McKinleys, with whom Gertrude would want to orchestrate an introduction. And yet. Gertrude was a much-loved member of their home, but they knew next to nothing about Strauss. Max had met him not long after the McKinleys moved to Berlin, but Strauss had elicited no strong opinions, other than the unhelpful observation that the man's skin had the texture of an undercooked Pfannkuchen.

"You might use your connections to look into him?" Lillian had casually suggested to Ernest.

Ernest looked both shocked and bemused. From the start of their marriage, Lillian had understood that there were certain aspects of his work he couldn't discuss with her, just as he understood that she used an overtly casual tone to describe something she'd overheard in the shops or the laboratory that he might find noteworthy. He strummed his mustache. "You're suggesting I task clandestine contractors of His Majesty's government to elucidate the marital suitability of a German pediatrician?"

Lillian smiled. Ernest could always make her smile. She recalled the word in all caps at the top of Mathilde's letter: *VER-TRAULICH*. Mathilde had sought her advice as a scientist, not given her permission to involve someone else. And shouldn't Lillian herself be able to find out how, precisely, doctors proposed to divorce a specific gene from the genotype? And attempt a *repair*? This sounded more like the sort of eugenics research being done at Kaiser Wilhelm, across town, and she knew how Max felt about this rival institution. Perhaps when she was back in Paris over Christmas, Ernest could come with her to the Sorbonne library, as translator. Perhaps the reason she'd never heard of this research was that it had all been published in German.

Their plan was to head back to France in December and stay through the New Year for the installation of Georges Vanier as special envoy at the Canadian legation. Gertrude would remain in Germany when the McKinleys were in France because, she told them with a guarded smile, her mother and father planned to visit Berlin. Ernest had offered for them to stay at the house on Tiergartenstrasse, managing to keep his face neutral. But after Gertrude turned to go, he raised an I-told-you-so eyebrow at Lillian.

After being out of town for Kristallnacht, Ernest insisted on staying put until they left for Paris. She could sense it, his malaise. The way he raked his fingers through his hair, making it stand in tangled tufts. If she woke in the night and listened, she could tell that Ernest wasn't sleeping. Worry was something Ernest now wore like a cape, gathering the children beneath it. One night, when she arrived home well past their bedtime, Lillian found her daughters curled fast asleep against him under a sagging configuration of blankets tented over the dining room furniture. When she lifted a flap to peer inside, he put a finger to his lips. She didn't hesitate, folding her tall frame to crawl into the fort beside them.

For a long time they lay in quiet. Then Ernest murmured, "There's a new posting I could put in for. India. It would take us a long way from this madness, wouldn't it?"

India! Lillian blinked. Was she dreaming? It wasn't like Ernest to want to run away. "We can discuss in the morning," he whispered.

But they didn't. When she tried to bring it up, he shook his head. "You've got your work to finish. Your degree. We're fine here for now."

CH10: NOVEMBER 1938

Berlin, by late November 1938, was no longer the city they first knew. More purposeful now; less lovely. It was an act of will to remember how it was before. So many old buildings were now draped in the red, black, and white flags. Others were boarded up or blackened. Everyone was marching, not just those in army uniforms and booted brownshirts but groups of boys ranging from teens to very young. Learning discipline. Practicing their salutes. Even the girls were taught to walk in formation, chests out, hair pulled back from their stern faces, legs swishing like scissors.

Only in the Tiergarten did the city feel mostly unchanged. When they went as a family on Sunday, their last before leaving for Paris, a foot of new snow was quilting the paths and meadow. Children were calling out in their high, pure voices, building snowmen, peeling off their own hats and scarves to dress their creations. Ernest pointed to the largest: four round balls instead of three, two black stones for eyes, and an army cap on its head. Beneath an icicle nose, the snowman had a square of black tree bark for a mustache. Thick branches were arms, one jutting into the air, the other wrapped with a handkerchief armband: red, black, and white.

Helen insisted they head to the playground first, but she stopped short some distance from the swings. Older boys had taken over the Spielplatz for a snowball fight and were dashing out from behind their barricades of snow. Comrades offered suppressive fire while a group of younger boys were rolling and packing ammunition for both camps. One of these junior recruits saw Helen approach and launched a volley of snowballs in her direction. A blatant warning, although none came close. Lillian started forward, calling out to Helen, but Ernest put his hand on her elbow, putting a finger to his lips.

Kit was already darting forward on her fast feet. She stopped at Helen's side, bent to scoop at the heavy snow with both mitts, then, with a blazing overhand throw, returned fire. Had the boy not ducked at the last minute, she would have hit him square in the face.

"Kit and Helen, that's enough," Lillian called. "This way." Lillian pointed toward the chestnut forest. Kit, another snowball already packed in her mitts, turned reluctantly to follow. Lillian wheeled on Ernest, who was trying to suppress a grin.

"Ten out of ten," he called to Kit as she raced past. "No rocks?"

"No rocks." She paused and drilled the snowball back at her father. Much softer, slower, than the one she'd beaned at the boy. It hit Ernest squarely in the stomach, making him laugh.

Lillian waited until the girls were well ahead. "What on earth, Ernest?"

He was puffed with pride. "She's gotten very good. You'll have to write Natalie. Her gift, all of our games of catch, have paid off."

Kit was already weaving through the trees, calling for Hodgepodge, ecstatic when the mutt skulked out of whatever nook he'd found as shelter, his coat matted with twigs and needles. Kit fished something out of her pocket that looked suspiciously like the toast Ernest had buttered for her that morning. The dog wolfed it down, then sank onto his hindquarters while she scratched his ears. In a moment Kit would be begging again to take Hodgepodge home, out of the cold. And Lillian, remorse already pricking at her like a thistle, would have to remind her that their landlord wouldn't permit them a dog. She squinted toward Mathilde's usual bench, but it was empty, still frosted with thick dollops of snow.

Helen hadn't run ahead. She still had a snowball in her mitten and was biting it like an apple. "When is that man coming to Paris, Papa? The special one."

Lillian and Ernest shared a look, equally bewildered. Helen rolled her eyes. "At the leg-leg-legation." She was pleased to have conquered the syllables.

"Ah." Ernest nodded, the word emerging as a swirl of mist. "You mean Georges Vanier. The King's Special Envoy Extraordinary and Minister Plenipotentiary." The long and highfalutin title had been a source of amusement in the McKinley household. "He and his wife, Pauline, should arrive in Paris a few weeks after we get back."

"Is Mr. Vanier like Kit, then?"

Ernest shot another puzzled look at Lillian, who shrugged.

Helen crunched her snowball in her teeth, her lips peeling away from the cold. "Special and extraordinary?"

Ernest managed a smile—rare these days. He laid a hand on her woolen hat. "It *is* a long and funny name, isn't it?" Then, turning to Lillian, he added, "But you couldn't imagine a more down-to-earth man to lead the legation than Georges Vanier, and his wife is cut of the same cloth. They've already been working with me on a petition to convince Canada to open its doors to Jewish refugees. I can assure you, he is every bit as concerned about Herr Hitler's policies and expansionism as I am."

CH11: DECEMBER 1938

Her last week in the laboratory before leaving for Paris, Lillian all but forgot about Mathilde and Frida Hesse. She was so behind in her analyses and would be even further behind by the time they returned. It felt more urgent than ever. She needed tangible progress to reassure herself she was doing the right thing by staying here, in Berlin, even as worry spread like mildew, like blight. She could see it now on the faces of neighbors and colleagues. The furrowed foreheads. Even sunny Fräulein Zimmermann, with her eager English greetings when Lillian stopped by the office to check for mail, had lost some of her light.

And the work itself felt . . . lost. Her distant goal had sprinted ahead, out of reach, more fleet-footed than any actual substantiating evidence. She usually had the sense of a rubber band, stretching and stretching, keeping the possible connected, however tenuously, to the proven. First, the hop from *Zea mays* to jumping genes, and from there, a nearly unimaginable leap to a young woman trapped in the mind and body of a child. But Lillian couldn't see a way to connect it all, let alone find a remedy. Not for Kit, or deafness, or any other trait inscribed in the genes. She'd certainly found no new information on this Brandenburg program. She'd made up her mind to run it all past Max, when they had the privacy to talk it through.

Lillian lifted her gaze to the long windows of the laboratory. The miserable smear of mustard-gray that passed for winter daylight in Berlin had long since been smothered by night. Unnoticed, darkness had crept over her bench like one of Fassbinder's molds. Her stomach rumbled. Had she eaten lunch? No. Yes—she remembered now. An apple and some cheese, but she'd shared that with King Louis. She needed to get home. She needed to find Max, scrape him from his own office, and convince him it was time to drive her back to Tiergartenstrasse.

As if summoned, Max surfaced in the murky gloom, a bundle of papers in his arms. He had dark circles under his eyes, and his mustache, in need of a trim, tugged at the skin of his tired face like cooling milk. He, too, needed a break. She and Ernest had invited Max to stay with them in Paris for Christmas. Gertrude's room would be empty in the flat on Rue Madame. Already Lillian was thinking of the medical library at the Sorbonne and what she might tell Max if she brought him there with her.

He set the stack of papers on her desk with a sigh.

"I've been rereading McClintock's notion that mutant sectorials are due to losses of specific regions within the ring chromosome. I think—"

Max broke off at the sound of a door opening. Voices speaking quietly in German. Footsteps. The clack of serviceable heels on the checkered limestone and slate. And then something else—the tack-tack and skitter of claws, a panting breath. And then yes, unmistakable: an animal whimper. Max raised an eyebrow at Lillian. Someone was walking a dog in the Dörr Lab. Lillian nudged the face of her wristwatch toward the moonlight: 9:00 p.m.

The quiet drone of voices continued, almost indiscernible. One was Amsel's, certainly. Others were male. And a growling contralto Lillian recognized as Frau Münter.

Max stood as still as a pillar, listening. Amsel and his guests had reached the north section of the lab, not bothering to pull the long drapes. There was the click of a cabinet, the spluttered protest of a stool being dragged. Underneath the weave of voices, the dog whined and panted. Never mind how irksome it was not to understand German: Lillian would have done anything, in that moment, to understand what the dog was trying so desperately to communicate. There was more scratching and scuffling, producing a more desperate yelp that made Lillian leap up. Straining and failing to catch the conversation, Lillian found she could hear only the animal and its rapid breath. Its fear.

And then, she realized, she didn't.

Max joined Lillian in the open space beside the rows of benches. They could both now be seen in the dim light. "Dr. Amsel," he called out. "Working late?"

A pause. Then, "Professor Dörr." The voice carried no hint of surprise or annoyance.

Max cleared his throat. He spoke slowly, and Lillian understood every word. "Dr. Amsel, I must remind you that no large mammals are allowed in this wing of the facility except for scientific purposes, and only after euthanasia and processing, according to strict protocols."

Lillian could see three men, plus Frau Münter: Amsel, another man she did not know, and then a younger man, practically a boy, who wore an army uniform. The young man looked on the verge of losing his supper and carried the dog in his arms. A small dog. Brownish, short fur, long, tattered ears.

"Ah, Dr. Dörr," Amsel replied in English. "In fact, these rules I believe apply to the Dörr Lab. Are you quite sure they apply to the Amsel Lab? I think not, but I shall surely check on these regulations in the morning. Frau Münter, you can verify this tomorrow?"

The men were headed for the doors; Lillian could hear the rap of Münter's sturdy heels. Max watched them go. "Is that dog okay?" he called after them, his arms rigid at his sides.

Amsel made a disparaging sound that still managed to sound amused. Lillian heard the creak of the opening doors. A surge of nausea roiled her stomach.

"No, Professor Dörr. The dog most certainly is not."

CH12: DECEMBER 1938

Back in Paris, Lillian felt her mood lifting. The sky seemed bluer, the talk prettier and more frivolous. In Berlin, everywhere you stepped was sludge and rubble, to be rebuilt as the city of Germania. Even Golden Elsie, the Victory Column in Königsplatz, had been yanked out by the roots and replanted in the Tiergarten.

The disorder of Paris, by contrast, seemed more human and harmless. Row upon row of *affiches illustrées* advertising everything from ear trumpets to cigarettes brought color to the drab streets. Even when the posters started to peel and fray, the decrepitude had a certain shabby grandeur. One for the Loterie Nationale, everywhere that December, featured a plump man and woman waltzing in springtime. The man clutched a bulging sack of francs in his hand, while the woman held a four-leaf clover. This was Paris. Lucky and untroubled. Predisposed to dance. Walking through their old haunts, Lillian felt as if the old stone buildings, blackened by the soot of living, looked like they'd reveled until dawn but could still blink open their rows of louvered shutters to bat their lashes at the rising sun. *Good morning*, they seemed to say. *Bonjour and welcome back!*

"People are smiling in the streets, do you see that?" Lillian said to Ernest. "They're not as cowed and fearful."

She turned to Ernest to find his face like plaster settling. "That's because they're fools."

The Vaniers arrived in Paris in mid-December and Georges was officially instated as the King's Special Envoy Extraordinary and Minister Plenipotentiary at the Canadian legation. Pauline Vanier fussed over Kit and Helen, confiding that she already missed her own children terribly, having made the decision to leave all four of them at boarding school in England. "But your girls are such a lovely age," she'd told Lillian, eyeing Kit and Helen tenderly. "They are fraternal twins?" Lillian didn't bother to correct her. "Enjoy this time with them—it passes in the blink of an eye."

By the time Max arrived, Ernest's official obligations at the legation were winding down, but without Gertrude to distract the children, Lillian found she rarely had Max to herself, let alone time to take him to the library at the Sorbonne. The girls circled him like Saturn's moons, dragging him to the displays in the department store windows and jabbering about Père Noël, pointing at the black barges strung with lights, swaying in the oily water of the Seine. Max allowed himself to be coaxed and tugged and hurried to the park, to the pond, to the ponies. Lillian found herself struggling to keep up, her chest squeezing at the effort.

On Max's last night, over dinner, it seemed she might never get a word in edgewise. Max and Ernest spent most of the evening hashing over the much-ballyhooed Franco-German declaration, signed by Bonnet and von Ribbentrop earlier that month and already fraying at the edges.

"But will it hold?" Max asked Ernest. "Can it?"

Ernest glared into his wineglass as if von Ribbentrop himself might pop out to defend his intentions. Lillian knew his response by the slump of his shoulders.

She met his eyes across the table and caught the swift, anxious look from Kit.

Max raised his glass. "To the Franco-German declaration. May it hold."

Only when Kit and Helen had slithered down from their seats at the table and Ernest had agreed to a storybook on the sofa did Lillian, at last, tell Max about Frida Hesse. All of it. The letter of invitation. The Brandenburg facility probing a cure for deafness. *VERTRAULICH* stamped at the top.

"Is it possible"—Lillian hushed her voice—"that German scientists, unbeknownst to you and me, have managed to target the locus for a specific genetic condition in man? And discovered a way to alter it?"

Max lifted his chin, the quake in his cheeks betraying disbelief and distaste. "My countrymen, as you know, are obsessed with the idea of hereditary defects, but this is the first I've heard that they think they have the power to correct the genetic coding in some way. And deafness? This is not a discrete phenotype, by any means. Besides, their obsession with eugenics has never had, as its aim, the correction of defects, only the propagation and perfection of uniformity."

Max snatched up his fork angrily. "I fear your Mathilde is getting her hopes up for nothing." He bayoneted the last morsel of tart. "She would be better off not getting caught up in this Nazi propaganda and keeping her girl at home. Where she can't be meddled with." He flashed a stern look at Lillian, then turned to follow her gaze through the double doors to the salon. Kit was trying to keep her weary eyes on the storybook in Ernest's lap. Helen's had already drooped closed, her head resting on Kit's shoulder.

"Perhaps," he continued in a softer tone, "these scientists have developed some new technology to amplify sound. Does the girl hear poorly? Or not at all?"

Lillian pictured Kit and Frida cavorting among the trees hand in hand, playing so silently they might be on film, Frida timing Kit's incessant laps on the necklace watch, oblivious to Kit's approach until she actually came into view. Frida and Kit, by now, seemed to commune on a level far beyond the furtive hand gestures they used when they were sure they couldn't be seen. In her mind's eye, Lillian could picture Frida's eager face, her keen attention, the way she always watched Lillian's lips as she spoke. She shook her head. "I don't think Frida hears a thing."

In the salon, Ernest extracted himself gingerly from his daughters before padding down the corridor to the lavatory. Kit had fallen asleep at last, her curly red head resting against Helen's dark one. Lillian and Max watched them for a long moment, then Max reached across the table to take Lillian's hand. "You know this better than anyone, Lilly, but whatever it is that makes Kit special, it's not something that you or I can change."

Lillian made to ease her hand from his, flitting an anxious glance at her children, straining to hear Ernest's footfall rejoining them. But Max only shook his head. "Lillian, don't. Please. In the years since we met, Helen has changed month by month, while Kit—physically—has stayed absolutely the same, even as her mind grows by leaps and bounds. It makes you wonder, as indeed you must, whether whatever it is that is keeping her from aging might also be where she gets her other gifts."

A lump rose in Lillian's throat. She waited until she could swallow it back down before whispering. "There's nothing wrong with Kit."

It was the line they'd told themselves over and over again, going on twenty-three years. She could hear how plaintive it sounded.

"Of course not." Max sounded so matter-of-fact that Lillian looked up at him, sharply. Maybe she'd misread his meaning. Then he said, "It's not something wrong, it's something different."

He patted Lillian's hand. "I can see you've twisted yourself in knots trying to understand it, and my guess is that this is why you ended up in my lab, in this field, in the first place. Trying to find answers. What I'm saying, Lilly, is that whatever it is, Kit's genetic signature, I don't think we can isolate it, and I'm positive we can't fix it. The more important thing is to keep anyone else from trying to find or fix it either."

Later, after Max had repaired to his room, and the girls, floppy in sleep, had been transferred to their beds, Lillian waited until Ernest had switched off the light before saying, "You heard him, didn't you?"

He shifted onto his side, drawing her close, and buried his nose in her hair until he found the nape of her neck. When he spoke, his voice was muted by hair and pillow. "What did Max mean by 'find it and fix it'? As in, fix Kit's leap year gene?"

Even in the whirring tumult of her thoughts, the phrase made her smile. She felt him rolling away, addressing his next question to the dark. "Is there any way you can finish off your thesis work, these analyses, without going back to Berlin? Can Max finish them himself?"

Lillian could hear in his voice everything he wasn't saying. Everything he feared. How could she explain it? How could she unwind the whole unknowable strand that connected what she and Max were doing to what Ernest wanted to know? A fault or a fix. A leap year gene.

CH13: JANUARY 1939

They thought of sending the girls home to Natalie in Canada. But Natalie's plans seemed nebulous, since she had recently severed things with John. Ernest proposed a boarding school, but Lillian rejected that outright. She and Natalie had hated being sent back to Canada by their missionary parents when they were children. In the end they decided it would be better for the whole family to return to Germany together, but to be ready to leave if the political situation worsened. Kit would return to her same school, Helen to Gertrude's lessons in the morning, kindergarten in the afternoon, and Lillian to her bench, where—Ernest was adamant—she must be willing to abandon her corncobs at a moment's notice.

Ernest would stay with them in the house on Tiergartenstrasse, traveling as little as possible, he said, his teeth scraping at his mustache. "I'm keeping our evacuation plan in place," he told her. "In case something happens and I'm not here." He made her take the card with the phone number from her pocketbook and show him.

"But I've memorized it, Ernest," she told him. "And Kit has, too."

Gertrude, too, seemed ill at ease, a gloom clinging to her like smoke. Happy enough to see the girls again, but that seemed a thin veneer. Maybe, Lillian reasoned, Gertrude was sorry to say goodbye to her parents, who left before the McKinleys returned.

They'd been back for a week when Ernest surprised her Saturday at the lab, the children in tow, pink-cheeked and windswept. She'd gone to the university with Max before dawn, the air so cold and damp it tasted like blood on her tongue. Once at the lab, she'd been so busy at her bench she'd failed to see that the sun had shouldered through the clouds. It was a familiar squeal and the patter of little feet that roused her from the microscope.

Ernest, flushing scarlet in the warm laboratory, pinched off his fur-lined hat so that his silver-and-gold curls came alive with static, straining for the ceiling. "We've come to take you to lunch," he said, trying and failing to pat his hair back into place.

Kit was conducting a slow surveillance of Lillian's bench, careful to keep her fingers to herself. Helen had clambered up on the stool to try to peer through the microscope. Lillian put out a hand to steady her, guiding her to the eyepiece.

Ernest turned to Max, spinning the brim of his hat in his hands. "Join us, Max. Café Adalheidis. I've booked their sunniest table."

Before Max could answer, the doors opened a second time. The lab was typically quiet now on Saturdays. Only Lillian and Max, as well as the inscrutable Dr. Amsel, tended to come in. Fassbinder had finished off the analyses for his *Neurospora crassa* experiments last month, in time to submit an abstract to a conference being hosted by the Rockefeller Institute in New Jersey.

Sure enough, it was Professor Amsel. Dressed smartly in a dark suit, he clearly intended to stride past without a twitch of greeting. For once, Frau Münter was not clattering in his shadow.

To Lillian's surprise, Amsel swiveled his head, back-stepping on his long, pinstriped legs. He nodded curtly at Ernest but addressed his question at Lillian. "They are twins, Frau McKinley?"

Lillian's heart pattered. This had happened several times since Helen's latest growth spurt. Pauline Vanier had also assumed they were twins, but on that occasion, the girls had been out of earshot. Kit could be relied upon to prevaricate, but Helen was a wild card. Already, Lillian could tell, Helen was sizing up the man, summoning the words to correct him.

From around the corner came the piercing crash of breaking glass. Lillian grabbled for Helen. Max darted around to the next workspace, Ernest right behind him. Helen started wailing as if she herself had been cut to ribbons. Amsel, a look of distaste on his face, reset his course for his office without a backward glance.

Lillian hastened to Fassbinder's bench. Kit was standing, unharmed, in the midst of a jagged field of shards. Ernest tiptoed through the broken glass to lift her into the air, then set her down at Lillian's side. Lillian's eyes quickly confirmed what she'd already suspected. An entire tray of sterilized flasks and beakers now lay in glinting pieces. Yet the tray, she knew, had been set well back from the edge.

Max had a look on his face that Lillian couldn't read: fright dueling with relief. "Go straight away," he said. "I'll tidy this and join you at Café Adalheidis."

At the restaurant, Helen drowsed in the warmth, the incident at the lab forgotten. But Kit was fidgety, steering her knife and fork around like steamships on a white linen sea. She picked up the spoon and gazed solemnly at her reflection, tilting her head one way, then the other, as if trying to right her face. Everything, with Kit, was always inside out and upside down. "Why did that tall man want to know if we were twins, Mummy?"

Lillian was craning her head to see the cakes. The question stopped her cold. "It is none of Dr. Amsel's business whether you are twins or not."

Ernest clasped his hands. "Such a spectacular day! Hopefully Gertrude makes the most of it. Maybe Strauss will take her to a sunny café as well."

Kit looked up from her cutlery barges. "Gertrude says that Dr. Strauss has another lady friend now. I heard her speaking on the phone with her mother. He doesn't call her anymore. She was crying and asking what to do."

Lillian darted a look at Ernest. Frankly, it would be a relief to know that the governess had not, after all, been forming a serious attachment with a man of whom they knew so little.

Kit's fingers abandoned the silverware and found their way to her mouth, where they set about wiggling her front teeth. Both baby teeth were, at last, loose and, indeed, the white tip of her right central incisor was coming in behind. "Is it Gertrude's teeth, do you think? That Dr. Strauss doesn't like? That's what Gertrude said to her mother. What if my teeth come in like Gertrude's?"

Lillian reached over and pulled Kit's hands away from her mouth.

"That's a shame if Gertrude and Dr. Strauss have had a falling out," Ernest murmured. His expression suggested anything but. Behind him, Max was bustling through the door, a gust of winter air sparkling like pixie dust behind him.

Kit, whose look drifted from her mother to her father before arriving at Max, missed nothing.

CH14: JANUARY 1939

The endless winter, the long days at the lab, the daily worry-worry-worry, not enough sleep at night, when her mind ticked like a furnace. It was no surprise that Lillian had run herself down. She'd kept going to the lab until her honking cough became intractable. Max had insisted it was time to stay home and get better. Just as well. Ernest was away again for another few days. Somewhere to the south or the east.

Lillian lay dozing in bed, listening to Gertrude and the girls quarreling in German, a lighthearted duet. The falsetto haggling from the children was offset by the deeper *scht-scht-scht* of Gertrude's lower register, kind but firm. Lillian was surprised to realize how much of it she could follow.

"If Frida is not there, Katharina, I will time your laps. But only after we go to the playground. Helen, little bunny, let's put on your stockings."

Lillian was drifting to sleep. But she was roused by Kit's next words, her voice glum. "Frida won't be there. Frau Hesse told us last time. Frida's gone away."

Lillian's eyes sprang open and she pushed herself up in bed. Had she understood that correctly? "Kit?" she croaked. "Come here, please."

A moment later Kit was at her side, watching her mother anxiously. Lillian tried to speak, but a fit of coughing waylaid her. Her eyes watered. "What do you mean, Frida's gone away? Gone where?"

Kit's face fell. "Frau Hesse said last week that Frida went to a special hospital to fix her hearing."

Lillian felt her heart thud. She sank back against her pillow. She'd meant to speak with Mathilde, had assured Max she would. But since getting back, she'd been so consumed by her work. The weeks had turned into the better part of a month. She hadn't joined her family at the park since before Christmas.

"Frau Hesse told me to tell you. She was excited." Kit bit her lip. "I forgot, Mummy. You got so sick. Gertrude said we needed to let you rest."

Lillian shivered. Kit plucked at the quilt, trying to pull it higher over her mother. "You don't think it will work, do you, Mummy? The cure for Frida. I heard you that night, with Uncle Max."

Lillian closed her eyes. There was nothing you could say that this child wouldn't pick up on. Lillian would have to track down the Hesses' address. She would write to Mathilde, ask to meet. Lillian could feel the fatigue swamping her again. She tried to turn her head to Kit, feeling like a creaky hinge. "If you see Frau Hesse again, please tell her to telephone me, will you do that?"

Kit nodded solemnly. Lillian tried to smile. "And you'll say hi to Hodgepodge and his friends for me."

Kit's face was pale, her features wriggling to suppress something. Sorrow. Worry. Lillian almost didn't catch her words. "Hodgepodge has gone away, too."

CH15: JANUARY 1939

It was days before Lillian felt well enough to bathe and eat properly and a full week before she was up to heading to the lab, queasy, not with fever, but with how much time she'd lost. Ernest had returned from his trip. It was clear from his sunken cheeks that whatever he'd learned from his network this time was worse than he'd feared.

But now it was Max who'd fallen ill. He called to say, through bouts of hacking, that he couldn't drive her today. Ernest insisted she take a taxi, not the tram. There was growing animosity toward foreigners. And when she'd finished for the day, she must call him and he'd come by taxi himself to fetch her home.

Back in her laboratory, she read through Max's notes, her eyes traveling from the words to the rack of orderly slides, each of their frosted edges neatly labeled in his elegant script. She guided each one to the microscope, her own thoughts shuffling like a deck of cards. Time fell away. She didn't notice dusk fall. When at last she stood and stepped over to the windows, the moon was washing the gray streets a chalky blue. She squinted at her watch. Almost 8:00 p.m. She cursed herself under her breath. She should have called Ernest by now. He'd be worried.

She used the phone in Fräulein Zimmermann's office. Ernest made her promise to be waiting at the main entrance by 8:30 on the dot. She returned to the lab and shrouded the microscope. Before leaving the Dörr wing, she stopped again in the office to check her pigeonhole.

It was crammed with mail, half of it probably intended for other people's cubbies. Catalogues and renewal notices, symposia invitations, two issues of *Genetics*, a large manila envelope addressed to the taciturn Herr Wittigard, who cared only for barnacles, a letter with a US postmark addressed to Fassbinder that she refiled into his slot, wincing. Hopefully it wasn't the acceptance letter from the Rockefeller conference he'd been so desperately awaiting, casually misfiled by Zimmermann.

Ernest. She'd lingered longer than she intended. The clock read 8:28. She switched off the lights and flew from the office. Down the stairs, past the admissions desk, and out through the front doors. Sure enough, a taxi was idling at the curb, exhaust frosting the air. She yanked open the rear door.

"Lillian." He spoke before she could say anything. A look of fond exasperation. "Where is your winter coat?"

She glanced down in surprise. She was in her white lab coat, not her wool. Ernest's mustache squiggled. "Here, climb in to hold the taxi. I'll get it."

Lillian shook her head. "They won't let you into the Dörr wing at this hour."

She retraced her steps, remembering she'd left the rest of her mail in the office. Sure enough, the big untidy stack still sat on the corner of Fräulein Zimmermann's desk. Heaven knows where the secretary might have refiled it in the morning. Her winter coat and purse she'd left in the lab. She reached for the light switch on her way out the door, then paused.

She'd turned it off, she recalled, when she dashed from the room. She hadn't turned it on again when she returned, had she? She peered around the cabinets that served to cordon off Frau Münter's domain. But Münter's desk was empty.

In the laboratory, the electric lights were off, but the moon was higher now, bathing the room in silver. More than enough light to make her way to her bench. She set down the sheaf of mail to sort through tomorrow. But snatching up her coat, she brushed the stack from the bench. Folded brochures and envelopes scattered like autumn leaves.

She was on her knees behind her desk when the lights came suddenly ablaze. She heard doors open, voices of men. One, two. A third, a fourth: she didn't know these men. She stayed crouched low. Then a fifth voice, authoritative. Amsel. She could hear their footsteps approaching on the limestone tiles, dress shoes, but also the heavier clack of jackboots, surely. She stayed hidden. How to explain what she was doing here, huddled on the floor of the laboratory? On her own, in the dark.

The voices fell quiet, leaving only footfall. A military cadence. And then another sound she'd heard once before. The softer patter of paws, toenails skittering on tiles. Peering out from under her desk, she could see Amsel striding past in his signature wingtips, polished to the nines. She heard him swish back the heavy curtains with a flourish. Then she counted four more pairs of legs pass by and, being dragged at the rear, four large paws. With electric light now flooding the room, she realized with a pang that she recognized these paws: one black, one gray, one brown, one white. A drooping tail dotted with the same four colors.

Hodgepodge has gone away, too.

She almost jumped to her feet, but Amsel was speaking. Truly, medical English must derive half its terminology from German or vice versa.

dose
vomiting
convulsions
lung
edema

She could follow Amsel's speech, with only the occasional phrase eluding her. Then she recognized the ugly word Kit had taught her, and Lillian went cold: *tödlich*.

"It has taken [. . .], gentlemen, to get the dosage right," Amsel was saying. "We tested it on smaller specimens first. As we've [. . .], it's essential that the action be lethal, swift, and peaceful. No emesis, no blood, no [. . .]. With an earlier formulation, we saw seizures, some cerebral edema, which might be noted if the family petitioned [. . .] to recover the [. . .] at autopsy, which [. . .]." The men chuckled. "None of those [. . .] have been noted with our current compound." Amsel made a phlegmy sound. Imperious. "Private, please restrain the mutt."

There was a scuffle and a whimper. As before, she could hear heavy panting.

Lillian felt the acid in her empty stomach rising into her throat. She could picture Hodgepodge—when was that?—seated at Kit's feet in the snow, his tatty bulk leaning into her legs. Spargo used to do the same. She started trembling.

"We have a little agreement with the dogcatcher," Amsel was saying. "He rounds up all the strays. This is how we keep the mongrels and shit off the streets of Germania. Well, this and the camps." Now the men hooted with laughter.

Lillian remained hunched on the floor, shivering, the cold of the stone tiles leaching into her knees. Amsel, as far as she could tell, was explaining that the white pills were effective up to 30 pounds, pink up to 60, and pale green up to 175.

"They look just like little candies," one man said.

"Exactly," Amsel said. "But we've found that under the tongue is best. Faster. And they can't try to retch."

Lillian's heart was throbbing thunderously, as if threatening to batter through her chest. If only she'd agreed to have Ernest fetch her coat or come with her.

But the panting and whimpering had stopped.

"There you have it, gentlemen. At the end of the Lebensunwertes Leben, a passive finish and the diseased germ line is severed."

Lillian curled herself into the recess under her desk. Her stomach grumbled, and she drilled her fist into her gut to silence it. *Lebensunwertes Leben.* The men were asking more questions. Then they were moving toward the door. The shoes and boots clomped past, the light was extinguished. And the door thudded closed.

CH16: JANUARY 1939

Lillian didn't go to the laboratory on Saturday. She rang Max first thing but got no answer. Later, when his housekeeper picked up, Lillian left a message for him to call as soon as he felt better. Then she paced the living room rug, waiting. Ernest had to remind her, in a mild voice, only loud enough for her to hear: telephones were not for private discussions.

Ernest had her repeat her story. She'd started blurting it to him as soon as she'd climbed into the taxi. He'd hushed her with a nod at the driver, so she bit her lip and he squeezed her hand. Once they were shut away in their bedroom at home, she told him everything. The whinnying fear, the horse laughs from the men, the lethal pills like green candies.

The next morning, with Gertrude and the girls still busy getting dressed upstairs, he asked her: Was there anything else?

In the watery sunlight of day, it wasn't so much fear as outrage that suffused her. Rage that Amsel and his wretched experiments could cast a pall like this on Max's lab, a space she loved. A place for science in its purest form. With the sun slicing through the shutters, it was hard to understand why she'd been so petrified last night. Why she'd done and said nothing. She stopped her pacing and crossed her hands over her chest, thinking. There were the words Amsel said that she hadn't understood.

"*Leben* . . . ," she said hesitantly. "Maybe *Leben-Leben*?"

"Life-life?" Ernest frowned. "I don't think so. *Lebens-raum*? Living space? Herr Hitler bandies that word around constantly, but I can't imagine they're killing off stray dogs to make space for more Germans."

"Shhh, Ernest!" Lillian gasped, stricken. If Kit were to catch wind of what had happened to Hodgepodge, that Lillian had done nothing to stop it, she'd never hear the end of it. Lillian could hardly live with it herself.

Ernest kneaded both thumbs along the bridge of his nose. "I'll ask around at the embassy, check in with a few contacts. They may know more." He glanced at his watch. "My train is at eleven," he said. "If we don't hear from Max, I'll postpone."

The phone rang as they were at breakfast. Lillian, usually sluggish in the mornings, bounced up like a jack-in-the-box to answer it, surprising everyone. But it wasn't Max.

"Guten tag, Dr. Strauss," Lillian said, trying to keep the disappointment from her voice. Gertrude, she noticed, had sprung from the table almost as quickly as Lillian. She broke out in a grin as she hurried to the telephone, making no attempt to conceal her higgledy-piggledy teeth. She was back a minute later, her composure 75 percent restored.

"Will you be staying home today, Madame McKinley? Heinrik—Dr. Strauss—is asking me if I'll join him for lunch."

"Oh, great," Kit harrumphed, prompting a stern look from Ernest.

"It seems Gertrude's mother's courtship tips paid off," Ernest mused as Gertrude flounced back to the phone.

Kit rolled her eyes. "Gertrude is more fun when she's not stewing about Dr. Strauss," she glowered. "Or her teeth."

Lillian turned to Ernest. "You go catch your train—you said you could be back by tomorrow afternoon at the latest? Gertrude can keep her lunch date. I'll take the girls to the gardens. We'll stop by Max's place en route, let him know I need to speak to him."

"About what?" Kit wanted to know.

"Our laboratory work." Lillian tried to sound casual. Ernest looked hesitant.

"We'll be fine," she said firmly. "Go and come back as fast as you can."

CH17: JANUARY 1939

Max came to the door himself, his frowsy housekeeper hovering in the corridor.

Lillian could hear "Casta Diva" drifting plaintively from the phonograph. "I saw you through my window," he said, his voice hoarse. He was wearing purple velvet slippers and a plush housecoat the color of peacock feathers, his thick hair tufted at the back. His skin was greenish-gray, with an oily glaze. There was no chance of him joining them in the park.

"Get some rest," Lillian said, trying to keep her voice light. "Perhaps stop by the house when you're up to it. Something to discuss in private."

In the park, Kit and Helen struck a pact. They would play for precisely thirty minutes at the playground, Kit keeping track on her necklace watch. She showed the watch face to Helen, who gazed at it solemnly before Kit slid it carefully back under her coat. Only recently had Kit summoned the patience to teach Helen how to read the steady creep of minutes and hours.

"Then"—Kit's voice was infused with more cheer than the plan deserved—"we'll go to my racetrack and you'll time my laps, okay?"

Lillian scanned the sprinkling of parents and minders on the benches that circled the Spielplatz. No sign of Mathilde. The snow had mostly melted in the streets. But here in the park, shoveled back from the gravel paths, the crusted heaps shone like gemstones, bluish in the sun.

At precisely 11:32, Kit coaxed Helen away from the swings to the wall where she kept her carefully foraged marker stones, each the size of a plum. She spaced them out meticulously on the ledge.

"Remember, each time I knock down a stone, you call out my time."

Helen took the watch soberly, looping it over her own neck. Kit pointed her boot to draw a straight line in the gravel and toed up behind it. Her legs lunged, her palms flat, her elbows bent. Then she fixed her eyes on the fountain, some two hundred yards away.

"Ready?" Helen squeaked. "Set? Go!"

Lillian watched Kit streak off, make her tight loop of the fountain, then zip back toward them. She didn't look like a girl when she ran, nor an adult either—too small and waifish, and yet. Her arms swung and her stride had a power to it that was nothing like Helen's hobbling gait when she was hustling to get somewhere. In leap year time, the sisters were now nearly identical in age; it would be Helen's fifth birthday that spring. In their base impulses and urges, their shrill needs, they were very evenly matched. But Kit carried her twenty-something years on earth not only as knowledge, Lillian mused. They were also in her limbs and in her grace. *But how?* The question was always with her, an undertow beneath every other waking thought. *How?*

Kit swooped past, swiping a stone from the ledge before continuing out on her next lap, Helen shrieking the minutes and seconds in her wake. Kit's wool cap was gone, her hair undulating like a flame behind her. Lillian shivered. A chill was sliding its cold fingers under her coat. She felt her chest, still tight from her illness, rattle ominously. Kit knocked the last stone to the ground, then slowed to a halt. Her narrow ribs heaved. Her breath, white gusts, punched at the air. Lillian called, "Run off and find your hat, Kit. We'll cut through the Wilderwald on our way home."

It felt milder out of the breeze, as if the trees themselves had gathered together for warmth. She hunched along the shaded paths behind her girls, saw Kit slow her stride and extend her mittened hand to her sister, who gladly seized it in her own. She felt the cinch of it in her heart and heard Ernest's warm voice in her head. *We tend to just think of it as love.*

Already the shock of last night was receding. The whine, the huff. Underfoot, the dry leaves crackled and the frost crunched. But amid the muck and decay, the first snowdrops were pushing through. So, spring still planned on returning.

"Lillian."

She hardly recognized the voice. And when she spied Mathilde on the bench, she looked nothing like she had the last time they'd met—so hopeful, aglow. Today, despite the icy air, she wore no gloves and no hat. Her honey hair, always so carefully styled, hung limply over her shoulders.

"Mathilde?" Lillian's gaze flitted to the woods, hoping to see Frida skipping among them in her quiet way. Her own daughters were inspecting the hollow of an old oak tree.

Mathilde had spied them, too, her eyes flooding. Then she buried her head in her pale hands. "She's gone," Mathilde managed.

Lillian took the seat beside her, pulling her friend's icy hands in hers. "I know. Kit told me, you decided to send her to the clinic in Brandenburg."

The statement produced a sound from Mathilde, a choking cry. She was shaking now, wracked by sobs. Her mouth was moving but no sounds came. The chill that Lillian had managed to shake on their brisk walk to the forest overtook her again, and she felt the painful torque again in her chest. Her face must have asked the question she couldn't put in words.

Mathilde nodded and tears flooded down her swollen cheeks.

Lillian pulled her close, hoping to shield her friend from the horror on her own face. Mathilde sobbed against her, her whole body jerking as if whipped. Over her shoulder, Lillian could see Kit and Helen weaving between the tree trunks, oblivious. *Keep playing*, she willed them. *Leave us be.*

Mathilde pulled away and swiped at her eyes. Lillian fiddled with the clasp of her purse in search of a handkerchief, but Mathilde had her own bag open.

She pulled out an envelope and passed it mutely to Lillian. With a stab of guilt, Lillian remembered the last time Mathilde had showed her a letter. The sun dappling the same bench they sat on now, Mathilde's beaming smile. How she'd intended to tell her what Max had said in Paris, that this was a ruse. Propaganda and grandstanding.

The envelope had no return address, and the postmark was faint, the ink blotted. The letter inside, signed by three physicians, was even more creased and blotched.

Lillian struggled to comprehend the words on the page.

Sehr geehrter Herr und Frau Hesse,

. . . Tochter, Frida Louise Hesse . . . Kinderstiftung . . . institutionelle Pflege

. . . Brandenburg . . . Infektion . . .

She scanned the rest of the page. Why did these words look nothing like their sound? She recognized *daughter* and Frida's name, along with *institution, children* something, *Brandenburg, infection*. Lillian felt sick with frustration. The very idea of asking Mathilde to translate this letter for her. She glanced at her daughters, still playing in the forest. She couldn't possibly ask Kit to read this aloud.

Mathilde shut her eyes, but the tears leaked out all the same. "It says Frida died of a burst appendix." A wet sob caught in her throat. "That it happened right after she arrived, too suddenly to inform us. They have taken the liberty of cremating her body at their own expense and will be delivering the-the-the—" She broke off, her lip trembling. "They *cremated* her. Before we could even say goodbye."

Lillian glared at the ridiculous long words choked with consonants. The official seal at the top, the foreign names at the bottom. Dr. Karl Brandt, Dr. Herbert Linden, and Dr. Ernst-Robert Grawitz. She passed the paper back to Mathilde and gathered the woman in her arms, her mind racing.

The girls were inching closer. They had surely spotted the women embracing, had noticed Frau Hesse's tears. Adults crying. This was always a source of upset and intrigue. She smoothed her friend's lank hair back from her brow, tried to wipe the tears from her face. The gesture only served to amplify the flood. Mathilde's shoulders heaved. She was trying to speak again. There was as much anger as pain flashing in her red-rimmed eyes, a madness taking root.

"This country," Mathilde managed finally. "This wretched, wretched place. These people. They've lost their way. *We've* lost our way. And there is no one, no one who will listen." Her guttural voice was surging louder.

"There's nothing you could have done," Lillian managed. "It could have happened anywhere. Even here." She reached for her friend's cold hands. Mathilde snatched them away, brandishing the letter at Lillian, fury and grief indistinguishable. She shook her head at Lillian.

"You don't understand." It came out as a snarl. "Our Frida did not die, in Brandenburg, of appendicitis."

Lillian blinked, opening her mouth and closing it. Mathilde's lips were blue and her grip on the wrinkled letter was so tight the paper was crumpling in her fist.

"Our Frida. Our beautiful Frida—" Her voice was a howl. "Our Frida had her appendix out when she was four years old."

CH18: JANUARY 1939

They stopped again at Max's house on their way home. This time an older woman answered the door, an even fleshier, unsmiling, female version of Max. Lillian had only met Max's sister, Anna, once before, and she hadn't been particularly friendly. According to Max, she cared only for her grandchildren, her radio dramas, and her afternoon cakes at Berlin's busiest Konditorei. And greatly disapproved of Max.

"He's gone to the hospital," Anna said brusquely.

Lillian's jaw dropped, picturing the bedraggled peacock who'd answered the door earlier that day. "To the laboratory?"

Anna flinched as if pained. "To the *hospital*," Anna repeated. "Michael, my husband, took him. The housekeeper called to say that his fever was much worse and she herself does not drive."

At home, Gertrude had returned from lunch with a new twinkle in her eyes, all but waltzing through the rooms. Lillian, shaken to the bone by her encounter with Mathilde, said that she needed to take a tram to the hospital to see Max. Gertrude merely nodded, her closed-mouth smile almost pretty on her lips.

Lillian found Max's ward and hurried to his bedside. He looked to be fast asleep in a pair of turquoise silk pajamas. He opened one eye when Lillian plunked herself by his bed, then closed it again, looking satisfied.

"I knew it," he breathed, his voice weak but clear.

Lillian felt her heart stutter with relief. She must have groaned, because his eye fluttered open again.

"Oh, Lilly." He pushed himself up on his satiny elbows. "Honeybee, I'm perfectly fine. Here."

He pressed her hand to his forehead. And indeed, it seemed the right amount of warm and his skin had lost its pallor.

His housekeeper had panicked, he said. At first he was having none of it until it occurred to him that having Michael drive him to the hospital—the university hospital—would put him in the same building as his laboratory.

"And I knew you'd come," he said smugly. "And whatever's in that"—he nodded at the drip at the side of the bed—"they should serve that in bars. Besides, I could tell something quite extraordinary must have happened in the lab. Did I make some monumental error? If it wasn't for this"—he gestured at the IV threading into his arm—"I'd have already scarpered up there. The nurses have us on lockdown." Max fluttered his fingers at an elderly man sleeping slack-jawed on the adjacent bed. "That guy. He tried to make a break for a cigarette, and they practically brought him back in handcuffs."

Lillian permitted herself a smile. Max was trying his best to placate her. Her eyes roved around the room, taking in the muttered complaints of the other patients, the white uniforms gliding in and out as if on casters.

"I can't tell you here."

He blanched. "Is it Kit? Helen?"

"What? No." The question unsettled her. She thought of Frida, the way she used to stand with her gloved hand extended primly, waiting for Kit to dash over and snatch it. How they would vanish, arms linked, under the dome of trees. She felt her throat grow thick.

His face crinkled with concern. "Don't worry about it for now. We'll fix it together, won't we. Stop in to check on me tomorrow before you head to the lab. If I can beg or bribe my way out of here, I'll come."

CH19: JANUARY 1939

That night, the skies laughed at the trick they'd played on Berlin, on the silly snowdrops nosing out of the cold earth. The clouds opened their great louvers and buried the city in snow the likes of which hadn't been seen all winter. And when the snow stopped, the wind came out roaring at the top of its lungs, as if it, too, had been the butt of the joke.

Schools were closed. So, too, were all government offices, the radio announced. Gertrude translated the broadcast into English for Lillian, parceling out the sentences as if printing them from a press. Her English had really come along. Businesses would remain closed until the Windsturm abated, Gertrude intoned. Trolley buses were canceled. Trams would run on a limited schedule. Trains were stalled on their tracks.

Lillian listened with a sinking heart. East, Ernest had said when she'd asked him where his train was taking him yesterday, but how far? He said he'd be back later today, but the east of the country was even harder hit. What if the trains stopped running? How soon would he get home?

She spent the morning at the living room window, drumming the ledge with her fingers. Outside the trees bent and whipped in the gusts barreling down the road like something unleashed. Snow was heaped against every wall and post. A man across the street was trying in vain to clear the snow from his front walk. Every shovel of snow he shifted aside, the wind would unceremoniously replace.

By ten o'clock, clouds were still shunting across the horizon as if being kicked. But a plow had made it the length of Tiergartenstrasse and she saw a tram round the bend at the end of the block. More and more people were venturing out, bent nearly double as they pressed through the invisible force, losing hats, umbrellas, briefcases, walking canes. Kit and Helen at the window, still in their nightgowns, treated the spectacle outside as if it were a Christmas pantomime, endlessly comical.

She found Gertrude upstairs in the nursery, preparing lessons for both girls. "I'm going to take the tram to the hospital now, Gertrude. To see Max. You'll keep the girls inside until the wind drops, no matter how hard they plead to go out?" "Of course," she said in her clipped fashion. There was more she wanted to say, Lillian could see it. She waited. Gertrude's pale eyelashes lifted to meet Lillian's gaze, then fluttered primly.

"Dr. Strauss had said he hoped to see me again today, perhaps afternoon tea. But probably . . . in this weather . . ."

Lillian stood awkwardly in the doorway, watching the color mount in Gertrude's cheeks. Strauss was clearly very much back in the picture. "I'll be back by midafternoon," Lillian found herself saying. "Then you can take the rest of the afternoon off. And evening if you like. And Ernest may get back here before me."

CH20: JANUARY 1939

At the hospital, she headed directly to Max's room. His curtains were pulled partly shut, but through the gap, she could see his eyes were closed. She took the chair by his side, watching the way his low-pitched snores were stirring his tidy mustache. After a few minutes, she crept away.

In the laboratory, the big glass windows were shuddering in their frames. No one else had ventured in. Lillian stopped by to check her pigeonhole before remembering no mail would have been delivered on a Sunday.

Get to work, she told herself, tidying the mail she'd dropped that awful night. She passed her thumb over the rows of slides in their neat racks, feeling the comfort of their blunt edges. Something solid and knowable in the face of so much unease.

"I knew I'd find you here." Lillian jolted on her seat.

Max was wearing his velvet slippers. She could spy, beneath his unbuttoned winter coat, his vibrant robe and pajamas, hairy ankles protruding from the turquoise cuff. Max watched her take in his ensemble and put a hand on his jutting hip, shrugging his shoulder to his chin.

"You were supposed to fetch me," he said, pouting, but his plummy baritone was back. He swabbed at his red nose with a handkerchief. "What was it you needed to tell me?"

They retreated to his private office and shut the door. She told him what had happened in the lab, after hours, Friday night. The men, their awful jokes, the paws of different colors. Then she told him about Mathilde in the park, about Frida's death, and the letter. When she was finished, Max's face looked closer to the color it had been when she'd knocked at his door yesterday morning.

"Lebensunwertes Leben." He said it so gently and with such sorrow, she almost didn't recognize the words as the ones she'd heard Amsel spit out that night, producing guffaws from the other men after he'd forced one of his candies under Hodgepodge's tongue.

"*Lebensunwertes Leben* means 'lives not worth living.'"

"A dog's life?" Lillian pictured Kit, searching tree hollows for the mutt that she'd pleaded to take home as a pet. "Who is Amsel to decide whether a dog's life is worth living?"

Max's soft eyes pooled and the slim line of his mustache trembled. He shook his head. "Not the dog's life, Lillian. Or not *just* a dog's life. I mean the deaf child. I mean Frida."

CH21: JANUARY 1939

Lillian was the sentinel. They did a quick lap of Amsel's domain, which he kept as tidy and gleaming as his ridiculous hair, his expensive suits.

"Close the drapes," Max said, pulling a pair of rubber gloves over his neat hands. Lillian yanked at the heavy black curtains that cordoned off Amsel's space. Working quickly, Max made his way through Amsel's benches, pulling each of the drawers out in turn. Lillian stood in the gap between the drapes and the wall. She kept her eyes trained on the two sets of double doors, her heart battering her breast. She desperately needed one of her Alka-Seltzers.

"Lilly," he said a moment later. She glanced over. He'd opened a shallow cabinet above the desk. Inside were three rows of little glass jars filled with small, flat pills. One row of white, one of pink, one of green, lined up as if in a candy store. Scarcely out of the reach of a child. Her eyes fell on a thick rubber mat covering one of the benches. She remembered how the skittering of the dogs' claws had fallen silent. A fresh wave of revulsion washed over her.

No one interrupted them.

Max made to pull the gloves from his fingers, his face unreadable. Then he stopped, glancing to the windows. Outside the sun still shone and the yowl of the wind was weaker. The tree branches had ceased their maniacal dancing. If the storm was moving on, they might not have the Dörr Laboratory to themselves much longer.

"We should check Frau Münter's office," he said grimly, snapping his gloves back in place.

In the secretaries' foyer, Lillian again stood sentry, the door firmly closed. If she heard anything in the corridor outside, they could swiftly reposition themselves and yank the door open, claiming it had slammed shut by accident on this drafty day.

Amsel, clearly, was a much more powerful man than she'd realized. This was why Max's prestigious lab had been slowly annexed out from under him. It was a wonder she, let alone Max, were allowed any space at all. Unless, she realized, their work, the mundane drudgery of pure science and erudition, provided exactly the sort of cover that Amsel needed.

"All of Münter's drawers are locked," Max muttered, frustrated.

Lillian's eyes scanned the room. There was the long bank of filing cabinets, the wall of pigeonholes near the door, framed photographs of stern, white-bearded men in dated suits. Her gaze rose to the high windows that let in the secondhand light from the laboratory next door.

"Watch the door," she said.

She stepped to the far wall, reaching her hand up to the high sills, out of reach for most mortals. Little Fräulein Zimmermann, certainly, would have needed to stand on a chair. Not Münter. Sure enough, on the ledge high above Münter's desk, Lillian's questing fingers stopped on a cold brass key.

Max went quietly to work.

"It's as I suspected," Max murmured from behind Münter's partition. He leaned back to peer at Lillian. He'd shed his overcoat and was now an eye-watering blur of blue, violet, and gold. "There is correspondence here between a number of prominent Nazi doctors and scientists. Some of it relates to Amsel's infernal twin genetics research, but there are also files marked top secret, related to the Children's Charitable Foundation for Cure and Institutional Care." His kindly face darkened. "I hate to think what *charitable* work they're doing." He held up a sheet of paper, frowning, then looked up at her, puzzled. "The address on all of this is Tiergartenstrasse 4. I'm trying to picture it. That's just down the street from my home, and yours."

Lillian watched his eyes darting left to right as he scanned the page, confusion swiftly replaced by disgust. He stretched an arm to pass her the file. "It's revolting. A pseudomedical list of genetic conditions judged irredeemable human degenerate diseases." He flinched. "Deafness, I notice, is one of them."

This file, too, was stamped *STRENG VERTRAULICH.* Strictly confidential. Top secret. The page was titled with other words that Lillian recognized, words she'd so recently learned and wished she hadn't. *Lebensunwertes Leben.* Her eyes ticked over the long list of terms as if "protracted aging" might be among them. Instead she was seized, vividly, by the memory of Ernest with Kit on his shoulders at a country fair in the Ottawa valley, years ago. The whitewashed hut with the tall sign listing all the eugenic conditions young people would want to steer clear of in courtship. Here, however, was an even longer list.

- *schizophrenia*
- *spastic conditions*
- *Down syndrome*

- *imbecility*
- *blindness*
- *deafness*
- *microcephaly*
- *hydrocephaly*
- *physical malformations of the limbs, head, and spinal column*
- *alcoholism*
- *idiocy*
- *delinquency*
- *homosexuality*

She looked up. Had Max scanned to the end of this list? He was frowning as he read from another brown folder. "This is madness," he said, his voice cracking. The tic that clamped his eye shut when he was nervous or angry had gone haywire, contorting the right side of his face like a concertina. "Doctors and nurses and midwives have been mandated by law to report a child born with any proven or suspected condition listed in the official Lebensunwertes Leben statement." He gestured with his chin at the paper in her hands, then held up the thicker folder in his, opening it and fluttering the sheaf with his thumb. "And they've been doing it! Letters and telegrams from across the country, all sent to Tiergartenstrasse 4. These all look to be copies."

He broke off to wipe his nose on his sleeve, a most un-Max-like gesture. He wasn't well. She needed to get him back to his bed. She opened her mouth to say as much, but he was speaking again, his voice ragged. "Most of them are babies, Lillian. But some of these reports are on older children, even teenagers."

He met her eyes. "There is a letter here from a mother reporting her adult son."

He held up an open folder containing what looked to be a magazine advertisement. It showed a handsome doctor standing behind the wheelchair of a young girl, her face twisted, her legs wasted and askew. Max translated the caption aloud.

"Sixty thousand Reichmarks is what this person suffering from a hereditary defect costs the People's community during her lifetime. Fellow citizen, that is YOUR money too!"

He snorted and went back to his work.

CH22: JANUARY 1939

For what felt like an hour, Max eased Münter's drawers soundlessly open and closed, riffling quickly through files. Lillian, straining for sounds outside the door, found her anxious gaze drifting over the pigeonholes. Order calmed her and Fräulein Zimmermann's pigeonholes were a far cry from orderly. She started squaring the mail more neatly in the slots, starting at Z, closest to the door. Several other pieces of mail, she noticed, had been misfiled by Fräulein Zimmermann.

The office clock chimed twice, and they both jumped. It was already 2:00 p.m.

"Max, I told Gertrude I'd get back in time for her to go out this afternoon."

He didn't reply. His nose and cheeks and the rims of his tired eyes were now the same aubergine shade as his slippers. He'd sunken into Münter's chair and was paging through a file. He passed it to Lillian with a grim sigh. "I fear you'll recognize this."

They were letters, or mimeographed copies. Scanning the German, Lillian realized she couldn't read them, but she knew what they were. Not merely the crest at the top and the names at the bottom—Karl Brandt, Herbert Linden, and Ernst-Robert Grawitz—she recognized the words themselves, even if she couldn't decode them. Only the dates and the names of the children and parents were different.

Sehr geehrter Herr und Frau Schloss . . .

She looked at the next page, and the next. Dear Mr. and Mrs. Bach, Dear Mr. and Mrs. Traeger.

"They're all the same," Max said. "Every last one of them, although some say the child died of pneumonia instead of a burst appendix. There are thirty-two separate letters, Lillian. I counted. Thirty-two deaths. And not one of them is addressed to the Hesses."

She tried to process this, her mind whirring. Then a sound in the corridor made them freeze. Footsteps. Max slid the drawer closed and ducked over to Lillian, standing in front of his pigeon-hole. She put her hand on the door, preparing to fling it open. But the footfall receded.

Lillian let her breath out slowly. "I need to get back, Max. I said I'd be home, and you—"

He held up a hand to stop her. "There's one more thing. Five minutes." He was already shuffling around Münter's partition. She went back to her tidying but turned when she heard him setting something down on Zimmermann's desk behind her. A cardboard box.

Max lifted the lid, tilting it toward her so she could read the big black words stamped on top. She didn't need a translation: *Spezial Projekte.*

Max's entire face was flushed and his hair hung long. He was lifting manila folders from the box one by one, glancing inside. The messy stack on Fräulein Zimmermann's desk was deeply unsettling. Unless there was method to his madness, he'd never get everything back in the box the way he'd found it.

Max made a strangled sound, and she wheeled around. All color had drained from his face. The door forgotten, she hurried to his side. He pointed to the words on the folder he held.

Project Leader, she translated. But the name below made her heart skip a beat.

Dr. Heinrik Strauss.

She stared up at Max. Sweat was beading in oily spots on his brow. He seemed incapable of speech. He opened the folder. Three sheets, neatly typed. Her eyes were drawn to a photograph clipped to the inside of the file. It showed a woman standing by a bench, a child on either side of her. Gertrude, Helen, and Kit.

Lillian let out a sound that started low and rose like the grind of gears. Only the terror on Max's face made her stop. *McKinley kinder* read the words at the top of the papers.

"What does it say, Max?" She looked frantically through the typewritten sheets, but they told her nothing. She repeated herself, a bleat. "What does it say?"

He took the file from her and put a steadying arm on her shoulder, then spoke in an urgent whisper. "Where are they now, Lillian? Is Ernest home? Where are the girls now?"

Lillian had already snatched up the phone. She watched Max as she waited for her call to be put through to Tiergartenstrasse, her panic mounting. Max was piling the folders hurriedly back in the box. The file marked *McKinley Children* he kept, folding it in half and cramming it in the pocket of his coat.

She heard only a deep nothingness over the phone line as she waited. Lillian's fear mounted, silence bloating like a sponge. A thought struck. Cradling the receiver to her shoulder with her chin, she strained her arm toward the first of the pigeon-holes, furthest from the door: Amsel's. She withdrew a slim stack. Her ear straining for any hints that her call might yet get through, she flipped quickly through Amsel's mail, then froze at the sight of the last envelope.

The phone fell from the crook of her chin. Max seized the letter from her hand and noticed what she had at once. Addressed to Amsel, the letter bore a return address in the left-hand corner that featured the logo of the loathsome Kaiser Wilhelm Institute. And the name beneath it: Dr. Heinrik Strauss.

"I'll go with you." Max's voice came out reedy, soaring toward panic. "We'll drive straight to your house, and if they're not home, we'll try the park." His eyes flitted to the high, bright windows as his breath labored and he fumbled to fit the lid back on the box. "They've surely gone to the park."

Watching her friend, Lillian realized she needed to take control. This fast-sublimating terror wouldn't help her, not in its current form, with its amorphous edges. She needed to force a phase change, depose it into icy resolve. Ernest would want that.

"Put everything back the way it was and lock it," she said. She pointed to Münter's chair, then the high ledge. "Replace the key. I need to fetch my things from the lab. Wait here."

Max nodded. Lillian raced back to the laboratory next door. Still mercifully empty. She grabbed what she needed, her hands shaking.

Max was waiting in the corridor, swaying with anxiety, when she returned. He'd buttoned his coat over his sleepwear too quickly. The left side hung lower than the right. He looked on the verge of tears, wringing his hands. "I'm so sorry, Lillian, I've just remembered. Michael drove me here, to the hospital. I don't have my car."

CH23: JANUARY 1939

There were no taxicabs outside the hospital. Max was high-stepping through the snowdrifts in his open-backed slippers, railing at himself for being stranded, today of all days. At the liminal edges of her own steely focus, Lillian could see that he was attracting too much attention, flagging down private vehicles as if they could be convinced to drive them to Tiergartenstrasse. At one point he reached for her face, cupping her chin in his hands, his eyes wild. His hands were bare in the chill breeze, yet still hot on her cheeks. His fever was surely back.

"When you find the children," he said, "leave. Leave at once. I can arrange everything else, your work, your things. You must get Kit out of Germany. This country is no place for her, for either of them."

Lillian thought of the awful list of Lebensunwertes Leben conditions and reached up to cover his hands with hers, pulling them from her face and squeezing them tightly. "You know as well as I do, Max. This is no country for you either."

Just then, a moto-taxi pulled up in front of the emergency entrance, fishtailing as it skidded around the corner. Max looked at it doubtfully as a man extricated himself and started limping toward the hospital doors. But Lillian had already hailed the driver, whose bike jounced forward, the empty sidecar jolting over the crusted snow. Max stammered his objections, but Lillian was already folding her tall frame into the single seat and reaching into her purse. She found the card, soft around the edges, that she'd been carrying for months.

"Meet me at the house as soon as you can," she said. "Bring your car." She glanced one more time at the card before passing it to Max. She already knew the number by heart. "If I'm not there, call this number," she said slowly and carefully. "Give Ernest's name and the location. Tell them it's urgent."

As the D-Rad snorted and chugged across the city, she noticed the awnings and signage torn and tossed by the storm. Cars were crumpled into street poles or abandoned in snow-drifts, mounded like sandcastles sloped by an incoming tide. She watched a man pick his way around a downed telephone pole, its wires tangled like fishing line. But the day was warmer now. She could see the sheen where the sun had managed to melt the snow, which had refrozen. There were few cars and even fewer people. Visions of what might happen next ticked through Lillian's mind as if through the viewfinder of her microscope, each starting hazy, brought into sharp focus, then discarded for the next possibility.

At home, she rushed up the steps, calling out for the girls, for Ernest, for Gertrude. Silence. She stopped to listen, her wet boots puddling the carpet. The only sound was the bass-drum boom of her heart.

But Gertrude, bless her, had left one of her neat notes on the table in the foyer. Her tidy handwriting explained that she had canceled her plans to go to tea, that she had listened to the radio forecast and made the decision to take the girls to the park. Lillian felt relief wash through her. But at the bottom of the notecard: an arrow. Lillian flipped the paper to read the other side.

If you are home before 3pm, perhaps you could meet us at the park and take the girls? Dr. Strauss is meeting us there and I could then join him for tea after all.

Lillian snatched up the telephone and was met with silence. This was why her call had not gone through: the lines here, too, were down. Lillian's glacial resolve returned even as her heart redoubled its pounding. She fumbled for a pen, dashed off her own note, then raced back onto the frosty street.

In the Tiergarten, trees were toppled. Branches littered the snowy paths. Clouds had scuttled back over the sun and the light was falling. Lillian hurried north, toward the Spielplatz, passing a trio of teenagers roughhousing, scooping up snowballs. But no one else.

The swirling wind was picking up again, emitting a low moan, chasing its own tail. The playground was barren. A large oak had come crashing down. Its long, black limbs tangled up in the swing set looked like an animal in a snare.

Lillian wheeled west, toward the meadows. Kit's Wilderwald. Here the close-set trees had ceded little to the funneling wind, but, for once, Lillian could see no dog walkers, no idling couples, no children playing in the meadow. No sign of her own girls, or Gertrude.

No sign of Strauss.

The panic she'd managed to suppress in the office came nipping back at her resolute calm. Was it possible that Strauss had already whisked her children away for his Special Project, whatever that was? Maybe this was her punishment for being so focused on her research—the desperate drive to understand every genetic thread woven into the human fabric that might explain a daughter like Kit—instead of being the kind of mother whose every waking moment was spent with her children. Mothering. She pushed the thoughts away. There were a million different ways to be in the world, and as many ways to love. And yet. She found herself sending up the kind of prayer she usually reserved for moments of enlightenment, those bridges of scientific insight that let her leap from the unknown to the possible. *Hurry, Ernest*, she thought, breathing deeply. In fact, she had no clue what resources Ernest had at his disposal. She'd never asked what would happen if she placed a call to that number she'd memorized. But what match would she be for Strauss, on her own, if it came to it? She needed Ernest's steely sureness, but also his boxer's fists. She didn't even know if the trains were running.

Hurry, Ernest.

Lillian took the shortcut through the forest, along the narrow, meandering trails that Kit claimed had been forged by fairies. They had been protected by the woven tree canopy above, and the snow here was neither deep nor icy. Lillian was practically running, her heart hammering, perspiration tacking her clothes to her skin, her breath inadequate for her heaving lungs.

She saw them before they saw her. All four of them. They were seated on one of the benches encircling the fountain. Kit looked cross, and Helen cold. Strauss was angling over the children, like a lid about to snap closed. Gertrude's expression, she could see, was strange even for Gertrude. Her eyes were wide and the hand in her lap fidgeted nervously with the buttons of her coat. Gertrude, Lillian realized, was terrified. If Lillian marched over and demanded her children, what would he do? The park seemed empty of everyone but this foursome on the bench. She started to shiver, the chill like a spider creeping through her veins to her very core.

Strauss was speaking and taking something from the pocket of his coat. Lillian couldn't hear his words or see what he held. She felt frozen in place, her thudding pulse so loud in her own ears it would surely betray her approach. Fear clenched a cold hand around her heart, as if to muffle it.

Strauss's ghostly face was the color of the snow itself, frost-white, but his pale lips were bent into a smile. She ducked deeper under the branches to get closer, creeping as silently as she could to travel the half circle in shadow until she was right behind their bench.

"Please, have one," Strauss was saying. The sound she heard was a metallic rattle she'd heard once before. Swastika candies in a tin.

"They're cinnamon," he said, prying open the lid. "Nice and spicy. They'll warm you up."

"I'd like to go home now." Kit spoke in a small voice, and Lillian felt her heart seizing. *Stop*, she wanted to cry out. But numbness, like plaster, was creeping up her arm as if to stay her hand, and through her jaw, as if to seal her lips.

Strauss's voice was saccharine, but firm.

"We are going soon, I promise, but you have not answered my question. Tell me, who is the special one? Is it you, Helen, or is it Katharina?"

Just as before in the lab, Lillian's fear suddenly evaporated, replaced with stony resolve. She stepped out from the trees just as Helen jumped down from the bench.

"I am!" Helen sang, sounding defiant. "*I* am the special one!"

The stabbing pain in Lillian's chest was back. Not cold, she realized with a dawning horror. Not fear. Not love. Certainly not anxiety or heartburn, or anything else that pompous doctor in

Paris had proposed. Nothing that Alka-Seltzer could touch. *Ernest!* She sank to her knees, clutching her breast, movement that Gertrude must have caught out of the corner of her eye. The governess turned her head a fraction, meeting Lillian's gaze and reading the warning that Lillian was trying so desperately to telegraph, even as the pain, now radiating into her chin, her face, became unbearable. Gertrude's head moved slowly, like an automaton, back to the scene unfolding before the bench.

Kit was getting to her feet, her small voice now sounding a thousand years old and an ocean away. Not scared, but resigned.

"No, she's not," Kit said firmly. "*I'm* the special one."

Helen stamped her feet, her voice rising. "No, *I'M* the special one."

Through the shroud of pain now setting over her, Lillian knew exactly what was coming: Helen's temper coming to a boil. She saw Strauss cast an irritable look at Gertrude, who sat frozen, ignoring Lillian, maintaining her petrified grimace. Lillian tried to stand but the pain in her chest was now a vice winching steadily tighter. Kit was glaring at her sister as if willing her to calm down, to be smart, to help them find their way out of this predicament, to muster the courage to grab her hand and dash away. But Helen couldn't or wouldn't cooperate. She had seen an opening and meant to take it. First she snatched at the little metal tin and helped herself to one of Strauss's sweets. Gertrude made a mewing sound, but Helen popped the candy into her mouth and bellowed at Strauss for the third time. "I AM THE SPECIAL ONE."

Whatever she'd ingested kicked in almost instantly. Helen's shout was still echoing in the treetops as her eyelids started drooping. A moment later, she was crumpling toward Strauss, who gathered her into his arms and held her with a brusqueness that hit Lillian like a whip. But she wasn't dead, surely. Strauss wasn't out here in the cold to poison her daughters.

"Nooooo." The word leaked out of Lillian unbidden as she tried to stagger to her feet. Strauss's head flicked toward her and he stood up.

"My goodness," he said calmly, but she could see he was rattled. "Frau McKinley. What an unexpected . . ."

"Kit, *RUN*."

Was it Lillian who said it? Or Gertrude? Lillian didn't know.

Strauss spun, Helen in his arms, but Kit was already sprinting away. He turned to Gertrude, her face a twisted knot of horror, guilt, and paralysis.

"Go and get her," he barked. "Now. My car is at the north gate."

Lillian managed to pull herself upright using the back of the stone bench. Her left arm was lifeless, as if anesthetized, the pain in her chest such a fine, pure sensation she felt almost warmed by it, as if by fire.

"You're not well, Frau McKinley." Strauss's wan lips formed a thin line. Helen was curled in his arms, her head on his shoulder. It was impossible to tell if she was breathing or not. Lillian scrabbled again at the cold stone bench, trying to keep herself upright. Ernest, she knew, would be too late.

"Oh dear," Strauss said, watching her futile efforts. "Better to have stayed home, Frau McKinley."

He turned and started striding to the north exit, Helen slumped in his wiry embrace.

Gertrude, too, was hustling in the same direction, Lillian realized. But Kit, by God, instead of heading into the safety of the trees, was pelting exactly the same line being taken by Strauss and Gertrude. Habit, Lillian realized, with a dawning despair. Kit was running her racecourse, her beautiful legs following the straightaway they knew and loved, toward her regular finish line. A moment later, she disappeared in the dusky gloom.

But Strauss, despite the weight of Helen in his arms, was also fast. Lillian started after him, every agonized step making her clutch at her chest. She saw Gertrude peel away toward the stand of lindens, Strauss barking a command. Lillian had to stop and put her hands on her knees, panting, watching the hazy scene play out from a distance, her own role in the drama now decisively off stage. This final act, it seemed, was merely Strauss with Helen in his arms, hurrying away, black against the white snow.

Then, out of nowhere, Strauss cried out, stumbled, and fell to the ground, where he lay motionless. It was enough to give Lillian the strength to lurch forward. As she did, she saw Kit creeping out from behind the low wall, clasping something in each hand. Strauss was facedown in the snow, Helen pinned underneath him.

Before Lillian could get to them, Kit was already easing her sister out from beneath the man, who looked to be out cold. Only when Lillian managed to drag herself alongside them did she see the blood blooming where Strauss had fallen. Beside his head, a black rock the size of a child's fist, gleamed like an eye in the snow.

Gertrude caught up with them, panting, her breath too ragged to speak. Lillian made a split-second decision: Gertrude loved the girls, she did. She wouldn't want them to come to harm.

"Home," Lillian pointed. "Run. Get Max. Tell him to bring the car to the gate. Not the north gate, the one at the Spielplatz.

Check. He may already be there." Gertrude looked rigid with terror, but nodded her head, then darted away.

Kit was struggling to pull Helen to standing. With a warm flood of relief, Lillian saw that her younger daughter was groggily moving her feet, her head lolling. Drugged, clearly. But alive. "Try to get her to the Spielplatz, Kit. I'm coming, I promise. But don't wait. If you see Uncle Max, get in the car and go."

Kit's face in that moment was not the face of a child, but infinitely wiser. With a blink, the faintest twitch of her head, she half pushed, half towed her sister away.

Strauss groaned but didn't move.

Lillian was on her knees again, blinking against the waves of pain in her breast that threatened to pull her under. She summoned concentration, her oldest friend. She was too weak to lift her head. Her hand scrabbled through her handbag, seeking by touch. Strauss made another sound and shuddered. He was coming to.

Lillian's hand closed around the glass jar in her purse. It took every ounce of strength to pry off the lid, to coax her numb fingers inside. She squinted toward the Spielplatz.

Did she grimace? Probably. Certainly she had to keep the bile from rising as nausea crashed over her like ocean breakers. It was the pain, partly, which was everywhere now. It had washed from her chest, through her limbs, to the tips of her toes. But more sickening still was the heat of Strauss's sticky mouth, his taut lips when she forced her fingers past them. When she used the last of her strength to poke the little green pill under his warm, wet tongue.

PART III

Helen

BRIEF OVERLAP, 1940–44

Helen remembered little about that day in the park in Berlin and how it ended, and no one ever talked about it. She had only a dim memory of a German doctor, pale as winter straw, who'd tried to kidnap them by drugging them with candies. This was all Mum would say, clamming up every time Kit started badgering her about whether the man might come looking for them after the war. As the years went by, all Helen could remember of Gertrude, for that matter, were alphabet blocks, German lessons, and a mouth overstuffed with teeth. As for the cities of Berlin and Paris, the two were blurred: chalky gravel paths that powdered her black shoes white, a swing set squeaking in the wind, ponies and miniature sailboats, forest paths flitting with fairies, and Kit's hand, always, reaching to take her own.

Of the mail boat fleeing France, crammed with legation staff and their families, Helen recalled cold and damp, constant seasickness, and so many salmon-paste sandwiches on stale bread that she and Kit would never again be able to stand the smell of fish. Of the Blitz, Helen remembered Dad's strong hand holding hers, keeping her upright as she stumbled over the rubble and the still-smoldering homes, their chimneys standing like vertebrae and their floors like fractured ribs, all the organs and flesh excised. How she was half an inch taller than Kit.

After they quit London for the relative safety of the Welsh countryside, Helen would recall, fondly, the pillowy hills dotted with sheep, thickly forested dells, and a month in autumn when both she and Kit had the same front tooth missing, although Helen's new adult tooth had come in much faster.

Maybe it was this brief overlap in their physical ages, the ever-present war, or the freedom of the countryside, but Helen remembered this as a golden time when she and Kit were at their closest. During the green, sun-dappled days of that first summer in Chirk, Kit taught Helen about the world as she knew it. How tadpoles became frogs, where babies came from, and how robins fed their young. And Helen (finally!) had the physical capacity to keep up. Not with Kit at top speed, of course. Helen knew no one who could run as fast as Kit, not even the boys at the village school. But for a day of exploring, Helen had the stamina and strength to climb the same trees, ford the same rushing brooks, and Kit was delighted to have her sister along. At night, with Dad away, it was Kit in charge of Helen's bedtime story: fantastic tales unspooled not from a book but from her own imagination. If Helen woke from a bad dream, it was Kit's bed she climbed into, Kit shuffling over and lifting the quilt so that Helen could curl into her warmth.

Memories of Mum were more shadowy. She'd taken years to regain her physical strength after her heart attack in the Tiergarten, and her sad moods seemed to last longer and plumb deeper—weighed down by worries over the war and whatever hush-hush role Dad was playing in it. But in Cambridge, where they moved in 1942 so Mum could work in the Cavendish Laboratory, their mother became their mother again, as if sharpened on a whetstone. Of Cambridge, Helen remembered fire buckets and sandbags lining the stairways, mullioned windows taped in place behind the blackout curtains, and the freshmen air raid wardens who practiced racing a pump and hose on hand-drawn carts. Kit enrolled at a public school, where she thrived, and Helen started as a bottom junior at the primary school just steps from their home. Once a week, Helen attended a special art seminar taught by a retired don, alongside a handful of other children deemed to show particular promise.

Hazy as they were, those in-between years would always stand out for Helen as the one time that Kit had been looking out for her, not the other way around: helping her tie her laces and stirring the lion's share of the cream into Helen's oats. As if Kit had willingly taken up the role of mother that Mum had temporarily stepped out of.

A year went by, then another. Kit still tried to convince Helen to go rambling in the woods, fly their kites in the meadow, or time her sprint along the banks of the Cam, but by then, Helen had made new friends her own age. That brief phase of scaling the same fences and wearing each other's shoes without noticing the difference—that was over without Helen even noticing when or how it ended.

TWO SISTERS, 1944–45

For Helen's tenth birthday, one of the first fine days of spring, they picnicked on the banks of the Cam. Other students and families were strolling along the towpath, watching the teams sculling in their pointy boats or lolling on bright blankets that patchworked the sloping lawns. While Mum set out their lunch, Helen was content to lie on her stomach with her pencils and sketchbook, doing her best to ignore Kit's pleading efforts to help her hunt for ladybugs, toads, crickets. Helen was still eating her sandwich when Kit fished her necklace watch out from under her blouse and handed it to their father. Dad made a big show of reluctance, but stood, dusted the crumbs from his hands, and agreed to a maximum of five laps. At Dad's count, Kit blazed off, nimbly dodging other walkers, who paused to watch the blur of limbs disappearing along the leafy lane that led to the bridge, then reappearing on the other side of the river before pelting back on the opposite bank.

Helen took up her pencil again and considered her father, standing barefoot in the clover, wriggling his toes. His curly hair looked almost white against the blue sky, although his thick mustache still glinted with copper. His face was deeply lined and his eyes looked puffy and tired.

"Is that not Ernest McKinley?"

Helen squinted in the direction of the voice, an aristocratic British accent, only warmer and lilting. A brown-skinned man, taller than her father and thin as a stick, was lifting his hat, a wide, white smile breaking across his broad face. His black hair was oiled severely to one side, the wind lifting it like a trapdoor, so that he hurriedly replaced his hat. In his dark green suit with matching bow tie and straw bowler with a yellow brim, he reminded Helen of a sunflower.

"Dr. Ayaan Gupta! I can't believe my eyes. What a terrific surprise! What on earth are you still doing in this part of the world? You told me you were returning to India, and I haven't heard a peep since. Indeed, I wrote you at your Delhi address to warn you we might be paying a visit."

The Indian man was pumping Dad's arm up and down as if drawing water from a well, the two of them grinning like long-lost brothers.

"I might ask the same of you, McKinley," the man scolded in his musical voice. "Surely you'd be better off back in Canada than enduring the rations and curfews here in England."

"You're one to talk of rations, Gupta. A puff of wind would bowl you over."

Just then Kit came whistling by, only managing to slow herself down to a trot after she'd traveled twenty yards past them. She tramped back, gulping at the air, her hands on her narrow hips and her elbows jutting. The reedy man had wobbled backward, but Helen could see his smile had widened further, his eyes bulging at Kit.

"My goodness, McKinley. This is your youngest, is it? Grown so tall! Helen if I'm not mistaken? Why she's the spitting image of Kit, isn't she? The same fiery hair, and the same speed, by the looks of things. Another tiny typhoon!" He pulled himself up stiffly and extended his hand to Kit. "You won't remember me, Helen. You were still in a bonnet and nappies when I met you on the SS *Montcalm*, and pretty green about the gills as I recall. That must be, what, seven years?" He turned to Dad. "No, eight years ago now, my goodness."

Helen stiffened and shot a worried look at Mum, who'd sat up on the blanket, lifting a hand to shield her eyes from the sun. But Kit, whose face had flicked alight like an electric bulb, seemed not to hear him.

"Dr. Gupta!" The man gladly accepted her embrace, but Helen caught the look of confusion and wonder rippling over his face. Then Kit pulled back, still beaming, and wheeled on Dad, snatching the necklace watch from his hands.

"I still have the watch," she said. "It's broken down twice and both times I managed to fix it myself. Papa even bought me my own staking set."

On the blanket beside her, Helen could sense that her mother had gone still, and Dad's face had frozen into a bland smile, one Helen had seen a dozen times. Helen felt the old tension poking at the pit of her stomach, as if she'd eaten something spoiled. Under his careful composure, Dad must have made a decision, because he beckoned to Mum, who stood.

"Gupta, you remember my wife, Lillian."

But the man didn't look up. He was still staring down at Kit, whose expression was still ablaze with goofy delight. He took the necklace watch from her hands and turned it over, his thumb stroking the etched face. Then his puzzled gaze snapped back to Kit, darting over her flushed and freckled cheeks, her bright eyes and wild curls. Unlike Dad, or Mum, for that matter, Dr. Gupta was no good at hiding the current of his thoughts beneath the surface of his skin. Then he glanced at Helen, sitting cross-legged now, the pages of her sketchbook fluttering in the breeze.

Kit tugged at his tweed sleeve, her eyes twinkling, then reached up as if she was about to lay a hand on the stranger's smooth, round cheek.

"My heavens," she said theatrically. "I've been searching all over for this!"

They all watched Kit as she raised herself on her tiptoes, stretching her arm toward Dr. Gupta's ear, while a slow realization spread across his features. Then she twitched her hand away and opened her palm, tilting it so a beam of sunshine seemed to seek it out, just like the searchlights that combed the night skies looking for bombers. The silver rupee coin that never left her pockets blinked brightly in the flat of her hand.

Dr. Gupta's face seemed to settle like a lake after a storm. "You haven't lost your touch, Kit McKinley." He said it proudly. "And fleet-footed as ever, by the looks of things."

He greeted Lillian, snatching his hat from his head a second time, then Helen. "And *you*, of course, are little Helen. Not so little now." His eyes did a quick shift between Helen and Kit, noting the difference—Helen, at last measure, was nearly half a foot taller than her sister.

"It's Helen's birthday," Kit chirped, pouncing on Helen from behind and wrapping her arms around her sister. "Look at her drawing of Papa, Dr. Gupta. Isn't she amazing?" Helen wriggled to dislodge her sticky sister, trying and failing to hide how pleased she was when Dr. Gupta stooped to take a look.

"Dr. Gupta should come for Helen's birthday supper, shouldn't he, Mummy?"

Kit started in on a fast-paced explanation of how they'd managed to source and barter for the ingredients for Helen's cake, no mean task with rations so strict, before Dad managed to interrupt, reminding her she still had three more laps and the clock was ticking.

"Will you stay?" she asked, suddenly anxious.

"Absolutely." He smiled and held up the watch. "I'll time you myself."

Kit charged off again at full tilt. The adults stood watching her, then Dr. Gupta spoke in a low voice, Ernest cocking his good ear to hear the words.

"I'm remembering now, Ernest. She told me back when we parted ways on the ship that she was a leap year baby, which I know to be rare, but I wasn't sure then if she was quite as rare as I suspected. She seemed so very wise, and so accomplished, for five. Because as I told you, I too know someone born on February twenty-ninth, but in India, long, long before Kit. It was this man, Tarun, and his rare condition that first inspired me to go into medicine, then to travel halfway round the world, seeking answers." Dr. Gupta grimaced, making a sweeping gesture that seemed to embrace the meadow, the river, and the picnicking couples. "Only to find that even the most advanced minds in medicine being churned out of this sodden, miserable country have never broached this particular transfiguration in the species. And if I'm not mistaken, Kit is every bit as special as this man, just as rare."

Mum had startled at the word *transfiguration*, but Dad wasn't fixing his glassy smile in place. He trusted this man, Helen could see that. She felt the churning in her stomach settle.

"Where is he now," Dad prompted, quietly, "this man, Tarun? Is he still alive?"

Now Dr. Gupta laughed. An exasperated laugh. "Oh, he's very much alive," he said. "Fit as a fiddle and pestering me relentlessly to come home to India." He looked up at Mum and Dad, his eyes crinkling in the corners. "This man is my father."

That night, over Woolton pie, as well as spinach and peas from the garden, followed by boiled raisin cake, the adults discussed Dr. Gupta's time at Oxford and the happy coincidence that had brought him to Cambridge that day. The McKinleys described their years in France and Berlin but said nothing Helen hadn't heard before. Still, she and Kit pushed their food quietly around their plates, hardly daring to chew lest they miss some interesting tidbit of information.

But later, much later, after the girls had been put to bed upstairs and Helen had drifted off to sleep, she was woken by the creak of a floorboard: Kit padding to the top of the stairs. Helen slipped from her bed and settled soundlessly on the top step beside her.

None of this grown-up conversation seemed particularly worthy of eavesdropping. Dr. Gupta was returning to Delhi next month to be married, he said, and planned to open his own practice. Dad, in turn, talked about Mackenzie King, the Canadian prime minister, who wanted Dad to be posted to India to pave the way for a high commissioner exchange. This was the first Helen had heard about India. But then, Mum was saying she was "close to something" with her work and couldn't leave. Cambridge was the place where she could truly make a contribution. Helen cupped her hand over her mouth, bending to whisper a question into Kit's ear, but Kit bugged her eyes at Helen, jabbing a finger to her lips to shush her.

Dr. Gupta was saying her name. "Helen is . . . ?"

Both her parents spoke at once. "Ten," Dad said. But under her father's firm voice, Helen caught her mother's answer: "Normal."

The word gave Helen her tummy ache feeling all over again, and she felt Kit go very still beside her. Dad said, "Helen does well in school, has friends, and you saw—she's got an artistic bent. She's very happy here."

"But Kit," Mum chimed in quietly. "She's done two years now at an excellent school and is more than able to keep up intellectually, but physically, she's falling behind. We considered a boarding school in Durham, but India seems a better option . . ." Mum's voice trailed to silence.

"Our time in Germany convinced us to be very . . . careful," Dad murmured. "At least until she looks a lot older than she does now."

Dr. Gupta made a sympathetic sound. "It's not merely a question of looking older, if you don't mind me saying. My father, Tarun, would be the first to tell you, knowledge and maturity are decisively different things. In his case, he spent many decades learning an extraordinary number of skills and trades and dialects, but he said he didn't feel grown until he was well into his sixties. He didn't marry my mother until he was seventy-two."

Helen heard Mum gasp. Helen, herself, felt a tick of irritation: now she wouldn't get to be the one to tell Kit about Dr. Gupta's father. She tucked herself close, trying to read her sister's expression in the light leaking up the stairs.

"So late in life," Dad said, his voice neutral.

Dr. Gupta tutted. "Quite the contrary. To hear my father describe it, this was the age at which he finally felt settled as a man, both physically and psychologically." He cleared his throat, adopting a more doctorly intonation. "Childhood and then puberty, if you can imagine, were both extraordinarily pro-tracted phases during which he acquired an enormous amount of knowledge and experience, but with the temperament of an adolescent. Only as he approached his seventies, around the time of his sixteenth or seventeenth leap year birthday, did his bodily changes stabilize, and along with them, the tempestu-ousness that had been a driving force for decades. He met my mother, they fell in love, and married."

He paused, as if to let the words sink in. When he spoke again, his English rose and fell so softly that Helen and Kit strained forward to hear. "My father had to keep a low profile for many years. Every culture in the world seeks to celebrate or denigrate exceptions to the norm. They are miracles or abom-inations, depending on the time and place. My grandparents, long dead now, tried for a time to be open about Tarun's con-dition, hoping he could be understood and accepted."

Silence. Someone set a teacup in a saucer. Helen was trying to picture the map on the wall at her school. India, she suspected, was a long way by ship, farther than France, for sure. She groped over Kit's flannel-clad knees, taking her sister's hand. Then Dr. Gupta spoke more cheerfully. "Of course, you would stand out in India, all of you, and as you say, there are turbulent times ahead for my country. But India has more tolerance for noncon-formity and for the full spectrum of humanity than England." A note of sadness now tinged his words. "There are many, many more shapes and colors and ways of being in the world than this godforsaken country has ever been willing to accept. Certainly my father, since coming of age, has managed to hide in plain sight in India for more than a century. I think you might find that India, given its sheer size and populace, is not a bad place to disappear for a while."

It happened far, far sooner than Helen expected. Within the year, she and Mum accompanied Dad and Kit to the airstrip to see them off, because they would be flying to India (in an airplane!), not traveling by ship. When the time came, Helen and Kit had clung to each other, sobbing, so swept up in their own grief that Helen almost didn't notice her mother and father. The way they, too, held each other so tightly there was no air, no gap, between any part of their two bodies. As if they were one solid thing that couldn't be cleaved. Until they were.

APART AND TOGETHER, 1947–50

Twice they'd made plans to visit Dad and Kit in Delhi, but sectarian riots caused them to cancel. As the time went by, Helen was ashamed to admit, you could start to forget that you'd ever had a sister like Kit, if only because your life could fall into its actual rhythm, easy and simple. *Normal*. The constant worry that someone might sometime pay undue attention to Kit, might ask about a sister or a daughter who never seemed to age: that anxiety lifted. For the first time ever, Helen had friends who came to her birthday and could stop by unexpectedly with their mothers on a Saturday afternoon without setting the household aflutter. Mum had her plants and fruit flies, Helen had her friends, her art classes, and a boy named Philip who asked her out for tea and a walk, all very proper, once she turned fifteen.

In his letters home, Dad told them about Ayaan Gupta's wedding and how they'd met his strange father, Tarun, who had the same leap year birthday as Kit, and later about Ayaan's son, Hari. *He takes after his father more than his grandfather*, Dad wrote. *In every way a normal baby boy, growing every day.*

Kit's letters blathered on about Hari too, focused more on his twinkling eyes and long, lush lashes, but also about snake charmers and sweet, spicy tea, always signing off by saying, *I love and miss you very much.*

Every Sunday Mum insisted that Helen sit with her at the dining room table to write to Dad and Kit. Mum wrote about her work in the Cavendish Laboratory—with Professor Crick and his sidekick, Watson, whom Mum referred to as the Cricket—long, incomprehensible descriptions (*deoxyribonucleic acid, self-replicating molecules, hereditary and somatic mutations*) that Helen skimmed over.

Presumably Mum wrote other letters to Dad too. Personal ones, expressing the sorts of private things that Helen imagined a husband and wife might write to each other, plus their quiet worries about her sister. Sometimes Helen wondered how Mum felt about being apart from Dad and Kit for so long, but it was impossible to tell how Mum felt about anything. Every now and then, Helen saw sadness, mixed with worry or confusion, fluttering in Mum's eyes—a lost look, brimming with uncertainty that seemed to have nothing to do with her work in the laboratory, or her family.

Helen chewed on her pencil or doodled in the margins of her mother's letter. *I've enclosed a sketch of the grape hyacinth in the front yard,* she wrote. *I caught a cold last month but it didn't spread to my chest. I love and miss you very much, Helen McKinley.*

Of course she missed them, she really did. But it would be okay, too, if her life continued exactly like this, with just her and Mum, her friends and Philip, one month melting into the next until she finished school and was off to university herself, to study art, or maybe nursing, which was more practical. She hadn't made up her mind. Three years stretched to four, then five, and she could hardly remember what it felt like to have all of them under one roof.

Which is why the letter from Dad in the spring of 1950, with the news that they were moving as a family to New York, was such a blow. All of her plans, Philip, her friends: all of that ruined. Not to mention Mum's own work, her helix thingy with the chains.

"Don't you even *care*?" Helen wailed. "You're always saying that Crick and the Cricket take credit for everything. And you still want to leave?"

Her mother, as usual, was unreadable. "Mathematically, we've verified it. It's the structure we can't agree on," she murmured. "I'm preparing all of my notes so they can understand my ideas and integrate my analyses. I'm confident they'll keep in touch."

As far as Helen could tell, apart from an even thicker layer of freckles, Kit looked and acted just as she had before she left for India, constantly pestering Helen to look, to watch, to come, to try, to do, even though she could see that Helen had outgrown all the games they used to play. Kit's eyes had grown wide, then soft, when she'd first glimpsed Helen at the port in Southampton, her gaze scanning her sister from head to toe and lingering on all the places where Helen was curvy instead of straight.

"You're all grown," Kit mumbled, her words hitching as she clamped her wiry arms around Helen, her chin sharp and her chest as flat and ribbed as ever. Helen had forgotten the feel of her sister's frame, but it was instantly familiar again: spiny and rigid and warm, like wrought iron in the sun. An unexpected emotion came loose inside her. Relief and something heavier.

During the Atlantic crossing, Kit had a million questions about Helen's life, her classes, her friends, Philip. (How had she even found out about Philip?) But she could barely hold still long enough to listen to Helen's answers. Or maybe something about the answers themselves set her off, like she wanted to listen, but then couldn't stand doing it. She was always dashing off, hooting in delight, saying she'd spied something in the gray and shifting sea. A whale, she insisted, poking Helen to get her attention. A dolphin, a mermaid, a school of flying fish. Another boat emerging ghostly on the hazy horizon was a pirate ship weighed down with plunder.

In the postcards Helen wrote to Philip and her friends back in Cambridge, she complained of nausea, of boredom, and of her tiresome little sister, because that's exactly what Kit still was. Kit's chronological age, her secret age, was thirty-five, but her leap year age, as Dad called it, was just eight and a half. Her new passport put her at ten years old. After a day or so of listening to all of Kit's nattering, Helen returned to her magazine, twitching the pages back and forth and trying her best to ignore her.

Her parents, on the other hand, Helen eyed with curiosity and grudging admiration. Kit, she noticed, was watching them too. They seemed to melt back together like pats of margarine in the sun, still itchy for each other's touch. And Dad didn't seem to notice the subtle ways in which Mum had changed, how she sometimes said one word when she meant another. How had they managed so many years of separation and stayed like this? Helen wondered. Not merely in love but straining closer. She saw it in the way they eyed one another when they thought they weren't being observed. The way her mother made excuses to "have a little rest" in their berth in the middle of the day while Helen stayed with Kit on the upper decks. How Dad would tuck a lock of Mum's thick hair behind her ear, then bring his mouth close, brushing his lips beneath her jawline. Philip had never once kissed Helen on the mouth, not even when she told him she was leaving.

BLAME GAME, 1950–51

If maturity was something ripening in Kit, straining under the skin and stretching her bones, you'd never know it. She was like orange soda shaken in a bottle, sweet and fizzing, occasionally volatile. She was always trying to rope Helen into games involving constant movement and a high chance of injury: a game of "don't touch the ground in the living room," meaningless sprints from one city crosswalk to the next, endless rounds of hopscotch on the cracked pavement behind their midtown apartment. Most of the time it was irritating, but every now and then the funny things Kit said or did tugged at Helen like an old song caught in snatches, drawing her back to an earlier, sillier version of herself, in Chirk, maybe, or Berlin. Which is how she ended up being the one teetering on the arm of the chesterfield, cackling like a chimpanzee, when Dad arrived home unexpectedly one day, gliding silently into the room, eyebrows raised, as Kit slithered, giggling, from her perch on the back of his armchair.

But if Kit's physical impulses were those of a kid, her curiosity about all things grown-up wasn't constrained. Puberty generally, but Helen specifically. Her armpit hair. Her monthly. Her bra size. Helen hadn't even told her parents yet about Dicky, but Kit had found out by tailing Helen all the way to Woolworth's Five and Dime on Fifth Avenue when Helen had told Mum she was meeting Amelia for a milkshake, even though Kit wasn't supposed to leave their neighborhood on her own.

Dicky, bold and shiny in the American way, was the total opposite of stuffy Philip back in Cambridge. A year ahead of Helen at school, Dicky played baseball, drove his father's convertible, and would be going out west, to Stanford, that fall. He'd given her his pin after their third date and made her pulse race when he stroked the baby hairs beneath her ponytail.

"Have you *kissed* him?" Kit whispered. "Do you open your mouth?" She'd crept into Helen's room after bedtime, inching her head onto Helen's pillow, the same way Helen used to do with Kit. Helen could feel her minty breath on her ear. A moment later, Kit's clammy feet had wormed their way into the crook of Helen's knees. Dicky's good-night kiss, the heat and push of it, the softness of his fingers on the curve of her hip—she'd wanted to hold on to these after switching off her lamp, but they vanished now as if wiped away by a wet cloth. She twisted away from Kit, but not before catching her wrinkling her nose, the tip of her tongue peeking through her lips in distaste.

On an icy morning in January, they boarded the subway at Lexington and 53rd, bound for the Columbia campus. Kit had her new Kodak Brownie 127 slung over her winter coat. There was no chance she still believed in Father Christmas (or Santa Claus as she'd started to call him), but she'd asked Santa for a camera and gotten it. It was the sleekest, most compact camera any of them had ever seen, with a black molded Bakelite body, rounded corners, and smooth, bulging sides that gave it the look of a large obsidian egg. Kit handled it like china, cupping it carefully in both hands when she held the viewfinder to her eye. In the subway, she refused to sit, keeping her skinny legs planted wide. Each jolt of the carriage swung her wildly from side to side so that she had to clutch the camera to her stomach with one hand while snatching for the pole with the other, grinning like a lunatic. Helen did her best to appear as if she wasn't related to her, sitting beside her mother with her ankles neatly crossed.

I do miss my rambles in the English countryside, Helen sometimes told her new friends. But she didn't really. She'd fallen in love with the clank and screech of this city, its hope and grime, the laughable mix of oversize buildings, cars, and people, all begging to be captured with a pencil. Everything and everyone managed to look simultaneously proud and disheveled. Even their art deco apartment building, complete with a doorman named Alvin, listed like a tipsy socialite. Window ledges drooped and the front door hung askew on its hinges so that its swing had scuffed an arc in the floor tiles. Helen tried to keep her bedroom neat as a pin, but to her frustration, the closet gaped open like the knees of the boys you shouldn't sit beside on the bus.

Though she worked to look blasé and poised, Helen was excited about their visit to the Columbia campus. Not only was it her first time touring the university, but Dad had said that afterward, since she would be seventeen that spring, she could take the subway on her own—something Kit would never be allowed to do—so she could meet friends at the New Amsterdam in midtown. Friends meant Trudy and Amelia (the ones she'd mentioned to her parents) but also Dicky.

A short, round ball of a man in a cherry-red coat was seated on the bench off Amsterdam Avenue, tapping a walking stick on the ground.

"Uncle Max!" Kit cried, and the man sprang up, a shock of silver curls bouncing behind his ears as Kit leapt into his arms. Maximilian Dörr, her mother's old colleague from Berlin, had made it out of Germany before the war, taking up a post at Baylor, but then transferring that semester to Columbia. When her mother reached him, her chin wobbling with emotion, Max shifted Kit to one arm and bundled Mum to his breast. After some protracted greetings, he set Kit back on her feet and turned his beaming smile on Helen.

"Look at you! Such a young lady now, Helen." He rubbed his hands together. "Shall we begin the tour?"

Kit raced ahead, wheeling back like a magpie to make Max pose for a photograph in front of a wall of mossy and crumbling brick. Helen walked with Dad while Max ambled arm in arm with Mum, the two of them alternating between laughter and earnest talk. At one point, Max stopped abruptly, halted by something Mum must have said, because he turned to her and his eyes combed her face, which wore that lost, blinking, but rebellious look that Helen had come to know.

Kit was drifting closer, Helen noticed. Snooping on other people's conversations, as usual. Max said something else, Mum replied in a low voice, and then they walked a few steps more before Max stopped again. This time every bit of jolliness had been scrubbed from his features. "But you should see a doctor, surely," he murmured.

Mum shook her head. "I'm taking all of the pills I can handle. You know me, Max. I've researched this. No one has proven a causal link between cardiovascular and cerebrovascular disease, but it would make sense, wouldn't it? Some degenerative or sclerotic process, possibly genetic. Some days I'm completely fine, and other days there are, well . . ." Mum spiraled her free hand in the air, frustrated.

"Gaps," Max offered.

Mum's face softened and she nodded. "Gaps."

Max raked a hand through his silver mane and shook his head, as if deciding something. "Well. Even with 'gaps,' your mind is keener than those of all of my colleagues and grad students put together. I insist you join the lab, informally if you prefer." He smiled up at her face, which was bent low toward him. "If you'd told me ten years ago that we'd have the chance to work together again, Lilly. That the war would end and we'd be able to continue . . . ."

Something in her face made him change the subject. "Do you ever hear from Gertrude?" he asked.

Mum nodded. "She lives in Ireland now, working as something called a dental hygienist, if you can believe it."

"Speaking of dentists . . ." Max peeled off a glove and pulled a pack of Lifesavers from his pocket. Kit was back at his side in an instant, but Helen shook her head.

"Very wise," he said. "Never take a candy from a stranger."

Mum stiffened and Kit shot a fast look at Helen. Max noticed and lifted his hands in apology. "I'm sorry, I'm not making light of it! Don't you mind me, Helen. I would have taken Strauss's candy myself." He patted his ample stomach. "I have a terrible soft spot for sweets."

He was talking about the day in the Tiergarten with the German who'd tried to kidnap them. Dr. Strauss. Helen's own memory of the man was so fuzzy it was almost translucent, a ghost. She'd taken a candy from Dr. Strauss? Mum never, *ever*, talked about what happened that day, but Max clearly hadn't been forewarned. He was smiling down at Kit, oblivious to the expression creeping over Mum's face, an anxious confusion. "I'm surprised you haven't been signed to the major leagues with that pitching arm of yours, little rabbit. And Lillian was the real hero. Even in the midst of a heart attack, managing to find the strength to get you both to safety."

Now Kit was shaking her head. "No, Gertrude went back in the park to get Mummy," Kit said carefully. "You made us stay with you, in the car."

Finally Max seemed to notice the current of tension running between Mum and Dad, the look of warning Mum was trying to transmit, and made a show of swiveling his head to get his bearings. "Ah-ha!" he said. "We're here."

Helen looked up at a four-story building fronted with red brick and a white limestone portico with four Corinthian columns.

"This is Barnard?" Helen said. "The women's college?" Max beamed and nodded.

Kit was sizing up the building with a dawning comprehension.

"I get to go *here*?" Kit said, excitedly. "College? Finally!" She gave a little hop and a whoop that was partly buried in Max's stomach after she threw her arms around him. "Did you arrange it, Uncle Max? For me?"

Helen watched Max's face flash from surprise to remorse as he crouched low with improbable nimbleness. "Oh, Katharina. I—"

Dad put his hands on Kit's shoulders. "No, Kit." He smiled at Helen. "We're here to show Barnard to Helen."

"Here?" Kit's words came out as a squawk. "*You?*" She shifted her wounded gaze from Dad to Mum before landing on Helen.

"You knew." Her eyelids drooped at Helen, her nostrils puffed. "You *knew*. You told me we were coming here to see Max when really the whole point of coming was *you*."

Kit wrenched herself out from under Dad's hands to face him, flinging an arm at Helen. "My grades are a million times better than hers! This is preposterous." The big word coming out in her childish chirp made Helen want to laugh. She didn't dare.

Dad still had both hands extended, palms down, as if trying to stop a Roman candle. "Someday soon, Kit, very soon, I promise. If not here, then at another college of your choosing. But you can't just yet, you know you can't. You're too—"

Kit had flushed a deep and mottled red. Her plaid hat was nowhere in sight, leaving her French braid to fight a losing battle with her curls and the wind. The Brownie camera around her thin neck looked huge and her woolen mittens dangled on strings from the cuffs of her coat. She bored a look of deep betrayal at Helen again, then shifted her accusing look back to Mum and Dad, launching into a steely synopsis of her accumulated skills and knowledge to date, the exams she'd run rings around if she was just given a chance, and the injustice of her predicament, her voice growing shrill.

Helen suppressed a growl. Kit was right, it wasn't fair. To Helen! This visit to campus *was* supposed to be for Helen, and hell's bells, what was so wrong with that? Kit always, always had to make everything about her. It wasn't Helen's fault, not remotely, that Kit was the way she was—that Helen's world was opening up while Kit's stayed closed. Nothing, no part of her life, ever seemed to truly be Helen's alone.

Only later, after they'd said goodbye to Max, and Kit, still sulking, had trailed behind them all the way back to the subway and Helen got to stay on the train until Times Square while Kit had to transfer with Mum and Dad at Columbus Circle; only after she'd met up with her friends at the theater and Dicky had escorted her home like a perfect gentleman and she'd brushed her teeth and shut her bedroom door so that Kit wouldn't try to crawl in beside her; only after she'd switched off her lights and pulled her quilt over her head, alone in her own private air, her own smell, only then would she have her thoughts to herself. Dicky. The darkened theater. The oddly thick feeling of his muscular tongue against her teeth, the way his fingers had fumbled to undo the top two buttons of her blouse, and the pressure of his mouth on her neck. This, she thought. This. *This* was something Kit didn't have. And couldn't take from Helen.

WANTING, 1951

A storm swept in while Helen and her friends were half-way through their burgers, one of New York's bombastic summer squalls: lightning and thunder, raindrops the size of quarters smashing into the hot pavement as if fired from a weapon, the smell of asphalt and garbage tinged with electricity. It was supposed to be dinner, then roller-skating in the park, or that's what she'd told her parents, who'd met Dicky by then and seemed relieved he was going to university on the opposite coast while Helen finished high school. Stuart had smuggled a flask of rye into the diner, splashing it discreetly into their Pepsi-Colas, so that by the time their bills came, Helen felt like she was balancing on the blade of a knife—invincibility on the one side, despair on the other. This would be the last double date she and Dicky would have with Amelia and Stuart. Dicky was leaving the next day for California, and Stuart to a college upstate.

The storm kiboshed their plans for the roller rink. But after they'd said goodbye to Stuart and Amelia, Helen could still feel the whisky, buoying her. Mum and Dad were meeting Max for dinner downtown and had insisted Kit go with them, since Helen would be out with her friends.

"Come to my place," Helen said to Dicky outside the diner, holding his eye. "My folks are out with my kid sister."

They dashed from awning to doorway through the rain, huddled close, Dicky pulling on her hand to tug her across the puddled streets. Under the wide canopy at Angelo's Launderette, they paused, panting, in the hot summer air. Rainwater was running down Dicky's face, a blond curl plastered to his forehead, his long eyelashes clumped and his shiny lips parted. Already he looked Californian. His eyes, marveling, drifted down from her face to her chest. She couldn't keep it from heaving up and down. The wet bodice of her dress, she knew, was clinging all wrong, or all right.

"I think it's easing up," she said, and he kissed her full on the lips.

Inside, the apartment felt both charged and hushed. The only sound was the ceiling fan paddling at the air, the stir of it lifting goose bumps on her wet skin. All the lights were off, but she called, "Hello, hello," just to be safe. No one answered.

"I need to get changed," she murmured, and led him to her room.

The sky through the wide window above her bed, slivered by the nearby buildings, was lavender and mauve, bruised by the storm. How strange and wonderful and terrifying to want something so badly without fully knowing what it was. She unbuttoned her damp dress slowly, her clumsy fingers pulsing hot and cold, then let it slip from her shoulders. Dicky sank onto the corner of her bed to watch, his mouth a sideways curlicue. And then time became pleated—moments, or minutes, or the better part of an hour passed, but all she heard was the faraway honk and swish of cars in the wet streets below.

She heard her own heartbeat banging at her like something trapped, and she heard the low purr that rumbled out of Dicky when he stood up from the bed and reached for the top button of his trousers.

Then, another sound. She angled her head, straining to listen. Nothing.

She allowed herself a quick look at his busy hands, the thrilling bulge in his jeans. She swallowed. She did want this, didn't she? To give him this. This beautiful boy, who'd be away from her tomorrow and perhaps forever, but was here now, thinking only of her.

She reached for the top button of his shirt, but he put a hand over hers and tried to pull it lower.

"Wait," she said, and tugged her hand out of his grasp. She had the sudden urge to cover herself, to fold her arm over her damp brassiere, her fraidy-cat skin. She swallowed, and her throat felt dry.

"You are so beautiful," Dicky mumbled, mashing his lips with hers. Stronger than before, his tongue bucking at her teeth. She didn't like it. *Wait*, she wanted to say again, but her mouth was under siege. He had her again by the wrist, more firmly now, twisting her hand back toward his open fly.

Then she heard it again, a grating sound, mechanical and muffled. Dicky's eyes were still closed when she jerked herself from his grip, striding to the closet and snatching at the folding door.

Kit had seen her coming, had ducked to a crouch and squirmed to one side as the closet door louvered open, managing to wriggle around her sister and across the room. As a bellow left Helen's lips, Kit had already yanked open the bedroom door. She was halfway down the hall before Dicky's eyes, open now and blinking in the bright wash of late-day sun, could make sense of this awful twist in the plot. Dicky saw only Helen, fumbling for her robe, but not the Brownie camera Kit had cradled to her stomach as she dashed from the room.

"She's a nut, a . . . a psycho, that's what she is!"

Dad, still in his dinner jacket, loosened his necktie and rocked thoughtfully on his heels, but said nothing. Mum turned her lapis bangle on her wrist as if she hoped to unscrew her hand from its socket, but she, too, stayed silent. Kit was slumped in a chair, glaring at the film that Helen had wrenched from the back of the Brownie, now lying in a tangled, amber coil on the kitchen table. Exposed to the light. Ruined.

"She was sneaking around after Dicky and me, Mum. Taking *photos*."

Helen did not say that Kit had been doing this from the dark vantage point of her bedroom closet, or what specifically she'd been trying to take photos of. "She spoiled our night— my last night to say goodbye."

Kit's rebuttal came out as a bleat. "Two pictures, maybe three. But she wrecked the whole film!"

Dicky was long gone by the time her parents got home. Kit had stayed holed up in the bathroom with her camera until Helen, in a stroke of inspiration, returned to the locked door with Kit's precious necklace watch and threatened to smash it with a mallet. What Helen should have done, when Kit unlocked the door looking suitably terrified, was destroy the stupid camera.

Mum looked exhausted, massaging her eyelids with her fingers. More and more these days, when Mum was tired, she tended to lose her way. "I don't quite understand," she murmured, her weary gaze bobbing from Kit to Helen and back to Kit. "Where? You were under strict instructions to not to leave the house, Kit. If you want more independence, you need to prove to us that we can trust you."

"But I didn't—"

Kit broke off. Helen glared at her. If Kit told Mum and Dad about Dicky, that she'd brought Dicky home, that she'd undressed in front of him, Helen would murder her sister on the Formica countertop.

Dad took his pipe out of his pocket and cleared his throat. Helen twitched. Chances were, he had probably pieced together more of the scene than Kit and Helen were prepared to admit to. To her relief, he directed his question at Kit.

"What were the photos for, Kit? Why didn't you simply tell Helen you wanted a picture of her and Dicky?"

Helen felt a hot wave of mortification swamp her, imagining what Kit's photos might have looked like.

Kit mumbled something unintelligible.

"I beg your pardon?" This from Mum.

Now it was Kit's face blushing scarlet. "I just wanted to *know*. Helen never wants to tell me what it's like." She slithered a sheepish look to one side. "Kissing and that stuff. Boys." Her voice was less than a whisper. "Love."

Dad abruptly stopped his rocking, and his pipe, unlit, bobbled in his clamped teeth like a springboard. He looked as if he'd rather be smuggling Cold War secrets than standing in his own kitchen. Helen had snagged on the word *love*, the surge of mucky churned-up feelings it gave her in that moment: fury, tenderness, resentment, joy, relief, longing, and even, she realized, fear. But Mum was watching her daughters as if they were pinned to one of her microscope slides, all her gauzy uncertainty gone.

"Girls, I think it's time we had a talk."

What transpired was awkward and bizarre, meandering first toward the regular business of the birds and the bees that Helen had already suffered through at school, which was a far drier, more alarming version of what she'd already learned from her girlfriends. But then her mother transitioned seamlessly into a lecture even more technical and humiliating. Helen had trouble following. Mum was talking about maternal transmission, heredity, dominant and recessive traits. The jumping gene theory she'd pursued with Max in Berlin, that no one else had fully accepted or corroborated. Thus the need to be cautious and judicious in the choice of a mate, life plans, timing of pregnancy. Not once did Mum flub her words or lose her train of thought. To her, clearly, this was a discussion about biology and chemistry, the capriciousness of genes—an experiment to be meticulously planned or left undone. Dad wore his bland, unreadable face, which had served him through two world wars. Kit was nodding, sitting up higher in her chair. As if all of this was informative if not quite what she'd been hoping for.

Helen's mouth fell open. This was not, after all, a sermon on virtue and chastity, the likes of which Amelia had got from her parents when they'd found out about her parking with Stuart at a make-out point overlooking the Hudson.

"But you've always said that Kit was a freak," Helen blurted. The word was the one she'd managed not to use earlier, but it spilled out now unchecked.

The look from Kit was like a lash from a whip. A sting followed by an undulating current of hurt and treachery. "No, sorry, I mean, not Kit, but how she *is*. Rare. A freak *accident*. You've always said you thought it was totally random. That the shock of Tom dying . . ."

Mum had been about to say something, her mouth was open, her hands already tracing her argument in the air, but Helen's words stopped her short. On Kit's face, too, the name of the father she'd never met transformed her injured disbelief into shocked sorrow. Mum blinked. Closed her mouth. Opened it again. Her eyes, suddenly, were swiveling and unsure, batting a helpless look at Dad.

He stepped forward and rescued her hands, still frozen in midair, mid-thought. "It's been a long night," he said quietly. "Everyone's tired. I think it's time we all head to bed."

GOING GOOEY, 1956

Helen made plenty of friends at nursing college, although she learned the hard way not to bring them home.

"Dad, do you know about magic fingers?" Kit asked once, at dinner, after Helen's classmate, Jeannie, had left. "Are they like sleight of hand, or more for music, like a pianist?"

"Either, I suppose," Dad said mildly.

Kit gnawed thoughtfully on a hangnail. "So then is Ken Pritchard a magician?" Helen colored at the name.

"I don't believe I know a Ken Pritchard," Dad replied, sounding mystified.

"Oh, I was asking Helen. He's in medicine at Columbia, but Jeannie used to date him and says he's a man of many talents," Kit said cheerfully. "Which I infer includes magic. Because now he's dating their other friend, Barbara, and Jeannie said that Ken Pritchard had magical fingers and that if Barbara let him go all the way, she wouldn't regret it." Kit's eyes, fixed on Helen, widened theatrically. "All the way, as in, saw her in half?"

Kit, on the other hand, had just the one friend, Deborah Katzen (not counting her pen pal, Hari Gupta, who was eight years old now and probably only wrote to Kit because his father made him).

Petite and doll-like, Deborah looked like a miniature version of her fashionable, fast-talking mother, Madge. But for all her grace and manners, her heart-shaped face and her small pink mouth that formed a polite O when other people were talking, Deborah was a devil. Set loose in Central Park, Kit and Deborah were Vikings hunting for polar bears, spooks who'd passed through the Iron Curtain to spy on the Reds, or Freya Stark (Kit's current obsession) charting the riches of ancient Ionia. Two years ago, when Kit had fallen out of an oak tree in the Ramble, breaking her arm for the umpteenth time, Dad offered to pay Helen to shadow Kit and her friend to make sure they stayed out of trouble. Never again, Helen had announced after flouncing home her first day on the job, having been battered by acorns. Deborah, it turned out, knew how to make a slingshot with hair elastics.

Today, Kit had convinced Dad to buy her a roll of color film and borrow a tripod so she could take a family photo on the bridge at the park. First, they were meeting up with the Katzens to see Deborah's new baby brother.

"Why is Kit so excited about the Katzen baby?" Helen grumbled to her mother as they hastened after Kit and Dad. They caught up with them at 59th, where Kit—the detestable Kodak Brownie yoked around her neck—was smiling from ear to ear and stroking the flank of a horse tethered to a gaudy carriage. The plaza reeked of horse piss and manure and over-cooked hot dogs. Helen tried not to breathe through her nose.

Madge Katzen sashayed into view along Fifth Avenue, pushing an oversize buggy and looking more like Brigitte Bardot than a thirty-five-year-old mother of two, her lipstick matched to a cherry-red dress with an off-the-shoulder neck-line. Deborah, who'd taught Kit the trick of loosening the top of the saltshaker and once left a puddle of apple juice on Helen's chair so that it left a yellow stain on her skirt, looked sweet as a summer rose, her dress the same shade as her mother's. She waved at them serenely with a cupping rotation of her palm as if she were Cinder-bloody-ella, and Kit dashed over.

Helen watched as Kit started to bend over the carriage and then froze as if she'd been zapped by one of the stun guns in her comic books.

"He's perfect," her voice catching as she finally let out a breath.

Helen peered into the pram. The baby had kicked off his crocheted blanket and was winking at the sunshine sifting through the canopy of leaves. He looked in every way like a regular baby, hairless and doughy. But Kit's eyes were nearly bursting from her head. "Look at his little hands!" she cooed. "Those teeny tiny nails."

"His name is Hezekiah. Hezekiah William Katzen," Madge was saying. "Hezekiah, of course, after my husband, and also my grandfather on my mother's side, believe it or not, who's long gone, of course, but we'll probably call this little tyke Billy, or maybe Bill, although I don't so much like Bill." Madge spoke in her fast New York accent, each word jamming up against the next.

"Baby Billy." Kit sighed, her eyes wide and soft. She tilted her head to one side to align her face with his. "Can I take his photo?" she asked, already gnawing on her lip and craning the camera this way and that.

She, Helen, had never given too much thought to babies, other than the need to never find herself in a position that might lead to having one by accident. This had so regularly been drilled into her by her mother that Helen, having not yet met any boy she'd consider settling down with, had never—not since the debacle with Dicky—considered letting anyone below the belt. As she watched Kit nod eagerly in response to a question from Madge, then Madge bend over the pram and lift up sturdy little Billy, who offered a wet chortle and jerked his chubby legs while he was being handed to Kit, Helen wondered if Kit, too, had absorbed Mum's lectures on Mendelian inheritance and judicious mating and was equally confused as to whether genes or random chance explained her strange makeup. Kit thrust her camera at Dad, then held out her arms as if King Arthur himself was about to entrust her with Excalibur. Was that what this was? Kit going gooey over Deborah's baby brother quite possibly stemmed from the worry she might never have a baby of her own.

Dad clamped his pipe between his teeth and held up the camera. "Smile, Kitty-Kat. I'll get a picture of you and Billy."

Afterward, when Deborah had pried Kit away from her brother to go buy ice creams (Helen, feeling very adult and ladylike, had demurred), Mum and Madge started to stroll into the park. Helen fell back with her dad. It was noisy along the path and on the grassy knolls. Children were shrieking, balls slapped at the pavement, dogs yapped. A busker under an archway was hacking at a fiddle.

Madge paused on the rise above the pond. She must have asked a question because Mum had gone very still and was staring at Madge, flustered, a look they had come to know too well. *Oh no*, Helen thought. Mum's gaps were happening more and more. She'd stopped working in Max's lab at Columbia, but he still came by every Sunday with blackout cake from Ebinger's, and they'd sit together at the dining room table, poring over the latest issue of *Nature* or *Genetics* and arguing about frameshift mutations and messenger RNA. Then, out of the blue, she'd ask a question about her old corncob experiments, or whether the trams were running, and once—Helen saw Kit go very still at the words—asking Max what had happened to Hodgepodge, the stray mutt they'd befriended in the Tiergarten.

Madge's red smile was stretched clownish across her face, and her perfect eyebrows had pleated closer on her brow, like inchworms on a leaf. Helen and Dad caught up in a few fast strides.

"Oh, Lillian, you're such a hoot. I mean, Kit's clever, but not *that* clever! And she's what now, twelve? She would have been born right at the end of the war."

Mum was blinking rapidly, on the edge of panic, her blue eyes like a cork in the sea. Madge turned her tinkling laugh on Dad. "I was asking Lillian where Kit learned her French, because she sounds almost fluent. Lillian just said that Kit picked it up in Montreal and Paris. But you were stationed in England, weren't you? Then India after the war?"

The questions seemed innocent enough. But Kit and Deborah had been friends for three years now. In that time, Deborah had shed her baby fat and sprouted from half a head shorter than Kit to two inches taller. The latest iteration of Kit's birth certificate gave her age as twelve years old, but unlike Deborah, she didn't look to be teetering on the brink of adolescence.

Dad would do what he always did: deflect with some half-truths—some fine tutors in Kit's childhood, the family sometimes speaking French at home. But Madge, with her Upper East Side radar, had noted Lillian's rising distress and tactfully dropped her line of inquiry, calling out instead to Kit and Deborah, their ice creams dripping down their chins.

Mum was jittery, unaware of what it was she'd said to Madge that was so funny or so wrong, caught somewhere in the rushing tide between the story they were supposed to tell and the story that really was. Kit, who missed nothing, raised an anxious eyebrow at Helen, who only said, "I have to get back to study. Are we taking this photo or what?"

Kit arranged them on the Gapstow Bridge, bossing Helen to the right and nudging Dad to the left, a backdrop of blossoms and skyscrapers jostling each other aside. In the resulting photo—Kit would keep it for the rest of her life—Helen looked like she was sucking in her stomach, Kit looked proud, her skinny chest puffed up and dotted with melted ice cream, and Dad was pulling his wife and daughters as close as he possibly could. Not visible in the photograph were the slim strands of DNA damaged by a lifetime of pipe smoke, instructing a small patch of cells in Dad's right superior pulmonary lobe to divide, divide, and divide again. Helen had learned all about these in third-year nursing. In two years, he'd be diagnosed with lung cancer; within six, he'd be gone. Mum would live two more decades, but the best parts of her would go with Dad, the rest to be nibbled away by her own terrible disease—her mind, her unproven hypotheses, and her vast intelligence disappearing crumb by crumb. But for now, Mum tucked as close as she could to Dad and looked to be smiling with her mouth, but her eyes were fixed just behind the camera or farther still, as if seeing something she was expecting, and was deeply sorry for, coming around the bend.

MISTAKES, 1962

Helen sat mutely beside Aunt Natalie and Mum on a vinyl chair in a peach-pink corridor that smelled like soup and industrial soap, faded watercolors lining the walls. To Helen, the pastel blobs in their plastic frames looked like the puddles of barf she used to have to avoid on Frat Row between Broadway and Amsterdam on Sunday mornings. Chamber music was oozing out of unseen speakers, scarcely loud enough for Helen to recognize the melancholy rendition of Mozart's "Rondo alla Turca," one of Kit's old favorites, now dragging its miserable way through the airwaves at half the intended tempo. Kit used to bang this particular sonata out at top volume, grinning while Dad waltzed Mum from room to room, laughing, her head thrown back so that her hair tumbled loose from its knot. Helen shot a look at her sister. Kit had not said a word to Helen since her outburst the day before. And Helen hadn't had a chance to say she was sorry. Aunt Natalie, in the drabbest outfit Helen had ever seen her wear, was uncharacteristically still, her eyes switching, worried, from one face to another. Mum, by contrast, looked as if all this excruciating sitting and waiting was causing her physical pain.

Yesterday Helen had made Kit come with her to the A&P to help with the groceries and Kit had shoplifted a packet of Juicy Fruit. Helen had only been taking a minute for herself, just thirty seconds, lingering over the welcome cool of the meat fridge.

"Is your daughter planning to pay for that gum?"

The cashier's words made her spin around in time to spy the wad of glistening beige between Kit's incisors—Kit's mouth, too, fell slack with surprise. *Daughter?* Helen was only twenty-eight!

Once they were out on the street, she'd planned to ask Kit, calmly, if she intended to reimburse Helen for the gum. Before she could say anything, Kit exploded.

"You're so self-absorbed. You always have been! You could have made Papa quit smoking. You could have made him see a doctor sooner."

What? Helen was incredulous. *She'd* been the one who looked after Mum the whole time Kit had been running wild on the streets of Delhi, and now it was Helen who was working around the clock to help care for their parents, not to mention Kit, who was nowhere near mature enough to be able to look after herself. She couldn't even help with the groceries.

"Want to know what really made Dad sick, Kit?" She snatched at Kit's arm. "Not smoking that pipe," she snapped. "Not India. You. *You* made him sick—worrying about you for all these years. Why you never grow, how long you've been a burden on them both, what on earth will become of you when they're gone."

She regretted the words instantly. Kit had reeled back as if smacked, the muscles of her jaw jumping, a mix of grief and fury adding years to her little-girl face. Then she'd spun on her heels, her fast legs dashing for home.

Now, at the hospital, Kit emerged from Dad's room, leached of all spark and color. She murmured something that Helen didn't catch before crawling into Mum's lap like a young child. "Your

turn," Kit repeated to Helen, exhaling the words, low and qua-
vering, before burying her head in Mum's hair.

When Helen slipped into Dad's room, he looked to be
sleeping and dreaming, the gray lids of his eyes twitching. His
cheeks and lips and the fingers splayed over his chest were all
tinged with blue.

Helen drew her chair as close to his bed as she could and
rested her hand on his. After a minute he turned his head and
opened his eyes.

"Helen." They sat quietly for what felt like minutes, Dad
watching her face fondly. He gripped her hand, a faint pulse of
pressure against her own, then he murmured, "I'm sorry."

She started to protest, but he cut her off, his words panting
and shallow.

"No. Listen. It's important. I'm sorry to leave. Like this."
He fluttered his fingers weakly. "Leaving so much on your
shoulders. Your mother. Kit." His chin contorted. "Natalie will
help with Lillian. When the time comes. But Kit. When Lillian
is gone. Kit will still need protection. Kit will need a mother."

Helen jolted as if she'd been pricked with a pin. *Protection?*
Kit could survive a Soviet missile attack. She was canny and
resourceful, too smart for her own good. But then Helen thought
of the cashier's mistake at the A&P yesterday. Kit's face after
Helen said those awful things. Her desperation and frustration,
her world-weary eyes. Helen blinked and another image swam
into view: Kit, all elbows and knees, arranging herself on their
mother's lap in the corridor, hiding her face from view.

Dad's eyes ached at her, as if he could read her mind. "Just
so," he whispered. "We know the years don't matter. She doesn't
just look young, she *is* young. Even now. She lacks the emotional

maturity to be able to make her way on her own. Others will take advantage."

He gestured feebly toward his bedside table. It was crowded with framed photographs that Helen herself had brought him. A faded cabinet card of Dad and his brother, Thomas, as schoolboys. Mum and Dad, posing for a photo on the banks of the Seine. Kit and Helen swaddled in woolens at the Berlin zoo. All four of them on the Gapstow Bridge in full color, ice cream blotched down Kit's front.

"The drawer," he whispered.

Inside: his old briar pipe, but no tobacco. She lifted it out quizzically, but he shook his head. There were several prescription pill bottles sitting on top of a copy of *The New Yorker*. She removed the magazine and spied a large manila envelope underneath. *Helen McKinley* it said in her father's hand. The flap was sealed with wax.

"Birth certificates. For Kit." Dad's eyes bored into her. "Dated from 1950 through 1970. A new one every four years. Unless the format changes drastically." He paused to cough into his fist, a wet bark that set him off so that Helen, despite all her training, felt helpless. When the fit finally subsided, his voice was strained. "There's also a list of colleges where I've made arrangements, just a handful—she'll have no trouble gaining admittance to these schools, no matter where her transcripts come from. And that's something I can't predict." He gave a wan smile. "Financially, I've made arrangements. Until she's old enough to work. All of this should see you through to the mid-eighties."

"The eighties," Helen repeated, although the word sinking in was *you*. By the mid-eighties, she'd be fifty, an unimaginable age. And her mother, she realized in the same moment, would almost definitely be gone. Certainly in mind if not in body. But Kit. Unless something miraculous happened to speed things up, Kit would still look like a teen and behave the same way. The thought of this made Helen feel impossibly heavy, as if her legs were filling with sand.

"I should have had more time."

He paused, then continued in short bursts of effort. "If you ever need something more. Help or advice. Get in touch with Ayaan Gupta. His contact information is there." He gestured with effort at the envelope. "You really only met him the once. And you never met Hari. But they know, about Kit. Ayaan's own father, Tarun—" He broke off, resting. "Tarun is also a leap year baby. Ayaan will understand. The transition from juvenescence. How long it took for Tarun." His words fell away a second time. "For Tarun to settle down."

Helen was staring at him. *Juvenescence?* It was the kind of obtuse word Kit would use. He meant puberty, of course. She thought of all the years she'd endured Kit's questions about kissing and boyfriends, about going all the way. Kit hiding in Helen's closet with her camera, taking pictures of Dicky. The thought dawned on Helen like a spray of sparks: Kit needed to suffer through adolescence like everyone else, but this stormy phase, for Kit (and for everyone around her), would drag on and on.

"But Helen. You need to promise me you'll look after her. And you'll keep others from finding out about her. Until she's old enough to decide for herself."

Helen found herself nodding at him dumbly, the envelope scorching her lap. Regret, apology, relief, sadness, fear, desperation, and pride were churning in his eyes, unblinking now, each emotion trying to muscle the other aside.

"I promise, Papa," she said, the babyish moniker coming to her lips, unused for so long, making her feel the way Kit must feel all the time: impossibly young and centuries old.

Then he was smiling again. He said, "Do you know what a fright you gave us? When your mother first found out she was pregnant? Again. We had no way of knowing. If you'd be like Kit. If her condition was an accident. Or genetic. We'd been so careful, for so long. Not to have a child together."

She laid her hand on his chest and could feel his heartbeat under her fingertips, so weary and straining.

"Everyone always tells you. You are your mother's daughter. And you are. You're the spitting image. You take after her. In so many ways. But you are also your father's daughter. Never forget that. I love Kit as my own. Just as Thomas would have. But I'm so, so grateful, Helen. To have had a daughter of my own."

His eyes, so sunken in their gray pouches, were glossy, carrying all the force and strength that was gone from every other inch of him. "By God, I've made a lot of mistakes, Helen. You were and always will be our absolute best, most perfect mistake."

Natalie stayed behind to wait for Mum, who'd gone back in to be with Dad and wouldn't leave until there was no more reason to stay. On the walk home, Kit dawdled, falling farther and farther behind, as if she might still duck back for another visit. Helen, too, could think of a thousand things she now wanted to say to or ask her father (and a dozen others she needed to say to Kit). The beige envelope was rolled in her purse.

She paused outside a store selling ladies' bathing suits, pretending to study the display until Kit caught up. As the March wind drilled up Second Avenue, Helen tried and failed to imagine herself trussed into a two-piece bikini.

Kit might have trudged right past without even acknowledging her sister, but Helen laid a hand on her shoulder. "Hey."

"Hey."

"Kit, I'm sorry. About yesterday. I didn't mean what I said."

She could feel Kit's shoulders quake in her coat. "Me too," she mumbled, and Kit's eyes, when she looked up, were flooding. No part of her face was dry. She took a timid step toward Helen, and Helen pulled her close. These days, in the ER, she was always handling bodies. Holding them and rolling them. Shifting their heft where they lay. Kit was the smallest, frailest body she'd held in ages. A bundle of kindling. Rods of glass. Her grief, or Helen's, might snap her in pieces. When had Helen held *anyone* like this? So gently. So ferociously.

"What did Dad want to say to you?" she murmured.

Kit shrugged in her arms. "He told me to behave, and to help look after Mum." They stood for a moment in silence. "What did he say to you?"

"The same," said Helen, her eyes on the mannequins in the window. Kit was quiet, then said, "He told you to behave?"

Helen snorted and pulled away. Kit's mouth, she saw, was curling up at the edges in a rueful smile, her red eyes drifting up to meet Helen's. Helen couldn't think of the last time she'd seen Kit smile, not even a wry one, but here she was, making an effort, trying to get a chuckle out of Helen, even if the look in her eyes betrayed sorrow's hatchet, poised to hack her in two. Helen, in that moment, felt exactly the same—a jagged, roaring sadness that made her pull Kit close. Kit, in turn, squeezed Helen as hard as she could.

A LIFE, HELD, 1964

Gunshot wounds, heart attacks, stabbings, strokes, poisonings, car accidents, factory traumas, accidental amputations, suicide attempts, not to mention New York City's steady pipeline of general lunacy, battery, and drunkenness: every shift in Helen's twelve-bed, heart-of-Manhattan ER offered the full spectrum of life-and-death emergencies, twenty-four hours a day. Helen thrived here. Blood stanched, gashes closed, bones set—acute problems fixed or alleviated before her very eyes, many times thanks to her own quick action.

Most of the other ER nurses were her own age or younger and came from a dozen different working-class backgrounds. Helen adopted their slang and their mannerisms, dodging any questions about her own upbringing and family, their international history. It helped that some of them had known her father, who'd spent months in a ward at this same hospital. They typically tiptoed around her personal life. One of the ER doctors, as fate would have it, was the suave and handsome Ken Pritchard, the medical student who'd broken the hearts and hymens of so many of her classmates at nursing college. He had joined New York Hospital not long before Helen. Pritch, as everyone called him, had a great build, dark eyes, and a boyish mop of sandy hair, but was also an attentive listener, endlessly curious about the lives of women: a combination that had made him devastating among Columbia undergraduates. But this was a new era. With all his talents and powers of persuasion in the fifties, Pritch had been ahead of his time. By 1964, unmarried and utterly unabashed in his reverence for all things female, Pritch was in his element.

"Oh, but you were the bossy brunette of *all* my undergrad fantasies," he crooned to Helen on their first shift together, then made a throaty sound, a chuckle that also managed to sound carnal.

Helen just batted away his steady compliments the way she'd learned to do from the other blunt-talking Irish, Black, and Italian nurses who took Pritch in stride. More intriguing to her was Dr. Robert Malloy, Pritch's best friend, who juggled his ER shifts with a pharmaceutical fellowship relating to prescription birth control. Robbie Malloy had wavy black hair and creamy skin that flushed rosy red when he was pressed or tired or angry. The oral contraceptive he was researching was intended for use by married women, as well as for "menstrual regularity," which, in Pritch's opinion, was a delightful loophole. But whereas Pritch exuded an inclusive, all-American warmth that drew everyone into his circle, Robbie Malloy was both shyer and pricklier: he could resist Pritch's constant ribbing, but also gave back as good as he got, often delivering a single smart retort that made them all laugh, even Pritch. Or wiped the smile from their faces.

"Do you have access to free samples, Robbie? There's not a single gal in this joint who wouldn't mind signing up for your clinical trials. You can put them down as married and they'll learn quickly. I can help."

In fact, Robbie replied, his interest in birth control was not for sex-for-the-sake-of-sex, but rather a solemn interest in maternal and infant mortality, which (he had argued in his thesis work) went hand in hand with unwanted and mistimed births. "I myself am the youngest of ten children," he said flatly. "My mother died in childbirth." He paused a beat. "I expect yours wishes she'd done the same."

The charged dynamic, the wordplay and innuendo, the flirty banter: these were as much of a rush to Helen as the heady, crisis-skirting pulse of the work itself. When Helen brushed up against the starched white sleeve of Robbie's coat in the supply room or had to lean across him to help with an unruly patient, she would catch a hint of his clean, warm smell, and everything else, her worries and her sadness, fell away.

It took months for Helen to get up the nerve to ask Robbie out. At first they just went to the malt shop, then to the cinema to see *My Fair Lady* with Audrey Hepburn and Rex Harrison. After that, so long as they both had the night off and Helen wasn't needed at home, their Saturday night routine became a film at the Rialto, the Rivoli, or the Capitol, and occasionally a live show. She met his father, a retired policeman, and Bernadette, the eldest of his many sisters. Twice Helen dragged Robbie to the Metropolitan Museum of Art, horrified that he'd never been before. Robbie, in turn, took her to the Hall of African Mammals at the Museum of Natural History.

They were standing in front of the herd of life-sized elephants, a marvel of taxidermy, when he said, "I'm going to Africa one day, you know. I'll travel the world. Anywhere I'm needed to improve perinatal health." Robbie said it lightly, confidently, but his eyes bored into hers. "Would you go with me?"

"Of course," she said, blushing. She thought of all the travel she'd already done (that she hadn't got around to telling him about). "I've always wanted to go to Africa."

But she didn't bring Robbie home to meet her family.
They'd moved again, farther uptown, just a block away from
Max. It was Max, who was well into his seventies by now,
who had arranged for Kit to attend yet another new school,
this one in New Jersey. It had a strong music program, and
she was enrolled as his granddaughter, Katharina Dörr. She
was also now allowed to go to Central Park, which was close
enough to their new apartment on 85th, on her own. She'd jog
there in the early morning to watch the most pampered dogs
of Manhattan racing around off leash on the East Meadow,
or after school, to run an agreed-upon loop—Max's reasoning
being that no kidnapper would ever be able to catch up with
her. Kit was still desperately sad and lonely, but Helen felt
powerless to do anything about it, given everything else on
her plate. Deborah Katzen was fully out of the picture. She'd
be what? Seventeen or eighteen by now—more interested in
boys and hairstyles, no doubt, than tree forts and whoopee
cushions. There'd been a brief time, when Dad first got sick,
that Deborah had kept calling for Kit, and Helen had decided
it was best not to pass along those messages. Not out of spite,
but kindness. Better, Helen decided, to let that friendship lapse
than to have it get to a point where their physical differences
became too obvious.

That's why Helen reasoned she couldn't tell Robbie about
Kit until she was absolutely sure about him. Apart from the
offhand comment he'd made about traveling the world, he
never talked about marriage or the future. Plus Robbie worked
so closely with the pharmaceutical company that was spon-
soring his clinical research. Dad had been especially wary of
drug companies. What if Robbie took an undue interest in Kit,

scientifically, before he'd even fully decided he was interested in Helen, romantically?

"But what is it *you* want?" Natalie had pressed her. Her glamorous aunt, visiting from Montreal for the summer of '64, was on her third sherry and had been goading Helen for details on Robbie, waving her long arms in the air, bangles jingling, and expounding about "modern freedoms" and what she did in her day. Mum was resting and Kit—Katharina—was shut away in her room playing the same melancholy passage over and over again on her cello. Natalie flicked a lock of her long gray hair over her shoulder. "Is it marriage you're thinking of, or just a bit of fun?—What!" She pouted at the expression on Helen's face. "These are different times. You can try on the dress, see if it fits."

In fact, Robbie had never pressured her physically, even though Helen had tried to make it abundantly clear that she was more than ready for all of it. She'd been ready for a decade. At work, Saundra and the other nurses had been teasing Helen about when she planned to "give it up," with tips for what she might want to try: how, where, and when. To be getting something along these same lines at home was even worse. She cocked her head, listening for Kit's cello. Years ago, Kit would have thundered into the room, thrusting her snout into the middle of this conversation. *Helen never tells me anything!*

She took a breath. "Robbie doesn't want to rush things."

"Does he want children?" Natalie asked.

"He doesn't, actually." Helen's voice was wobbly, not too different from how Robbie's had sounded when he first brought it up. He'd said he hoped she might feel the same way, too, since she never talked about children, never gawked at babies the way other girls did. "Robbie believes, quite rightly, that there are so many children in the world already, in Central America, Asia, sub-Saharan Africa—everywhere, really—born into families that can't feed them. He wants to spend his life helping those children, and their mothers. It's the reason he's so passionate about his work in maternal-fetal health and universal birth control."

"Oh, *that's* the reason, is it?" Natalie hiccuped.

"And no." Helen swallowed. "Before you ask. He doesn't know about Kit."

Natalie's teasing smile and hopping eyebrows settled into something more somber. "You know you can't put your life on hold forever, Helen. If you're serious about Robbie. If he's the one. All this responsibility—your mum, Kit—shouldn't fall to you. They've asked me to postpone my retirement a few more years at Trafalgar, but that's not set in stone. We can make a plan."

THE BREAK, 1966

She felt like an autumn leaf wafting down Second Avenue, or a musical phrase, something fluty and whimsical. Natalie had stayed with them again all summer, taking some pressure off Helen. Kit seemed more settled. Mum was no better, but no worse either. And today was two years to the day since she'd gotten up the nerve to ask Robbie to go for milkshakes, and she knew he knew it. Helen was practically skipping, a smile ticklish on her lips.

Pritch was standing at Admissions, his elbows planted on the high counter, bantering with the receptionist, his lips curling roguishly. Pritch still flirted with Helen the way he did with the other nurses, laying a hand on her shoulder, her arm, or the hollow of her back. But Robbie and Helen's romance had also given Pritch a gold mine of new opportunities. The other day all three of them had been bracing a patient with a dislocated shoulder when Pritch asked Robbie in a sprightly tone whether he'd read the Masters and Johnson three-part review of the clitoris published in the *Western Journal of Surgery, Obstetrics, and Gynecology*. Helen went beet red, but not before seeing the patient's eyes widen above his oxygen mask, his pain forgotten, while Robbie, his own cheeks flushing, yanked the joint back into its socket.

Today, Helen sailed past Pritch, ignoring his entreaties.

"He's in radiology talking about Bed C," Saundra called in her hearty voice when Helen strode by. Bed C (C for "confidential") was the private post-surgery bed for patients whose care needed more discreet discussion. "But I swear he's gotta bulge the shape of a ring box in his pocket." Helen had already decided: if Robbie asked, and she was certain he would, she would take him home to meet her family that very night.

She found Robbie and the radiologist, Steven Bard, conferring over a series of X-rays clipped against the light box. Dr. Bard was tracing a barely visible fissure across what looked to Helen to be an ulna. The way the dim light filtering through the X-rays accentuated Robbie's cheekbones and his plush lips made her insides flutter.

Dr. Bard waved her over. His pinkie finger moved to another scan, and here she had no trouble seeing the jagged edge of the bone protruding from the arm. "And again here." His finger moved to the third X-ray, a hand. "Four, maybe five years ago, nicely healed. But you can see the thicker band of new bone." Helen leaned closer, using the opportunity to breathe in Robbie, all but closing her eyes.

The grit in Robbie's tone snapped her back to the room. "We're thinking we need to bring in social services when the family arrives, if we're right about this. She says she tripped and fell, but with so many other older fractures—five at least, according to Dr. Bard, all at different stages of healing . . ."

Helen edged closer, squinting at the scan but mostly so she could feel Robbie's elbow knock against her own, and the electric charge that produced. She tried to sneak a glance toward his pocket.

"The little tyke was funny about her name. Said one thing, then something else."

Whatever warmth Helen had felt standing so close to Robbie vanished when her eyes slid to the name on the X-rays. Robbie and Dr. Bard continued to murmur, but their words receded as if down a tunnel. If social services started digging around, asking for medical records, wanting to interview the mother . . . Helen could feel the hairs standing up on her arms. Her voice came out as a squeak.

"Can I speak to you in private, Dr. Malloy?"

Robbie looked surprised, and his eyes slid from Helen to Bard, who was still stroking his cropped beard. "Thanks again, Steven. I'll keep you posted."

When Dr. Bard was gone, Robbie hooked a finger through hers, managing to look apologetic, distracted, and concerned, all at once. "I wasn't ignoring you," he started. She cut him off.

"Robbie, don't call the social worker. Please. I can explain."

She clasped his hand in both of hers and pulled it toward her as if begging. Which she was. "Please. I know this girl." She swallowed. "I know Katharina Dörr."

Just then, Saundra poked a head around the door. "Sorry to interrupt, lovebirds." Thanks to Saundra, every nurse on this shift probably had money riding on whether or not Robbie would pop the question. "Bed C," Saundra said. "Her family is in the waiting room."

Helen let go of his hand. "I'll get them, Robbie. We'll meet you there." She locked eyes with him before hurrying out the door. "Just don't call social services."

Mum looked adrift under a faded painting of sailboats in a harbor. Too large for the waiting room's chrome chair, she still managed to seem shrunken and ill at ease. When she saw

Helen, her face brightened but not, Helen thought, with actual recognition. Helen's heart sank.

Natalie, meanwhile, was pacing. "Oh, thank goodness!" she said, lifting her long arms theatrically. "I couldn't remember when your shift was starting, and we got the call about Kit and rushed down here. Is she okay then? Is she in a lot of pain?"

Both women were properly dressed, Helen noticed with relief. She'd half-expected her mother to have hustled to the hospital in the long cardigan that doubled as a housecoat, but she was wearing a decent dress, faded but clean. Natalie wore an oriental scarf swept over her shoulders and wide-leg trousers paired with a billowing peasant blouse that was belted around her tiny waist with a chain of interlocking brass hoops that matched her earrings, everything tinkling as they walked down the corridor. With her hair braided in two long plaits, Natalie looked like a sexagenarian schoolgirl playing dress-up. Helen opened the door to the recovery room and led them to Bed C.

Later Kit would tell them the same story she'd told Robbie, that she'd been running in Central Park, her regular loop around the reservoir, then took a shortcut through the bushes to get down to the road. Helen could picture the other walkers and birdwatchers, hoping for a pleasant stroll away from the hot snarl of midtown traffic, only to have this reckless blitz of girl zing past them. Kit had slipped on a stone or a stick, she said, and come down hard on her arm.

The curtain around the bed was already pulled aside when they got there, and Helen could see Robbie, smiling, a chart tucked under his arm, his hands thrust into the pockets of his white coat. Pockets that otherwise looked empty. Kit glanced past him and saw the three of them hurrying over.

"Mummy!"

Helen could hear the fear and relief woven into Kit's cry, but they didn't touch her. Instead she saw the effect of the word on Robbie. His face flattened with shock, then creased with confusion, then soured with something close to anger. Helen could picture, suddenly, what this looked like to him. She, Helen, bustling to the bedside of a young child—just twelve years old according to the date on the radiographs—flanked by two towering grandmothers. And Kit calling out for her mother.

She acted on instinct, ducking past Robbie, effectively blocking his view. Then she laid a hand on Kit's shoulder and planted a kiss on her brow. If Kit looked puzzled, her gaze darting to her mother and aunt, Robbie looked ready to explode, the little muscles in his temple hopping.

"You have a child?" he growled. Helen saw Natalie flinch. Kit's sharp ears would also have heard.

"A *child*?"

Helen's mind swerved, rebelliously, back to her walk to work that morning, how she'd felt like a leaf dancing, like a song.

"Robbie—" She reached for his hand but he yanked it away. But then Natalie was wheeling around, her thin braids swirling in an arc.

"You're *Robbie*!" Natalie exclaimed. For a moment it seemed Natalie might be about to fling her long arms around him, her blousy sleeves flapping like the wings of a bat. Then she seemed to remember the charade they had unwittingly set in motion and her arms dropped to her sides, her mouth snapping shut.

Robbie struggled for a moment and regained his composure, but he didn't smile. "Dr. Malloy." He extended his hand to Natalie, who took it, then stammered a reply. "Natalie Kenilworth. And this is my sister, Lillian McKinley."

His eyes flickered at the name. Helen spoke up softly. "My mother."

She could see the hurt in his eyes. He couldn't think—he couldn't *possibly* think—that Helen would ever hurt a child, any child. But he now had the chart pinched so tightly between his fingers and thumb that his knuckles were white. Inside, she knew, were the X-rays showing five or more broken bones belonging to Katharina Dörr.

Helen could see Mum's eyes had drifted away from Robbie and were roving over the curtains at the foot of the bed, the milk-white walls that always looked like they needed another coat of paint, the thin, over-laundered sheets on the bed, and the plaster cast encasing Kit's arm all the way up to the armpit. On a plastic tray at her bedside were Kit's house key, her necklace watch, the rupee coin, a rubber ball—all her prized possessions. The entire scene was so ridiculously familiar, Kit's many misadventures having landed her in hospitals in at least three different countries on both sides of the Atlantic. This alone might set Mum off on the wrong path, unearthing a name in her scrambled brain that Helen didn't know or hadn't heard in years. *Where's Max? Where's Gertrude?* Or, more likely, given the room's harsh overtones of Ajax and antiseptic (Helen braced for it, knowing the effect it would have on Kit), *Where's Ernest?*

Instead Mum's gaze snapped like a switch back to Robbie. "In fact, we've been waiting a while now to meet you," she said brusquely, with none of the flimsy uncertainty Helen had anticipated. "I hadn't expected it to be at your place of work." Mum tilted her head, a brisk nod, at the folder in Robbie's hands. "X-rays, I presume. It's not what you think. Can we speak somewhere in private? Natalie, you'll stay with Kit, while Helen and I go with Dr. Malloy." At her full height, Mum could look at him eye to eye. "Robbie," she said, and her mouth turned up at one side, a sad smile. "If you're joining this family, you need to know a bit more about my daughter."

Robbie looked from Lillian to Helen, hesitating.

"Not my daughter Helen," Mum said gently. "My daughter Kit."

FOOLING, 1968

n the end, Robbie, having been spared the decades of Kit's protracted childhood, accepted her at face value: as a *kid*. Albeit an exceptionally bright and athletic one, inching closer to the cusp of womanhood. Even after a night shift, Robbie could always be convinced to listen to Kit's rapid-fire questions and opinions about the Vietnam War protest in Central Park, the Aberfan landslide in Wales, about Martin Luther King Jr.'s assassination in Memphis. He always had the energy to time her laps at the track or race their go-cart along the Hudson River greenway. Scientifically, Robbie had an endless list of questions for Helen and Lillian (on the days Mum was up to answering them), and Helen suspected he'd spent hours thumbing through the musty medical journals in the hospital's basement library, looking for anything similar to Kit. But Robbie was also profoundly influenced by one of his former mentors, Henry Beecher, who'd published an exposé of all the studies involving human experimentation that had been conducted without adequate patient consent: penicillin withheld from soldiers with strep throat, disabled children infected with hepatitis. "Researchers can be ruthless in pursuit of that signature contribution that will make their careers worthwhile, and children are the most vulnerable," Robbie told Helen. "I've seen respected physicians set aside their fundamental humanity in their quest for scientific acclaim, forgetting their vows. *Primum non nocere*. First do no harm."

Robbie was adamant that Kathy—he was the only one who consistently remembered to call her that—might be a medical miracle, but whether she wanted to share this with science was a decision she could make when she was fully grown and capable of consent. Here, Helen was sure of it, she detected a whiff of eagerness that Robbie couldn't quite suppress. "If in fact it's a genetic trait that prolongs youth, there may be implications for fertility."

That surprised Helen. "I thought your interests were in helping to keep women from getting pregnant in the first place."

"Maternal choice," he said. "For some women, that's having none, or fewer. For others, it's the ability to have them if they want."

On a Saturday in October, Helen arrived at the park to find Robbie was already sprinting around after the Frisbee with Kit and another kid. Natalie and Mum were sitting on a bench in the shade of a chestnut tree, rusty leaves still clinging to their branches. Lillian had dozed off, her lips parted and her chin falling to her chest.

"Who's that, with Kit and Robbie?" Helen said, dropping herself onto the bench.

Natalie, who'd taken up knitting and did it badly, looked up from her lumpy mound of wool.

"That's Will, her little friend from the track team at Hutchison."

Hutchison Academy was an elite boarding school in Connecticut specializing in premed and athletics. Helen and Robbie had registered Kit there as their daughter, Kathy Malloy. Kit was the happiest Helen had seen her in years, bubbling over with talk of her coach, ladder workouts, and negative splits. The Olympic Games had kicked off in Mexico that week, and Kit, home with Mum and Natalie for the weekend, would no doubt spend it planted in front of the new color TV, transfixed.

"He's only twelve," Natalie was saying, "so he must have skipped a grade, and he's a middle-distance runner, too. A match made in heaven, I'd say, although she'll bite your head off if you call him her boyfriend. He lives nearby, apparently."

Helen did the math. If this boy was twelve now, he'd be nearing retirement by the time Kit was ready to marry. The thought made her shudder.

Helen watched Kit winding up to hurl the Frisbee. Kit was well over five feet tall now. Jigging on her toes, she still looked gawky and gangly, like a marionette on a string. But sprinting across the grass, she had a grace and athleticism that made people stop and watch.

Then Helen frowned, shielding her eyes with her hand. "Is Kit . . . developing . . ." Her lips balked. The idea that Kit's body might, at last, be catching up with her curiosity made Helen feel a mix of relief and trepidation.

Natalie nodded. "Oh yes, Kit—*Kathy*—is pleased as punch. She informed me she bought herself a 'Bobbie bra.' Whatever that is."

A row of stitches threatened to slip from Natalie's needle and she tucked her bony elbows back to her sides. "How are you and Robbie? You seem happy, but your mother worries."

Helen considered her mother, fast asleep on the hard bench. Were Mum's dreams as jumbled as her waking thoughts? Last week, Mum had twice said with rising anxiety that she'd forgotten her dolphin at home, and would it rain, did they think? She'd need her dolphin if it rained. It was hard to imagine Mum, these days, inquiring about Helen's marriage. But you'd never know it to watch her sleep. Her twitching eyelids and the sweep of her tall forehead gave Helen a sensation she'd all but forgotten, and it rolled over her now like the peal of a bell, gratitude edged with looming loss. Even now, Helen's greatest thought or impulse, the biggest idea she could ever muster, would never come close to the intellect and wisdom shut away in the mind of her mother.

Natalie read her thoughts, giving her a chiding jab. "She does have lots of good moments. Some mornings she goes dark, but others she'll spend hours leafing through her journals and reading through old notebooks. The other day she insisted I listen to a long explanation of a groundbreaking achievement to do with something-or-other synthesis. But I got the exact same lecture three days later, delivered with the same breathless excitement."

Natalie held up her knitting so that it fell in a shapeless curtain of purple, then bundled it into a carry bag. "You dodged my question. You and Robbie. No change of heart on babies? That means you're taking the pill. My god, if the pill had been around in my day." Natalie smirked into the bag of wool, as if she'd hidden her lover inside. "Mind you, I don't think I'd remember to take something every day."

"It's not a pill I'm taking, actually. I kept forgetting, too. This one is an injectable Robbie has been working on, with Upjohn. One needle every three months."

"John who?"

"Upjohn, a pharmaceutical company. They're funding Robbie's clinical trial. The results look excellent so far and the FDA is reviewing the interim data now."

Natalie looked appalled. "You're taking something experimental?"

"DMPA. Depot medroxyprogesterone acetate," Helen said cheerfully. The words had taken practice.

"Are there side effects?"

Helen hesitated. Headaches, muscle aches, dizziness, breast tenderness, joint pain, fatigue, insomnia, weight gain, acne, depression, bloating, decreased sexual desire, irregular menstruation, no menstruation—anyone enrolling in Robbie's study was practically encouraged to find something to complain about. "Not really, no." Her aunt looked skeptical.

"It's safe, trust me, and Upjohn is a key SAMM sponsor, providing financial support and DMPA."

If anything, their baby was SAMM—Stopping Avoidable Maternal Mortality: Robbie and Helen would soon be heading to South Africa to set up the first SAMM clinic, and Robbie's dream was to expand it across the continent within ten years.

"Hmph." It had been Natalie's decision to move from Montreal to live with Mum and Kit when she finally retired from Trafalgar, the same year Helen and Robbie were married, but she had mixed opinions about their plans to move abroad. But her foxy look was back, turning up her sealed mouth. "So how is it, then?"

It really was ridiculously warm for October. Helen's feet felt hot and swollen, her thighs sticky. "The shot? Not bad. A bee sting."

"No, you ninny. The *sex*." Natalie sizzled the word through her teeth. "Sex at your age, free of consequences and commitment." She turned her eyes skyward, inviting the treetops, utter strangers, to agree with her. "Imagine!"

Helen looked at her aunt, thinking, not for the first time, that Kit wasn't the only one in the family able to bend the rules of aging. The truth was, sex was neither good nor bad with Robbie. They probably weren't doing it often enough to get good at it, as Helen's magazines advised. Most nights she nestled her back toward Robbie's chest and he would pull her close, his arm threading over her waist, but that was it. Helen couldn't actually remember the last time he'd nudged her onto her back, or sometimes her stomach, and done the very thing that warranted her getting this injection in the first place. She couldn't imagine explaining this to Natalie, who was already basking in an answer Helen was in no position to provide.

"Look at you." Natalie was grinning. "You're red as a tomato!"

Kit saved her, sprinting the last thirty yards to their bench. Close up, Helen could see the half-dozen angry red spots dotting her chin and between her eyebrows, the damp blotches at her collar and under her arms. When, exactly, had Kit started with the pimples and perspiration?

"Can Will come for dinner to see the new TV, Aunt Natalie?"

Helen turned her eyes on the boy, who was watching Kit with a goofy, oversize smile on his face. He was a few inches shorter than her and just as gangly, although his big shoes and the breadth of his bony shoulders suggested he was headed for a growth spurt. His hair was dirty blond, flopping long over his forehead and behind his ears. He looked like he could be the kid brother of a British pop star, the kind who trailed after the band, making a nuisance of himself. But he was beaming at Kit, his eyes twin spotlights and her center stage.

"Aww," Natalie murmured. "Look at them."

"We can ask my mom," the boy said. "She should be here soon, with my brother and sister. They wanted to meet you."

Kit seemed to remember her manners. She turned to Helen first, pointing with the Frisbee and saying, "This is my—" Then she paused and her giddy look was replaced by something more guarded. "This is Helen," she said simply. "Robbie, Natalie, and Lillian."

If Will was confused by what roles these adults played in Kit's life, he didn't show it. "Pleased to meet you," he said politely.

"Who are you?" Mum said, looking the boy up and down. "Are you friends with Thomas?"

Now Kit's face fell like a stone. She touched Will's arm to distract him. Natalie chimed in. "Will is a friend of Kathy's, Mum. From school." Mum's eyes widened. "Kathy? Will what?"

Suddenly Helen felt bushed and gloopy. A leaden lump of warm dough. "We should probably get Mum home for a rest," Helen said. She glanced back up the knoll. Still several hundred yards away, two women were making their way slowly down the walk with a young boy being yanked by a poodle on a leash.

"Will Katzen, ma'am."

As the name sank in for Helen, she saw its effect on Kit, who turned to look at the two women making their unhurried approach. Her cheeks turned fuchsia, and she shot a panicked look at Helen. Natalie was smiling blandly, the faintest ripple of confusion crossing her face. Robbie, who'd slumped on the bench and closed his eyes, looked on the verge of a nap. When Helen pinched him on the shoulder blade, he jumped. "It's lovely to meet you, Will, but we actually need to dash off."

Will's sweet lips formed an instantly familiar O and he glanced from Helen to Kit. But Kit was already slinging Natalie's knitting bag over her shoulder with a look on her face that Helen had never seen there before: heartbreak mixed with terror. "I'm so sorry, Will, I didn't realize the time."

Something in Kit's tone was enough to tip off Robbie and Natalie, who swung into action so that the whole family had hustled off before the two women, the boy, and the poodle had drawn much closer. When Helen looked back, Will was trudging up the slope toward his family, dejected.

"Does someone want to tell me what just happened?" Natalie asked.

Kit stayed silent. Instead it was Mum who spoke in her old, sure way, so rare these days that all of them stared as if she'd recited the names of the thirty-five American presidents. "That was Madge and Deborah Katzen, wasn't it." A statement, not a question. "Deborah"—Mum directed this at Natalie—"was Kit's best friend, years ago, when Will was a baby."

Helen wheeled on Kit. "You didn't know, *Kathy*. How could you not know?"

"I didn't!" Kit chirped. "I swear! They didn't call him Will back then. And he's two grades below me. I don't have any classes with him. I doubt he knows my last name either."

"Hezekiah," Mum said mildly. "Of course he doesn't call himself that." She tipped her chin skyward. "Will it rain, do you think? It feels like rain."

When they got home, Robbie and Kit, as predicted, glued themselves to the television, Mum took a nap, and Natalie got the

roast in the oven. Helen used the hour to sort through the last
of her things still stored at the back of Kit's closet.

It was the poster above Kit's bed that put the question in
her mind: a peace sign made of yellow daisies and the words
Make Love Not War in rainbow lettering. Did Kit even know
what that meant? Helen snorted, then checked herself. Of
course she did. Kit had likely known as long as Helen had.
Probably longer.

So had Kit started fooling around? She'd been so curious,
for so long. Sheesh, she'd been curious more than a decade and
a half ago when she'd spied on Helen's ill-fated striptease with
Dicky. Helen flinched at the memory. Kit's little friend Will
looked like he'd be far more interested in Kit's go-cart than
anything so gross as a kiss, but maybe that was old-fashioned
thinking. Kids in the sixties were much more worldly than she'd
ever been in her teens. They grew up faster. Well. Regular kids
grew up faster. Even if little Will Katzen wasn't interested, there
would be other boys, older boys, at Hutchison who'd be only
too happy to provide an education. Helen thought suddenly of
Pritch and what he must have been like in high school. There
were always boys like Pritch in high school. Like Dicky, she
realized with a rush of feelings she could not, even now, understand. That night, she'd thought she wanted him, that she was
ready. But she wasn't. Her jaw tightened. This was exactly the
kind of mistake Kit might go barreling into.

She wondered, did Kit still keep a diary?

The bureau and closet proved to be jammed with well-worn
clothes, the bookshelves with notebooks full of vocab lists in
half a dozen different languages, binders of sheet music, and
two mementos set in frames that Helen hadn't seen in years:

the letter of condolence they'd received from Prime Minister Diefenbaker after Dad's death, thanking him for his long years of service, and the yellowed "Votes for Women" pamphlet that used to hang in her parents' bedroom. An old Howdy Doody lunch box, its buckles rusty, was filled with yellowed newspaper clippings that Helen realized with a pang were obituaries. Had Kit really known all these people? How? How well?

She checked the drawer in the nightstand last, tutting to herself. Maybe this was a little-known side effect of DMPA: a prurient interest in her sister's protracted sexual development.

What had she expected? Little kid stuff, maybe—matchbook cars, bottle caps, marbles, cherry-flavored ChapStick, the rupee coin, or the set of marked cards that Kit used for her magic tricks. Instead, the drawer was crammed with ribbons and medals. There was even a small trophy engraved with the words:

1st Place, 800m, Under 16s, 1968 Katherine Malloy

Helen sank down on Kit's bed.

She knew, of course, that Kit was fast. *Very* fast. And running, other than possibly Will Katzen, might be the one thing Kit truly loved. So why had it never occurred to Helen that Kit might be entering races? This, these ribbons and prizes hidden in a bedside drawer—this was why the color TV and the Olympic Games were so important.

Sweeping up the golden cup along with a handful of ribbons and medals, Helen marched to the living room.

"Have *you* won a prize now?" Natalie said. "What for?"

"You knew about this? These races?"

Robbie took the trophy, reading the inscription on its base. Natalie sucked in her cheeks and her gaze floated past Helen. "Right. You should know, a Mr. Drummond, that's the head coach, has called several times—"

"Those are mine!" Kit's words were muffled by a wad of what looked to be bread and jelly in her mouth. "You were snooping!"

"Congratulations, kiddo." Robbie spoke in the voice he usually reserved for the man hospitalized after a bar fight who finds out his adversary is in the next bed. "Why didn't you tell us?"

Kit snatched the cup from Robbie and took a step back, fixing them with her puppy-dog eyes. "I didn't *not* tell you," she said. "You know I'm doing track—this is track."

Helen felt the old exasperation rising up in her like a sneeze. Kit always had to act so hard done by! As if every single thing this family had ever done hadn't been because of her, always to protect her. Helen could admit she'd been nervous about the move to Africa, in spite of Robbie's runaway excitement and all their years of fund-raising and preparation for SAMM. But Kit's aggrieved self-righteousness—Helen couldn't wait to get away, to start her own life (finally!).

Robbie started again. "We're proud of you, Kathy, for sure. It's just, well, these look like pretty serious races, where your name might get written down in some kind of record? That makes people take notice."

Kit cut him off. "I already broke the record, twice. For the 800 *and* the 1500." A haughty look crept over her face. "Then I broke my own records."

A shrill ping from the kitchen interjected.

"That's the roast." Natalie smacked her hands together, falsely cheerful. "Why don't we talk this all through over supper."

Kit crushed her peas under the tines of her fork, lifting them upside down to her mouth, and jabbed at her meat as if, in life, it had done something to her personally. But she couldn't be prodded into conversation. After ten minutes, she said, "I'm not hungry."

Helen rolled her eyes and started to speak, but Robbie tapped a finger on her knee and she startled. They had been arguing more than usual, her and Robbie—the stress of the move, the last-minute arrangements for SAMM. Still, it shouldn't have felt so unexpected to feel her husband's touch under the table.

"You're going to let me keep doing it, right, Aunt Natalie? Doing track? The races and everything?"

Natalie's eyes met Helen's over the table. Robbie cleared his throat, but Kit had her arguments already locked and loaded, firing them as a spray of bullets. "There's no point in training if I can't race. No point getting faster! And Will's going to be racing, too. I have to race with Will, I *have* to."

Helen tuned her out, wondering again just how close Kit and Will had become. She was struck by the thought of Will blazing around the track, Madge and Deborah Katzen under matching sun hats in the stands, becoming suddenly aware of the jumble of red hair and a familiar voice cheering him on.

The telephone rang, breaking the tension. Natalie jerked her arm to glance at her wristwatch, nearly upsetting her water glass.

Kit was already snatching up the phone. Her face lit up. "Of course! Send him up."

She set the phone down, ecstatic. "It's Coach Drummond!" she squealed, then looked down at her outfit, her smile fading, then dashed from the room.

Everyone turned to Natalie, who looked sternly at Helen and Robbie. "This is what I was trying to say earlier. Coach Drummond has called here repeatedly about a form he needs signed. Our telephone number must be what they have on file, but *you* are Mr. and Mrs. Malloy. And your daughter is Kathy Malloy," she reminded them, her voice firm, her eyes on Robbie. It had been his idea to register Kit at Hutchison as his daughter. "I told him to stop by. That's why you had to come here tonight."

Mr. Drummond, ruddy and affable, settled eagerly into the chair he was offered in front of the television. He had a sprightly accent that at one time must have been Scottish and now was even more so. "Hello there, lass," he said to Kit when she reappeared wearing what looked like a sporty pair of terry cloth pajamas with stripes down the side. To Helen's relief, Mr. Drummond proved to be one of those men she knew well from the waiting room at the hospital, the kind who lost all thought of what they might have been intending to say or do as soon as they had a television screen in front of them. Two commentators at a desk with the Olympic rings behind them were summing up the day's gold-medal count for the US team, but when they cut to a commercial break, the coach seemed just as riveted by the advertisements and their jingles, his lips mouthing the words.

He only tore himself away when Robbie cleared his throat.

"So, about Kathy." Mr. Drummond rubbed his palms. "As I said on the telly-phone to Mrs. Malloy"—he directed this remark at Helen—"Kathy is a phenomenal talent. Phenomenal. You must be very proud. Now, there's no telling how things will change for her as she, you know, fills out a bit." He cupped his hands momentarily in front of his chest, giving a toothy laugh. "But I think it's possible she could join the ranks of them."

Here, he jerked his thumb over his shoulder at the television, which Helen took not to mean the rolls of three-ply toilet paper gaily dancing the cancan.

"Hutchison has strong ties to the Yale biomedical program, partnering with the American Athletics Association. But for Kathy to be in the study, get the scans, give the samples, and the like, we do need the forms signed."

"Samples?" Robbie repeated.

"Blood samples, VO2 max, urine analysis." Mr. Drummond waved a hand in the air. "All of the most advanced tests—just like a real Olympian! But she can't be in the study without parental consent."

He looked from Robbie to Helen, and when neither of them spoke, flashed a yellow-fanged smile at Lillian and Natalie. A premonition was creeping over Helen like the slug trails of memory. She'd felt this before—when they lived in their first East Side apartment in New York City, then had to move to a new neighborhood, farther uptown. She'd had the same feeling in Cambridge when they first got Dad's letter from Delhi, uprooting them to sail to America. And before that, surely, in Paris, in Berlin, in London, in Chirk—that too many years had passed and the time had come for the circus to pull up its tent pegs. Kit, she realized, couldn't stay in New York City much longer.

She glanced at Robbie, whose eyes were on Kit. Helen already knew his views on informed consent in underage research subjects. She wouldn't even need to ask.

Mr. Drummond was rattling on about fast-twitch muscles and beats per minute. "You want to be tested, right, Kathy? Anything to make you faster, hmm? And your man Will has already signed up."

Kit's eyes crumpled at Will's name, as if she could sense what was coming. Her shoulders drooped. Even Helen felt a flash of empathy for her kid sister. No. Her older sister.

How Robbie managed to pinch his lips into such a thin line Helen would never know. He caught her eye and she nodded, a faint swish of her chin, which was all she could manage.

Robbie cleared his throat. "Time for tooth-brushing, Kathy." The wiry coach sprang to his feet and Kit mumbled an uneasy good night. Mr. Drummond seemed about to revive the discussion about Kit's blood tests, moving to pull what must have been the unsigned forms from the pocket of his baggy trousers. Robbie held up a hand. "I'm afraid Kathy can't join your study and won't be attending any more track meets," he said firmly. "In fact, next month, Kathy is moving with Helen and me to South Africa."

A LIFE, 1971–75

I t couldn't work, of course. Shifting Kit from place to place like a parcel lost in the post until she could be dropped at some future destination, where she'd be her own responsibility and no one else's. Kit, after spending a year with them in Ladysmith, lasted just two years at the all-girls boarding school in Johannesburg before she was expelled for organizing an anti-apartheid rally. After that, Helen had been forced to pull out the manila envelope her father had given her so long ago. By 1971, Kit had moved to England, where Hari Gupta was wrapping up his undergraduate degree at Oxford. By 1974, she had moved again to Montreal, to which Natalie had returned, having found a facility that could provide the round-the-clock care that Mum now needed. Kit was close enough to New York to return in March of '75, when Max passed away. Helen herself didn't go to the funeral, but Kit, with her morbid fascination for obituaries, had sent her Max's, the newsprint creased and soft, as if she'd carried it with her for days.

Helen (finally!) was living her own life. They had spent their first few years abroad setting up the pilot SAMM clinic in Ladysmith, which is where Will's letters had found them. Had Natalie given Will their address? If so, that was reckless. There was no way this puppy love could last, given the circumstances, and the sooner it ended, the better. For almost a year, the letters had arrived, sometimes twice a month, and Helen, to her credit, resisted the urge to read them. At first she thought she'd save them, for when Kit could read them with maturity and nostalgia, but in the end, she burned them in the fire, and eventually the letters had stopped.

By '71, SAMM's growth allowed them to move to Geneva, where their board had decided to base the administrative offices—nestled among the other heavy hitters in the international aid community and the corporations they depended on for funding. She'd thought Robbie might finally want to settle down with her, in a leadership role, but she'd forgotten the blazing look in his eyes the day he took her to the Museum of Natural History. *I'm going to Africa one day, you know. I'll travel the world.*

Helen, mostly, did not go with him. It was safer, he always said. Think of the malaria and typhoid, rabies and opportunistic crime, the dangerous roads and unreliable transport. Besides, he felt better knowing that logistics, operations, and finances were under Helen's watchful eye, somewhere stable and secure. She was essential to SAMM's success.

SAMM's success. SAMM's growth. SAMM's impact on the lives of mothers and babies in the world's neediest corners. If anything, Robbie had become even more intense and driven than the man she'd fallen for in the NYH emergency room. Within five years, SAMM wasn't just Robbie's baby—it was his life. Even when he was back with her in Switzerland, his meetings with corporate sponsors, NGOs, and research collaborators consumed his days, while his nights were devoted to the never-ending grant writing needed to keep the entire endeavor afloat. Never mind that she'd gone to the trouble of having her hair done, that she'd splurged on a flimsy quarter-cup bra she'd seen advertised in *Elle*, that she'd been eating nothing but grapefruit (or pineapple or hard-boiled eggs) for weeks before he came home. On those nights, Helen could lie awake for hours in the bed they were supposed to be sharing while he hunched over his desk in the downstairs office, only to lose her battle with sleep before he crept in beside her. Nothing she could do or say would convince him to take his foot off the gas. Helen had made the mistake, just once, of proposing that SAMM might align its efforts with the World Health Organization, but Robbie had dismissed her with a snort.

"You're not serious. So much red tape! Plus the WHO is way too picky about private sector contributions. We could never get anything done with the DMPA rollout if the WHO was involved! No, we won't be taking direction from bureaucrats and pencil pushers."

When are you coming home to see Mum?

Kit's letters, after she'd moved back to Montreal, were relentless; she wrote separately to Helen and Robbie every week. But just like when Kit had been in India, Helen found she didn't have much to write about. If anything, Robbie was a more reliable correspondent, or so she intimated from Kit's letters. Possibly because he had more exciting things to tell her.

Mum gets so confused when we visit. Sometimes she's happy to see us, but other times she's obviously distressed. She's talking less and less, but when she speaks, she uses the wrong words, then gets upset when we don't understand. You need to come while she still knows who you are. When will you come?

At first Helen made excuses. Her work, her duties. SAMM was opening its first clinic in Chad and finances were tight.

Please, Helen. Come. I love and miss you very much.

Helen finally made arrangements for the autumn of 1975, tacking a side trip to Montreal onto the flights she and Robbie would take to Washington, DC, where Robbie had meetings with the US FDA. Over the years, Upjohn had repeatedly applied to get its contraceptive shot approved, but the FDA kept balking. Now the agency wanted reassurances about a signal of cervical cancer, which Robbie dismissed as baloney. By then (and this was what he'd tell FDA officials), he'd been administering DMPA shots to women all over Africa; their lives, he insisted, and the lives of their families were utterly transformed for the better.

The plan was for Helen and Robbie to spend a few days in Washington, then take the train to New York to see Robbie's family and some of their old friends from NYH. Pritch had invited them to stay with him before they continued on to Montreal.

In the end, the FDA, unmoved by Robbie's data, had again declined to approve DMPA as an injectable contraceptive, and Robbie was urgently summoned to the Upjohn offices in Kalamazoo, Michigan. "You'll have to head to New York and Montreal without me," he told her, his eyes dark.

When Helen disembarked from the train at Grand Central and spotted Pritch underneath the big clock, in a short-sleeved shirt with his arms crossed, she couldn't help but notice the corded muscles of his arms and the hollow of his throat where it disappeared into his collar. Pritch would be what now—in his early forties? But his hairline was holding its position, and he still had the slim waist, broad shoulders, and sly lips that had proved so irresistible to Barnard undergrads. A trio of college girls in miniskirts pushed through the turnstiles just ahead of Helen, and she waited for Pritch to flick the switch on his old languorous charm: the upturned lips, the wolf whistle under his breath. Instead his eyes seemed to barely snag on them, his face blank until he spied Helen and broke into a fond smile.

"Who are you and what have you done with Pritch?" she chided as she stepped toward him. He looked puzzled, so she pointed at the three twenty-somethings now flouncing toward the exit. "You've mellowed."

"I have not!" He feigned offense at the suggestion, leaning in to peck her lightly on the cheek, scarcely long enough for her to smell his aftershave, before stooping to take her bag. He winked at her. "It's just that all the good ones are taken."

She rewound and replayed those words to herself many times that night. They'd stayed up late talking about her life in Geneva in the leafy shade of his front stoop, but mostly Pritch wanted to talk about Robbie: his success with SAMM, his ever-growing bibliography, his disappointment at the FDA meetings last week. Robbie, Robbie, Robbie. Pritch would never, in a million years, think that she and Robbie had drifted so far apart they were practically different continents. She sat on the hard step, close enough to Pritch that she could have brushed a casual hand against his thighs, bare and golden where his quads bulged below the hem of his shorts.

How easy this felt. How effortless. A summer evening with an old friend. In a few days, she'd be seeing her mother again, so changed, so diminished. She'd be facing the regular barrage of questions from Natalie. And she'd be back in Kit's fierce grip, those skinny arms wrapped around her again like a tree frog, pulsing with all of her unspoken words and needs. Helen couldn't bear to think of it. Not yet.

That night, in the swelter of Pritch's tiny guest room, she tried to listen for any sounds from his bedroom. Helen smirked to herself in the dark. *This* was a tangible side effect of stopping the DMPA. Not that anyone was asking. Weight loss. Better sleep. Increased sexual desire. She hadn't got around to telling her husband. What was the point? For years, Robbie had seemed more concerned with tracking possible side effects than he had with personally involving himself in any tests for efficacy.

She threw aside her sheet so the eddying air from the ceiling fan could lick over her skin where she lay. She put a finger in her mouth, sucking at its tip, then let her hand graze down her chest, past her navel, goose bumps rising to the buzz of her touch. If she closed her eyes, she could conjure Pritch's face amid the crowds in Grand Central Station, his questing look, his eyes lighting up at the sight of her.

WORLD-WEARY, 1977

Oh, the muck of this. The stabbing sadness, the disbelief, the self-pity, the guilt, the blame, the lumbering resolve like a pair of stone boots, and the clanging injustice of it all. Oh, Robbie. It wasn't supposed to be this way. This wasn't the ending they'd negotiated.

How dare he? She couldn't stop herself from thinking it. Especially when the death they'd so long been expecting and bracing for was Helen's mother. How dare *he* die, making everything even messier than it was already.

And now Kit, on top of everything, angry. "Kit, I don't want to fight."

Kit's eyes shone with hurt as her questions boiled higher and higher, aggrieved, but still, a woman's voice, not a girl's. "But why didn't you tell me?"

Helen's own voice came out a holler. "I DON'T WANT TO FIGHT."

Because fighting was what she and Robbie had done the night before he flew to Abuja. And Helen had kept that anger neatly folded in her heart to make everything tidy and so it would be easy to leave him, once and for all. Pack her last things and go.

The call came from the Nigerian embassy two nights later, asking to speak with Mrs. Robert Malloy. Such a gentle voice. So deeply sorry. Dr. Robert Malloy had been in a serious vehicular accident. Dr. Robert Malloy had succumbed to his injuries.

When the phone rang, close to midnight, Helen was standing in the kitchen, making her way through an entire box of Wernli Choco Petit Beurre, because why not? Robbie wouldn't eat them if she left them behind. It took the Nigerian man repeating himself for Helen to understand, her anger refolding itself as a blade so that she collapsed against the cabinets and slid to the floor.

And he had *just* been here. Standing with her in the Geneva office that they'd built together and shared, even after they'd partitioned everything else. Robbie had just been *here*. Alive. With her.

Arguing.

"What is this, Robbie?" She hadn't been able to keep her hand steady, the papers quivering in her grip. Ostensibly, she and Robbie had been going through files, sorting through ten years' worth of records and itemizing any last details, pending sponsorships and grants, open correspondence and RFPs: everything required for Helen to fully extract herself from her duties at SAMM before moving back to New York. And they'd been doing it like civil adults. Colleagues. How fitting, Helen had thought, that these last tangled tendrils of SAMM were all that remained of their threadbare marriage.

At first she assumed Robbie was hunting through the cabinets and files for something he thought she'd hidden from him, which was ridiculous. She'd been faithful. She had no secrets. Only when she waved that particular document in the air, DRAFT PROPOSAL stamped in bold letters on the front page, had she realized, no. He'd been looking for this.

She'd almost overlooked it, just one slim sheaf in a stack of active, completed, or canceled applications:

Return of Fertility After Cessation of Depot Medroxypro-gesterone Acetate in Northern Tanzania

Hair Loss vs Hirsutism with Long-Acting Injectable Agents for the Regulation of Fertility

Then:

Candidate Genetic Markers for Delaying Natural Meno-pause and Extending the Reproductive Window: A Case-Based Study

"Robbie," she repeated. A parchment voice. Rasping and ancient. She did not know this man, not anymore. She'd reached that grim conclusion a year ago, when she'd learned that Upjohn had no plans to pull out of South Africa, even though every other major pharmaceutical multinational was honoring the international sanctions. And that Robbie, who'd always, *always* been an unbudging defender of racial equality and human rights, had rationalized Upjohn's position, insisting that continued access to safe contraception trumped the United Nations' calls for divestment.

At the time, her disappointment in him had prickled under her skin like a fever. "Are you still tracking the women in the registry, with all the original protocols in place?" she'd demanded. "Informed consent? Awareness of alternatives?"

"Of course," he snapped, rolling his eyes, the same way he used to do with Pritch in the old days, their barbed and funny banter amid the chaos of a Saturday night ER shift at NYH.

She didn't believe him. "But they actually *want* contraception, Robbie? They're coming of their own accord?"

Robbie met her skepticism with a shake of his head, as if astounded by her shortsightedness. "*Primum non nocere*," he said, as if speaking to a child. SAMM was sparing women the harm and burden of endless pregnancies. It didn't matter who was paying for it, or why.

That's when she'd told him she wanted a divorce.

And now this.

Their last night together, she fluttered the pages of the research proposal at him, enraged. Could he possibly have already secured the funding? She'd glanced at the abstract, already registering Robert Malloy as the sole author. She wanted to flip through the whole thing on the spot, speed-read the methods, the proposed aims, and endpoints before he could snatch it from her hands.

"Candidate genes for extending years of fertility, Robbie? And who, exactly, is your 'Case-Based Study'?"

When Helen called Montreal long-distance to tell Natalie and Kit about the accident, that Robbie had *succumbed*, Kit had instantly said that she'd come out on the next flight.

All on your own? It was on the tip of Helen's tongue to question Kit's independence, her ability to make such a trip. But that was silly. Kit had been navigating the world without Helen's oversight for nearly a decade. Standing at the window of her Geneva flat and watching Kit step out of the taxi she'd taken from the airport, Helen's tears had bubbled up, blurring everything, but she could easily see that Kit was poised and unruffled. Not so much adult as ageless: an antique doll, slim and porcelain white, with a mane of hair cascading down her back and every limb, every shapely curve, in its proper proportion. Nothing about this young woman pressing the buzzer at Helen's doorstep suggested she wasn't perfectly capable of flying halfway around the globe on her own. What Helen felt, acutely, was relief. Kit would stay for as long as it took to get everything packed up in Geneva, then would fly with Helen to New York. Pritch, who had called every day since getting the news, had already told Helen they were welcome to stay with him until after the funeral. He had plenty of room at his new place.

Oh, and they'd done so well, she and Kit, almost the whole week in Geneva. No tension, no biting words. They leaned on one another the way they hadn't done since Dad died. Crying, sure, but also sharing laughter and memories: The "restaurant" they'd built for elves in the Tiergarten, complete with miniature tables and cake crumbs, and returning to find it overrun by ants. The grass snake they named Leaf Erikson living by their backyard pond in Chirk. The scruffy cocker spaniel Kit had found on the streets in Cambridge that they'd smuggled home, assuming they'd kept it a secret until Mum had come home with a poster peeled from the window of the greengrocer's, reporting the dog as missing.

"I couldn't tell if Mum was mad or sorry or relieved—"

"Or happy," Helen broke in. "Or bored, or hungry. You could never tell with Mum!" Kit's smile was faint, no doubt thinking that however inscrutable their mother had been in the past, she was even more unreachable now.

Helen changed the topic. "But you must have your own dog now, finally, don't you? In Montreal?"

Kit shook her head. "Maybe next year, when I get back from India. Did I tell you Hari is getting married?"

It was funny and wonderful but also a little unsettling to think of all the things Kit remembered about Helen that Helen herself had forgotten or never knew. It didn't work as well the other way around. Most of the memories Helen offered up for

Kit were things Kit seemed to already know, and the stuff she didn't? Now didn't seem the time. Helen did not, for instance, tell Kit that she and Robbie had almost completed divorce proceedings at the time of his death. She didn't say that she knew Kit had written to Robbie with questions about DMPA and whether he thought the injectable was better than daily pills. Robbie had treated Kit's letter as if her questions themselves were hypothesis-generating, something to be held up and inspected from all angles, and not, as Helen saw it, Kit effectively broadcasting that she'd become sexually active, or was considering it. Maybe that's when Robbie got thinking about his case-based study. Kit, her interminable *juvenescence* behind her. Fully grown and capable of consent.

And that, very definitely, was the last thing Helen would be sharing. That her own husband had written a grant proposal for a case-based study describing a young woman who aged one year for every four: *candidate genes for extending years of fertility*.

With nothing else she felt she could offer up, Helen decided to tell Kit about Will's letters.

It had been nearly a decade, for Pete's sake, since the letters had stopped. Little Hezekiah William Katzen was a grown man by now, in his early twenties. How could Kit possibly still care? On top of everything else Helen was going through, she did not need Kit's wounded incredulity.

But tears, livid ones, were streaming down Kit's face. "But why, *why* didn't you tell me?"

"Kit, think about it. It could never have worked. We were living halfway around the world and you were still far too young for anything serious."

"Too *young*?" Kit scoffed, then repeated the words in a shout, fury a gurgle in her throat. "We both know how ridiculous that sounds, Helen! And since when was it up to you who I have in my life, who matters to me, and why?"

"Of course it's not up to me." Helen could hear how her voice sounded. Dry as tinder. She tried to let some warmth back in. "I was only doing what I knew was in your best interest. You weren't ready, you just weren't."

Maybe Helen should have told Pritch everything, right away. About why things had ended between her and Robbie in the first place, and about Kit, her secret. Pritch was no longer the man her best instincts had warned her to steer clear of in the past. He was more mature now, more responsible, less under the sway of his base instincts. He had picked them up at JFK airport, driving a sleek sedan, midnight blue, not the Shelby Cobra he'd been zipping around in when she'd last visited. He'd moved uptown to a spacious brownstone on a staid street that was quiet after 10:00 p.m., so as to be closer to his aging mother. He'd taken up golf. Not once in the weeks they stayed in his beautiful home did he allude to anyone he was dating or bedding.

"You can stay as long as you like," he'd said when he greeted them at Arrivals, wrapping Helen in his arms.

"Kit," he'd said, pulling away from Helen and extending his hand to her sister, then changing his mind and gathering her into an awkward hug.

The whole transatlantic flight, Kit had curled her back to Helen, answering any questions in monosyllables. Now, looking at Helen over Pritch's embrace, Kit's eyes were so salt-puffed and red-rimmed that the color of her irises was piercing, an almost chemical green.

This was the reward she would get for her lifelong self-lessness. Widowed at forty-three, Helen had a mother needing round-the-clock care and an eccentric aunt who was bearing the brunt of that now but couldn't for much longer. That meant that sometime soon, Helen would be the sole guardian for a sister who clearly hated her guts and barely looked old enough to hold a job.

But maybe that was just Helen's perception: Kit as the perpetual sulky child, always needing to be babied. Everyone else meeting Kit for the first time—Pritch, Robbie's sister Bernadette, Helen's old friend Saundra from the hospital—had no trouble making the mental leap that put the two sisters closer in age. Where Helen saw petulance, blame, and all the old friction that had kept her and Kit like two magnets, propelling each other apart, everyone else saw a young woman, world-weary, matured by grief. *So striking and self-assured*, they murmured to Helen. *Such a comfort, I'm sure.*

Helen got hired almost right away as a temp at Mount Sinai, then started looking for an apartment. Pritch didn't hurry them along or ask Kit when she was returning to Canada or give Helen even the slightest impression that they were underfoot or cramping his style, even when his own work kept him coming and going at odd hours. He was considerate, always ready to listen. He'd reach out and fold Helen in his strong arms when she cried, always sensing she needed physical touch.

Most days, nursing again after all those years felt useful and distracting. But on a night when her shift began with an Upper East Side blue blood who'd slashed her own wrists and whom they managed to stabilize, followed by a child struck by a car whom they couldn't save, she told her supervisor she felt fluish and went home barely two hours into her shift. That night, returning to Pritch's upscale brownstone felt like coming home. She kicked off her pinching shoes and, still wearing her coat, sank into a soft chair. She closed her eyes.

And then she heard it: an unmistakable rhythmic creak, a low laugh, and then a murmured voice—female. Helen's eyes fluttered open, registering the bottle of wine on the table, the two glasses pinked by dregs. She cocked her head, straining to listen. It took a long moment for the sounds to sink in, and then she was drawn to them, pulled as if by rope to the door of Pritch's bedroom, slightly ajar. She stood in her nylons in the corridor, a chill creeping up her spine despite her winter coat. Pritch's words on the other side of the door, deep and rumbled, were familiar to her. She'd heard them in her imagination and in her fingertips, countless times, starting on that hot summer night when she'd slept in his guest room and wondered what he'd do if she tiptoed down the hall to his bed. She blanched.

The creaking quickened and she heard a shuddering grunt akin to the carnal chuckle she recalled, almost viscerally, from Pritch's teasing in the emergency room at NYH. She almost expected to hear Robbie's tart retort. But what she heard was another voice, also familiar. Not a girl's voice. A woman's. And the chill she'd felt a moment ago was replaced by a prickling heat that was part shock, part rage, part shame.

PART IV

Kit

Robert Ian Malloy, MD
April 10, 1935 – June 26, 1977

Robert "Robbie" Malloy, 42, passed away last month in a tragic road accident in Kaduna, Nigeria. Robbie will be remembered for his committed service in the emergency rooms of Boston and Manhattan, and for championing the rights of mothers and babies both at home and abroad. Memorial contributions may be made to the Stopping Avoidable Maternal Mortality foundation.

1977: DELHI, INDIA

Her fellow passengers on the long flight from London carried her in a tide of noise through the glass doors from customs, calling out for loved ones, porters, and drivers. She'd almost forgotten this, all of it, but it came flooding back: the fuzzy mix of fatigue, grief, and shock that greeted her the first time she'd arrived in India, more than thirty years ago, her eyes raw from crying. The kerosene stink of the hot tarmac, the kindly pilot all the way from North Bay, Ontario, who spoke with a stammer, the staircase being wheeled to the side of the plane—how desperately she wanted to scramble back up the steps, into the plane, and back to Helen and Mum in England. Kit let her eyes rove over the throngs of indefatigable touts, families, and taxi wallas and felt the years roll over her like a wheel.

What she needed was for someone to tell her that one day, she'd be fine. That the hurt would be less. That heartbreak and loss are muscles that get stronger the more you train them. Put in the effort, push through the pain, and that becomes its own remedy, and reward. How could she do this otherwise? Continue on? Loving people and losing them, over and over and over.

"Kit! Over here!"

Dr. Gupta—Ayaan—was grinning from ear to ear. Seeing him again after all this time summoned the ghost of her father like a punch to the stomach. Papa and Ayaan, razzing each other over chessboards and croquet sets on the back lawn at the consulate or striding side by side in the Lodhi Gardens, deep in conversation, each with his hands clasped behind his back. Fresh tears bubbled from her eyes and she forded the human stream until she could barrel into him, just as she had on the lurching deck of the SS *Montcalm*. With her ear pressed to his warm chest, the din was muffled and time cartwheeled in her mind once more. Now it was 1950, not 1977, and this was Ayaan's goodbye, not hello, because Kit and her father were leaving India after five years, to start over, as a family, in America.

She pulled back to look at him. He was, as always, wearing a natty jacket, a shirt, and trousers rather than the more traditional kurta or lungi better suited to the humid morning. And he was as lean and lanky as he'd been at Papa's funeral, his teeth straining out of his smile. His hair, still lush and glossy, glinted with streaks of silver.

Hari, she realized, was at his father's side. Clean-shaven but with the same round face as Ayaan, the big, oval glasses, and the same thick hair swept obliquely over his scalp, Hari had completed his graduate degree in mathematics after she'd left England for Montreal; now he was mere days from marrying the woman he loved.

"We were so very sorry to hear of Robbie's death," Hari said, and his eyes shone.

Grief soared up in her again like a bushfire, devouring. This was Robbie, of course, the shock of his accident still raw. This was Mum, unrecognizable and unresponsive in her bed, being fed and drained by tubes. This was Helen, what she'd done: destroying her mail, making Kit think Will had been ignoring all the silly, sad, boastful, don't-worry-about-me letters she'd sent him for months from South Africa. She had spent hours on the streets of Manhattan after Helen left for her shift, ringing buzzers, badgering doormen, and scanning the names on building directories in the four-block radius of where she thought Will had lived, because someone, surely, would know where the Katzens had gone. And then there was the stupid, stupid thing she'd done with Pritch, trying so desperately to feel something other than misery. Other than abject failure.

Hari was looking more and more sorrowful. *Get hold*, she told herself, trying to stop her juddering chin.

She was aware, abruptly, of how bedraggled she must look and edged away from the Guptas. She probably smelled like a hippie! She'd meant to freshen up in the tiny bathroom but had woken up with a jolt when the plane touched down. Now her pants were limp and baggy, her blouse sticky where the straps of her pack sawed into her armpits, and her hair was hanging over her shoulders in two untidy hanks. She'd been hoping to convey something of a Raquel Welch when she met Hari's fiancée for the first time. She'd ended up more like a damp and frowsy Anne of Green Gables.

Beside Hari was the most beautiful woman Kit had ever laid eyes on. She wore a blue-and-silver kameez over a pair of bell-bottom jeans and platform shoes. She looked nearly as tall as Hari, especially with her hair piled in a loose coil on her head. Her eyes were fringed by a set of lashes so long that on anyone else, they'd have looked artificial.

"Udita, I'm pleased to introduce you to my oldest friend in the world. This is Katherine—Kit—McKinley." Hari paused and took a deep breath, his eyes aglow. "Kit, this is Udita Chowdhury."

Udita. You'd have thought, given how tight the weave of her life and Udita's would become, there'd be something suitably ceremonious heralding this moment—flashing lights, the blare of a trumpet, all eyes turning to watch. Instead, Kit just shimmied out from under her backpack so it dragged on her sleeve and she had to yank her blouse back over her bra strap while her bag toppled sideways with a thud. .

She'd heard so much about Udita. Twenty-one years old, Udita was still finishing her undergraduate studies at Oxford; Hari, having completed his doctorate, feared he was too old for her, or too subcontinental. She'd grown up in London, where her father taught Asian history at Imperial College but had an extended family in India, where the Chowdhury name was big in construction. Hari's lineage was more suspect: a widowed doctor for a father who'd never remarried and had chosen to hang up his shingle in an underserved part of Delhi rather than stay in Britain after the war. No aunties and uncles. And Hari's only living grandparent was unseemly in a manner Hari sensed the Chowdhurys felt they'd never satisfactorily fleshed out. Udita, by contrast, had an entire dynasty behind her, all of these fawning relations preparing to descend on Ayaan's Delhi home for the wedding. Kit had read about every stage of Hari's courtship in his letters—his fretful angst before he'd gotten the blessing of her family, the giddy joy when she'd said yes—all of it a welcome departure from his usual ramblings about applied math and fuzzy logic.

Udita grabbed Kit's hands, then leaned forward, smelling of jasmine. "You must be exhausted. We'll get you straight to a bath and a rest, unless you're hungry? A bath and lunch maybe? A stiff drink? Bath, lunch, drink, bed?" She flashed a smile. "You decide."

Kit couldn't help but worry about her stale breath and general economy-class miasma, worsening by the minute. Udita had mentioned bathing. Three times. But Udita was still holding her by both hands, as if she intended to waltz her to the luggage carousel. "I've wanted to meet you for so long, Kit. Can I call you Kit? Finally! Hari has told me so much about you."

Kit caught Ayaan's eye behind her and sensed, more than saw, an infinitesimal shake of his head. So no. Hari had not told her everything.

The final preparations for the wedding were in full swing. An army of workmen trooped in and out of Ayaan's home, delivering tables and chairs and erecting a dais and tents. "We've only invited a hundred and fifty, but I'm estimating another two dozen, on my side, might show up if they find out the date," Udita told Kit. They were hiding—ineffectually—behind a peepul tree on the back lawn to smoke a cigarette; Mr. and Mrs. Chowdhury had arrived from London the day before. "On Hari's side, it's mostly school friends. Hari hasn't seen his baba—Ayaan's father, Tarun—in years. Did you know he's become a sadhu?"

This was news to Kit. A sadhu was a Hindu holy man, an ascetic who forsook all of his worldly possessions in order to devote himself to the gods, wandering the length and breadth of India in tattered robes. She knew a thing or two about the need for constant relocation, but Kit couldn't remember Tarun being particularly religious. She didn't say this to Udita. In fact, Kit found she kept tripping over her tongue every time she opened her mouth to speak to Hari's bride-to-be. Udita was doing her best to make Kit laugh, swearing like a sailor when Ayaan was out of earshot, the words sounding posh in her upper-crust British accent. Infectious energy seemed to spiral outward from some secret source at her core. She was lightning-quick with pithy comebacks, but goofy and self-deprecating, too, her heart pulsing neon on her sleeve. The whole combination was deeply endearing in someone so physically striking. Kit desperately wanted Udita to like her.

Udita expelled two chic columns of smoke through her nose and bugged out her eyes. "Can you imagine if Tarun shows up for the wedding all dreadlocked and pongy, covered in ash?" She hitched a perfect eyebrow at Kit, amused. "My friends from St. Anne's will choke on their fucking chai."

Hari didn't know what to do with himself. He lurked like Banquo's ghost—saying very little, but crucial to the plot. Kit couldn't help but notice the tenderness between Hari and Udita, as if they were drawing some kind of charge from each other with every quick touch, necessitating constant refills. Last night, Kit was sure of it, she'd heard the swish of Udita's bare feet padding down the hall to Hari's room. She hadn't seen or sensed this kind of connection between two people in ages, certainly not between Helen and Robbie, and it hit her like a blow: Udita and Hari reminded her of her mother and father, tending a fierce and invisible bond the way you would the coals of a fire.

Inevitably Hari found them in the garden. His bride-to-be flashed him a devilish look as she took a last drag on her cigarette, ground it out with the toe of her sandal, then kissed him brashly on the lips.

"I think my father might flee to the hills," Hari said. "Rescue him, won't you, Kit?"

She found Ayaan fielding a barrage of questions from Mrs. Chowdhury about his late wife, about Tarun, about Kit herself. Hari had already told the Chowdhurys that Kit's "old-fashioned accent" was the result of her international childhood, and that he'd met her as a baby in the fifties, when her family had been briefly posted to India. He didn't specify who'd been the baby. Helen used to say they needed handbooks in their family, updated yearly, to keep up with all their lies and omissions. Hearing Hari and Ayaan covering for her made Kit feel deeply weary—another layer of weariness, plastered over the old.

"Shall we take a walk to the Bara Gumbad?" Kit suggested to Ayaan, and he went to grab his hat.

In the gardens, a brawny man in short-shorts with white Adidas socks pulled up to his knees was doing jump squats and push-ups in the shade of a crooked rosewood, reminding Kit, for the millionth time, of her father.

Ayaan laid a hand on her arm. "Slow down, Tiny Typhoon. I'm in no rush to get back."

He himself had slowed down in general. He'd turned sixty-one that year and she could see it in his stiff gait and the grimace he made as he lowered himself to a bench to tie his shoes. She couldn't bear to think of Ayaan getting old. "Don't look at me like that," he chided. "I tweaked my back playing tennis last week, but I'm otherwise magnificent."

They walked for a while in silence before he said gently, "How is your mother?"

Kit worked to swallow the sudden lump in her throat. The latest series of strokes had left Mum more or less paralyzed and it had been years since she'd spoken. If any of her genius remained, it was locked away for good. Kit would sit for hours beside Mum's bed, willing her to blink her eyes open: her mother's eyes had always been able to see the one thing nobody else had thought to look for. But Mum didn't know Kit anymore. She didn't know Natalie, and she'd long ago stopped asking about Helen.

"Go to the wedding, Kit," Natalie had insisted after Kit got home from New York. "There's nothing you can do by staying."

Before flying to Delhi, on the suggestion of a nurse, Kit had brought in a cassette tape she'd bought from Cheap Thrills on Bishop and played it for Mum: Maria Callas singing Bellini's "Casta Diva," which had never failed to leave Max honking into his hankie. Mum didn't open her eyes, not once, but her lips formed an almost smile, and when Kit leaned close, she thought she could hear her humming.

Now tears were rolling down Kit's face again, although she hadn't managed to say any of this aloud. Ayaan stopped and cradled her face with one hand while he dabbed at her tears with the other.

"I know, I know." He nodded. "Too many goodbyes."

They started walking again and silence lapped between them until Ayaan halted a second time, tapping at his many pockets with both hands so that she could almost feel the roll of the ship beneath her feet. Finally, he pulled out a wristwatch in rose gold with psychedelic sunburst dials and held it to his ear before passing it to her, smiling. "My latest project," he said, "a VC chronograph."

She admired it for a moment, then hooked her thumb under the scarf at her throat and pulled out the necklace watch. His eyes bulged, delighted, then he said, "How is Helen holding up?"

Kit's smile dropped. Helen. It was no effort, none at all, to call to mind her face that night in New York, mottled with anger, the set of her jaw, her eyes as frozen as Kit had ever seen them. How was she to know Helen had feelings for Pritch? She was supposed to be grieving Robbie.

"She's fine," Kit said flatly. Ayaan twitched a look her way. "Well, as fine as possible. She's working a lot of shifts. Trying to keep busy."

"And what about you. Anyone special?"

Udita had asked her the same thing in the back garden, mugging at Kit when she hesitated. Kit hadn't been able to shake her frustration at not finding Will in New York, or to stop wondering how he looked now, what kind of man he'd become.

"Ooooh, spit it out," Udita had prodded.

"It's nothing, no one. We went our separate ways, ages ago. No one thought we were a good match, anyhow."

"Pffft." Udita rolled her eyes. "Who cares." She wrapped an arm around her slim waist so she could rest her elbow on the back of her hand, hovering her cigarette near her lips. "Look at me and Hari. My parents were dead set against him—they wanted me to marry the drip they'd picked out for me, but I put my foot down."

Kit thought of Hari's letters, how nervous he'd been about asking the Chowdhurys for Udita's hand and his jubilation when she'd said yes, not realizing she'd already been pleading their case on his behalf.

"And nothing in the works now?" Udita winked. Kit thought of the boys—men— she'd been eyeing shyly in Montreal. The trombone player who waited tables at the new Bistro à JoJo on Saint-Denis. The young doctor who worked at her mother's nursing home, so soft-spoken and gentle, the taut skin above the ledge of his collarbone . . .

These kinds of thoughts were exactly how she ended up letting herself be deflowered by Pritch. Invited it, even. His hungry hands, his hot snuffles. The ruddy folds of skin like loose hide sagging at his stubbled throat. She felt awash in the same queasy mix of humiliation and disappointment she'd felt when he slumped back down against her and she'd heard the creak of Helen's step in the hall.

Ayaan was still waiting for her answer. He'd no doubt misconstrue the blush reddening her cheeks. A dog strained past them on a leash, pulling a man in a Princeton sweatshirt and a flowing dhoti. The man dipped his head in greeting, but his brisk gaze snapped from her to Ayaan and back again. In jeans and a T-shirt, with her red, homesick eyes and her hair pulled back in a ponytail, she could have been a foreign exchange student walking with her high school principal. She looked up to Ayaan like an uncle, but they'd realized long ago they were born just a few years apart.

She decided to change the topic. "Would it be so bad, do you think, to just be myself now? No secrets. Everyone's always so worried about me—you, Hari, Natalie, Helen. But the world is different now than it was for Tarun, I think. More tolerant. Maybe it's time to just stop hiding and tell the truth."

One of Ayaan's eyebrows popped up to peer at her over his glasses. "You'll tell people you were born in 1916?"

"No. But from now on, I'll just be me. No more lies, no more moving around. I've seen what it does to the people trying to protect me."

She couldn't read his expression. "I'm not going to put an ad on TV or anything," she said. "And I haven't completely made up my mind. But I'm thinking about it." She twisted her head skyward to the admonishing trees, the cheeping objections of birds.

"How is Tarun, anyhow?" she asked before he could speak. "Is he really coming to the wedding?"

Ayaan plucked at a thread on his sleeve. "I don't know."

"How he is? Or whether he'll come?"

"Both." He poked his glasses back up the bridge of his nose. "I don't know where he is, and I have no way of knowing whether he even got the invitation."

"Udita thinks Tarun is a sadhu."

Ayaan chuckled. "We had to come up with something peculiar enough that the Chowdhurys wouldn't want him at the wedding, but commendable enough to be redeeming if he turned up. He used to keep in better touch, sending us postcards from his travels. And he came back to see Hari the last time he was home, but that's what? Four years ago now. And he was much changed. Not outwardly, I have to say. He still looked fit, with a full head of hair, although he'd let his beard grow long. But he seemed slower and sadder. His vision had really declined, his teeth were mostly gone, and every step looked like it was against his best interests, although he wouldn't let me check him over. If you ask me, he should have learned to slow down years ago."

Then he frowned. "What's this I hear about you going to an ashram after the wedding? Not that place in Pune."

"No, the Sri Aurobindo Ashram in Pondicherry. It was Natalie's idea. She wants me to find a little peace and enlightenment." She could sense Ayaan's skepticism and offered a smile. "Maybe I can learn to slow down."

They walked for a long minute in silence, and she was careful to match her step to his. Then Ayaan said, "I haven't had a note in over a year now, actually. From my father. I'd love for him to show up at the wedding just to know he's okay."

"How could you invite him if you don't know where he is?"

Ayaan had his hands clasped behind his back. "Poste restante," he said. "I've done this for years. I write my letter, then Xerox twenty-two copies so I have one to send to each of the GPOs—the general post offices—in India."

He saw her confusion. "You've never used poste restante? I suppose you always had a home address during your travels. Most countries have it in some form, and it's very handy if you're traveling from place to place. You can have mail sent to the GPO and they'll hold it for you for months. Funnily enough, that's how Tarun stayed in touch with me when I was traveling across Canada, before I met you on the boat to England. I have a very clear memory of handing over my British Indian passport at the post office in a place called Saskatoon. Imagine my delight when the nice woman behind the counter handed me a package containing a letter from my mother, two dozen packs of Parle Kismi Toffee, and a fresh supply of candied ginger for the Atlantic crossing."

"So you have no way of knowing if Tarun even got your letter."

Ayaan tried to purse his lips, but she could hear resignation leaking out.

"If he got it, he'll find a way to come. And not just to see Hari and his bride, or me, for that matter." Ayaan shot her a look. "He'll come to see you."

A Commemoration
in Honor of
Lillian Doris McKinley
January 16, 1897 – July 1, 1978

The American Society for Clinical Genetics invites geneticists and hobbyists to attend a symposium of science and remembrance celebrating the life of Lillian Doris McKinley, PhD, who died after a long illness. Her elucidation of the suppression and expression of genetic information, as well as her lifelong commitment to the advancement of women in science, will be honored with a special seminar featuring some of the most dazzling minds of the era.

1:00 PM, July 15, 1978, St. Paul's Chapel, Morningside Heights, New York, NY.

1978: NEW YORK, NY

Everyone was wearing dull suits and somber dresses with the exception of Aunt Natalie, who was resplendent, as always. She'd wound the gold and turquoise scarf Kit had brought her from India into a turban and matched it with a shimmering gold jacket and a pair of satiny, colored trousers. There was enough fabric for a full skirt in each pant leg; they billowed wide before cinching tightly at the ankle.

"They're parachute pants," she told Kit. "Stick close. If the speeches get too boring, we can jump."

Kit was still at the ashram when one of the other devotees came to tell her she had a guest. When she'd last seen Ayaan after the wedding, he'd been glowing, not only from seeing his son so happy and all the Chowdhurys out of his house at last, but because Tarun had made it, after all.

When Ayaan materialized in Pondicherry, his face so gloomy and grave, she knew instantly what he'd come to tell her.

He nodded. "Peacefully, in her sleep. Natalie called. She could have sent a Telex to the ashram, but she wanted you to hear it from me."

Ayaan had insisted on accompanying Kit to New York, saying it would give him the chance to visit Hari and Udita in Boston. They'd rented a house in Harvard Square, within walking distance of campus, but they would take the train down to New York to come to the commemoration.

"A *commemoration in honor*?" Kit had repeated the phrase back to Natalie when she got through on a long-distance line from Delhi.

"I was surprised, too, believe me. We had her cremated, no service, according to her wishes. But this is being organized by someone at Columbia."

Here they were, then, commemorating. Kit was doing everything in her power to hold herself together. St. Paul's was a cavernous chapel built of yellow and rust-red bricks that arched up the walls and over the domed roof like a gigantic pizza oven. Light streaming through the tall panels of stained glass in red, green, and blue mottled the faces of the guests to make them look alternately sunburned or sickly.

Helen was struggling with it all, too. She was wearing a navy blue two-piece that looked too hot for the July heat and a matching pillbox hat that could have been teleported from the fifties. Kit and Helen hugged, woodenly at first, but their contact exerted some kind of chemical effect, turning them both mushier and stickier. Kit couldn't quite let go. "I wasn't sure you'd come," Helen mumbled. "God, you're skinny. Don't they feed you at an ashram?"

When they finally pulled apart, Helen must have caught Kit's zigzagging look to the left and right, because she said, in a flat voice, "You maybe heard, Pritch moved to San Francisco in the spring."

Kit reintroduced Helen to Ayaan Gupta, whom she hadn't seen since Papa's funeral, then to Hari and Udita. Helen did a double take at Udita—everyone did—gaping at her movie-star looks a beat too long. Udita didn't notice, or pretended not to, plunging into some tactful condolences before transitioning into polite questions about Helen's work at the hospital, the thrills of living in Manhattan, and her favorite Broadway shows. Natalie, who'd arrived the day before, was appraising the scene contentedly, her gaze bouncing from Helen to Udita to Hari, no doubt on the verge of opening her own interrogation of Hari, whom she'd never met and used to tease Kit about mercilessly. But she caught Kit's eye and knew instantly what Kit wanted to ask.

"She never woke again, not once," Natalie said firmly.

Kit let her aunt fold her in her ropey arms, thinking that for all her bedside waiting, Mum had departed before any of them fully realized she was gone, without saying farewell. She'd left as if slipping out the door of a crowded room.

"She's at peace now," Natalie murmured. "Wherever that is. I hope your father got the place kitted out with a Bunsen burner and a fume hood before she arrived, otherwise there'll be hell to pay."

Kit nestled into Natalie's embrace and sensed Helen sidling closer, hoping to horn in on the circle of sympathy. Natalie lifted an arm to draw her in, her sixth sense as sharp as ever. "You're good, you two, right?"

Udita looked enthralled by this emotional reunion of people she didn't know and was clearly sizing up Helen. Hari, meanwhile, had a stiff set to his jaw, instinctively piecing together the half-truths he'd need in order to answer Udita's questions later. This had to stop. Kit didn't want to keep this from Udita or anyone else for that matter. Udita and Kit had kept in touch since the wedding, and next year, when Kit headed to Boston, where she'd been accepted at the Berklee College of Music, she hoped she and Udita could be friends, proper friends, without secrets. She'd had plenty of time to think this through at the ashram and she'd made up her mind. No more hiding. No new birth certificates. No more annual updates for the handbook of lies. This was the reason Kit had decided she'd go up to the microphone with Helen today, here, to say a few words. She wasn't planning to stage some dramatic, showstopping reveal and trot out the long story of her life. She wasn't even going to delve into the specifics. Kit merely wanted to say, publicly, that she was born different, invisibly so. And that Mum, always adamant that the bounds of normal were endlessly elastic, had worked tirelessly her whole life to figure out why.

An electronic squeal snapped their attention to the small stage, where a leggy man in too-short trousers was struggling to raise the microphone, throttling the device as if wrestling with a cobra. A second man hurried over to help but tripped on the cord.

"Some of the most dazzling minds of the era," Natalie murmured. She caught Kit's eye and winked.

A sharp intake of breath made them all turn to Udita.

"That's Barbara McClintock!" she said, pointing at the small crowd gathered near the stage. From the look on her face, it might have been Barbra Streisand. "And that's George Wells Beadle!" Helen's mystification must have been the most encouraging because Udita turned to her, gushing. "*You* know, Beadle won the 1958 Nobel Prize with Lederberg and Tatum for their work confirming the link between genes, heredity, and enzyme structure in *Zea mays*. Beadle knew your mother? Aagh!" Her eyes swerved back to the stage and her hand slapped her breast. "I bet you that woman with the big teeth is Ruth Sager. I'm taking one of Sagar's classes for my master's."

Helen was eyeing Udita up and down again, looking affronted. As if it wasn't enough that Udita should have runway-model looks, she'd also been gifted a brain. Udita gave another titter of disbelief. "That's James Watson, look! In the green tweed."

"The Cricket," Helen murmured. Udita ignored her, craning her neck.

Natalie had turned to Ayaan and was saying she planned to take a trip, destination unknown, when Mum's affairs were settled; she'd always meant to travel after she retired. The idea of Natalie, at her age, donning a backpack and thumbing her way around Europe made Kit smile, although she was certainly spry enough. Then she was struck by the memory of Aunt Natalie arriving with her trunk and hatboxes at their creaky old East Side apartment after Helen got married, her cheerful smile pinned in place. It was because of Kit that Natalie never went traveling after retirement, Kit and Mum. Natalie had stayed to look after them. Kit looked from Natalie to Ayaan and from Helen to Hari and felt her throat grow tight. This was the way time played its tricks, yoking two totally separate moments so close together you could forget everything you'd lost in its folds.

"Excuse me. Kit?"

Something about this voice. Turning around felt like trying to tighten a rusty screw. And she felt too thin-skinned, too close to implosion as it was. The hair prickled on the nape of her neck.

The man standing behind her was tall and slim, dressed in the requisite dark suit, but of a better cut and hue than those of the bearded, middle-aged men clumped throughout the chapel like microbial cultures. He was younger, too, broad-shouldered and clean-shaven, with skin a rosy gold, as if he spent time outdoors, not stooped over agar plates and graduated cylinders. His sandy-brown hair reached his collar, with a soft Luke Skywalker curl behind his ears and over his forehead. He brushed it from his eyes with a nervous swish. He was staring at her much the same way Helen had gaped earlier at Udita, as if under the sway of a powerful potion, his big, wide mouth fighting off a smile. She knew him instantly.

"Will?"

His lips lost their battle, splitting into a grin, his eyes wide. "It *is* you. I can't, I mean, I . . ." He broke off, his mouth still moving, his entire face struggling toward a different shape. "Your mom. I am so, so sorry. We saw the announcement in the paper and . . ."

Kit would cry now, she could feel it swamping her. How could she stop it? *Will Katzen. Will!*

"I, I wouldn't have recognized you," she lied. The floppy hair, the wriggling lips. "I looked for you, last year. I never got . . ."

She broke off, darting a glance at Helen. She was deep in conversation with the man they'd seen earlier at the microphone, nodding her head and pointing to the side of the stage. Kit had told Helen on the phone last night that she wanted to go up with her, to say a few words when the time came. That she was ready for this. Helen, she could tell from her silence on the line, wasn't convinced.

We saw the announcement, he'd said. Kit's gaze did a quick scribble around Will, but he looked to be alone. She wanted to ask him a million things, but it was as if she'd forgotten their language. She of all people.

"You came . . . to pay your respects to my mum?" she said, then grimaced. This was so far down the ladder of things she wanted to say, it was beneath the earth's crust. He pawed at the air between them briefly as if he was about to reach for her, then thought better of it.

"No." He smiled, more tenderly now. "I came looking for you."

Onstage, the man pecked his head toward the microphone, offering a hello that boomed, making everyone jump. "If you can take your seats, everyone, I'd like to introduce . . ."

Kit saw that Udita had spied her and Will, goofy-faced and bumbling their words. Any minute now, she would be swooping over to them like a bee to nectar. Kit leaned close to Will and caught the faintest smell of him. Pine and sunshine and salt. "Afterwards, okay? I'll find you."

It was all she could do to keep herself still and not swivel her head to see where Will had found a seat. The lights dimmed and scientists started trooping onstage, one after the other, raking their fingers through their thinning hair, then professing their gratitude, admiration, and respect for the late Dr. Lillian McKinley, whose insights had paved the way for their own. This, Kit quickly saw, was just a launching pad for detailed descriptions of what their own work entailed. This commemoration was as much a celebration of scientific progress as of her mother. Mum would have loved it.

Assembled in the front row, off to one side, a trio of younger men and a woman were looking alternately perplexed, then bored, then busy. Three of them were taking notes while one man was snapping pictures. Their hair and dress, even their demeanor, suggested they weren't just from a different decade, but a different species altogether. "Reporters," she heard Udita hissing gleefully to Hari. "I was chatting up the woman in the loo. She writes for *Scientific American*! You never told me Kit's mum was such a trailblazer!"

Udita, who was paying much more attention to the science-speak than Kit, must have sensed her restlessness. "You okay?" she whispered, ducking her head to catch Kit's eye. "Who was that cute boy?"

"An old friend. I didn't expect to see him here, is all."

Udita caught the snag in her voice, because her smooth brow furrowed and she linked her arm through Kit's.

"Your mum sounds like an amazing woman," Udita said, still whispering. "All these famous people!"

Kit could judge their star wattage by how long Udita held her breath while they spoke and how hard she clapped when they were done. "Beware the woman scientist so confident of her discoveries she doesn't feel the need to publish them," said the woman Udita had recognized as Barbara McClintock, and the crowd chuckled appreciatively—Udita loudest of all.

Kit's thoughts kept zinging back to Will. The back of her head felt scalded at the thought of him watching her. Everything she planned to say when she went up to the microphone now seemed that much more important and loaded.

She missed the name of the next man, dressed in a chestnut-brown suit and braying about his technique for coaxing bacteria to produce foreign proteins, although she noticed Udita sloping forward, a rapt expression on her face.

"It's the culmination of so much of what Dr. McKinley set in motion so many decades ago," the man was saying. "The ability to synthesize genetically modified bacteria."

Kit snapped to attention. *Genetically modified?*

"Imagine," the man boomed, "restriction-enzyme scissors that can snip out the DNA segment of interest to amplify a desirable trait or to suppress something unwanted. The possibilities are endless. Our company was founded on the belief that the future of medicine and pharmacotherapy lies in genetic engineering."

Kit turned these phrases over in her head. This was the stuff of science fiction, wasn't it? And yet a company, a private enterprise, was actively working on this. Synthesized insulin, the man was saying. Commercial markets. Artificial growth hormones. Patent pending. Improving the defects of man.

It was harder now to take the temperature of the room: no one prior to this company man had drifted into talk of pharmaceutical blockbusters. Udita was frowning slightly, but she had the focused intensity of someone who wouldn't notice if her own shoes were stolen from her feet.

Gripped in Kit's hand were her notes for what she wanted to say when she went onstage with Helen.

a daughter born different from other children . . .

a conviction that mutations were not abnormalities but possibilities . . .

a mother whose motives were not to transform her daughter, but to know her . . .

The words swam on the page.

Kit couldn't do this, she realized. Not here. She couldn't face all these eager men and women of science, the journalists with their furious notes and photos, the executives hunting for base pairs with commercial potential. She couldn't stand up and say, *I am Lillian McKinley's unpublished data—her mutant, never*

decoded. Mum in her lifetime had never gotten close to understanding why Kit was the way she was, or if she had, dementia
had stripped her of the chance to explain it to anyone else. But
that wasn't the case for all these eminent minds, waiting expectantly for the family of Dr. McKinley to step up and say some
final words. Mum wouldn't want Kit to do this, not after the
lengths she'd gone to keep her hidden, to keep her safe—the
realization hit Kit like a slap. Her thoughts jolted to the journalists and their hovering pencils. Papa wouldn't want it either.

Kit eased her arm out of Udita's and twisted the other way,
toward Helen, who turned and met her gaze. The look in Hel-
en's eyes, soft and sorry, told Kit that she had already reached
the same conclusion, had likely had to stop herself from saying
something last night over the phone. Having already spent so
much of her life shielding Kit from scrutiny, Helen now put her
hand over Kit's, lacing her fingers through like a claw.

Kit felt a first tear, tears she'd been fighting all day, seep
from the corner of her eye. What was she thinking, saying she'd
find Will afterward? In what world, in what universe, could she
and Will make sense?

She wiped at the tear with a knuckle.

"Oh, hey." Udita was dipping her head again to look up at
Kit, then delving into her bag for a Kleenex pack. "Oh, sweetie,
it's okay."

Farther down the row, Ayaan whispered something to Natalie
that made her tip her gleaming turban back, her laugh swooping
through the nave so the stodgy scientists turned their heads.

But they weren't drawn by Natalie's laugh, Kit realized.
They were looking expectantly at their little group. Then Helen
was rising from her chair in her ill-fitting suit, clutching her

own notes. She shone another look at Kit, blinked, and nodded, the lump in her throat visible as she started to edge past the other chairs toward the aisle. A wave of feeling rose up in Kit. Anger, frustration, and grief, flapping their frantic wings.

Kit turned back to Udita and spoke under her breath. "I need to get out of here. Now."

Carrie Buck
July 3, 1906 – January 28, 1983

Carrie Elizabeth Buck went home to be with the Lord on the 28th day of January, age 76. Carrie, who loved crosswords and reading the newspaper, made history as the plaintiff in the 1927 case of *Buck v. Bell* in which the US Supreme Court upheld the constitutionality of compulsory eugenics-based sterilization laws on the grounds of hereditary feeblemindedness.

1984: BOSTON, MA

The ophthalmologist, Dr. Eriksson, was young, lean, and woolly-faced—unfashionably so for 1984. He leaned in to swivel the dials on the phoropter. Despite the breath mint she could hear clacking against his teeth, his blond beard smelled of sandwich meat.

The student health clinic overlooked the playing fields. Kit could make out furrows of mud where someone had driven a truck onto the tawny grass, wheeling in drunken loops. Today, people were running back and forth in random directions, forming quick twosomes with their arms flailing, then sprinting apart. Whatever game this was, the players were blurry. Which is why she was here.

"F-*E*," he said. "Not F-B. And you said you're premed?"

She nodded. "But first I'm going to travel, do some volunteering overseas. Leaving tomorrow, actually."

Laughably, at the med-school interviews she'd done so far, the admissions officers had universally taken one look at her and said she needed more life experience.

"You're how old?"

Sixty-eight. But she didn't tell him that. Or that, in February, she'd celebrated her seventeenth leap year birthday. She still got carded getting into bars, but no one else had trouble believing the age on her current ID. "Twenty-two," she said.

The doctor tsk-tsked, making it sound diagnostic. "These changes show all the signs of pre-cataract, but cortical cataracts typically don't manifest until the fifth or sixth decade of life. A number of genetic diseases can lead to premature cataracts, but you have no other signs of the phenotype. We could get some blood tests to be sure."

She wouldn't be getting any blood tests.

"Do either of your parents have vision loss?"

She thought of her mother gesturing at a crow on a lamp-post and calling it a cantaloupe. Poor eyesight would have been a much more welcome explanation. She shook her head.

His beard rearranged itself. "We're actually doing a study of congenital cataracts. I'll give you some information in case that's of interest."

He pulled a slip from the pad he'd been writing on. "You can get a rush pair made up before your flight. You'll need to monitor regression closely. If I'm right, at some point you'll probably need surgery."

More shouts and cheers from the field outside made them turn to the window. Dr. Eriksson saw her squinting. "Frisbee football," he said. "Ultimate Frisbee is what they call it. Some big college tournament. There's teams in town from all over the place."

Udita was waiting for Kit at their usual bench overlooking the sports field. "Have you seen this? Dashing around after Frisbees!" She sounded mystified. Udita was a big fan of aerobics, Lycra, and leotards, but she spurned all forms of strenuous outdoor activity. "So?" Udita hopped her eyebrows at Kit. "Dr. Eriksson. Cute, eh? Like a Viking in a doctor's coat."

Kit groaned. In the years since Kit had moved to Boston, Udita had been relentless in her efforts to see her "get a bit of action," as she'd put it, lapping salaciously at her lower lip. Kit had invariably found herself seated by the only single man (and once, a woman) at Udita's potlucks: basketball players and poets, breakdancers and accountants. One time Udita had purposely blocked Kit's bathroom sink, then passed along the number for the plumber whose physique she'd admired in her Jazzercise classes. Some were awful, some were fun, and some were very sweet, which made it harder to keep her heart in check. Sometime, very soon, she'd have to tell Udita—she should have told her years ago—why she always kept things casual. But as time went on, the fact that she hadn't shared this part of herself from the outset felt like a betrayal, bigger and bigger every year. Hari said he'd stand by whatever Kit chose to do, but she knew this was unfair to him, probably the only secret he had from his wife. At this point, Udita couldn't understand why none of her introductions seemed to stick, and Kit couldn't explain her fear of falling for someone who'd eventually outgrow her, that she'd have to find a way to leave. Or be left behind.

At LensCrafters, Udita talked her into oversize frames in malachite green that "set off her eyes," then they headed to the American Express. Kit's first stop would be Houston for a med-school interview at Baylor, then she'd fly back to Toronto for a belated birthday with Helen, who'd already sent Kit a birthday card containing her horoscope for February 29, cut from the *Toronto Star*, adding her own handwritten prophecy at the bottom: *You will visit your sister before heading off on your adventure.* That adventure would begin in Britain, with stops in Chirk and Cambridge, then on to parts unknown. India, definitely. Ayaan was insisting on it.

While Kit went in to get her traveler's checks, Udita waited for her in a beam of sunshine, turning her face to the sun, one hand already clawing through her purse for a cigarette. But by the time Kit got back, Udita's wraparound sunglasses were off and she was blotting her mascara with a tissue. She made a phlegmy sound, part laugh, part moan, then flung her arms around Kit, hiccupping her words. "I don't want you to go."

Kit was acutely aware of Udita's quaking hug, her bony spine, and the citrusy scent of her shampoo even as she found she could also step outside of this moment, to watch it from a distance, like a memory, marveling that this was *her*, Kit McKinley, best friend, deeply loved, and sorely missed, before she'd even left. Leaving was always, always hard, and she'd done it so often. This time would be the hardest.

They found Hari alone in his computer lab, slouched in front of a bulky black screen, the cursor winking. He'd yanked the heavy curtains closed against the lemon-yellow sun so the shadowy room was a chaos of computer parts. Wide strips of gray cable like pulled taffy were tangled between consoles, disk drives, and mainframes. Deconstructed circuit boards, folding lamps, and magnifiers competed for desk space with coffee mugs, spiral-bound manuals, *Byte* magazine back issues, and a dog-eared comic book collection. Hari's natural habitat.

Udita stooped to read the type appearing on his screen as if by magic.

Channel > 3
C> **Chat w Sysop:** KwantumKing

Topic > Marvel Xcellent
/? for Help
<**MightyHerk67**> Professor X wouldn't stoop
<**Supamann**> p17! tell me Im wrong
<**2hot2touch**> hey boyz

"This is it. My BBS," Hari said proudly, rolling his chair to one side. "My Bulletin Board Server. I'm the SysOps. That makes me God of the BBS."

Udita mussed his hair. "KwantumKing," she read aloud. "I should get that for you on a T-shirt."

He looked pleased but shook his head. "The beauty of a BBS lies in the anonymity. This one's a BBS chat for Marvel X-Men fans, but I go by 'DataDelhi48' on the Super Highways BBS."

Hari passed Kit the floppy disk he'd insisted she take with her on her travels. As long as she could find a computer with a modem, he said, she could dial in to his BBS and they could stay in touch from wherever. He started tapping at the arrow keys to move the cursor. "Udita, this is the Chemical Brothers BBS I was telling you about."

Udita glanced at the blinking text on the screen, her nose wrinkling. "I'm holding out for the Chemical Sisters," she said, and started for the door. "We'll meet you at the Lark and Whistle, okay? Kit's buying the first round."

Hari watched her go with a look of pride mixed with longing. Married seven years and they still shared a chemistry that couldn't be found on the periodic table, not even by Udita. Hari had confided to Kit that they were planning to start a family after Udita had defended her PhD.

Just last week Kit had gone to see Udita give a practice talk about her research. Watching her in her black crepe suit at the podium, looking knife-sharp, radiant, and sexy as hell, it was hard to imagine how Udita would transition to motherhood. Kit knew her mum had struggled trying to juggle her family alongside the work that seemed to set her alight. Udita's talk was on salicylate molecules as chemical filters in dermatological photo-protection—the future of suntan lotion, she'd translated—and for the entire thirty minutes, she spoke directly to the audience, doodling an occasional line at her slides with the laser pointer. A nonchalant wizard in shoulder pads, charming everyone with her languid spells.

Sometime in the small hours, after Kit had stumbled home from the Lark and Whistle, but before she'd managed to pry herself out of bed the next morning, heavy clouds had shouldered past the moon. By the time Kit stepped outside, a good two inches of heavy spring snow had accumulated in the streets and more was tumbling from the sky. Kit looked and felt terrible. At least two drinks over her limit last night. Her pounding head felt cottony and her stomach loose and queasy. "Rum runs" was Udita's cheerful term for the gastrointestinal payment exacted for nights like yesterday's. This felt crampier. Typical, Kit thought. She got her period so seldom, three or four times a year, max. It would be absolutely classic for it to show up today, just in time for her night flight to Texas.

Udita, looking implausibly perky and coifed, was in line at The Tasty, alone. "Where's Hari?"

Udita shook her head, exasperated. "His junk cave, of course. He'll come eventually."

The cloying fried-egg bacon-grease maple-sugar-pancake smell wafting from the diner made her stomach slosh ominously. Kit glanced at Udita's pointy boots, their nonexistent tread. "You get seats, I'll get Hari."

Kit paused at the fields. The Frisbee tournament was clearly undeterred by the weather. Several dozen men and a handful of women looked to be warming up, the many-colored discs soaring like slow-mo confetti back and forth across the dirty, churned up snow. Hari, she saw, had emerged from the computer lab and was hurrying toward her on the sidewalk, raising his arm in greeting.

An errant Frisbee landed near her feet and Kit picked it up in her gloved hand. It made her think of Robbie, all those times they'd played at the Hudson River Parkway. Could she still throw a Frisbee without embarrassing herself? Worth a try, she figured, pulling off her glove, winding up, and letting loose. She was so focused on her throw, she didn't hear the calls of warning from a different part of the field. The Frisbee hit her square in the forehead. Not hard, but enough that she stepped backward, stumbling into the low bank of snow that had been cleared from the walk.

Her eyes fluttered open again to find two familiar faces hovering above her. She blinked her eyes closed again, as if she might not really be awake. She must be dreaming.

Hari was already taking her arm to help her to her feet. The other man was flushed, his eyes ablaze with worry, damp sandy hair curling out from under his tuque. He hastened to take her other elbow, then his face sprang open in surprise.

"Kit?"

She hadn't been winded by the fall, not at all. Yet she felt suddenly breathless, as if she couldn't quite remember where breath came from in the first place, how oxygen can be coaxed into a body. She knew, intimately, the way this man folded his limbs, these jutting knees. He'd had to crouch much the same way to cram himself into her go-cart to race along the parkway, the sticky buds from the chestnut trees tacky on the soles of their sneakers.

"*Will?*"

Hari flashed Will a quick look, astonishment pricked with worry. Kit shrugged their hands from her arms and pushed herself up. "I'm fine, totally. I just tripped." She touched her forehead. She'd have a bruise, but not a bad one. "Will, what on earth?"

"You know one another?" Hari looked between them.

Will couldn't keep his smile battened down any longer. It pushed upward and outward, even as he ran his hand down his face to hide it.

Kit found her tongue. "Will and I used to run track together, at a school in Connecticut. Before I moved away."

She noticed now that Will was wearing red long johns under a pair of jogging shorts and a soggy K-Way jacket, mud streaked down its front. "You're part of this tournament," she said, gaping. What were the chances? All those first dates orchestrated by Udita—Kit had said yes over and over in part to forget *this*, this feeling. How Will made her feel. How could she explain slipping out of Mum's commemoration with Udita, without saying goodbye?

She stalled by introducing Will to Hari, saying she'd met him at Oxford, a partial truth. Hari, she said, taught in the computer science program here at Harvard. Will, who looked to be eyeing up Hari, trying to gauge the nature of their relationship, said he was doing his PhD in marine biology at UCLA; he'd long ago traded his track shoes for turf cleats and this funky new game, played with Frisbees.

Will pulled off his wet hat and tried to muss his hair so it didn't look slicked to his scalp. "You've been here, Kit, at Harvard, this whole time?" She couldn't think of the last time someone had looked at her like this. With such a glow.

She shook her head. "I did a bachelor's in music at Berklee. Now I'm picking up some courses for med school. But not right away. I'm taking a year or so to go traveling."

She watched the effect of her words, the light fading in his smile.

Hari must have seen it too. "Want to join us for brunch, Will?" he said.

"Oh, I'd love to—" Will gestured at his muddy front, everything snow-soaked and hanging, but his face wrestled with indecision. "My team, I can't, I don't think—I can't miss my game."

She turned to Hari. "Can you head to The Tasty? Udita's holding our spots. I'll be right behind you. Two minutes."

Will stooped to pick up the wayward Frisbee, managing to inch closer in the process. His cheeks were even more flushed now, the same raspberry pink as his lips, which wouldn't stay still. His tousled hair looked long on top but was shaved short at the back and sides. She remembered what Helen and Natalie had said about him when they thought she wasn't listening, after they'd had to dash home from the park. That he looked like Eddie Brigati of The Rascals, but with better teeth. And Mick Jagger's lips.

Will was slowly shaking his head, without dropping his gaze. "Two minutes won't be enough, Kit McKinley."

She blushed.

"You're always vanishing, aren't you." He said it wistfully. "Where are you headed? And when?"

Her words were rattling so loudly in her head that it was impossible, after, to remember what she'd said aloud. But when she came up for air, she finished with, "And I leave today. Tonight."

"I know you're going to be jumping from place to place, but this time, can we try to keep in touch?"

Kit swallowed. "Will, in Africa, I did, I wrote to you. But I thought you weren't writing back. Helen, she thought . . ."

How to explain this.

She held Will's eye and it seemed as if some great hand were tearing her gently in two. She didn't know if it was because she knew she would disappear again, or try to, or it was time to *stop* disappearing, or if it was because Will had already decided that her disappearing was something he cared about. She remembered the floppy disk Hari had given her, how she only needed a modem to connect to his computer bulletin board. How she'd be able to post notes and updates to anyone or everyone. Including Hari the SysOps, the KwantumKing, who could see everything, and missed nothing.

She said, "Do you know about poste restante?"

April 12, 1985

Dear Kit,

I asked a friend what to send in a care package to someone back-packing around Europe and she suggested fresh socks, underwear, and a mixtape. Fun as the shopping might have been, I've settled on the mixtape, but included songs about socks (Aretha Franklin's "Respect") and undies (The Pretenders' "Time the Avenger"—okay, it's a stretch, but clean underwear IS mentioned). I have no idea what your musical tastes are or if you even have a Walkman, but somehow, somewhere, I'm sure you can listen.

I'm waiting to hear back on my post-doc applications and doing the final analyses requested by my committee. Very borrrring. Unfortunately I made the mistake of buying the new Anne Rice novel and it is MUCH more interesting. I've also been reading all about geoducks, which I've never paid much attention to (their habitat is mostly north of here). Did you know the name "geoduck" comes from the Salish Indian word that may or may not involve the word for "penis"? Also, they're the largest burrowing clams in the world and live more than 100 years. Who knew!

Big idea: I've submitted an abstract to the European Marine Biology Symposium in Denmark in September. I don't know where you'll be in the fall, but does Denmark appeal? Underwear shopping?

Tell me if I'm wrong, but I think we have some unfinished business from Boston.

I'd love to meet up.

Safe travels,
Will

1985: NAINITAL, INDIA

India was overwhelming for Helen, Kit could tell. When beggars plucked at her skirt outside the airport, miming hunger by lifting their fingers to their cracked lips, her face tightened. On their way to the Gupta home in the taxi, Helen kept her window closed but couldn't tear her gaze from the broken streets and putrid puddles—Delhi's oozing wounds.

It was Natalie's idea. For her 85th birthday, she wanted Helen and Kit to take her to visit Ayaan in India—Helen and Natalie would meet up with Kit in Europe to fly the final leg from Amsterdam to Delhi together. Natalie's eyes had lit up like a flashbulb when she recognized Kit at Schiphol airport, despite her cornrow braids and tattered hi-top hikers, appearing on the other side of the planet like a rabbit pulled out of a hat. She had twitched her pointy nose at Kit and winked.

"You've changed," she whispered in Kit's ear when they embraced. This was something no one ever said to Kit, and it made tears spring to her eyes. Natalie had pulled back, her eyes still twinkling. "You've met someone, haven't you?"

Kit already knew she'd end up telling Natalie about Will, but she hadn't made up her mind about Helen. The crazy coincidence of bumping into him again, right before leaving on her trip. How she'd spent her last half-day in Boston watching him sprint around after a Frisbee before getting roped into playing herself. Ever since, Will had been sending her sweet and funny postcards and letters to poste restantes and American Express locations all over Europe, and now a mixtape, which must have taken him hours to make. Kit was a year into her long and aimless jaunt, the sole purpose being to gain life experience and postpone feeling like the oldest student in her med school classes while looking like the youngest. But Will's letters had taken the spontaneity out of her travels: she was basically routing her trip based on the city she'd told him, in her last letter, she'd be going to next. His latest suggestion, that she meet up with him in Denmark in the fall? Geoduck penises? Underwear shopping?! And who was this "friend" who'd told him what to send? She desperately needed advice and wasn't quite sure who to ask. Or whether she'd like what they told her.

The plan was to spend just one night in Delhi with Hari and Udita, who'd flown in from Boston, load up on supplies, then have a hired van take them the following day to Nainital, where Ayaan now lived from spring through autumn.

Helen opted to stay home when they went out to do the shopping, pleading jet lag, but Natalie met them at the door with a camera slung around her neck on a gaudy strap. When Kit had admired it on the plane, Helen had mumbled to no one in particular: "Kit used to be into photography," but didn't meet Kit's eye.

Everything enthralled Natalie. Her face went slack at the sight of a man selling marigold garlands from a hand-drawn cart, but she seemed just as moved by the two-story shop selling stereo systems and ghetto blasters, marveling at their coexistence just as she had at the woman flicking a switch at a cow plodding through the honking Fiat Padminis and Hindustan Ambassadors. Every few steps, Natalie would point her

Pentax at a teetering tower of oranges, a child frying sweet jalebi in a wok spitting with grease, a man transferring rice and dal from a banana leaf to his mouth with a deft flick of his thumb. Natalie had made Udita promise to teach her how.

Udita thought Natalie was adorable, hamming it up for her photos with an array of theatrical Bollywood poses. God, Kit had missed Udita—her lavish affection and her quick laugh. Hari, too. Kit had missed his steady calm and his slow smile— the quiet way he made her know he always had her back. Hari and Udita, she knew, had been trying to start a family: Udita would be thirty next year and had twice told Kit in her letters she was the oldest female in her MBA program, which she'd started as soon as she'd finished her PhD. But she'd also confessed that she was worried about what childbearing would do to her body.

"Does Helen have kids?" she'd asked—happily not within Helen's earshot. Kit had already heard Helen complaining to Natalie about how tight her clothes felt, in the heat. But Udita had only met Helen the one time in New York and clearly noticed that Kit and her sister were wearing their years differently. "You and Helen had different dads, right?" Udita pressed.

"Yep," Kit said, feeling the old spasm of guilt. "And my mum had us almost twenty years apart."

Which was, after all, true.

Kit found herself searching the faces in the crowded streets for Tarun, which was nonsensical. She hadn't seen him since Hari and Udita's wedding in '77. He'd slipped in, unobtrusive, not in the orange robes, long grizzled beard, and powder-white face of a sadhu that Udita had plainly been thrilling for, but in regular clothes and a set of false teeth, his dark hair cropped. Of course Tarun had come to see his son, Ayaan, and his grandson, Hari, all grown up and marrying exactly the kind of woman—smart, sassy, and exquisite—that Tarun himself might have chased during the years he spent reinventing himself as the most eligible widower in the Union Territory. But, as Ayaan had predicted, Tarun had also come to see Kit. Back when Kit and her father had lived in India in the late forties, Tarun had displayed only a passing interest in her—a pesky kid who just happened to share his birthday. But he'd come to Hari and Udita's wedding to see for himself a half-century's worth of proof that there was, after all, another person in the world like him. Also to remind her of the same. In the years since, she'd occasionally gotten his letters, asking who she had allowed into her secret, and her heart. How was she keeping herself whole when all of the friction of living was trying to wear her down?

In her replies, Kit always asked if he'd crossed paths with others like them. He hadn't. But, like Kit, he'd always heard there *were* people like them in the past and probably others now, though infinitely rare, doing what they themselves were doing. Keeping a low profile, staying on the move, and protecting themselves from the kind of attachments that would later need to be broken.

But what about love? That's what she wanted to ask him now, searching every face as if he might magically materialize on the teeming streets of New Delhi. What do you do when you're in danger of falling in love?

Ayaan was seated on a chair under a trellis of bougainvillea when their van pulled up. The sunlight filtering through the flowers cast a rosy glow over his features, but when he stepped forward to greet them, his brown face looked more of a jaundiced gray and, she noticed with surprise, he was leaning on a cane. Kit waited while he greeted Hari and Udita, then let herself be gathered in his string-bean arms, unable to stop happy tears from soaking into his cotton shirt. His letter had reached her in Stockholm. *Time to visit*, he'd written. She wasn't ready for this, Ayaan old. She could feel it in his brittle embrace. How could he be old?

Later, while Natalie took a nap and after Hari and Udita had shooed her out of the kitchen, Ayaan bossing them around from a stool at the counter, Kit found Helen in the relative cool of the back garden, her sketchbook in her lap. Kit passed her a gin and tonic and settled on the bench beside her. They could see Naina Peak, furred with trees and slumbering like a bear above the green gleam of the lake, and in the distance, the frosted meringue of the Himalayan foothills. Overhead, palm fronds jostled with stiff pine branches and delicate stems clumped with berries. Two butterflies, black-winged with red swatches, drifted like ashes against the late-day sapphire of the sky. They could hear the clink of plates and cutlery—Helen would be relieved to know that silverware was on offer—as well as the Guptas laughing, Hari's big, round bark and Udita's musical peal. Kit was glad. The business of baby-making was causing them tension, she could tell.

Helen spoke first. "Is it true, what Natalie said, that you've met someone? While traveling?"

Kit hesitated, then flapped her hand. "Nothing serious." Until receiving his latest letter, Kit had presumed Will had a girlfriend back in LA, and the thought of that had fueled a handful of tipsy entanglements. "Everyone's always got different plans, or wants to go somewhere you've already been, so it's easy not to get involved."

Helen was frowning. "I hope you're being careful."

Kit nudged her with her knee. "You sound like Mum," she said, and saw the side of Helen's mouth curl upward again. "Trust me, everyone's paranoid about AIDS. It's easier to find condoms in Europe than contact lens solution."

Feeling the sturdy warmth of her sister beside her and seeing her wry smile—with the blanket of mist sliding through the valley as if to tuck everything in for the night—Kit had the urge, after all, to tell Helen about Will. That they were back to writing letters. That he was wrapping up his PhD at UCLA and would be picking a job out east, or out west, he hadn't decided. Kit, meanwhile, had at least five med-school offers. Even if she decided to retrace her steps to Denmark, she had no idea what could possibly happen next. Simmering at the top of her mind, always, was their goodbye in Boston, when he'd borrowed Hari's car to drive her to the airport himself. He'd leaned close, and she thought he was going to peck her on the cheek, but at the last second, he put two fingers under her chin to tilt her lips to his, impossibly warm and soft. It felt as if time had stopped, someone pausing the VCR to leave them twitching and jaggy. She'd rewound and relived that kiss in her mind so many times the memory was almost worn through.

Helen's gaze slanted in her direction and she murmured, "Did you hear Pritch died?"

The tingle of Will's kiss evaporated. They'd never talked about Pritch. He was always the uninvited guest whenever she visited Helen, the unwanted passenger inserting himself in an invisible seat between Helen and Kit on the long flight from Amsterdam, then again on the drive to Nainital. Now he was here on this bench, trying to ruin their sunset. She should have been the one to mention him long ago, to be sure he was vanquished for good. She felt a sudden lump in her throat. It turned out Pritch was already gone.

Helen nodded at her expression. "I heard from Saundra, at NYH."

Kit could see the tiny muscles of Helen's mouth working, her eyebrows trying to keep still. Kit sought out her hand.

"Oh, Helen, I'm so sorry."

Helen shook her head, still pinching her lips. "We weren't in touch. Not for years."

Kit swallowed. "But I mean, I'm sorry about what happened. Pritch and me. It was so stupid. *I* was stupid. It was just, Robbie's death. Mum. And I didn't realize you had, or you were hoping . . ." Kit paused, willing the warble in her voice to settle. "It was just, everything in my life felt so on hold."

"I know." Helen flipped her palm under Kit's, weaving her fingers through. She smiled sadly. "You probably saved me from making a fool of myself."

Kit willed her eyes to stay on her sister, knowing if she closed them, she'd be assailed by images she'd tried and failed to erase. Pritch, kneeling between her thighs and nudging her wider with his hairy leg as he rolled the condom onto himself, his veiny cock turning purple and waxy. Kit, propping herself up on her elbows to watch, stupidly eager for him or thinking she was. Him pinching the slick tip of his tongue between his teeth and drawing back his lips to make his first thrust. She'd made him think she wanted it that way—all that frenzied clutching and squeezing, their urgent unbuttoning. Kit had twisted her face to one side, clamping her eyes against the pain, and he mistook that for pleasure.

Kit shivered. "But he died? How?"

Even as she said it, it dawned on her what they'd been talking about before she'd drifted into thoughts of Will—Helen asking her if she was being careful. And she was, always. Even with Pritch, she'd been sure they were careful.

Kit raised her eyebrows and Helen nodded. "I always knew Pritch loved sex and he loved women, revered them," said Helen. "But I think his love was even bigger than that, spanning everyone, even Robbie." She floated a peek at Kit. "Not that Robbie knew what to do about that, I'd say. Pritch did. I think Pritch took pleasure, took love, wherever he could find it. I guess that caught up with him, in the end."

They fell quiet. Kit kept her hand tangled in her sister's, thinking how familiar this felt. How right. The light was falling; the mist that had seemed so gauzy and distant was slinking now through the garden.

Then out of nowhere, Helen said, "I'm adopting a child."

Kit's head whipped sideways. A child? She'd always assumed Helen had no interest in children.

"Ah, you see, Udita?" Natalie's voice. "This is already a *much* more interesting conversation than dial-up speeds and databases." She had donned an orange and fuchsia salwar kameez, the dupata wound around her head and throat, and she had her arm linked over Udita's to navigate the lumpy lawn. Udita made googly eyes at Helen, having caught her last words, but Kit suspected from Natalie's calm reaction that Natalie already knew.

Helen explained that the adoption was taking place through an organization based in England that helped to place mixed-race children born in South Africa, where interracial marriage was illegal.

"It's haunted me, sometimes, certain aspects of the SAMM project," Helen was saying to Udita, but her gaze kept trailing back to Kit. "Robbie believed so fervently in what he was doing, but I . . . I guess I question that now. Anyhow. His name is Phumlani and he's four years old, although he'll be five by the time everything is finalized.

"Helen, that's *amazing*." Udita clasped her hands. There was a note in her voice Kit couldn't quite place. "You see, Kit? You're going to be an auntie no matter what."

Udita hadn't smelled the strong whiff of neem oil or noticed the splash of lamplight from the lanterns Hari had been carrying carefully on a tray. His eyes flashed with a crumpling hurt and his lips seemed to twist, although that might have been the flames and shadows playing on his face.

"I'm not sure what you're cooking up out here, ladies, but the menfolk have been toiling away. Dinner's ready."

Natalie must have leaked Kit's news about Will to Ayaan, because he offered to drive her to the post office, his mustache failing to cover his smile.

"Does Tarun ever write to you here?" she asked as they waited in the queue alongside people clutching brown paper packages, folded bills, an anxious chicken.

Ayaan's face fell. "In fact, I haven't heard from him in a while. I sent my photocopies to all the postal circles back in 1979, saying I'd bought the place here and inviting him to come, but he never did. Any mail sent to Delhi is set up to forward to Nainital, although who knows how well that works. Up until last year or so, I got the occasional letter, but his handwriting is almost unreadable. I wrote him to say your travels might bring you to

India, but heard nothing. My guess is time finally caught up with him, as it were." Ayaan's big somber eyes blinked at Kit. "I'm only surprised he didn't find a way to say goodbye."

The postmistress shook her head at Ayaan, but at the sight of Kit, with her freckled skin and copper braids, she bustled away, returning with a postcard. She made a big show of officiously checking Kit's passport against the name in all-caps. Kit had already recognized the big, boxy script: Will.

Dear Kit.

Big news! I accepted the post-doc at the University of British Columbia, in Vancouver, Canada. You're Canadian, right? Take the Stanford or UCSF offers when they come (which they will). Then we'll be in the same time zone! Maybe you already got the postcard I sent to Delhi, but if not, don't go out of your way—it says pretty much the same thing.

Will

P.S. If you can't meet me in Denmark, no big deal (hopefully you got my package, and my offer didn't freak you out). But you have to make a trip to see me next year, okay? It's the World Expo in Vancouver. Great excuse to visit. Geoducks, here I come!

On the day the van was coming to drive them back to Delhi, Kit found she couldn't leave Ayaan, not yet. There was nowhere she needed to be. She helped Ayaan with the shopping and went on the occasional run around Naini Lake, drawing astonished looks and solemn applause from the locals. But most of the time, she sat and listened to Ayaan's stories about growing up with Tarun, about his friendship with her own father. She devoured Ayaan's memories as if she might never eat this particular treat again. And, she knew, there was a chance she might not.

"It's the craziest thing," Ayaan said the day before she left. They were sitting on the back terrace watching the cotton-ball clouds snaring on the forested flanks of the mountains. "I don't feel old, I never have," he said, sounding philosophical. "It's just somewhere along the way, I stopped feeling young."

"Oh, you're still fit as a fiddle," she chided, desperately hoping this was true. To her, it wasn't so very long ago that Ayaan had patiently pointed out the constellations blazing over the mid-Atlantic on the SS *Montcalm*. *Isn't it hard*, Papa used to ask, *time moving like a rickshaw for you while everyone else dashes past on the train?* Not at all, she thought, watching Ayaan turning his cane in his hands. Nothing feels slow for me, time doesn't drag its feet. I am the one going the speed limit while everyone else rockets by too fast.

"And what have you decided?" Ayaan asked gently. "Will you go meet this young man in Denmark?"

Kit chewed the inside of her mouth. "I don't know. I already have my ticket to Melbourne."

He watched her, fondly. "Tickets can be changed, can't they? You have all summer to make up your mind. Or winter, I suppose, in Australia."

Leaving him almost broke her. Taking local buses, which took twice as long as it would have in Hari's hired van, Kit cried for most of the trip, prompting others on the crowded bus to pass her handkerchiefs, cold drinks, and slices of mango.

Back in Delhi, she couldn't resist going past the general post office to check the poste restante before heading to the airport. But the promised postcard from Will wasn't there.

Instead she was handed a letter from Tarun, addressed in a hand so spidery it was almost unreadable. The post office had held it for her far longer than they usually would, because, according to the man in the frayed uniform who pointed reverently with his pen, the letter was marked with the symbol that meant it had been sent from a holy man, a sadhu. These men cannot be held to rules or time, he explained. Nor to a return address.

She read Tarun's letter at the airport, weeping openly as his words sank in.

Dear Kit,

We are blessed, you and I, to get far more than our share—both the good and the bad. Cherish that. I should have cherished it more. I told you at Hari's wedding not to make the same mistakes I did. This is the last time I'll remind you. Look after yourself the way you would if your days were numbered, but don't live as if it doesn't matter how. Brush your teeth. Don't let a wound fester. Love as if it's your last chance, even if there may be other chances.

When it's time to go: leave. You'll figure it out when you need to, but there are ways to do it quietly and peacefully. On your own terms. That's what I'm doing now. I can't bring myself to tell Ayaan: I'm hoping, as one last favor, you can do that for me.

—Tarun

Death of an
Unknown Sadhu
?? – 1986

The death of an unnamed sadhu has prompted an outpouring from assiduous readers who claim the mysterious Holy Man is Sadhu Sunder Singh, declared dead by the Government of India in 1933. Others say he is Sadhu Brahmachari, best known for his ten-and-a-half-hour static wall-sit at the Netaji Subhas Institute of Sports in 1974, or possibly the famed Pushkar Fair sadhu, whose unorthodox feat of strength has not been corroborated by our journalists. In fact, the late ascetic is described as having a fair complexion, a long beard, and was tall and trim, thus challenging contentions that he could be any of these men.

1986: VANCOUVER, BC

nother airport, another Arrivals hall: Will's face was bobbing above the others, hopeful and eager, not nervous in the least. He was wearing a pair of black cargo shorts with a white button-down shirt and black Converse high-tops. Not preppy, thank God. She'd toned down the eye makeup, but she figured her spiked hair was a challenge of sorts, a test.

He recognized her, no problem. They hugged, but only after an awkward hesitation that made them both laugh. It had been more than two years since the Frisbee had hit her in the head outside Hari's lab in Boston. Despite Will's reference to "unfinished business" in his postcards, she hadn't changed her flight to meet him in Denmark, and in the end, he'd decided not to attend the conference. *Too busy with the move to Vancouver*, he'd written. *It's beautiful here! You're definitely coming to visit.* They'd kept up their correspondence, but to Kit, his letters had become less flirty and more contemplative, as if he liked putting his thoughts on paper. No more mention of underwear. Neither of them, in their letters, had so much as hinted at their farewell kiss or suggested this was anything more than friendship. To test the waters, she'd made some passing mentions of the guys she'd met on her travels and he, too, referred to different "friends" he'd met after moving to Canada. This airport hug in Vancouver seemed merely sociable: long, but not full pressure, as if he were holding himself slightly apart. He smelled delicious, like a forest in springtime, velvety and green. He brushed his hands over the spiked top of her hair and said, "I love it!" And they headed out to his car.

Will lived with a roommate, sharing an older home in North Vancouver with a view of the high-rises downtown and the lights of Lions Gate Bridge, laced like a string of pearls across the bay.

"The lighting on the bridge is new," Will said, pointing it out from the porch. "For Expo 86. And Brent, my roommate, is hardly ever here. He's happy to stay at his girlfriend's place so you can have his room."

She hoped disappointment wasn't strung on its own marquee lights across her face.

He didn't touch her the entire day, other than their blundering airport hug. That night, he made fettuccini with pesto, then offered her the big poofy chair in the living room that swiveled toward the view while he himself took the couch with his long legs extended. They talked about her travels, his work, med school. Then he said, "You must be exhausted!" And they went to their separate rooms.

Will was just as funny and thoughtful in person as he'd been in his letters, but his intense way of looking at her, which she'd held in her heart like a parallel pulse—she didn't see it now, didn't feel it. He still had the habit of trying not to smile, which was adorable, and when they went out to the street to get in his car, he always opened her car door first before walking around to his, which was beyond charming. But he didn't reach for her hand over the gearshift or put a palm in the curve of her back when they lined up to get their tickets for Expo, even though her skin was screaming for it.

Halfway through her visit, she phoned Udita while Will was at work. Kit was heading to visit Udita and Hari in Seattle next, taking the Greyhound bus from Vancouver. The Guptas had moved to Seattle not long after getting back from India last year, Microsoft Corporation having recruited Hari away from Harvard. Udita had peddled her combo MBA/PhD to land a job heading up the innovation division at Coccinel Cosmetics, in Redmond, not far from Hari's office.

"Expo is a lot of fun. My favorite is probably *Rainbow War* at the Canadian Pacific Pavilion, but Hari would get a real kick out of the Omnimax, an enormous orb that looks like it's built of mirrors. The theater inside shows a movie in 3D—you have to wear these special colored glasses."

"*And?*" Udita pressed. "You're just spending all your time at Expo?"

No. Will also took her to the wilder corners of Vancouver: its windswept beaches and old-growth forests. One day they took a ferry up the strait to a densely wooded stretch of coastline that Will said was his favorite place on earth. "I want to live here one day," he said in a quiet voice. "When the time is right."

Closer to home, on the North Shore Mountains, he introduced her to his regular trails: spongy with mud, gnarled with roots, studded with granite. Standing under Douglas firs as tall as her old New York apartment building, their bark like a prehistoric pelt, long fossilized, Kit thought she might not, after all, always live in a city.

"That's it," Udita squeaked, incredulous. "You've been putting off this guy for years, you finally visit him, and all he does is roll out the red carpet and become some handsome, hands-off tour guide. Nothing more?"

The next day, Will and Kit took the bus, then a sea bus, to get to the Expo and spent the entire day touring around, getting her passport stamped by all the countries whose pavilions they visited. Never in her life had Kit traveled with so little anxiety about her identification papers. It took every ounce of self-control not to snatch at Will's hand when the Scream Machine roller coaster inched with an agonizing slowness up the slope and over the crest before plunging down. Later, at dinner, with a view over False Creek, Will reached to run his open palm over her spiky hair the way he'd done at the airport, but said nothing as he did it, just slid his smile into the dimple of his cheek and watched to see what she'd do next.

Kiss him, you ninny! That's what Aunt Natalie was squawking at her in her head. *What are you waiting for?!* But she didn't, not with their dinner plates strewn with salmon bones and smeared potato, and not later when the night turned cool and the fireworks started, lit from a barge out in the bay. She'd never seen fireworks so close overhead: you could see the flares of light tracing the air before bursting into color and flame, each explosion mirrored and refracted on the inky ripple of the sea. Kit leaned toward him, so that after a moment, he lifted an arm, and she thought he would pull her against his warm body, but instead he merely took off his jacket to drape over her shoulders. The urge to twist her face toward him, to yank at his head and pull it to hers, was so strong she thought he could have felt it passing telemetrically between them. But all he did was stand impossibly still, so close behind her she could feel his solid warmth from her calves all the way to her shoulders.

By the time they got back to his place, it was after midnight and the cold of the May evening had settled into her bones, making her teeth chatter. "I'm so sorry, I'm such an idiot. I should have known it would get cold." Will, unlocking his front door, couldn't stop apologizing, his own cheeks ruddy, his eyes anxious. "How about I get a fire started for us and make some cocoa. Or do you want a hot bath? I can run you a bath. Whatever you need."

Udita would have known to say yes to all of it. Udita would have emerged from the bathroom flushed and tousled, wrapped only in a towel, having remembered to floss the fish from her teeth. She would have padded on her smooth, manicured feet to the fireplace, turned her back to the blaze, wet her lips before blowing softly over her hot chocolate, and then, when the moment was right, let the towel slip to the floor.

Kit didn't say yes to any of it, she'd lost all knack for simple talk. Instead, she closed the front door behind her and snatched at his hand before he could reach for the light switch. She tugged him clumsily toward her, then buried her face in his warm neck, sliding her hands under his untucked shirt, her cold touch, or her urgency, making him jump. She breathed him in, a gulp, as if she'd surfaced from a dive, and she felt him shiver, then groan the words, "Oh, thank god," before dropping his face to her lips.

The next few minutes were fumbled and sloppy: two days' and two years' worth of jokey, uncertain foreplay now detonating against the coat closet. At one point, he pulled away, panting, and said, "Are you sure? I thought . . . From your letters—" He cut himself off with a low moan because she was undoing the buttons of his shirt, making her way lower, her warm lips eager to follow the fast trail of her icy fingers. But then he said, "Wait. Stop." So she did. He smiled at the frustration and want that must have been churning on her face, then led her down the hallway to his room.

Time slowed. Or rather, Will slowed it, slowed her. And she'd never done this slowly. He made her stand at arm's length with nowhere to put her fidgety hands, so they hung useless and trembling. With his eyes on hers he finished undoing the buttons of his shirt and slipped it back over his shoulders. Then he did the same with hers, one button at a time, leaving her skin feeling frosted, but also aflame. Then he stopped, his eyes twinkling, as if to say again, teasing, *Are you sure?* Only then did she reach out to him, tucking the tips of her fingers under the waistband of his jeans and pulling him toward her.

On her last morning, the day she'd be taking the bus to Seattle, Kit snuggled into him under the covers while he slept, her fingers making a slow glissando over the keys of his ribs, through the taut valley of his waist, before rising up and over his glutes, trying to memorize every angle, every slope.

"You better watch yourself," he murmured, reaching to take her hand.

She nuzzled closer and said, "When did you know you liked me? As in, like-liked."

No hesitation. "I like-liked you the day I first saw you," he said, his voice a sleepy rumble. "Coach Drummond was making everyone run fartleks and you were wearing a green-and-yellow-striped shirt and green shorts and you had a green ribbon woven through your braid, which was flying behind you, horizontally, because you were so flippin' fast. I thought you looked like a salamander and I loved you instantly."

She laughed, but she felt a tiny pricking in her heart. She was picturing baby Billy, his little booties pedaling to get out from under his blanket, his eyes blinking against the sunlight.

He rolled onto his back. "You?"

Karl Herman Amsel
November 8, 1907 – July 12, 1987

Karl Herman Amsel, a former Nazi SS colonel who helped design Hitler's Aktion T4 euthanasia program, died at age 80 of natural causes yesterday in Santiago, Chile. A self-proclaimed "mercy killer," Amsel oversaw the systematic extermination of an estimated 200,000 German babies, children, and young adults with incurable or hereditary diseases and disabilities between 1939 and 1941. President Augusto Pinochet had repeatedly denied requests for Amsel's extradition.

1988: SEATTLE, WA

Udita's friends from Coccinel Cosmetics had flower child names like Amber, Luna, and Autumn, better suited to a sunny meadow than a fortieth birthday party. They drank wine coolers and wore Swatches, fishnet gloves, and jelly shoes. They weren't chemists, like Udita. They were too young for PhDs. They worked in strategy and facilitation, brand analysis and market research. Kit had no more idea what their workdays actually looked like than she did her skin tone and color chart.

It was Hari's birthday, but Udita was the life of the party. When Hari bustled past with spinach dip and pizza bites, the Coccinel girls paused their chatter and blinked at him, smiling polite, close-mouthed smiles as if he were someone's father. In their midst, Udita's laugh was overloud, her eyes glossy, and her face had a heat to it Kit remembered from the dance floors and crowded bars of their Boston years. Something had done the rounds here other than shooters and California Coolers. Hari mostly stayed out in the yard with Will and a motley collection of neighbors and bespectacled computer types. Kit caught a glimpse of Hari through the window at dusk, his hunch, his hands balled in the pockets of his soft cords, and the thought that reared up in her was he *did* look like a dad. Or like he should be someone's dad.

Udita had showed them to their bedroom earlier, apologizing for the mess and decor—they hadn't gotten around to redecorating. The papered walls were adorned with monkeys, jungle vines, and toucans, while the desk teemed with Hari's computers, cords, and cables. When Udita left, Kit noticed the faint pencil lines and dates inching up the doorframe, hidden when the door was ajar. This was a little boy's room, or had been, and none of it looked too worn or outdated. Hari and Udita weren't planning to redo this room; they were still hoping to use it as is.

Kit had flown into Vancouver earlier that week, then she and Will had driven south that morning. Now, Will kissed her, long and slow, then went to help Hari set up the tent and tables in the backyard. Kit dropped back on the quilt with a groan, pulling a pillow to her chest. She was a *mess*: all jangling hope and saw-toothed hunger. Being with Will was like being constantly jolted by a cattle prod. She wasn't on the brink of getting a medical degree, she had no mind of her own. She was just flesh and want.

A gentle knock made her sit up. Udita was carrying bath towels, her eyes dancing and curious. But her face fell at the look on Kit's.

"What's wrong?" She dropped down beside Kit, the towels in her lap. "I told you, these walls are thick, practically sound-proof. You guys should have taken a nap."

Kit thwacked her with the pillow, but Udita managed to snatch it away, intending to wallop her back, but she dropped it when she saw the tears spilling over the rims of Kit's eyes. Kit swiped at them with her sleeve, no doubt smearing her mascara. "I just don't think it can work."

"Oh, sweetie." Udita took a facecloth from the stack on her lap and started dabbing tenderly at Kit's cheeks. "You see? All this drugstore makeup is going to wreck my linens."

Udita could always, always make her laugh. It came out stuttered and snotty. "Why can't it work—because of school? Long distance? That's only for a few more years."

Funny. Hari had already alluded to Udita's "ticking clock" when she was out of earshot, and Udita had joked about thirty-two being "over the hill" at a cosmetics company. Things wouldn't work out with Will precisely because his years and hers were entirely different units of time. Kit just shook her head.

"Come on," Udita said gently. She reached out to tap tentatively at Kit's crispy, spiked hair as if she were a deep-sea invertebrate in a touch tank. "Let's wash out all this crunchy shit. You need an Udita makeover."

At the end of the night, Will insisted on doing the dishes, rolling up his sleeves so she could see the smooth underbelly of his forearms. Kit found Hari exactly where she expected: in the smudgy gloom of his office—the guest bedroom—his big, brooding face lit only by two boxy monitors.

"Busted," she said, plunking herself on the blue quilt and willing the birds and animals in the wallpaper not to hop and spin. A sure sign of a successful party. The neighbors and Hari's colleagues had left, but some of Udita's Barbie doll workmates remained, propping themselves up on the pool table downstairs. They could hear Udita's trilling laugh through the floor.

Hari flinched. Whatever it was Udita had taken so she could drift above the fray like a helium balloon, Hari clearly hadn't joined her. He pushed his glasses up his forehead to rub at his face. "At least we know she's not pregnant—she's got a lifetime's worth of pregnancy tests in our bathroom. We could have given them out in goody bags."

At one point, late in the evening, Kit, Will, and Hari had found themselves on the backyard swing set—another gut-punch left behind by the previous owners—passing a twenty-sixer of vodka back and forth. Hari was talking about Ayaan, who was stubbornly resisting their efforts to get him to immigrate to the US and move in with them in Seattle. After, they fell silent, neither Hari nor Kit able to contemplate a world with no Ayaan in it. Then, out of the blue, Hari told them he was trying to convince Udita they should see a fertility specialist. Maybe they could try some kind of treatments, he'd said, glaring down the neck of the bottle.

Now, turning away from his computers, Hari waggled his head in apology. "I'll clear out of here. Just wanted to check on a few things."

"No rest for the SysOps," Kit said, and he pulled a face that still managed to look pleased she'd remembered.

"Who are they?" Kit asked, gesturing at the screens behind Hari. He brightened. "This one has a dedicated line so I can use it to explore other boards—lots of other slabheads out there. Right now I was checking in on Marvel-Marchers." He pointed at the other system. "This one's my BBS. Helen was on just now, actually." Hari had convinced Helen of the need to get on his BBS years ago, in Nainital. "We broke into chat for a bit. Sounds like she's over the moon about Phumlani."

Kit nodded. "He's a great kid, and Helen is amazing with him. Like a different person."

Hari turned away quickly, as if to draw comfort from his blinking monitors. He was happier here, she realized, in the company of his cables and keyboards, than among the guests who'd been gathered earlier around his backyard hibachi. Or the shiny young things downstairs even now, a few of whom were staggering outside to barf in the rhododendrons.

In a neutral voice that reminded her of Ayaan, Hari asked: "So did you tell Will?"

Kit looked at her bare knees, jutting naked and knobby from the dress she'd borrowed from Udita, and shook her head. Earlier, when Will had gone inside and she and Hari had been dangling drunkenly on the swing set, Hari had said: "Do you ever wonder how many more of you there might be out there in the world, living amongst us, with your invisible superpower?" It was the same question Kit used to put to Tarun in her letters. Hari had said softly, "All you need to do is find another person like you, and you guys can live happily ever after."

Now, at his desk, he was scratching at something on his jeans, avoiding her eye. "What's your plan, then. Is this serious?"

"Maybe? I don't actually know. I don't know what Will wants."

"We talked for a bit. He sounds pretty serious. The house, the dog. Kids."

His last word was so heavy, Kit wasn't sure she could hold it. Will wanted kids? He'd never said. Or was this just Hari, projecting?

"What do *you* want, Kit?"

Ah. They'd gotten here quickly. What *did* she want? She wanted to see where she and Will could take this. She wanted this feeling to last as long as it could, her whole life. Her every instinct told her that wouldn't be possible.

Hari leaned forward, pushing the door mostly closed. He was already wrestling with the logistics on her behalf. "Will thinks you're, what, in your thirties, right? Ready to settle down.

What does he think you've been doing all this time? Why you're only finishing med school now?"

His voice was gentle, but she could hear the undercurrent of concern.

Instead of answering, she said, "I've decided I'm going to tell Udita. Tomorrow. You haven't said anything, right? Just today, when she was doing my makeup, she kept going on about my skin."

Hari gave a firm shake of his head. "I would never say anything to Udita without asking you first."

"Say anything d'me about wha?" Udita pounced into the room and tackled Kit on the bed, laughing, so that Kit fell back. Udita smeared a slobbery kiss across her cheek before rolling onto her back beside her, breathing hard. She smelled of booze, hairspray, and menthol cigarettes. Then she sat up just as abruptly, wobbling unsteadily.

"Whater you two plotting?" She narrowed her eyes at Kit, then Hari, pushing her lips together in mock suspicion.

"Inviting Will to stay on a few extra days," Hari said smoothly. "I wouldn't dream of suggesting it to you without first checking with Kit."

"In-vi-ting Will-i-am," Udita repeated, singsong and teasing. "I'm na-sure Kit wans us here, Hari. She wans him aaaaaaaall to herzelf."

Hari stood up. "I'm going to relieve Will of cleanup duty," he said, throwing a pointed look at Udita.

She ignored him, flopping back on the pillow and nesting her head against Kit's. They lay there quietly for a minute, then Kit said, "I do need to tell you something, Udita."

"Wha." Her voice slushy and sleepy.

"Not now. Tomorrow. Okay?"

"Okay." Then, "Hari's madda me."

"He's not mad at you."

"Yesh. He's mad 'cause I'm not pregnant."

"He's not mad. He's sad, that's all. Birthdays can be sad."

Udita managed to lift her head up, twisting toward Kit, bugging her eyes. "Are *you* pregnan? Thas what you wanna tell me?" She tried to push herself up on her elbows. "You pee on a shtick. I have shtick. Lemme get you."

"No, Udita." Kit pulled her back down so Udita's head was on her shoulder. "No sticks. I'm not pregnant. Really."

Kit could feel Udita relaxing, her head heavy. "Okay. But. If you needta take care of it. I know. I know where to go. Shh-hhh." She tried to lift a finger to her lips, making it as far as her chin. "Shhhh."

Oh no.

Udita was still muttering something, words Kit couldn't decipher. The hand that got lost on the way to Udita's mouth dropped back in the gap between them, and she worked her fingers under Kit's, curling them like a mouse in her palm. Deep inside, Kit felt something open as if slashed. The way Hari, on the swing set, had glared down the throat of the vodka bottle as if their unborn child might be hiding at the bottom.

Kit sensed Udita's eyes flutter open again, her body jerking. "But you canna tell Hari. You. Can. Not. I'm gonna have our baby for him soon. Okay? Soon. I jush couldna do before. New job, new place, new friends, new-new-new-new-new."

"Hey, *hey*. It's okay. I won't tell." Kit stroked her hair. "You need to get some sleep."

"Is your turn," Udita mumbled.

"My turn what?"

"Your secret."

"I'll tell you tomorrow."

Kit thought she was asleep, but Udita nudged her with a knuckle. "Promise."

"I promise."

Barbara McClintock
June 16, 1902 – September 2, 1992

Botanist and Nobel Prize Laureate Barbara McClintock, best known for describing the ability of genetic fragments to transpose or "jump" between chromosomes in *Zea mays*, passed away Friday of natural causes, age 90. Dr. James Watson, co-discoverer of DNA, hailed her as one of the three Great M's of genetics along with Gregor Mendel and Thomas Hunt Morgan.

1993: TORONTO, ON

Kit leaned in the doorway watching Natalie and Phumlani at the piano, Natalie's fingers dancing over the keys as if they'd never known a day's stiffness. Natalie had moved in with Helen in Toronto in '86, not long after Helen had brought Phumlani home. He was eleven now, crazy for spaceships and Nintendo, but quite musical, too. Listening to their duet, Kit had one of her vertigo moments, tumbling back through time so that it was her seated at their old Bush and Lane upright in Ottawa, Natalie swaying on the bench beside her. *Bravo!* She could hear her father calling, pride swelling in his voice. *Bravo.*

"You're not playing anymore?" Natalie had asked.

"I don't have a piano at the moment."

"Don't let it slide." Natalie patted her hand. "Music can always be a comfort. The person who can make her own music will never be truly alone."

Kit turned away so Natalie couldn't see her face. Helen must have told her. Will and Kit were off again: off for good this time. She had been doing the same thing she'd done with Udita for years, stalling, so the longer she stalled, the harder it was to tell him. It was as if she were hoping for crow's feet and gray hairs—some sign her seventy-seven years of life might at last be catching up with her. Or, alternatively, for some irrevocable rift between her and Will to prove they were destined to split, making it appropriate and reasonable that she had never succumbed to the urge to tell him the whole, long sob story of her life.

She'd been the one to break it off. Will was thirty-seven, for god's sake; he deserved to start a family with someone normal and settled. She hadn't even landed on what she wanted to do for a career, let alone where she could do that, or for how long. Plus she and Will couldn't keep up the long-distance thing, back and forth, especially now that she'd decided to go the MD/PhD route at Queen's University, rather than pursue her residency. Plus Kingston, Ontario, wasn't particularly easy to get to from Vancouver. Plus, plus, plus.

Kit had changed into her running gear, planning a quick 10K before supper, but she lingered long enough in the kitchen that Helen put her to work. "She's amazing, isn't she?" Helen said, gesturing through the window. Natalie and Phumlani had gone outside onto the postage-stamp lawn, Phumlani zipping around spearing the croquet hoops into the grass. "At ninety-two! Still creaming us at croquet. Mind you, she keeps herself so slim and trim. Here, grate this."

Helen passed Kit a block of cheese large enough that you wouldn't want to be pinned underneath it. *Pecorino* Kit read on the label. At Stanford, Kit had seen a dermatologist named Pecorino who specialized in rare skin disorders. He'd been horrified by her actinic keratosis and mottled pigmentation in the utter absence of elastosis. "At age thirty-three!" Dr. Pecorino had gasped. "And you said you spent time in India?"

Helen was saying that Natalie had joined a seniors club that swam practically year-round at Cherry Beach. "She must have at least some of your leap year genes, I'd say."

Helen was the only one who ever used that phrase of their father's. There was nothing, not *one thing* Kit had ever learned at med school to support the theory of trauma mutating a person's genetic code weeks or months after conception. She said as much to Helen, who set down her knife, pushing her hair back from her face with the back of her hand.

"You know, I don't think Mum ever really believed that."

Kit felt trepidation prickle in the pit of her stomach. "What do you mean?" She knew what was coming.

"All of Mum's warnings about being careful, choosing your mate. None of that made sense if she really believed something happened to you in the womb. There was one time when I was first dating Robbie, when Mum could still be really lucid and sharp—she told me she and Thomas had 'fooled around' for years, well before they got married."

Helen picked up the knife again, the blade clacking at the board. "My guess is she was pregnant some time before they tied the knot, she just wasn't showing." Helen glanced over her shoulder at the Matterhorn of cheese Kit was mounding. "Oh, that's plenty." Helen caught Kit's expression and set down her knife again, pulling Kit toward her. "I'm not telling you anything you haven't already thought of yourself, am I?" She pulled back to look at Kit's face. "I can take it from here, if you still want to jog in this heat."

When Kit got back, drenched in sweat, her mind still whirring, she walked around the house and straight into the sprinkler, wearing her shorts and sports bra, letting the jets of cold water rake the length of her body. Phumlani thought this— a grown-up, in clothing, in the sprinkler—was hilarious. He streaked out to join her before his mother could stop him, and

Kit spent the next five minutes darting and jumping through the oscillating wall of water with her nephew, both of them getting soaked from head to toe.

Neither Kit nor Phumlani heard the doorbell. She was toweling herself off when she caught Natalie's voice, lilting and gracious, leading someone out of the house to the backyard.

"Will?" Kit's face must still have been the color of Helen's tomato sauce, freckles standing out like a pox. Her socks and shins were covered in lawn clippings and her thatched, wet hair wasn't so much surfer-girl chic as drenched beaver dam. She smelled like garden hose and was wrapped, fetchingly, in Phumlani's Thomas the Tank Engine towel.

Will seemed delighted to have caught her waterlogged, half naked, everything clinging. Natalie, too, looked ecstatic. "I've heard so much about you, Will, it's just wonderful to finally meet you. Of course you'll stay for Helen's lasagna? Kit, you never mentioned Will would be in town?"

He was wearing a short-sleeved shirt and light trousers with a jacket slung over his arm, as if he was on his way to a faculty meeting. He looked good. *Really* good. Clearly Natalie was of the same opinion as she scanned him up and down, her smile strung like bunting from her cheekbones.

Kit kissed him on the cheek, breathing him in, then instantly regretted it. She'd broken this off. It had ended, she'd ended it. "What are you doing here? How did you find me?"

Helen was bustling toward them, drying her hands on a dish towel. "He called while you were running," she said flatly. "I would have told you, but . . ." She shot a pointed look at Kit's wet socks. "Phumlani, out," she called. "It's dinner in five." She smiled at Will now, lips pursed. "I remember you, Will

Katzen, when you were this small." She held a hand at chest height. "I've set another place at the table."

Oh, Helen. With her dimpled arms and loose knits, her bossy face: she must have looked more like Kit's mother than her sister. And Kit looked more at home squealing through the sprinkler with Phumlani.

"So what *are* you doing here?" Kit asked again when Helen had shooed Phumlani back inside and she had Will to herself, the towel over her shoulders like a cape. The sun was slanting through the yard, golden and hazy. Will reached up and brushed a blade of grass from her cheek, his thumb lingering on her jaw. She wanted to bite it.

"Just a stopover. I'm en route to New York tomorrow night. It's Mom," he said quietly. "She's in the hospital again." He made a face, his breath sighing out of him. "It's not good."

Kit could picture Madge Katzen in her Chanel suit and long cigarette, sashaying through Central Park as if a movie crew might be trailing behind her. It was impossible to imagine her doing anything so unstylish as dying.

He put his big hands on her shoulders, the heat of his touch making her want to slot herself against his chest. But he tucked his chin to make sure she held his eye. "I've decided. I'm done with this, Kit. Being apart. You keeping us apart. I want my mom to meet you, especially if she's close to the end. I want us to be *us*, all the time, and for everyone to know it. Everything else . . ." He shrugged, tilting his head to encompass the sky, the gathering dusk, all of the unknowable things. "Everything else doesn't matter."

His eyes were so close, it almost hurt to keep them in focus. It would be easier to tumble into them—to be absorbed in their depths rather than see them watching her casting around for the right words, the right answer. She loved this man too much for her own good, and his. She always had.

"Why?" she whispered.

He blinked at the word.

"I mean, why *me*? Will—you could have anyone."

He smiled his crooked smile, half his mouth pursed to one side, considering. "Because you're not anyone, you're different. Different from everyone I've ever known."

Kit froze. But his face still wore its lopsided smile.

"Sure, you're fast, when you want to be, but what I love is how you spend so much time dawdling, not wanting to miss out on a single thing. The way you look up at the clouds, then tell me an entire story from their shapes; the way you pause to check how a cobweb has been woven; the way you lay your hands on the bark of an old tree in passing, like you're transmitting a message. I love how, in a crowded room, you'll always seek out the oldest person and get them talking, and how you'll never interrupt, even if they're slow to finish a sentence. I love how you start a book by reading the acknowledgments at the end, because you want to imagine all the people in the background, the hidden hands, getting their due. I love how you make a big deal out of everyone's birthday except your own. I love how you're never late for anything, because you hate to keep people waiting. I love how opera makes you cry, but then, so does Frankie Valli, Roberta Flack, and The Cure. I love how much you care about how long your tea steeps but can't be bothered to match your socks." He pulled her, at last, against him. "Maybe I'm selfish, but I love how fiercely you love."

Natalie's musical voice rolled out toward them. "Dinner is served. Kit, hurry and get changed. Will, what can I get you to drink?"

Kit tucked her head under his chin. His warm hands roved down the damp towel stretched across her back but stopped short of heading lower where her clammy shorts still clung to her bum, even as she willed his hands to keep sliding. Natalie was lingering in the gloaming, watching them, as if offering a blessing, or a nudge.

"Okay," Kit mouthed, inaudible. She cleared her throat, pulling away. Louder, "Okay." His eyes crinkled again, and he started to speak, but she shushed him, pressing a finger to his lips. "But tomorrow," she murmured. "Before you go. It's important. There's something I need to tell you."

DISCONNECT >>> **CHANNELS** >>> ***HELP***
*****spacemilano** has joined #fridays
*****rockinmountains** has quit #fridays (XML Socket Connection closed)
<**melbatoast17**> ya spacemilano!
<**spacemilano**> ciao mthrfkers
<**KwantumKing**> FOR HELP TYPE #ophelp
*****speedycarrot123** has joined #fridays
<**speedycarrot123**> Hey KKing: break into chat?
<**KwantumKing**> Hi speedycarrot123! Yes. Gimme 2 min.
. . .
[PRIVATE]
<**KwantumKing**> Hey Kit!
<**speedycarrot123**> Hi Hari. TY. were you in the middle of something?

\<**KwantumKing**\> No prob. How's Toronto? how's Helen and the fam?

\<**speedycarrot123**\> Toronto good. HOT. Helen and Natalie good. Phumlani fun. Y'd like him, he's insane with computers. Already writing programs etc. Natalie is Natalie — ie amazing. How r u guys?

\<**KwantumKing**\> Udita just back from big dermatology conference. get this. someone has figured out you can inject botulism into the face to cure wrinkles.

\<**speedycarrot123**\> WHHAAT?

\<**KwantumKing**\> U is all jacked about it. theyre acquiring the tech for Coccinel

\<**speedycarrot123**\> as long as she doesnt try it on hrself

\<**KwantumKing**\> . . .

\<**speedycarrot123**\> NO!

\<**KwantumKing**\> . . .

\<**speedycarrot123**\> oh wow. I'll call her ok? Tomorrow. But Hari, theres something else. Will surprised me, showing up here at Helens. Tonight.

\<**KwantumKing**\> I know

\<**speedycarrot123**\> What do you mean you know?

\<**KwantumKing**\> :):):) I told him to

\<**speedycarrot123**\> !!!!!!!!!!!!!!

\<**KwantumKing**\> :):):)

\<**speedycarrot123**\> Hari I'm going to tell him. about me. Everything. tomorrow before he flies to NY. am I crazy?

\<**KwantumKing**\> We alrdy know u r crazy. Crazy is bside the point.

\<**speedycarrot123**\> Hari . . . Im serious.

<**KwantumKing**> Kit, can i tell u something? 100% serious.

<**speedycarrot123**> ?

<**KwantumKing**> people luv you, even when u make that hard. Me, Dad, Udita, Helen. We luv u, even tho u r a total brat. We CARE. And yes, WILL. that guy luvs you so much its like youve rewired him. The more u push him away the more he luvs. And u HAVE been pushing him away (you psuh everyone away!) because ur afraid of feeling 2 much, getting hurt etc. But actually feeling 2 much is EXACTLY THE POINT And when u have people that feel so much for u, u r fucking lucky

She sat for a long moment, watching the cursor blinking, its heartbeat steady while her own bucked in her chest.

<**KwantumKing**> I better go.

<**speedycarrot123**> ok. Say hi to Udita for me. Tell her botulism for wrinkles is bad. and Hari?

<**KwantumKing**> yeeees

<**speedycarrot123**> I love you 2.

She disconnected, then sat for a while lost in thought. Natalie. Hari. Udita. Will, Will, Will. The desk was littered with proof of regular habitation by Phumlani, who'd been the one, lightning quick, to connect with Hari's BBS earlier. There were comic books, his battered purple Game Boy, a grotesque flesh-colored toy with a shock of orange hair. Helen was equally in evidence: her Rolodex, a jar of nail polish, and messy stacks of magazines that looked to be mostly *Chatelaine* and *Home-makers*. The cover of a well-thumbed *Time* caught her eye. It featured a repeating picture of a human fetus, each one shaded a different hue, its face twisted from view. "Solving the Mysteries of Heredity," the cover promised, followed by smaller text that read: "The drive to map human genes could revolutionize medicine but also raises troubling ethical questions."

"Oh, I left that out for you, actually." Helen's quiet voice, out of nowhere, made her jump. "Phumlani brought it home from school."

"Do you need to get on here? I logged off."

Helen shook her head and gestured at the magazine. "It explains the whole rationale for the Human Genome Project—you've probably been following it."

Kit was and wasn't following it. Millions of government dollars and private donations had been committed to the goal of identifying every gene and its function in the string of DNA coiled inside the twenty-three human chromosomes. To Kit, the project seemed too broad in scope, too intangible to relate to her in any way, but she could well imagine how dismissive her mother would be of that stunted thinking. She'd take her ignorance personally, the way anyone else's mother might chide a child for questioning the existence of Santa Claus.

"Take it," Helen said. "It's mostly mumbo jumbo to me."

Jesse Gelsinger
June 18, 1981 – September 17, 1999

Son of Paul and Pattie Gelsinger, Jesse, 18, loved pro wrestling and Adam Sandler movies, and lived life to the fullest, despite being diagnosed shortly after birth with ornithine transcarbamylase (OTC) deficiency, a rare genetic condition. Jesse died of multiple organ-system failure after volunteering to be the first human to receive an experimental treatment intended to introduce a corrective segment of genes into his DNA using a "vector" based on the common cold virus. Jesse, whose condition was well-managed by diet and drugs, said he was doing it "for the babies."

1999: SUNSHINE COAST, BC

"You can't ask me to marry you."

She couldn't look at him. Instead, she stared at the knobbles of his toes where he stood barefoot on the beach. They'd picked their way down to the water over the granite, its knuckles and folds gnarled with barnacles and slimy yellow tongues of bladder wrack growing bloated in the sun. When they'd reached this small swath of sand, Will had kicked off his flip-flops before pulling the ring box from his pocket, a confident smile playing on his lips. She'd known this was coming, had known from the moment he'd suggested they rent a place for a week on the exact stretch of coastline he'd taken her to back in '86. She'd known what was imminent from the restless, eager thrum of him as he packed their picnic. There was almost definitely a bottle of champagne in his nylon packsack, which had hung low and heavy on his back.

Hari and Udita were supposed to drive up to meet them later in the week, but they'd bowed out. Udita, who'd continued her rise through the ranks at Coccinel, said she was in the midst of a big launch. Hari, meanwhile, was leading the team scrambling to patch any Microsoft systems vulnerable to the millennium bug before the stroke of midnight on December 31. As far as Kit could tell, Udita spent any spare time she had at spin classes, leaving Hari to cruise dying chat rooms dedicated to Aerosmith and Marvel Comics, mourning the demise of independent BBSs, crushed by CompuServe and AOL. Kit was sorry they weren't coming. She'd like to see firsthand whether Udita and Hari, more than twenty years married, still had that invisible circuitry crackling between them.

Kit felt the tide rushing foamy up the beach, straining to reach them, and risked a peek at Will's face. He looked like she'd slapped him.

She eased the lid closed on the white satin ring box as if it was an oyster agape on the shore. "I love you, Will Katzen. You know I do."

Next, his shoulders would roll and his head would rear back so as to direct his exasperation at the cosmos. This, too, she'd expected, because she'd seen it before: their regular argument, prompted by one of her idle remarks loaded to the hilt with her deepest fears: that he'd grow away from her, that the gap between them would widen and become a burden, that she'd eventually be left all alone. Aging slower, at a fraction of the speed of everyone she'd ever loved, was like having gangrene, a slow rot. She would lose her limbs at some point, it was just a question of when and how much she'd need to lop off. Her mum had understood this. Papa, too.

Every time they argued, Will would say, *We're here, now, aren't we? We need to live in the* now. It was the same argument he'd used back when she'd first told him about her leap year gene, the morning after he'd shown up unexpectedly at Helen's in Toronto. She told him everything. About Heinrik Strauss, the German doctor who'd tried to abscond with Helen, thinking she was the "special" one, and how Kit, to this day, still had nightmares that he might one day track her down. She told him what Helen had finally told her, years after their big fight over

Will's incinerated letters in Geneva, about Robbie applying for research funding for a "case-based study" looking at genetic markers for delayed menopause. She told him about the fledgling company she'd first heard about at Mum's commemoration making restriction-enzymes scissors and synthetic insulin, now a huge corporation scraping human DNA for clues to the next blockbuster drug—that made her sneak out of the chapel without saying goodbye.

Will had gaped at her and said, "It's 1993, Kit. People from your past aren't chasing you down for your DNA. The Nuremberg Code, informed consent, privacy laws—your health, your genes, your medical history are completely *yours* unless you yourself decide you want to figure out what makes you different."

Figuring out what makes her different. That notion had felt like a pebble in her shoe since the night before, when she'd read the *Time* magazine Helen had given her. "We used to think our fate was in our stars," James Watson was quoted in the article. The Cricket, Mum used to call him—Francis Crick's chirpy sidekick. "Now we know, in large measure, our fate is in our genes."

Kit had said, "What about kids, Will? If that's not in the cards." She'd seen what that was doing to Hari and Udita.

Will's face had been so close to hers, she could see his pupils tracking back and forth, trying to scan both her eyes at once. "But you just told me Hari's grandfather is like you, but Hari isn't, and his dad isn't."

She shook her head. "It's not an option. Even if it were physically possible for me, which I'm not sure about. I know I can't take the risk. I've always known."

He leaned in, pressing his lips against her forehead. "What we're deciding on today is us. You and me. Everything else can wait."

Now on his favorite beach, next to the sea with its soothing stroke, she took the ring box from Will's hand and tucked it gently back in the pocket of his shorts. A crab eased itself sideways from behind a rock like the good guy in a gunfight making a break across the open ground.

Kit took from her own pocket her most prized possession. She'd rehearsed this in her mind, how she'd say, *I will love you to the end of time,* before lifting her necklace watch over his shaggy head.

Instead she fumbled with the satiny ribbon, her corny speech forgotten. "My whole life, Will, people have been making decisions about what happens for me next, even you."

She reached up and he bowed just slightly, not breaking eye contact, and she made to loop the watch over his head.

"So, William Hezekiah Katzen. Will you marry me?"

She paused. His wriggly lips were already breaking into a smile. "Also," she added, letting the watch drop into place against his chest, "I've decided we're getting a dog."

Ayaan Gupta
May 5, 1912 – October 12, 2003

In Loving Memory of our TREASURED DOCTOR AYAAN GUPTA who left for the Heavenly Abode to be Deeply Missed by: Son, Hari, Daughter-in-Law Udita (Chowdhury), his Many Patients, and the Chowdhury Family of Chowdhury Construction Pvt. Ltd. Kerala. (phone/fax: 91 484 412 0666, chowdhuryconstruction@yahoo.in).

2003: SEATTLE, WA

The Guptas now lived at the edge of the city, where a handful of giant houses had been hammered like pegs into a sloping bluff overlooking Puget Sound, all jutting beams, endless windows, and automatic gates. Hari greeted them at the door, his round face pimpled and ashen. A scruff of beard was creeping along his jawline, and his hair, having fled the high ground at his crown, was regrouping manfully behind his ears. He didn't so much hug as collapse into Kit, like he'd swum some distance to shore. He blamed the time difference and the long flight home to Seattle from Delhi with Ayaan's ashes in his carry-on bag, but Hari clearly hadn't slept properly in months.

And he'd been drinking, they both had, and maybe something more. Udita looked tasteful and immaculate as always, but she had the brittle, jangling energy Kit remembered from some of their big nights out in the past. Udita, the chemist, always had a number without a name in her Filofax, filed under F for fun. She'd already made a big show of how "stunning" Kit looked, letting her jaw hang open and her eyes pop, clucking in disbelief. "You brat! I hope you know how lucky you are, Will."

Udita looked great, too, lithe as ever but more chiseled. Will noticed too and must have said something Kit didn't catch because she heard Udita say, "Oh, but I have to work at it," tilting her chin and fluttering her eyelashes like a Betty Boop cartoon. Udita had run a 10K last month, she said, and was hoping to do a half marathon in the spring. Kit thought she was joking and chuckled; Udita had always made fun of Kit for her "obsessive" running. But Kit felt bad, because Udita looked hurt or mad. It was hard to tell which: Udita's face seemed so much less expressive than Kit remembered.

On that first night, Kit stuck with wine at dinner and so did Will. Hari said almost nothing, filling and refilling his glass with steady resolve. Udita's white-toothed smile and throaty chuckle seemed overdone. Something was off with Udita. Hurt feelings, possibly. Last year she'd wanted Kit to meet her for a girls' getaway in New Orleans, just the two of them, but Kit hadn't been able to make it happen.

"How's Helen, how's Phumlani?" Udita asked brightly.

"They're great. Helen's got one more year in her fine arts program at York and Phumlani's finishing up his honors degree at U of T. You'd love his project, Hari." She was desperate to draw him in. "All of his computer hacking skills are coming in handy. I don't fully understand it, but it's some kind of mathematical modeling looking for areas of gene overlap in sickle cell disease. Very hot stuff, apparently. Helen says he'll have his pick of grad schools next year."

When Hari said nothing, Udita flapped him an irritated look and said, "And Natalie, still healthy as a horse?" Natalie, at 103, was still walking without aid, still playing bridge, still sharp. But it was the wrong thing to say.

"Maybe we should call it a night," Hari said. He pushed back his chair, then half-stood, half-stumbled from the table.

The next morning, when Kit and Will wandered out into the fish-tank living room, they found a note from Udita saying she'd gone for a jog and that Hari had gone into work. Kit almost jumped out of her skin when an older woman in an apron stepped into the room carrying two caffe lattes on a tray. So the Guptas had a maid.

"Do you think they even want us here?" Will asked, a thread of milk foam on his upper lip. They were standing at the window. A white ferry, far below, was chugging through the gray-green harbor.

Kit wasn't sure. It had been Udita who'd called, begging them to come. They'd put Basil in a kennel and driven down to Seattle that same day. But now Udita was being so frosty. "I think Hari is glad we're here, right?"

Will continued to watch the ferry turning like a toy in a bath. He nodded and tipped the last of his coffee down his throat.

The Guptas drank too much every night Kit and Will were in town. Kit couldn't tell whether this was habit or grief. Hari drove into the Microsoft campus for part of the day most days while Udita played host, occasionally disappearing to "catch up on email" somewhere else in the house. Kit joined her on a jog their second-to-last morning so they could get some time to themselves, but when Kit asked how she was holding up, Udita made a face and said, "I can't do chitchat at this pace."

After they got back and showered, Kit found Udita in the kitchen making them protein smoothies, dressed in a clingy purple top and full makeup, having taken the time to straighten her hair. Kit assumed she needed to head into the office, but Udita said, "Just get Hari out of here, won't you? Maybe he'll open up a bit more if you two are alone. Will and I can head into town."

When Hari nosed the Range Rover into a line of idling cars at the Burger King drive-through, Kit raised an eyebrow.

"Whopper, onion rings, and a Coke," he told the microphone. When had Hari started eating meat?

After they'd picked up the food, he steered the car around to the parking lot so they were facing a cement wall crawling with bindweed that was also laying siege to an overflowing dumpster.

"No," Kit said, and snatched the paper bag from his lap. "No way. Not here." She held out her hand for the keys.

They ended up at Seward Park, overlooking Lake Washington. The clouds to the south had lifted and they could see the white snub nose of Mount Rainier in the distance. Hari snapped at his food in bites that looked forced, swallowing with effort, finally saying, "Udita doesn't let me eat this."

Mentioning her seemed to open the floodgates. He and Udita were having trouble, if that wasn't obvious. Trying for children for so long had pushed them over the limit. He'd tried to convince her they could adopt, he'd be fine with that—look how happy Helen was with Phumlani.

"You know what she said?" Hari asked, looking wretched. "She said she'd never adopt because you have no idea what kind of kid you might end up with. As if you ever do." He leaned his temple on the window and let out a long sigh that fogged the glass, then vanished. "Udita has been so focused on her career, an immigrant—an Indian!—climbing to the top of the ladder. And she's done it in an industry fixated on impossible beauty ideals." His last words—"I'm not sure Udita even wanted children in the first place"—leaked out of him like stale air from a punctured tire.

The milkshake was leaving a waxy-sweet varnish on Kit's tongue, making it even harder to form the right words. Hari saved her the trouble.

"You and Will seem good." He balled the greasy wrappers and shoved them in the pocket of his door. "He's okay then, not having kids?"

This question. It had been chasing its own tail, around and around, ever since she'd first grappled with telling Will her secret, pulling a million other questions into its vortex. Back in 1999, not long before she'd proposed to Will, it had seemed like gene therapy using viral vectors might prove the miracle solution for countless conditions, even "fixing" babies before they were born. Instead, more and more people had died. The US FDA had put a moratorium on all gene therapy trials after another "bubble boy" in France developed cancer following his so-called cure. It was abundantly clear to Kit that for all the genius minds and billions of dollars spent so far, the human blueprint was far more intricate and convoluted than anyone had ever anticipated. She and Will loved each other, and for whatever time they had together, they'd decided it wasn't worth the risk of an experimental fix that might possibly permit Kit to carry a child, or attempt to repair the DNA of a child born the same way as her.

She couldn't say all that to Hari, given how things were going with Udita. "No," she said, as neutrally as she could.

"So how are you for ID?"

It was such an abrupt change of topic her milkshake spluttered in her throat. For years now, and at no small risk, Hari had helped with a few forgeries and made sure all of her online records were synced. On the World Wide Web as well as on the cards she carried in her wallet, she was thirty-six. She looked younger. No one had mentioned this in recent memory.

"Um, fine," she said, surprised. "I don't think I'll need anything anytime soon."

He was quiet again, lost in thought. Then he ran his palm down his face, closing his eyes, and nodded at the keys in the ignition. "There's something I need to show you back at the house."

Will and Udita were on the covered patio overlooking the bay, Udita stretched out on the chaise under a thick fleece blanket, her expression unreadable. Will was nursing the remains of a beer and Udita was drinking vodka sodas—Kit saw the bottle of Absolut and two empty cans rolling on a low table. It was two thirty in the afternoon. Kit cast a questioning look at Will, but he did not meet her eye.

Hari ignored them, heading straight down the stairs to his office. "Shut the door," he said, and rolled his chair toward a keyboard.

It took her a long while to understand what she was looking at. This didn't look like the retro BBS-style chat rooms dedicated to comics and seventies arena rock. This page was orderly and modern, but clearly a throwback to the chat bulletin boards Hari had loved.

A discussion was active on-screen, type skittering across the white page.

Everyone "chatting" on here was using the same winky-wink code names Udita and Kit used to poke fun at almost two decades ago. @SplitPinyata, @slimboyfat, @CardinalPecorino, @idreamofgene, @SCDefrag. And they seemed to be talking over one another like in the chat rooms of old, having multiple conversations at once, the difference being these aliases were conversing in a more serious, solemn manner than Kit could remember from Hari's old BBS.

@CardinalPecorino:
Recall the Danish Twin Study (Herskind. *Hum Genet.* 1997). In that analysis, the heritability of longevity was estimated to be 0.26 for males and 0.23 for females, with a greater impact of non-shared environmental factors seen in the females.

@SplitPinyata:
Even if you take environment 100% out of the equation wouldn't there be, in very rare phenotypes, a series of genes, not a single mutation, responsible for delayed aging?

@junkyardDNA:
Has anyone looked into metabolism distinct from adiposity, as a confounder in #ELG?

"What *is* this site?" Kit said, scanning the top and bottom of the screen for clues.

"It's a subbranch of a gated international research chat room. The idea, I gather, is to hone papers prior to journal or grant submissions. This particular branch"—Hari hesitated, darting a look at her over his shoulder—"is focused on the genetics of longevity. #ELG, I gather, stands for 'extreme longevity,' or maybe 'extreme longevity gene.'"

Her brain was spinning. "Cardinal Pecorino," she said aloud. She remembered the oversize block of cheese Helen always had on hand for her lasagna as well as the dermatologist at Stanford who'd been so transfixed by her old-young skin. Stanford's football team was called the Cardinal.

But what of @SCDefrag? SCD, she knew from Phumlani, was shorthand for sickle cell disease, the subject of his honors thesis. Phumlani, computer whiz, always offering to "remote" into her computer to check for bugs. How many math geeks studying the genetics of sickle cell disease and who also knew how to defrag computers were into chat rooms, *and* actively calculating their grad school prospects?

But then, of course, there were colleagues in her own epidemiology department at UBC, who for years had teased Kit for looking like a perpetual grad student, and the ophthalmologist with his study of premature cataracts in Boston. She could hear, in her head, the soft footfall of her heart picking up its pace.

Hari scrolled farther and Kit caught snatches of the conversation, all centered on genes and aging: junk DNA, telomere shortening, free radicals, heterochromatin, somatic mutations. @idreamofgene had recommendations for long-term storage of centenarian blood samples. @SCDefrag predicted CONFIDENTIALLY that the "pharmaceutical outputs" from the #HGP would be in clinical testing by next year.

#HGP, Kit knew, meant the Human Genome Project mapping every conceivable cranny and crook of the human blueprint.

"Anonymity is guaranteed," Hari was saying. "Some users are pretty forthright about their publications, so it's not hard to attach a name to an alias. Others, I've honestly got no clue."

He scrolled a bit farther, then stopped. With a swipe of his mouse he highlighted a single comment.

@SplitPinyata:
I've identified an early #ELG candidate distinct from any of the established Blue Zones, female, currently in

7th or 8th decade of life but with a phenotype consistent with the 2nd or early 3rd. So an observed/expected longevity ratio of roughly 1:4. Seeking tips for approaching case for study inclusion or DNA sampling.

A lump rose in Kit's throat. Hari swiveled his chair to face her, his face so sad and serious she felt a rush of guilt. On top of everything, Ayaan's death, the child that never was, his crumbling marriage, Hari was worrying about *her*.

"I know you've toyed with 'going public' about this. But if you're not ready . . ." He took a deep breath. "It seems like someone on here either knows about you or knows someone else like you. This is why I asked you about your ID, if it's up to date. If you're not ready to do this, kind of, on your own terms, then . . ."

She thought of her home, her leafy street, her beloved Basil pining for them at the kennel, and finished the sentence for him.

"Then it might be time to disappear again for a while."

Hari T. Gupta
April 6, 1948 – September 1, 2008

Hari Gupta, a former Microsoft leader and micro-computing impresario, died on the morning of September 1, 2008, at Swedish Hospital in Seattle, leaving behind his loving wife, Udita (Chowdhury). An avid collector of rare Marvel comics memorabilia, Hari was an early star at Microsoft, leading the launch of OS/2 and later pioneering the DirectX platform for Windows 95. His real "baby," says Microsoft cofounder and philanthropist Bill Gates, was MSN Messenger. Donations in lieu of flowers to www.children.org.

2008: SEATTLE, WA

U dita looked wild. Not Udita-wild, not the glittering jewel of a thousand sparks, neon-bright Udita of the eighties, or the prowling jungle cat of the nineties, fierce and strutting. She was hollow-cheeked and drawn, her beautiful hair knotted and snarled.

Years of Botox around her eyes, her lips, and her forehead had given her a flatter look, as if she'd been rolled over by a street paver, but the effect without makeup made her look blank and unfinished. She opened the door to Kit, saying nothing, her red-ridged eyes ablaze and her arms drawn over her chest.

Only after Udita had shut the door—a shove that sent it clapping—did she speak. A low and thready voice, ragged at the edges.

"Kit McKinley. Sorry, Kit *Katzen*. Returned from the wherever. Once more, same as before."

Will had tried to come with her, but Kit said she needed to go alone, she'd be fine. She wasn't. A bubble of panic might pop in her breast. She couldn't open her throat, couldn't coax her lungs to fill. She would drown, she would drown, she would drown.

And she needed someone to blame. "How," Kit heaved. "Did. He. Die."

Udita flicked a bloodshot look at Kit and arched her wrist back, beckoning Kit into the gleaming, sterile box of glass that was the living room. There were cups and plates strewn over the tables, clothes on the floor and over the arm of a chair. A blanket lay bundled on the couch, as if Udita had been sleeping there. No sign of the maid in the apron.

"He saved all your letters, did you know that?" Udita asked. "Over years and years. I'm sure you haven't done the same with his, living your nomad life. I found them when Hari went to India to collect Ayaan's ashes. He'd accused me of cheating on him, which I hadn't. I convinced myself he felt guilty about something *he'd* done, so I went looking for proof."

Udita gnawed on her lip, flicking Kit a defiant look. "You know, by then, he hadn't touched me in a year? I repulsed him. As if we'd only ever had sex as a means to an end, and when we decided that was done, well."

She dropped herself onto the couch. Even unwashed, unkempt, yellow stains like bruises in the underarms of her T-shirt, almost certainly Hari's, Udita was still elegant, falling onto the cushions like a cashmere shawl. She drank deeply from a tall glass, no ice, that could have been water, but Kit had a better guess. At least she was using a glass. Udita pleated her lips and ticked her chin to point at the bar in the corner. Kit shook her head.

"I went through his emails, finding nothing remotely interesting or incriminating. But he'd always been a letters kind of guy, right? So I dug through box after box of his crap, computer shit, reams of manuals for processors and printers long dead, his old comic book collection." Her eyes flashed brighter with these last words. They could both picture Hari engrossed in a frame-by-frame battle between good and evil, slowly turning the pages, his eyes growing wider and wider. "That's where I found them, your letters, with his precious comics. Fitting, no? You keeping company with all the other mutants."

Udita snatched up a pack of cigarettes and shook one out with a flourish. A glimpse of her old flair.

"It was always so hard to get used to it, you showing up looking so freakishly young, even after you told me your big secret. Before that, I guess I thought it was your whiteness. Your big green eyes, your flat chest and skinny legs. I figured it was the look you were going for, and you worked hard at it—all that maniacal running and sunblock. Somehow it took me reading those letters to really *get* it. To understand that you have always been this way, it wasn't something you had any control over, and how much you leaned on Hari and everyone else around you to make yourself feel safe."

Sunshine was slicing through the windows to spotlight this performance. Kit was cooking in her jacket but left it on. Some distant version of herself—a dot in the cosmos, a speck—was reminding her that this was Udita, her best friend, and she was grieving. Kit didn't care. Her own grief felt animal. Feral. Untamable.

Udita spoke now with her lips clamped around the cigarette, swishing the lighter, then sucking a breath as if to keep aloft. "At first I thought, *man*, Kit wrote to him every other week, how desperate! A precocious little kid, writing these rambling letters about music lessons and Frisbees, month in, month out, always using five big, old-timey words when one small one would do. But you actually weren't writing that often, were you. A few times a year, at most? It's just that very little changed for you between letters. School was still too easy. Helen was still boring and bossy. But you couldn't resist bragging about your fancy American life. The *West Side Story* premiere, those poor monkeys getting sent into space. I was still playing with dolls, but in your letters, you were Peter-fucking-Pan, in your umpteenth year of school and jogging around Central Park with Jackie O. Before she was even O! Jesus, Kit, you've been running away from everyone for a hell of a long time, always leaving it to Hari to cover your tracks."

Kit opened her mouth, but Udita cut her off.

"Did you ever think for a second what that was like for him, for us, everything always on your terms? You used to chirp on the phone about how much you missed me, but not so much that you'd actually come and visit, not when the second round of IVF failed, not even when everything with Hari was going to shit. I was supposed to be *it*, Kit. His it. And I thought I was, honestly. The sun to his earth. He sure as hell was mine. But those letters, I can tell. Hari's whole fucking life, you were there all along. Right from the start, you were this other gravitational pull."

Kit sat down at the table, not trusting herself to stay standing. "It wasn't like that, Udita. You know that. We were always just friends."

She snorted. "*Just* friends. What does that even mean? After everything he did for you . . . You know, you should have had his baby. Everything probably would have gone tickety-boo in your tender young womb. Oh, that's *right*. You and Will *decided* not to have a baby. You know what, Kit? *You* decided not to have a baby. Will gave that up for you, too. I asked him. Everyone gives up everything for you."

Then, her voice changing key, Udita said, "You know, the last time you were here, they'd 'let me go' at Coccinel." Udita made bunny ears for quote marks with her chipped fingernails, the glow of her cigarette poking dangerously close to her tangled mane. "HR had been trying to get rid of me for a while—too old, too brown. My most successful R&D work was no longer hitting the mark, in their view, even though there was a huge market for skin-lightening products. Too *off-brand* for Coccinel." She winced. "Ironically it was someone at Microsoft who came up with the software to selectively lighten skin tone so no one in a Coccinel ad ever looked too dark."

She stood abruptly, striding to the bar, then grabbed a bottle by its neck and filled her glass. Then she walked slowly back to stand over Kit. Up close, the whites of her eyes were pink, the sockets sunken and dusky. Udita scanned Kit's hair, her skin, her throat; on Udita's face, a look of resentment did battle with contempt.

"You should see yourself," Udita sneered. "All self-righteous. Did it ever occur to you *not* to run? Not to be constantly asking people to cover for you? That maybe there's something about you that could actually *help* people? Medically speaking, your genes might hold the secret recipe for DNA repair, telomere maintenance, whatever. Fuck *me*, I'd have gotten my job back in a heartbeat if I'd brought Coccinel the secret for perpetually youthful skin, but I bet there's other ways your genes could actually do some good if you ever paused to think of anyone other than yourself."

Of course Kit had. Every single day. The anger that had fueled her when she charged up to the front gate had all but left her now. She didn't feel afraid or enraged. She felt deeply, desperately tired.

"It was you, wasn't it," Kit said. Udita's words had reminded her of the aliases she'd seen that day in Hari's office downstairs, when he showed her the longevity chat room.

"@CardinalPecorino or @idreamofgene. Discussing telomeres and mutations linked to 'extreme' longevity. That was you asking how to 'approach' me."

Udita took a swill of her drink and spun in a slow arc, almost a dance, her cigarette tucked in the corner of her lips. "Come on, Kit," she chided. "@SplitPinyata. You know I'm always the life of the party." Her voice turned snide. "What the fuck, Kit. We were friends, or I thought we were." Udita sank again onto the couch and dropped the cigarette in the cup she'd been using as an ashtray. Kit caught a faint extinguishing hiss. "What I don't get," Udita said, drawing out the words, "is why on earth you always went running to Hari, even after you told *me*. You kept him spinning in your orbit. After everything we've been through. You're my oldest friend." She made a face. "Literally."

Kit said nothing. Felt nothing. And no words came. Udita still hadn't told her how he'd died. Wherever Udita had been steering this conversation, she seemed now to change her mind.

"You know, I tried to fuck Will the last time you guys came down. After Ayaan died. You left in such a hurry, I figured he must have told you." Udita was watching her face for a reaction and Kit did everything she could to keep it blank. Udita shrugged. "Later, when it was obvious even Hari didn't know how to reach you, I figured you must have gotten on that chat room and twigged to @SplitPinyata. And maybe Will never told you about my failed seduction."

When Kit said nothing, she made a gritty, sneering sound. "Whatever. I'm telling you now. I guess William only likes them young."

The urge to drive her fist into Udita's mocking face came swinging back. She had guessed Udita was the one on the chat room, although she'd never told anyone, not even Will. But Kit didn't know Udita had come on to him, he'd never said. She felt a scattershot pain, everywhere at once. She knew why Will had never told her. Because he knew what Udita meant to her. She was one of her only friends on earth.

Whatever Udita could see now on Kit's face prompted a mirthless sound, a fragment of a laugh, a shard. "Look at you. And I remember when I thought you were incapable of love."

Her anger seemed to wane with this last word. Kit didn't need to split her face to hurt Udita. It was already there, pain raking her features the way a tide scrapes at a shingle beach. Udita gulped.

"An overdose, Kit. He OD'd. I don't know where or how he got it. It wasn't any of our usual stuff. I came home and found him. It was an accident, I swear. One hundred percent. It had to be an accident."

Now tears were streaming down her face, brimming over the raw rims of her eyes as if they couldn't get out of her fast enough: a dam about to burst. Udita took another jagged breath that sputtered in her throat, then buried her head in her hands.

Natalie Estelle Kenilworth
April 25, 1901 – February 24, 2012

Beloved aunt, great-aunt, and great-great aunt, Natalie Kenilworth passed away two months shy of her 111th birthday, becoming one of Canada's oldest centenarians. A longtime headmistress at Montreal's Trafalgar School for Girls, Natalie was a dedicated member of the Everyday Dippers swim group, an accomplished pianist, and a formidable bridge foe. The family will bid her farewell at a private ceremony.

2012: TORONTO, ON

"Happy Leap Year Birthday, Kit."

Helen set the gift on her lap, her cheekbones bobbing with anticipation. Even her hair seemed to bristle with excitement: a masterpiece of tight salt-and-pepper curls, the work of a cherished hairstylist named Shavonne, who also did Helen's nail art. Today, February 29, two weeks after Valentine's, Helen's nails were still fire-engine red, dotted with little pink hearts and cupids.

Phumlani, living in California now, had flown in the day before the service with his wife, Julie, and their baby girl. No one was overly distraught—more like grateful that Natalie had been a part of their lives for so long, even getting to meet her great-grandniece, Savannah. Natalie had not, in the end, beaten the record for the oldest Canadian ever. Marie-Louise Meilleur died in 1998 at age 117, but in a nursing home, whereas Natalie had still been living with Helen. Always a class act, Natalie had washed her teacup, set it in the dish rack, then passed away peacefully in her sleep.

The others were at the window, watching the dog outside, while Savannah slept in Will's arms. Basil was feigning indifference to the sub-zero Ontario temperatures, solemnly inspecting each naked shrub as if by professional duty. She was too old to be kenneled now, but flying her with them to Ontario had clearly wreaked havoc on her sluggish digestion. Will, swaying with Savannah, had complained of a headache earlier, but seemed to have rallied and was asking Phumlani and Julie how their CRISPR research was progressing. CRISPR was the gene-editing technology that scientists at Berkeley were developing, much safer and simpler than the viral-vector method that had caused so many problems in the early 2000s. Kit knew from her own reading that CRISPR was like gene scissors—if scientists could pinpoint the exact stretch of DNA of interest in any cell or organism, they could snip it out or replace it with something else. Phumlani and Julie were exploring ways CRISPR could be used to delete the gene responsible for warping blood cells in sickle cell disease. Will gave Kit a thumbs-up. Basil, at last, was staggering arthritically in a hunched semicircle at the edge of Helen's vegetable box.

Kit watched Will with Savannah and felt awash with love. It upset him, she knew, the sidelong looks they got in restaurants and movie theaters, as if he'd left a more suitable wife for his young secretary. He would be fifty-six this year and worried more and more about his physical shortcomings, as if he might age out of her affections, even though he still kite-boarded, he still ran his beloved trails. Kit could argue until she was blue in the face that inwardly, they were traveling at the same speed, that mentally they were perfectly matched. The truth was that they were both struggling with opposite ends of the same fear. She felt it every time Will winced when he knelt to pump a bike tire, when he rattled two extra-strength ibuprofen into his palm before a run. Never mind Basil, Kit counted the extra minutes Will spent on the toilet, too. If she couldn't somehow catch up with Will, or he couldn't slow down to her speed, then what in the end would take him from her?

Kit opened Helen's beautiful handmade card first: a watercolor of Basil in her prime, an oversize stick in her mouth. The customary horoscope was tucked inside, and Helen had written "Happy 24th!" in block letters. Helen's little joke.

But Helen's math didn't account for the friction of living—Tarun's phrase. Gravity's pull, daylight's pierce, sunshine's sear. It seemed Kit's body, stubbornly programmed for youth, was only capable of so many innate repairs against external assaults. She wore wide-brimmed hats and SPF 50 on every scrap of freckled flesh, prescription sunglasses on all but the cloudiest days. When she finally saw a specialist about the dull pain in her knees, the doctor had pointed at her scans with a mix of disappointment and hurt on his face, as if he'd caught her joints and tendons plagiarizing an exam—so fundamentally out of character.

"To see such advanced arthritis at such a young age," the doctor murmured gravely. "I assumed there'd been a mix-up with the files."

Helen was still quivering with impatience. Kit unwrapped her gift.

The book was old. Its pages were yellowed at the edges and the frayed dust jacket, its colors faded, had an illustration of a hand cupping an ear. The title, *HAVE A LISTEN*, was printed in an italicized all-caps style that reminded Kit of the supermarket novels Natalie used to power through in the sixties. The author's name, below the title in a smaller, spidery font, was not one Kit knew: Gertrude Jameson. She flipped the book over to scrutinize the black-and-white photo on the back. Gertrude Jameson was rocking the saucy schoolmarm look with a sweater buttoned up to a crocheted collar, beehive hair, and cat's-eye glasses set over a cheerful expanse of glossy teeth. Kit could sense Helen's smile growing wider to the point of splitting, and Will, ever the bookworm, had drifted closer, still gently joggling the baby. Kit looked up, bewildered, but Helen, her eyes looking like they might pop from her head, bit her tongue.

Kit scanned the blurb on the inside cover. This was a memoir, she gathered. The author, a dental hygienist, had found her true calling after her husband's death, when she opened the Jameson Institute for the Deaf. Kit felt a prickling realization that made her flip again to the photo on the back.

"This is Gertrude? *Our* Gertrude? Our nanny? With the teeth?" Kit yanked off her useless glasses and held the book at a distance, trying to bring the image, the perfect teeth—dentures, surely—into focus. She looked up at Helen. "Gertrude founded an orphanage for deaf children in Ireland?"

Later, after Helen's legendary lasagna, Phumlani and Julie insisted on tackling the dishes while Will took his stubborn headache to bed, leaving Kit and Helen some time to themselves.

Helen settled herself on the sofa beside Kit. "So how's Udita?"

"Good. Really good. We did a long weekend in Boston last fall, visiting our old haunts. She's still working for that nonprofit in Seattle. Nearly four years sober now. Spending a fortune in therapy."

Helen nodded approvingly, but she was only half-listening. She'd taken Gertrude's book from the table and was stroking the cover on her lap.

"I read it first, I confess. Would you believe Natalie had this on her shelves the whole time? As if she was waiting for us to notice."

There was more, Kit could tell. Helen nodded.

"We're in here, briefly, two sisters in her care, although she's changed our names and the dates are vague. She writes in detail about your friend Frida, the little deaf girl who got sent away. She's a bit more cryptic about you and me: she writes that one of us was artistic, but the other had a trait even more unusual, something she knew the Germans would take an interest in. Gertrude blamed herself, obviously, for Frida, because she told her Nazi boyfriend she was deaf—which she describes as a reckless attempt to woo him back."

Lebensunwertes Leben. Life not worth living.

"Strauss's name isn't mentioned either, and it's clear why. Because she also told him about you."

Kit took the book from Helen and flipped it open, the fluttering pages offering up their secretive musk.

"Mum would never tell us what happened in the Tiergarten that day," Helen continued. "I always thought it was both of us he'd drugged, but it was just me. Max let that slip once, but I didn't understand." She tapped the book with a fingernail and smiled, her whole face creasing, her eyes full. "You saved me. I was being a needy little brat, craving attention, wanting for once to be 'special.' And you saved me."

Kit opened her mouth to ask the question they had always wanted to ask their mother: Why on earth did she never worry Strauss would come for them? Helen read her mind. She tapped the book a second time, and Shavonne's nail-art hearts pattered for them both. "Gertrude saw it, when she went back into the Tiergarten, to get Mum. Everything. It's all here."

2015: VANCOUVER, BC

She'd never seen him so angry or struggling so hard to contain it, a live wire, whipping and thrashing. Kit was still sitting on the bench overlooking the ocean, but Will had bolted up when she finished speaking and now couldn't stand still. He was pacing back and forth in his running tights, long jolting strides so that everyone else on the seawall, blindly zombie-walking while texting or swishing past with dogs, glanced up, then gave him a wide berth. Already he looked thinner, as if hewn from wood, all planes and angles—his matchstick arms swinging back and forth might topple him from the stilts of his Lululemon legs.

On her lap she had smoothed the papers that explained everything he needed to know about his upcoming procedures, the biopsy, the blood samples, the gene tests. Phumlani had done a far better job explaining it to Will than she could have, that cancer was fundamentally a disease of the genes, whatever the trigger: a signal gone awry, telling cells to reproduce themselves for no reason, or telling other genes not to intervene. Gene testing might help them target drugs not to specific types of tumors, necessarily, but to the genetic problem at their root. Today he'd get another PET scan, get his chemo and radiation schedule, and do the sperm-banking, if they decided that was something they wanted to do.

Which was why they were fighting.

She had a decent idea of what kind of inspiration might be on offer in the "production rooms" at the sperm bank, but for fun, she'd nipped down to the hotel lobby while Will was in the shower to buy the August issue of *Playboy*. She figured they might as well try to make this fun or funny. The cover featured a blonde in a black cowboy hat, breasts erupting over the top of a denim bikini, practically tumorous in their own right. Kit had it squirreled away in her purse.

But Will wasn't finding any of this funny. He spit his words like buckshot. "Why would I bank sperm *now*, Kit? If this was something you were even considering, we should have started down this path years ago. Decades! But you made me think you couldn't get pregnant, or you wouldn't be able to carry the baby, or the baby might end up like you. Now, after everything, you want me to jerk *off*, in a test tube, all so you can be sure to have my baby *later*? After I'm GONE?" He broke off with a gasp of pain, bashing his fists at his temples. She couldn't tell if it was fury or their new enemy, confirmed on the MRI last month, reminding them how they got here in the first place.

She felt her predictable tears threatening to spill out, which was infuriating. She'd promised herself she wouldn't cry today. She had to be strong, for his sake. But then, suddenly, anger was like a balm, much easier and more satisfying than crying.

"I wasn't ready earlier!" she hollered back at him, sending another dog walker scuttling past. "I thought maybe one day, I *would* feel ready, and then I would do this for you, if I could. But that hasn't happened, I haven't 'changed.'" She waved the forms, half crumpled in her fist, at him. "That's why maybe you should do this before the chemo and radiation. Because I know, Will. I know you wanted a family. Hari told me. Ages ago. Udita, too."

She couldn't stop them now, her salt tears a veritable tide unto themselves. Will was still marching in a furious circle on the seawall, still squeezing his head in the vise of his hands. "I'm just talking about *options*. For later."

The word made him stop his manic pacing as if his power cord had been cut, and he crumpled beside her on the bench. They both so desperately wanted a later.

And just like that, the anger was gone, gusted out of them both.

She put an arm around him and they looked out at the anxious, shifting surface of the sea, the waves swiping at the breakwater with their frothing claws. The pewter sky threatened rain. She could tell from the strain in his forehead that his headache was still there in full, beating at his skull with its bludgeon.

She brushed her lips, feather-light, to his temple. "You don't need to do it—it's a total waste of money if there's no chance we'll change our minds down the road."

She reached into her purse for the magazine and saw his eyes bug out at the sight of the glossy, swollen breasts unfurling on her lap. "Either way," Kit said, "I got you a present."

FEBRUARY 29, 2016:
SUNSHINE COAST, BC

Kit is sitting up against her pillow when she hears tires on gravel. Will does not. He's fallen asleep again at last, his head lolling to one side so she can see the angry, puckered crescent moon of his scar. For a while she'd been sitting beside him, listening to the marvel of his breath. The twin hollows of his eyes seem darker, almost bruised, but his lips, faintly parted now, are still plush and bendy, still quick to curve into a million eager, silly, hopeful, impish, dumbfounded, heartbreaker smiles. Kit glances at the wall where the clock should be, forgetting they'd taken it down when the 9-volt battery died.

We're stopping time, Will had said. Their little joke.

"Yoo-hoo, anyone home?" Udita lets herself in the front door. There are no real rooms in the cabin, just a few walls and nooks—no privacy except for the toilet. Kit stands and the bed celebrates with a loud squeak. That sound more than Udita's hello is enough to make Will's eyes flutter open.

"Oh! I didn't wake you, did I?" Udita flashes Kit a look, stricken.

Will props himself up with effort. The sunshine falling across his face, feathered by the branches of the cedars, turns his pallid skin a yellowy blue. But he twists his lips into a sideways come-hither so that Udita bustles forward, her eyes soft. Trust Will to make cancer look swashbuckling.

"Oh, you. Lying around in bed with someone half your age."

It's hard to know whom she's referring to because Kit realizes Udita is carrying a tiny cake, scarcely big enough to hold the three glittery numbers planted in the icing: 1 0 0. Helen, who'd moved in with Phumlani and Julie in Berkeley after Natalie died (better weather!), had sent Kit her "If It's Your Birthday" horoscope tucked into the customary birthday card, wishing her a happy 25th. Udita's 100, today, feels far more accurate.

"Happy birthday, old girl." Udita thrusts the cake into Kit's hands, then drapes an arm over her shoulders, planting a loud kiss on her cheek. "Hang on." Udita steps aside and palms her iPhone out of the back pocket of her skinny jeans, waving her hand to make Kit stand closer to Will, who has pulled himself out of bed. He grabs his baseball cap from the bedpost, dropping it sideways over his fuzzy head.

"I'm not posting it, don't worry. This is just for Helen." Udita raises her head to smile at them, her eyes suspiciously bright, the phone hovering. "And for me."

Will takes his time getting to the kitchen counter, where Udita starts unpacking bags of dry goods and fresh produce, milk that is sure to be organic, cheeses she's triple-checked were pasteurized. Kit can smell mangoes and coffee beans, fresh baked bread.

"We can't possibly eat all of this," Will says, his face blanching at the growing mound of groceries, already grieving the overbuy on spinach destined to turn viscous in the vegetable drawer.

Udita swats affectionately at the air near his shoulder, careful not to touch, and her mocking voice vaults Kit backward, decades. "Well, it's not all about you, is it Will-i-am?" If Kit were to turn around, she'd surely see Hari, slope-shouldered, standing up from his desk.

Time is not neatly coiled. This is what Kit says when Helen asks her to remember some detail from her big, long life. You can't run your hand smoothly along it like a rope. Memories, and the people you love, are the knots you hold on to along the way.

"Oh, and these." Udita takes a packet of 9-volt batteries from her purse. "I remembered."

Kit and Will both sent off their samples last year. Will's were analyzed so his treatment could be tailored to his results—Phumlani had got him included in a small clinical trial, and they wouldn't know until he went back for additional imaging whether it was having the hoped-for effects. But Will does, to her, seem a bit better. More hopeful. She tells herself the treatment is working, the renegade cells have thrown their hands in the air to surrender. Phumlani has also warned them, gently, that whatever discoveries might come from fishing through Will's brain tumor genes might be too late for Will, but might help the next person, or the next. Kit has chosen to think otherwise.

As for learning what lurks in her own DNA—this is a slow dance Kit has been having with herself for as long as she can remember, long before it ever crested the horizon of human possibility. Certainly long before Coach Drummond suggested his biomedical tests or Helen sent her the ad calling for Human Genome Project volunteers. Kit has a crystal-clear memory of her own mother gazing at her in that stern and steady way, as if she couldn't see the face in front of her but was instead scanning every curve and twist of triplet and codon, every chain link and base pair for which no one yet had ascribed names or functions. As if Mum could read the entire map of what made Kit who she was. Whatever Phumlani finds in her DNA he'll keep confidential until she makes a decision on what to do about it. Here, too, Kit wouldn't be doing it for herself, but for the next person, or the next.

When Will climbs back under his quilt, having barely managed a few bites, Kit and Udita set out on the trail down to the water. They pick their way through the mud now steaming itself dry, grabbing at the salal bushes to keep from slipping. High above, the tall trees tap on each other's shoulders, pointing at the friends as they pass and creaking their eerie regards. At sixty, Udita has stopped coloring her hair, which now glints silver, and her long lashes are the ones she was born with. She's slower but every bit as graceful. She has a peace to her, a quietness, that Kit wishes Hari had lived to see.

They reach the shoreline. The sea, high and calm today, kneads steadily at the stones and the cedars curtsy their skirts above the tide. Deep, deep beneath the surface, a Pacific geoduck, Kit is certain of it, will also be celebrating a subdued centennial.

Udita says: "So? How are you doing? Really."

It was nearly six months ago that Kit and Will had their fiery argument on the seawall. They had taken the elevator up to his first appointment, *Playboy* sizzling a hole in her bag, but they didn't speak about it afterward, not on the ferry or during the long drive up the coast to the cabin. She started to make dinner, everything unsaid still sparking between them, but then Will had laced up his shoes, gesturing that she should too. When they were out of the trees at the beach, he plunked himself down, crossing his gangly legs and patting the rock for her to sit. It's the same thing Kit does now with Udita, who folds herself neatly beside her.

"It's not like I've been carrying around this great sadness of not becoming a father," Will had said that day. "You have always, always been enough. More than enough. Let's get through this first, okay? Then anything is possible." He tucked her under his arm. "Look at Hugh Hefner. He's got to be what, 132? That guy was still having kids when he was, like, 105."

Kit smiled, burrowing closer. "And those are only the ones we know about."

They stayed like that until the light began to sink beneath the ocean's hem and it seemed possible that everything might turn out okay.

Udita is watching her, waiting.

"Well, to be honest," Kit says, "I feel like I'm a hundred years old."

Udita shoots her a crooked smile in the old way, open to gladness, game for anything. "Well, thank the fucking gods. *Finally*."

When Helen, Phumlani, and Julie call tonight to wish her happy birthday, Phumlani will ask about Will and they'll talk everything through, whether or not there are any signs of progress. Then he'll ask about Kit and whether she's ready to hear what he's found. Also: that it's okay if she's never ready. "I know one of my parents was Black and the other white, but I know nothing more, and I've made peace with not knowing," Phumlani will say.

She is ready. It took Will getting sick for her to properly realize there might be something in her own jumbled DNA worth hunting for, worth sharing. So many people braver than her, who inherited much more difficult burdens, have offered up their genes to science and paid the ultimate price. She thinks about Alzheimer's, osteoporosis, and all the other quiet maladies of aging that she has managed to stave off so far, distinct from the friction of living, let alone any diseases of the future—new pathogens or viruses for which youth might provide some protection. Maybe there's something in her genes that could help.

The bigger question is whether she'd want to do anything about it, her leap year gene. Or genes. Or repeats. Or fragments. Whatever it is they find. Whether she, too, would want to be fixed—that's what Udita's really asking. Phumlani's team is close to a breakthrough with sickle cell, using CRISPR to delete the gene responsible for the warped blood cells. Udita's prediction is that Phumlani and Julie will win the Nobel Prize for their sickle cell work within the next four years, with implications for the entire field. Four years is *nothing*. Four years is the blink of an eye. By 2020, maybe CRISPR will be repairing all the defects and dysfunction plaguing our herds, our crops, ourselves. *Imagine*, Kit thinks. *All of our unwanted segments pruned and grafted, leaving them shining and flawless and whole.*

Even if her units of time could be recalibrated, she could never catch up to Will— they accepted that long ago. But she does wonder sometimes about a child and what it might be like to march in lockstep with someone she loved, year by year, decade by decade. To live without the dread of that leapfrog moment that always, always leaves her behind.

Udita, her eyes on the sinking sun, is telling her she's lost touch with almost all of her old friends from Coccinel, which was acquired by Decléor, then sold to L'Oréal in 2014 for nearly half a billion dollars. Kit is scarcely listening. She's thinking: If they'd had a child, Udita and Hari, it would be easier, wouldn't it, to go on without him? Udita would have something of him still, a partial blueprint, a living piece. Even the wisp of this thought, the shape of it, can't be held or endured.

Now Udita is waving her hands in the air, sweeping gestures, outsized contempt. "Can you believe it," she says. "L'Oréal now has an entire bloody division dedicated to genetics and aging? They've hired whole squadrons of scientists to concoct creams and injections, potions and peels designed to keep jawlines tight and skin supple, to coax hair to grow from the root in exactly the right shade. As if there's a cure for aging! What a waste of brainpower. They could be out there curing cancer." She sneaks a glance at Kit, a look packed so snugly with love and worry that Kit leans against her, letting Udita hold her tight.

Kit knows this better than anyone: it's not eternal youth we need, but love and the chance to hold on to it for as long as possible. Who among us gets to synchronize their ticking heartbeat to their heart? Not Udita and Hari, who never got the chance to run down their clock together, not Helen and Robbie. Certainly not her mother, who, as the clouds gathered in her mind and the walls of her world crept closer, outlived her father by fifteen years, losing even her memories of him. How lucky, how precious, how rare it is to grow old with the people we love. Science, she thinks, should be hunting for something very different: a way of being in the world for as long as you feel yours is a life worth living, then a door to slip away through, when it's time to leave.

AUTHOR'S NOTE

Kit's "leap year gene" is fictional and all of the principal characters in this novel are entirely imaginary. Real names of historical figures, corporations, and scientists woven into this story are used for authenticity, often in the spirit of acknowledging their contributions.

My novel takes a number of liberties with facts and time-lines. Carrie Derick was the first female full professor at a Canadian university and the founder of McGill's genetics department, where there is still a teaching award in her name; in my novel, her campus lecture in 1918, as well as the op-ed Ernest reads aloud to Lillian in 1927, are entirely imagined but inspired by newspaper coverage of Derick's many speeches and publications dating back to the mid-1910s (e.g., "Segregation of the Feeble-Minded; Prof. Carrie Derick Suggests Royal Commission to Investigate Mental Deficiency," *Montreal Gazette*, December 21, 1915). Derick's opinions were by no means an anomaly among educated women: Canada's National Council of Women, for example, pushed for the vote, but also passed a 1925 resolution calling for the sterilization of "mental defectives."

Vincent Donaldson and his radio show are fictional, but the *Buck v. Bell* case, unfortunately, was real and precedent-setting. The program's name, *Times Like These*, is a nod to the title of the Nellie McClung book Lillian is reading in 1916. In it, McClung sets out arguments she later employed to lobby (successfully) for sterilization legislation in her home province: under the Alberta Sexual Sterilization Act, enacted in 1928 and not repealed until 1972, 2,822 sterilizations were performed, including many in prepubescent children, with a disproportionate representation of women, Indigenous people, ethnic minorities, and people from low-income groups.

The eugenics movement reached its most vile and notorious application in Nazi Germany's Aktion T4 program, which was quietly launched under Karl Brandt in September 1939—slightly later than in my novel—and dismantled in 1941, although the "involuntary euthanasia" continued. Roughly a quarter of a million children and adults deemed to have undesirable traits were ultimately killed with poisons, lethal overdoses, starvation, and the first use of improvised gas chambers.

The propaganda Max discovers in Münter's drawers in January 1939 estimating the societal costs of a person with a hereditary defect is real; I tweaked my description to suggest that the image featured a young girl.

When Kit explains her secret to Will in 1993, she recalls James Watson's remarks from an article by Leon Jaroff titled "The Gene Hunt" (*Time*, March 20, 1989). "The Cricket" is Lillian's nickname for Watson, not a real-life sobriquet, as far as I know.

The speech by a company scientist at Lillian's celebration of life is 100 percent fictional, but I hope it captures the historic, cat-among-the-pigeons moment of a geneticist explaining to his more purist peers the commercial potential of recombinant DNA technology. Genentech, now one of the world's largest biotech companies, unveiled the first genetically engineered medicines, including synthetic insulin, in the early 1980s. Sally

Smith Hughes's essay "Making Dollars Out of DNA" (*Isis* 92 [2002], 541–75) is a brilliant synopsis.

I lost myself in everything from PubMed to Coursera to try to better understand genes and genomes, as well as the ways family planning, prenatal and preimplantation genetic testing, recombinant DNA, and CRISPR, all have eugenic roots. Particular thanks to S. Mukherjee's *The Gene: An Intimate History*, M. Sandel's *The Case against Perfection*, and G. Aly et al.'s *Cleansing the Fatherland: Nazi Medicine and Racial Hygiene*.

ACKNOWLEDGMENTS

I'm hugely grateful to the people who suffered through too many words, continents, and characters before I whittled this book into shape: Ray Wood, Tyler Dyck, Joanne Carey, Corinna Chong, Alix Hawley, Adam Lewis Schroeder, Ashley Howard, and Jorie Soames. JC, without our all-weather, on-foot Distillibus discussions, I might not have survived this novel.

Samantha Haywood: your stamina, confidence, and unflagging faith in this project lifted me up, over and over—thank you.

I'm indebted to my US editors, Claire Wachtel and Barbara Berger at Union Square & Co., for falling for this story and helping it shine; Iris Tupholme at HarperCollins Canada, who pushed me to dig for the diamond in the rough; and the incredible team members on both sides of the 49th parallel: Lorissa Sengara, Natalie Meditsky, Ivy McFadden, and many more. Amanda Lewis, your insights were the tough love I didn't know I needed. A Project Assistance Grant from the British Columbia Arts Council aided me hugely at a critical early stage of this manuscript.

Countless people helped me grasp topics I don't know deeply enough. Thank you Chris Thompson for the telomeres, Eric Topol for pre-/post-zygotic mutations, John Medina for biological aging, Patti Richardson for the Bach inventions, Reiner Brecht for the German, and Nona Navin for the lab gadgets.

My uncle, Dudley Richmond, shared memories of his childhood for a part of the book that didn't make the final manuscript; he died in 2022. I'm so glad to have heard his stories.

I am forever grateful to my mum, for everything; to Pat and Tony Dyck for the loan of the Crab Shack (and the proof that family is more than bloodline); to the Super Six for tolerating my 9 p.m. bedtime; to the many Tuwanek cooks who fed me during solo writing jags; to the trail angels of Hidden Grove, where so much plotting was solved by plodding; to Joey, for urging me from my chair. Thank you to the many PACERs who endured my book babble over untold miles, especially Rene, whose trail-running maxims (with minor edits) continue to be lifelines for writing. A sentence is just a sentence and can be changed.

This book is dedicated to my father from whom, alas, I inherited just a fraction of his creativity and intelligence, but did get his blue eyes, wanderlust, predilection for pesto, compulsion for storytelling, and love of the sea. As I child, I wished my dad was more like other, normal dads; as an adult, I know that normal is both boring and elastic. Also: I'm the luckiest daughter alive.

This is a book with medicine and science in its DNA. I was extraordinarily fortunate to be able to hole up during the pandemic to write and rewrite this book, far from COVID-19's front lines. My profound thanks to the researchers, physicians, nurses, hospital staff, and other frontline workers who lived (and died) through horror, to keep the rest of us safe.

Lastly, to Tyler, who read all the drafts and never doubted. You are all my fish in the ocean and my sunlight on water. You are my ear-to-ear grin.